Praise for *New York Times* bestselling author Diana Palmer

"Diana Palmer is one of those authors whose books are always enjoyable. She throws in romance, suspense and a good story line."
—*The Romance Reader*

"Palmer knows how to make the sparks fly!"
—*Publishers Weekly*

"Diana Palmer is a mesmerizing storyteller who captures the essence of what a romance should be."
—*Affaire de Coeur*

Praise for *Publishers Weekly* bestselling author Lee Tobin McClain

"*A Family for Easter* by Lee Tobin McClain is a beautiful story of deep friendship, and how it turns into lasting love and brings two families together into one."
—*Harlequin Junkie*

"Everything I look for in a book—it's emotional, tender, and an all-around wonderful story."
—RaeAnne Thayne, *New York Times* bestselling author on *Low Country Hero*

Author of more than one hundred books, **Diana Palmer** is a multiple *New York Times* bestselling author and one of the top ten romance writers in America. She has a gift for telling even the most sensual tales with charm and humor. Diana lives with her family in Cornelia, Georgia.

www.DianaPalmer.com

Publishers Weekly bestselling author **Lee Tobin McClain** read *Gone with the Wind* in the third grade and has been an incurable romantic ever since. When she's not writing angst-filled love stories with happy endings, she's probably cheering on her daughter at a gymnastics meet, mediating battles between her goofy goldendoodle puppy and her rescue cat or teaching aspiring writers in Seton Hill University's MFA program. She is probably not cleaning her house. For more about Lee, visit her website at www.leetobinmcclain.com.

New York Times Bestselling Author

DIANA PALMER

MERCENARY'S WOMAN

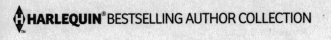

HARLEQUIN® BESTSELLING AUTHOR COLLECTION

ISBN-13: 978-1-335-01516-7

Mercenary's Woman

Copyright © 2019 by Harlequin Books S.A.

The publisher acknowledges the copyright holders of the individual works as follows:

Mercenary's Woman
Copyright © 2000 by Diana Palmer

His Secret Child
Copyright © 2016 by Lee Tobin McClain

Recycling programs for this product may not exist in your area.

Printed in U.S.A.

CONTENTS

For a complete list of books by Diana Palmer,
please visit dianapalmer.com.

MERCENARY'S WOMAN

Diana Palmer

For the Habersham Co. (Georgia) sheriff's department, and the Habersham Co. emergency medical service, with thanks.

CHAPTER ONE

EBENEZER SCOTT STOOD beside his double-wheeled black pickup truck and stared openly at the young woman across the street while she fiddled under the hood of a dented, rusted hulk of a vehicle. Sally Johnson's long blond hair was in a ponytail. She was wearing jeans and boots and no hat. He smiled to himself, remembering how many times in the old days he'd chided her about sunstroke. It had been six years since they'd even spoken. She'd been living in Houston until July, when she and her blind aunt and small cousin had moved back, into the decaying old Johnson homestead. He'd seen her several times since her return, but she'd made a point of not speaking to him. He couldn't really blame her. He'd left her with some painful emotional scars.

She was slender, but her trim figure still made his heartbeat jump. He knew how she looked under that loose blouse. His eyes narrowed with heat as he recalled the shocked pleasure in her pale gray eyes when he'd touched her, kissed her, in those forbidden places. He'd meant to frighten her so that she'd stop teasing him, but his impulsive attempt to discourage her had succeeded all too well. She'd run from him then, and she'd kept running. She was twenty-three now, a woman; probably an experienced woman. He mourned for what might have been if she'd been older and he hadn't just come back from leading a company of men into the worst bloodbath of his career. A professional soldier of fortune was no match for a young and very innocent girl. But, then, she hadn't known about his real life—the one behind the facade of cattle ranching. Not many people in this small town did.

It was six years later. She was all grown-up, a schoolteacher here in Jacobsville, Texas. He was…retired, they called it. Actually he was still on the firing line from time to time, but mostly he taught other men in the specialized tactics of covert operations on his ranch. Not that he shared that information. He still had enemies from the old days, and one of them had just been sprung from prison on a technicality—a man out for revenge and with more than enough money to obtain it.

Sally had been almost eighteen the spring day he'd sent her running from him. In a life liberally strewn with regrets, she was his biggest one. The whole situation had been impossible, of course. But he'd never meant to hurt her, and the thought of her sat heavily on his conscience.

He wondered if she knew why he kept to himself and never got involved with the locals. His ranch was a model of sophistication, from its state-of-the-art gym to the small herd of purebred Santa Gertrudis breeding cattle he raised. His men were not only loyal, but tight-lipped. Like another Jacobsville, Texas, resident—Cy Parks—Ebenezer was a recluse. The two men shared more than a taste for privacy. But that was something they kept to themselves.

Meanwhile, Sally Johnson was rapidly losing patience with her vehicle. He watched her push at a strand of hair that had escaped from the long ponytail. She kept a beef steer or two herself. It must be a frugal existence for her, supporting not only herself, but her recently blinded aunt, and her six-year-old cousin as well.

He admired her sense of responsibility, even as he felt concern for her situation. She had no idea why her aunt had been blinded in the first place, or that the whole family was in a great deal of danger. It was why Jessica had persuaded Sally to give up her first teaching job in Houston in June and come home with her and Stevie to Jacobsville. It was because they'd be near Ebenezer, and Jessica knew he'd protect them. Sally had never been told what Jessica's profession actually was, any more than she knew what Jessica's late husband, Hank Myers, had once done for a living. But even if she had known, wild horses wouldn't have dragged Sally back here if Jessica hadn't pleaded with her, he mused bitterly. Sally had every reason in the world to hate him. But he was her best hope of survival. And she didn't even know it.

In the five months she'd been back in Jacobsville, Sally had managed to avoid Ebenezer. In a town this size, that had been an accomplishment. Inevitably they met from time to time. But Sally avoided eye contact with him. It was the only indication of the painful memory they both shared.

He watched her lean helplessly over the dented fender of the old truck and decided that now was as good a time as any to approach her.

Sally lifted her head just in time to see the tall, lean man in the shepherd's coat and tan Stetson make his way across the street to her. He hadn't changed, she thought bitterly. He still walked with elegance and a slow arrogance of carriage that seemed somehow foreign. Jeans didn't disguise the muscles in those long, powerful legs as he moved. She hated the ripple of sensation that lifted her heart at his approach. Surely she was over hero worship and infatuation, at her age, especially after what he'd done to her that long-ago spring day. She blushed just remembering it!

He paused at the truck, about an arm's length away from her, pushed his Stetson back over his thick blond-streaked brown hair and impaled her with green eyes.

She was immediately hostile and it showed in the tautening of her features as she looked up, way up, at him.

He raised an eyebrow and studied her flushed face. "Don't give me the evil eye," he said. "I'd have thought you had sense enough not to buy a truck from Turkey Sanders."

"He's my cousin," she reminded him.

"He's the Black Plague with car keys," he countered. "The Hart boys wiped the floor with him not too many years back. He sold Corrigan Hart's future wife a car that fell apart when she drove it off the lot. She was lucky at that," he added with a wicked grin. "He sold old lady Bates a car and told her the engine was optional equipment."

She laughed in spite of herself. "It's not a bad old truck," she countered. "It just needs a few things…"

He glanced at the rear tire and nodded. "Yes. An overhauled engine, a paint job, reupholstered seats, a tailgate that works. And a rear tire that isn't bald." He pointed toward it. "Get that replaced," he said shortly. "You can afford a tire even on what you make teaching."

She gaped at him. "Listen here, Mr. Scott…" she began haughtily.

"You know my name, Sally," he said bluntly, and his eyes were steady, intimidating. "As for the tire, it isn't a request," he replied flatly, staring her down. "You've got some new neighbors out your way that I don't like the look of. You can't afford a breakdown in the middle of the night on that lonely stretch of road."

She drew herself up to her full height, so that the top of her head came to his chin. He really was ridiculously tall...

"This is the twenty-first century, and women are capable of looking after themselves..." she said heatedly.

"I can do without a current events lecture," he cut her off again, moving to peer under the hood. He propped one enormous booted foot on the fender and studied the engine, frowned, pulled out a pocketknife and went to work.

"It's *my* truck!" she fumed, throwing up her hands in exasperation.

"It's half a ton of metal without an engine that works."

She grimaced. She hated not being able to fix it herself, to have to depend on this man, of all people, for help. She wouldn't let herself think about the cost of having a mechanic make a road service call to get the stupid thing started. Looking at his lean, capable hands brought back painful memories as well. She knew the tenderness of them on concealed skin, and her whole body erupted with sensation.

Less than two minutes later, he repocketed his knife. "Try it now," he said.

She got in behind the wheel. The engine turned noisily, pouring black smoke out of the tailpipe.

He paused beside the open window of the truck, his pale green eyes piercing her face. "Bad rings and valves," he pointed out. "Maybe an oil leak. Either way, you're in for some major repairs. Next time, don't buy from Turkey Sanders, and I don't give a damn if he is a relative."

"Don't you give me orders," she said haughtily.

That eyebrow lifted again. "Habit. How's Jess?"

She frowned. "Do you know my aunt Jessie?"

"Quite well," he said. "I knew your uncle Hank. He and I served together."

"In the military?"

He didn't answer her. "Do you have a gun?"

She was so confused that she stammered. "Wh… what?"

"A gun," he repeated. "Do you have any sort of weapon and can you use it?"

"I don't like guns," she said flatly. "Anyway, I won't have one in the house with a six-year-old child, so it's no use telling me to buy one."

He was thinking. His face tautened. "How about self-defense?"

"I teach second grade," she pointed out. "Most of my students don't attack me."

"I'm not worried about you at school. I told you, I don't like the look of your neighbors." He wasn't adding that he knew who they were and why they were in town.

"Neither do I," she admitted. "But it's none of your business…"

"It is," he returned. "I promised Hank that I'd take care of Jess if he ever bought it overseas. I keep my promises."

"I can take care of my aunt."

"Not anymore you can't," he returned, unabashed. "I'm coming over tomorrow."

"I may not be home…"

"Jess will be. Besides, tomorrow is Saturday," he said. "You came in for supplies this afternoon and you don't teach on the weekend. You'll be home." His tone said she'd better be.

She gave an exasperated sound. "Mr. Scott…"

"I'm only Mr. Scott to my enemies," he pointed out.

"Yes, well, Mr. Scott…"

He let out an angry sigh and stared her down. "You were so young," he bit off. "What did you expect me to do, seduce you in the cab of a pickup truck in broad daylight?"

She flushed red as a rose petal. "I wasn't talking about that!"

"It's still in your eyes," he told her quietly. "I'd rather have done it in a way that hadn't left so many scars, but I had to discourage you. The whole damned thing was impossible, you must have realized that by now!"

She hated the embarrassment she felt. "I don't have scars!"

"You do." He studied her oval face, her softly rounded chin, her perfect mouth. "I'll be over tomorrow. I need to talk to you and Jess. There have been some developments that she doesn't know about."

"What sort of developments?"

He closed the hood of the truck and paused by her window. "Drive carefully," he said, ignoring the question. "And get that tire changed."

"I am not a charity case," she said curtly. "I don't take orders. And I definitely do not need some big, strong man to take care of me!"

He smiled, but it wasn't a pleasant smile. He turned on his heel and walked back to his own truck with a stride that was peculiarly his own.

Sally was so shaken that she barely managed to get the truck out of town without stripping the gears out of it.

JESSICA MYERS WAS in her bedroom listening to the radio and her son, Stevie, was watching a children's after-school television program when Sally came in. She unloaded the supplies first with the help of her six-year-old cousin.

"You got me that cereal from the TV commercial!" he exclaimed, diving into bags as she put the perishable items into the refrigerator. "Thanks, Aunt Sally!" Although they were cousins, he referred to her as his aunt out of affection and respect.

"You're very welcome. I got some ice cream, too."

"Wow! Can I have some now?"

Sally laughed. "Not until after supper, and you have to eat some of everything I fix. Okay?"

"Aw. Okay, I guess," he muttered, clearly disappointed.

She bent and kissed him between his dark eyes. "That's my good boy. Here, I brought some nice apples and pears. Wash one off and eat it. Fruit is good for you."

"Okay. But it's not as nice as ice cream."

He washed off a pear and carried it into the living room on a paper towel to watch television.

Sally went into Jessica's bedroom, hesitating at the foot of the big four-poster bed. Jessica was slight, blond and hazel-eyed. Her eyes stared at nothing, but she smiled as she recognized Sally's step.

"I heard the truck," she said. "I'm sorry you had to go to town for supplies after working all day and bringing Stevie home first."

"I never mind shopping," Sally said with genuine affection. "You doing all right?"

Jessica shifted on the pillows. She was dressed in sweats, but she looked bad. "I still have some pain from the wreck. I've taken a couple of aspirins for my hip. I thought I'd lie down and give them a chance to work."

Sally came in and sat down in the wing chair beside the bed. "Jess, Ebenezer Scott asked about you and said he was coming over tomorrow to see you."

Jessica didn't seem at all surprised. She only nodded. "I thought he might," Jessica said quietly. "I had a call from a former colleague about what's going on. I'm afraid I may have landed you in some major trouble, Sally."

"I don't understand."

"Didn't you wonder why I insisted on moving down here so suddenly?"

"Now that you mention it—"

"It was because Ebenezer is here, and we're safer than we would be in Houston."

"Now you're scaring me."

Jessica smiled sadly. "I wouldn't have had this happen for the world. It isn't something that comes up, usually. But these are odd circumstances. A man I helped put in prison is out pending retrial, and he's coming after me."

"You...helped put a man in prison? How?" Sally asked, perplexed.

"You knew that I worked for a government agency?"

"Well, of course. As a clerk."

Jessica took a deep breath. "No, dear. Not as a clerk." She took another deep breath. "I was a special agent for an agency we don't mention publicly. Through Eb and his contacts, I managed to find one of the confidants of drug lord Manuel Lopez, who was head of an international drug cartel. I was given enough hard evidence to send Lopez to prison for drug dealing. I even had copies of his ledgers. But there was one small loophole in the chain of evidence, and the drug lord's attorneys jumped on it. Lopez is now out of prison and he wants the person responsible for helping me put him away. Since I'm the only one who knows the person's identity, I'm the one he'll be coming after."

Sally just sat there, dumbfounded. Things like this only happened in movies. They certainly didn't happen in real life. Her beloved aunt surely wasn't involved in espionage!

"You're kidding, right?" Sally asked hopefully.

Jessica shook her head slowly. She was still an attractive woman, in her middle thirties. She was slender and she had a sweet face. Stevie, blond and dark-eyed, didn't favor her. Of course, he didn't favor his father, either. Hank had had black hair and light blue eyes.

"I'm sorry, dear," Jessica said heavily. "I'm not kidding. I'm not able to protect myself or you and Stevie anymore, so I had to come home for help. Ebenezer will keep us safe until we can get the drug lord back on ice."

"Is Ebenezer a government agent?" Sally asked, astounded.

"No." Jessica took a deep breath. "I don't like telling you this, and he won't like it, either. It's deeply private. You must swear not to tell another soul."

"I swear." She sat patiently, almost vibrating with curiosity.

"Eb was a professional mercenary," she said. "What they used to call a soldier of fortune. He's led groups of highly trained men in covert operations all over the world. He's retired from that now, but he's still much in demand with our government and foreign governments as a training instructor. His ranch is well-known in covert circles as an academy of tactics and intelligence-gathering."

Sally didn't say a word. She was absolutely speechless. No wonder Ebenezer had been so secretive, so reluctant to let her get close to him. She remembered the tiny white scars on his lean, tanned face, and knew instinctively that there would be more of them under his clothing. No wonder he kept to himself!

"I hope I haven't shattered any illusions, Sally," her aunt said worriedly. "I know how you felt about him."

Sally gaped at her. "You…know?"

Jessica nodded. "Eb told me about that, and about what happened just before you came to live with Hank and me in Houston."

Her face flamed. The shame! She felt sick with humiliation that Ebenezer had known how she felt all the time, and she thought she was doing such a good job of hiding it! She should have realized that it was obvious, when she found excuse after excuse to waylay him in town, when she brazenly climbed into his pickup truck one lovely spring afternoon and pleaded to be taken for a ride. He'd given in to that request, to her surprise. But barely half an hour later, she'd erupted from the passenger seat and run almost all the half-mile down the road to her home. Too ashamed to let anyone see the state she was in, she'd sneaked in the back door and gone straight to her room. She'd never told her parents or anyone else what had happened. Now she wondered if Jessica knew that, too.

"He didn't divulge any secrets, if that's why you're so quiet, Sally," the older woman said gently. "He only said that you had a king-size crush on him and he'd shot you down. He was pretty upset."

That was news. "I wouldn't ever have guessed that he could be upset."

"Neither would I," Jessica said with a smile. "It came

as something of a surprise. He told me to keep an eye on you, and check out who you went out with. He could have saved himself the trouble, of course, since you never went out with anyone. He was bitter about that."

Sally averted her face to the window. "He frightened me."

"He knew that. It's why he was bitter."

Sally drew in a steadying breath. "I was very young," she said finally, "and I suppose he did the only thing he could. But I was leaving Jacobsville anyway, when my parents divorced. I only had a week of school before graduation before I went to live with you. He didn't have to go to such lengths."

"My brother still feels like an idiot for the way he behaved with that college girl he left your mother for," Jessica said curtly, meaning Sally's father, who was Jessica's only living relative besides Sally. "It didn't help that your mother remarried barely six months later. He was stuck with Beverly the Beauty."

"How are my parents?" Sally asked. It was the first time she'd mentioned either of her parents in a long while. She'd lost touch with them since the divorce that had shattered her life.

"Your father spends most of his time at work while Beverly goes the party route every night and spends every penny he makes. Your mother is separated from her second husband and living in Nassau." Jessica shifted on the bed. "You don't ever hear from your parents, do you?"

"I don't resent them as much as I did. But I never felt that they loved me," she said abruptly. "That's why I felt it was better we went our separate ways."

"They were children when they married and had you," the other woman said. "Not really mature enough for the responsibility. They resented it, too. That's why you spent so much time with me during the first five years you were alive." Jessica smiled. "I hated it when you went back home."

"Why did you and Hank wait so long to have a child of your own?" Sally asked.

Jessica flushed. "It wasn't...convenient, with Hank overseas so much. Did you get that tire replaced?" she added, almost as if she were desperate to change the subject.

"You and Mr. Scott!" Sally exploded, diverted. "How did you know it was bald?"

"Because Eb phoned me before you got home and told me to remind you to get it replaced," Jessica chuckled.

"I suppose he has a cell phone in his truck."

"Among other things," Jessica replied with a smile. "He isn't like the men you knew in college or even when you started teaching. Eb is an alpha male," she said quietly. "He isn't politically correct, and he doesn't even pretend to conform. In some ways, he's very old-fashioned."

"I don't feel that way about him anymore," Sally said firmly.

"I'm sorry," Jessica replied gently. "He's been alone most of his life. He needs to be loved."

Sally picked at a cuticle, chipping the clear varnish on her short, neat fingernails. "Does he have family?"

"Not anymore. His mother died when he was very young, and his father was career military. He grew up in the army, you might say. His father was not a gentle sort of man. He died in combat when Eb was in his twenties. There wasn't any other family."

"You said once that you always saw Ebenezer with

beautiful women at social events," Sally recalled with a touch of envy.

"He pays for dressing, and he attracts women. But he's careful about his infrequent liaisons. He told me once that he guessed he'd never find a woman who could share the life he leads. He still has enemies who'd like to see him dead," she added.

"Like this drug lord?"

"Yes. Manuel Lopez is a law unto himself. He has millions, and he owns politicians, law enforcement people, even judges," Jessica said irritably. "That's why we were never able to shut him down. Then I was told that a confidant of his wanted to give me information, names and documents that would warrant arresting Lopez on charges of drug trafficking. But I wasn't careful enough. I overlooked one little thing, and Lopez's attorneys used it in a petition for a retrial. They got him out. He's on the loose pending retrial and out for vengeance against his comrade. He'll do anything to get the name of the person who sold him out. Anything at all."

Sally let her breath out through pursed lips. "So we're all under the gun."

"Exactly. I used to be a crack shot, but without my vision, I'm useless. Eb will have a plan by tomorrow." Her face was solemn as she stared in the general direction of her niece's voice. "Listen to him, Sally. Do exactly what he says. He's our only hope of protecting Stevie."

"I'll do anything I have to, to protect you and Stevie," Sally agreed at once.

"I knew you would."

She toyed with her nails again. "Jess, has Ebenezer ever been serious about anyone?"

"Yes. There was a woman in Houston, in fact, several years ago. He cared for her very much, but she dropped him flat when she found out what he did for a living. She married a much-older bank executive." She shifted on the bed. "I hear that she's widowed now. But I don't imagine he still has any feelings for her. After all, she dropped him, not the reverse."

Sally, who knew something about helpless unrequited love, wasn't so quick to agree. After all, she still had secret feelings for Ebenezer…

"Deep thoughts, dear?" Jessica asked softly.

"I was remembering the reruns we used to see of that old TV series, *The A-Team*," she recalled with an audible laugh. "I loved it when they had to knock out that character Mr. T played to get him on an airplane."

"It was a good show. Not lifelike, of course," Jessica added.

"What part?"

"All of it."

Jessica would probably know, Sally figured. "Why didn't you ever tell me what you did for a living?"

"Need to know," came the dry reply. "You didn't, until now."

"If you knew Ebenezer when he was still working as a mercenary, I guess you learned a lot about the business," she ventured.

Jessica's face closed up. "I learned too much," she said coldly. "Far too much. Men like that are incapable of lasting relationships. They don't know the meaning of love or fidelity."

She seemed to know that, and Sally wondered how. "Was Uncle Hank a mercenary, too?"

"Yes, just briefly," she said. "Hank was never one to rush in and risk killing himself. It was so ironic that he died overseas in his sleep, of a heart condition nobody even knew he had."

That was a surprise, along with all the others that Sally was getting. Uncle Hank had been very handsome, but not assertive or particularly tough.

"But Ebenezer said he served with Uncle Hank."

"Yes. In basic training, before they joined the Green Berets," Jessica said. "Hank didn't pass the training course. Ebenezer did. In fact," she added amusedly, "he was able to do the Fan Dance."

"Fan Dance?"

"It's a specialized course they put the British commandos, the Special Air Service, guys through. Not many soldiers, even career soldiers, are able to finish it, much less able to pass it on the first try. Eb did. He was briefly 'loaned' to them while he was in army intelligence, for some top secret assignment."

Sally had never thought very much about Ebenezer's profession, except that she'd guessed he was once in the military. She wasn't sure how she felt about it. A man who'd been in the military might still have a soft spot or two inside. She was almost certain that a commando, a soldier for hire, wouldn't have any.

"You're very quiet," Jessica said.

"I never thought of Ebenezer in such a profession," she replied, moving to look out the window at the November landscape. "I guess it was right there in front of me, and I didn't see it. No wonder he kept to himself."

"He still does," she replied. "And only a few people know about his past. His men do, of course," she added, and there was an inflection in her tone that was suddenly different.

"Do you know any of his men?"

Jessica's face tautened. "One or two. I believe Dallas Kirk still works for him. And Micah Steele does consulting work when Eb asks him to," she added and smiled. "Micah's a good guy. He's the only one of Eb's old colleagues who still works in the trade. He lives in Nassau, but he spends an occasional week helping Ebenezer train men when he's needed."

"And Dallas Kirk?"

Jessica's soft face went very hard. At her side, one of her small hands clenched. "Dallas was badly wounded in a firefight a year ago. He came home shot to pieces and Eb found something for him to teach in the tactics courses. He doesn't speak to me, of course. We had a difficult parting some years ago."

That was intriguing, and Sally was going to find out about it one day. But she didn't press her luck. "How about fajitas for supper?" she asked.

Jessica's glower dissolved into a smile. "Sounds lovely!"

"I'll get right on them." Sally went back into the kitchen, her head spinning with the things she'd learned about people she thought she knew. Life, she considered, was always full of surprises.

CHAPTER TWO

EBENEZER WAS A MAN of his word. He showed up early the next morning as Sally was out by the corral fence watching her two beef cattle graze. She'd bought them to raise with the idea of stocking her freezer. Now they had names. The white-faced Black Angus mixed steer was called Bob, the white-faced red-coated Hereford she called Andy. They were pets. She couldn't face the thought of sitting down to a plate of either one of them.

The familiar black pickup stopped at the fence and Ebenezer got out. He was wearing jeans and a blue checked shirt with boots and a light-colored straw Stetson. No chaps, so he wasn't working cattle today.

He joined Sally at the fence. "Don't tell me. They're table beef."

She spared him a resentful glance. "Right."

"And you're going to put them in the freezer."

She swallowed. "Sure."

He only chuckled. He paused to light a cigar, with one big booted foot propped on the lower rung of the fence. "What are their names?"

"That's Andy and that's... Bob." She flushed.

He didn't say a word, but his raised eyebrow was eloquent through the haze of expelled smoke.

"They're watch-cattle," she improvised.

His eyes twinkled. "I beg your pardon?"

"They're attack steers," she said with a reluctant grin.

"At the first sign of trouble, they'll come right through the fence to protect me. Of course, if they get shot in the line of duty," she added, "I'll eat them!"

He pushed his Stetson back over clean blond-streaked brown hair and looked down at her with lingering amusement. "You haven't changed much in six years."

"Neither have you," she retorted shyly. "You're still smoking those awful things."

He glanced at the big cigar and shrugged. "A man has to have a vice or two to round him out," he pointed out. "Besides, I only have the occasional one, and never inside. I have read the studies on smoking," he added dryly.

"Lots of people who smoke read those studies," she agreed. "And then they quit!"

He smiled. "You can't reform me," he told her. "It's a waste of time to try. I'm thirty-six and very set in my ways."

"I noticed."

He took a puff from the cigar and studied her steers. "I suppose they follow you around like dogs."

"When I go inside the fence with them," she agreed. She felt odd with him; safe and nervous and excited, all at once. She could smell the fresh scent of the soap he used, and over it a whiff of expensive cologne. He was close at her side, muscular and vibrating with sensuality. She wanted to move closer, to feel that strength all around her. It made her self-conscious. After six years, surely the attraction should have lessened a little.

He glanced down at her, noticing how she picked at her cuticles and nibbled on her lower lip. His green eyes narrowed and there was a faint glitter in them.

She felt the heat of his gaze and refused to lift her face. She wondered if it looked as hot as it felt.

"You haven't forgotten a thing," he said suddenly, the cigar in his hand absently falling to his side, whirls of smoke climbing into the air beside him.

"About what?" she choked.

He caught her long, blond ponytail and tugged her closer, so that she was standing right up against him. The scent of him, the heat of him, the muscular ripple of his body combined to make her shiver with repressed feelings.

He shifted, coaxing her into the curve of his body, his eyes catching hers and holding them relentlessly. He could feel her faint trembling, hear the excited whip of her breath as she tried valiantly to hide it from him. But he could see her heartbeat jerking the fabric over her small breasts.

It was a relief to find her as helplessly attracted to him as she once had been. It made him arrogant with pride. He let go of the ponytail and drew his hand against her cheek, letting his thumb slide down to her mouth and over her chin to lift her eyes to his.

"To everything, there is a season," he said quietly.

She felt the impact of his steady, unblinking gaze in the most secret places of her body. She didn't have the experience to hide it, to protect herself. She only stood staring up at him, with all her insecurities and fears lying naked in her soft gray eyes.

His head bent and he drew his nose against hers in the sudden silence of the yard. His smoky breath whispered over her lips as he murmured, "Six years is a long time to go hungry."

She didn't understand what he was saying. Her eyes were on his hard, long, thin mouth. Her hands had flattened against his broad chest. Under it she could feel thick, soft hair and the beat of his heart. His breath smelled of cigar smoke and when his mouth gently covered hers, she wondered if she was going to faint with the unexpected delight of it. It had been so long!

He felt her immediate, helpless submission. His free arm went around her shoulders and drew her lazily against his muscular body while his hard mouth moved lightly over her lips, tasting her, assessing her experience. His mouth became insistent and she stiffened a little, unused to the tender probing of his tongue against her teeth.

She felt his smile before he lifted his head.

"You still taste of lemonade and cotton candy," he murmured with unconcealed pleasure.

"What do you mean?" she murmured, mesmerized by the hovering threat of his mouth.

"I mean, you still don't know how to do this." He searched her eyes quietly and then the smile left his face. "I did more damage than I ever meant to. You were seventeen. I had to hurt you to save you." He traced her mouth with his thumb and scowled down at her. "You don't know what my life was like in those days," he said solemnly, and for once his eyes were unguarded. The pain in them was visible for the first time Sally could remember.

"Aunt Jessica told me," she said slowly.

His eyes darkened. His face hardened. "All of it?"

She nodded.

He was still scowling. He released her to gaze off into the distance, absently lifting the cigar to his mouth. He blew out a cloud of smoke. "I'm not sure that I wanted you to know."

"Secrets are dangerous."

He glanced down at her, brooding. "More dangerous than you realize. I've kept mine for a long time, like your aunt."

"I had no idea what she did for a living, either." She glared up at him. "Thanks to the two of you, now I know how a mushroom feels, sitting in the dark."

He chuckled. "She wanted it that way. She felt you'd be safer if she kept you uninvolved."

She wanted to ask him about what Jessica had told her, that he'd phoned her about Sally before the painful move to Houston. But she didn't quite know how. She was shy with him.

He looked down at her again, his eyes intent on her softly flushed cheeks, her swollen mouth, her bright eyes. She lifted his heart. Just the sight of her made him feel welcome, comforted, cared for. He'd missed that. In all his life, Sally had been the first and only person who could thwart his black moods. She made him feel as if he belonged somewhere after a life of wandering. Even during the time she was in Houston, he kept in touch with Jessica, to get news of Sally, of where she was, what she was doing, of her plans. He'd always expected that she'd come back to him one day, or that he'd go to her, despite the way they'd parted. Love, if it existed, was surely a powerful force, immune to harsh words and distance. And time.

Sally's face was watchful, her eyes brimming over with excitement. She couldn't hide what she was feeling, and he loved being able to see it. Her hero worship had first irritated and then elated him. Women had wanted him since his teens, although some loved him for the danger that clung to him. One had rejected him because of it and savaged his pride. But, even so, it was Sally who made him ache inside.

He touched her soft mouth with his fingers, liking

the faint swell where he'd kissed it so thoroughly. "We'll have to practice more," he murmured wickedly.

She opened her mouth to protest that assumption when a laughing Stevie came running out the door like a little blond whirlwind, only to be caught up abruptly in Ebenezer's hard arms and lifted.

"Uncle Eb!" he cried, laughing delightedly, making Sally realize that if she hadn't been around Ebenezer since their move from Houston, Jessica and Stevie certainly had.

"Hello, tiger," came the deep, pleasant reply. He put the boy back down on his feet. "Want to go to my place with Sally and learn karate?"

"Like the Teenage Mutant Ninja Turtles in the movies? Radical!" he exclaimed.

"Karate?" Sally asked, hesitating.

"Just a few moves, and only for self-defense," he assured her. "You'll enjoy it. It's necessary," he added when she seemed to hesitate.

"Okay," she capitulated.

He led the way back into the house to where Jessica was sitting in the living room, listening to the news on the television.

"All this mess in the Balkans," she said sadly. "Just when we think we've got peace, everything erupts all over again. Those poor people!"

"Fortunes of war," Eb said with a smile. "How's it going, Jess?"

"I can't complain, I guess, except that they won't let me drive anymore," she said, tongue-in-cheek.

"Wait until they get that virtual reality vision perfected," he said easily. "You'll be able to do anything."

"Optimist," she said, grinning.

"Always. I'm taking these two over to the ranch for

a little course in elementary self-defense," he added quietly.

"Good idea," Jessica said at once.

"I don't like leaving you here alone," Sally ventured, remembering what she'd been told about the danger.

"She won't be," Eb replied. He looked at Jessica and one eye narrowed before he added, "I'm sending Dallas Kirk over to keep her company."

"No!" Jessica said furiously. She actually stood up, vibrating. "No, Eb! I don't want him within a mile of me! I'd rather be shot to pieces!"

"This isn't multiple choice," came a deep, drawling voice from the general direction of the hall.

As Sally turned from Jessica's white face, a slender blond man with dark eyes came into the room. He walked with the help of a fancy-looking cane. He was dressed like Eb, in casual clothes, khaki slacks and a bush jacket. He looked like something right out of Africa.

"This is Dallas Kirk," Eb introduced him to Sally. "He was born in Texas. His real name is Jon, but we've always called him Dallas. This is Sally Johnson," he told the blond man.

Dallas nodded. "Nice to meet you," he said formally.

"You know Jess," Eb added.

"Yes. I…know her," he said with the faintest emphasis in that lazy Western drawl, during which Jess's face went from white to scarlet and she averted her eyes.

"Surely you can get along for an hour," Eb said impatiently. "I really can't leave you here by yourself, Jess."

Dallas glared at her. "Mind telling me why?" he asked Eb. "She's a better shot than I am."

Jessica stood rigidly by her chair. "He doesn't know?" she asked Eb.

Eb's face was rigid. "He wouldn't talk about you, and the subject didn't come up until he was away on assignment. No. He doesn't know."

"Know what?" Dallas demanded.

Jessica's chin lifted. "I'm blind," she said matter-of-factly, almost with satisfaction, as if she knew it would hurt him.

The look on the newcomer's face was a revelation. Sally only wished she knew of what. He shifted as if he'd sustained a physical blow. He walked slowly up to her and waved a hand in front of her face.

"Blind!" he said huskily. "For how long?"

"Six months," she said, feeling for the arms of the chair. She sat back down a little clumsily. "I was in a wreck. An accident," she added abruptly.

"It was no accident," Eb countered coldly. "She was run off the road by two of Lopez's men. They got away before the police came."

Sally gasped. This was a new explanation. She'd just heard about the wreck—not about the cause of it. Dallas's hand on the cane went white from the pressure he was exerting on it. "What about Stevie?" he asked coldly. "Is he all right? Was he injured?"

"He wasn't with me at the time. And he's fine. Sally lives with us and helps take care of him," Jess replied, her voice unusually tense. "We share the chores. She's my niece," she added abruptly, almost as if to warn him of something.

Dallas looked preoccupied. But when Stevie came running back into the room, he turned abruptly and his eyes widened as he stared at the little boy.

"I'm ready!" Stevie announced, holding out his arms to show the gray sweats he was wearing. His dark eyes were shimmering with joy. "This is how they look on television when they practice. Is it okay?"

"It's fine," Eb replied with a smile.

"Who's he?" Stevie asked, big-eyed, as he looked at the blond man with the cane who was staring at him, as if mesmerized.

"That's Dallas," Eb said easily. "He works for me."

"Hi," Stevie said, naturally outgoing. He stared at the cane. "I guess you're from Texas with a name like that, huh? I'm sorry about your leg, Mr. Dallas. Does it hurt much?"

Dallas took a slow breath before he answered. "When it rains."

"My mama's hip hurts when it rains, too," he said. "Are you coming with us to learn karate?"

"He's already forgotten more than I know," Eb said in a dry tone. "No, he's going to take care of your mother while we're gone."

"Why?" Stevie asked, frowning.

"Because her hip hurts," Sally lied through her teeth. "Ready to go?"

"Sure! Bye, Mom." He ran to kiss her cheek and be hugged warmly. He moved back, smiling up at the blond man who hadn't cracked a smile yet. "See you."

Dallas nodded.

Sally was staggered by the resemblance of the boy to the man, and almost remarked on it. But before she could, Eb caught her eyes. There was a look in them that she couldn't decipher, but it stopped her at once.

"We'd better go," he said. He took Sally by the arm. "Come on, Stevie. We won't be long, Jess," he called back.

"I'll count the seconds," she said under her breath as they left the room.

Dallas didn't say anything, and it was just as well that she couldn't see the look in his eyes.

IT WAS IMPOSSIBLE to talk in front of Stevie as they drove through the massive electronic gates at the Scott ranch. He, like Sally, was fascinated by the layout, which included a helipad, a landing strip with a hangar, a swimming pool and a ranch house that looked capable of sleeping thirty people. There were also target ranges and guest cabins and a formidable state-of-the-art gym housed in what looked like a gigantic Quonset hut like those used during the Second World War in the Pacific theater. There were several satellite dishes as well, and security cameras seemingly on every available edifice.

"This is incredible," Sally said as they got out of the truck and went with him toward the gym.

"Maintaining it is incredible," Eb said with a chuckle. "You wouldn't believe the level of technology required to keep it all functioning."

Stevie had found the thick blue plastic-covered mat on the wood floor and was already rolling around on it and trying the punching bag suspended from one of the steel beams that supported other training equipment.

"Stevie looks like that man, Dallas," she said abruptly.

He grimaced. "Haven't you and Jess ever talked?"

"I didn't know anything about Dallas and my aunt until you told me," she said simply.

"This is something she needs to tell you, in her own good time."

She studied the youngster having fun on the mat. "He isn't my uncle's child, is he?"

There was a rough sound from the man beside her. "What makes you think so?"

"For one thing, because he's the image of Dallas. But also because Uncle Hank and Aunt Jessie were married for years with no kids, and suddenly she got pregnant just before he died overseas," she replied. "Stevie was like a miracle."

"In some ways, I suppose he was. But it led to Hank asking for a combat assignment, and even though he died of a heart condition, Jess has had nightmares ever since out of guilt." He looked down at her. "You can't tell her that you know."

"Fair enough. Tell me the rest."

"She and Dallas were working together on an assignment. It was one of those lightning attractions that overcome the best moral obstacles. They were alone too much and finally the inevitable happened. Jess turned up pregnant. When Dallas found out, he went crazy. He demanded that Jess divorce Hank and marry him, but she wouldn't. She swore that Dallas wasn't the father of her child, Hank was, and she had no intention of divorcing her husband."

"Oh, dear."

"Hank knew that she'd been with another man, of course, because he'd always been sterile. Dallas didn't know that. And Hank hadn't told Jessica until she announced that she was expecting a child." He shrugged. "He wouldn't forgive her. Neither would Dallas. When Hank died, Dallas didn't even try to get in touch with Jess. He really believed that Stevie was Hank's child. Until about ten minutes ago, that is," he added with a wry smile. "It didn't take much guesswork for him to see the resemblance. I think we won't go back for a couple of hours. I don't want to walk into the firefight he's probably having with Jess even as we speak."

She bit her lower lip. "Poor Jess."

"Poor Dallas," he countered. "After the fight with Jessie, he took every damned dangerous assignment he could find, the more dangerous the better. Last year in Africa, Dallas was shot to pieces. They sent him home with wounds that would have killed a lesser man."

"No wonder he looks so bitter."

"He's bitter because he loved Jess and though she felt the same, she wasn't willing to hurt Hank by leaving him. But in the end, she still hurt him. He couldn't live with the idea that she was having some other man's child. It destroyed their marriage."

She grimaced. "What a tragedy, for all of them."

"Yes."

She looked toward Stevie, smiling. "He's a great kid," she said. "I'd love him even if he wasn't my first cousin."

"He's got grit and personality to boot."

"You wouldn't think so at midnight when you're still trying to get him to sleep."

He smiled as he studied her. "You love kids, don't you?"

"Oh, yes," she said fervently. "I love teaching."

"Don't you want some of your own?" he asked with a quizzical smile.

She flushed and wouldn't look at him. "Sure. One day."

"Why not now?"

"Because I've already got more responsibilities than I can manage. Pregnancy would be a complication I couldn't handle, especially now."

"You sound as if you're planning to do it all alone."

She shrugged. "There is such a thing as artificial insemination."

He turned her toward him, looking very solemn

and adult. "How would it feel, carrying the child of a man you didn't even know, having it grow inside your body?"

She bit her lower lip. She hadn't considered the intimacy of what he was suggesting. She felt, and looked, confused.

"A baby should be made out of love, the natural way, not in a test tube," he said very softly, searching her shocked eyes. "Well, not unless it's the only way two people can have a child," he added. "But that's an entirely different circumstance."

Her lips parted on the surge of emotion that made her heart race. "I don't know…that I want to get that close to anyone, ever."

He seemed even more remote. "Sally, you can't let the past lock you into solitude forever. I frightened you because I wanted to keep you at bay. If I didn't discourage you somehow I was afraid that the temptation might prove too much for me. You were such a baby." He scowled bitterly. "What happened wouldn't have been so devastating if you'd had even a little experience with men. For God's sake, didn't they ever let you date anyone?"

She shook her head, her teeth clenched tightly together. "My mother was certain that I'd get pregnant or catch some horrible disease. She talked about it all the time. She made boys who came to the house so uncomfortable that they never came back."

"I didn't know that," he said tautly.

"Would it have made any difference?" she asked miserably.

He touched her face with cool, firm fingers. "Yes. I wouldn't have gone nearly as far as I did, if I'd known."

"You wanted to get rid of me…"

He put his thumb over her soft mouth. "I wanted you," he whispered huskily. "But a seventeen-year-old isn't mature enough for a love affair. And that would have been impossible in Jacobsville, even if I'd been crazy enough to go all the way with you that day. You were almost thirteen years my junior."

She was beginning to see things from his point of view. She hadn't tried before. There had been so much resentment, so much bitterness, so much hurt. She looked at him and saw, for the first time, the pain of the memory in his face.

"I was desperate," she said, speaking softly. "They told me out of the blue that they were divorcing each other. They were selling the house and moving out of town. Dad was going to marry Beverly, this girl he'd met at the college where he taught. Mom couldn't live in the same town with everybody knowing that Dad had thrown her over for someone younger. She married a man she hardly knew shortly afterward, just to save her pride." She stared at his mouth with more hunger than she realized. "I knew that I'd never see you again. I only wanted you to kiss me." She swallowed, averting her eyes. "I must have been crazy."

"We both were." He cupped her face in his hands and lifted it to his quiet eyes. "For what it's worth, I never meant it to go further than a kiss. A very chaste kiss, at that." His eyes drifted down involuntarily to the soft thrust of her breasts almost touching his shirt. He raised an eyebrow at the obvious points. "That's why it wasn't chaste."

She didn't understand. "What is?"

He looked absolutely exasperated. "How can you be that old and know nothing?" he asked. He glanced over her shoulder at Stevie, who was facing the other way and giving the punching bag hell. He took Sally's own finger and drew it across her taut breast. He looked straight into her eyes as he said softly, "That's why."

She realized that it must have something to do with being aroused, but no one had ever told her blatantly that it was a visible sign of desire. She went scarlet.

"You greenhorn," he murmured indulgently. "What a babe in arms."

"I don't read those sort of books," she said haughtily.

"You should. In fact, I'll buy you a set of them. Maybe a few videos, too," he murmured absently, watching the expressions come and go on her face.

"You varmint...!"

He caught her top lip in both of his and ran his tongue lazily under it. She stiffened, but her hands were clinging to him, not pushing.

"You remember that, don't you, Sally?" he murmured with a smile. "Do you remember what comes next?"

She jerked back from him, staggering. Her eyes found Stevie, still oblivious to the adults.

Eb's eyes were blatant on the thrust of her breasts and he was smiling.

She crossed her arms over her chest and glared up at him. "You just stop that," she gritted. "I'll bet you weren't born knowing everything!"

He chuckled. "No, I wasn't. But I didn't have a mother to keep my nose clean, either," he said. "My old man was military down to his toenails, and he didn't believe in gentle handling or delicacy. He used women until the day he died." He laughed coldly. "He told me that there was no such thing as a good woman, that they were to be enjoyed and put aside."

She was appalled. "Didn't he love your mother?"

"He wanted her, and she wouldn't be with him until

they got married," he said simply. "So they got married. She died having me. They were living in a small town outside the military base where he was stationed. He was overseas on assignment and she lived alone, isolated. She went into labor and there were complications. There was nothing that could have been done for her by the time she was found. If a neighbor hadn't come to look in on us, I'd have died with her."

"It must have been a shock for your father," she said.

"If it was, it never showed. He left me with a cousin until I was old enough to obey orders, then I went to live with him. I learned a lot from him, but he wasn't a loving man." His eyes narrowed on her soft face. "I followed his example and joined the army. I was lucky enough to get into the Green Berets. Then when I was due for discharge, a man approached me about a top secret assignment and told me what it would pay." He shrugged. "Money is a great temptation for a young man with a domineering father. I said yes and he never spoke to me again. He said that what I was doing was a perversion of the military, and that I wasn't fit to be any officer's son. He disowned me on the spot. I didn't hear from him again. A few years later, I got a letter from his post commander, stating that he'd died in combat. He had a military funeral with full honors."

The pain of those years was in his lean, hard face. Impulsively she put a hand on his arm. "I'm sorry," she told him quietly. "He must have been the sort of man who only sees one side of any argument."

He was surprised by her compassion. "Don't you think mercenaries are evil, Miss Purity?" he asked sarcastically.

CHAPTER THREE

SALLY LOOKED UP into pain-laced green eyes and without thinking, she lifted her hand from his arm and raised it toward his hard cheek. But when she realized what she was doing, she drew it back at once.

"No, I don't think mercenaries are evil," she said quickly, embarrassed by the impulsive gesture that, thankfully, he didn't seem to notice. "There are a lot of countries where atrocities are committed, whose governments don't have the manpower or resources to protect their people. So, someone else gets hired to do it. I don't think it's a bad thing, when there's a legitimate cause."

He was surprised by her matter-of-fact manner. He'd wondered for years how she might react when she learned about what he did for a living. He'd expected everything from revulsion to shock, especially when he remembered how his former fiancée had reacted to the news. But Sally wasn't squeamish or judgmental.

He'd seen her hand jerk back and it had wounded him. But now, on hearing her opinion of his work, his heart lifted. "I didn't expect you to credit me with noble motives."

"They are, though, aren't they?" she asked confidently.

"As a matter of fact, in my case, they are," he replied. "Even in my green days, I never did it just for the money. I had to believe in what I was risking my life for."

She grinned. "I thought maybe it was like on television," she confessed. "But Jess said it was nothing like fiction."

He cocked an eyebrow. "Oh, I wouldn't say that," he mused. "Parts of it are."

"Such as?"

"We had a guy like B.A. Barrabas in one unit I led," he said. "We really did have to knock him out to get him on a plane. But he quit the group before we got inventive."

She laughed. "Too bad. You'd have had plenty of stories to tell about him."

He was quiet for a moment, studying her.

"Do I have a zit on my nose?" she asked pleasantly.

He reached out and caught the hand she'd started to lift toward him earlier and kissed its soft palm. "Let's get to work," he said, pulling her along to the mat. "I'll change into my sweats and we'll cover the basics. We won't have a lot of time," he added dryly. "I expect Jess to call very soon with an ultimatum about Dallas."

JESS AND DALLAS had squared off, in fact, the minute they heard the truck crank and pull out of the yard.

Dallas glared at her from his superior height, leaning heavily on his cane. He wished she could see him, because his eyes were full of anger and bitterness.

"Did you think I wouldn't see that Stevie is the living image of me? My son," he growled at her. "You had my son! And you lied to me about it and wouldn't ask Hank for a divorce!"

"I couldn't!" she exclaimed. "For heaven's sake, he adored me. He'd never have cheated on me. I couldn't bring myself to tell him that I'd had an affair with his best friend!"

"I could have told him," he returned furiously. "He was no angel, Jess, despite the wings you're trying to paint on him. Or do you think he never strayed on those overseas jaunts?" he chided.

She stiffened. "That's not true!"

"It is true!" he replied angrily. "He knew he couldn't get anybody pregnant, and he was sure you'd never find out."

She put a hand to her head. She'd never dreamed that Hank had cheated on her. She'd felt so guilty, when all the time, he was doing the same thing—and then judging her brutally for what she'd done. "I didn't know," she said miserably.

"Would it have made a difference?"

"I don't know. Maybe it would have." She smoothed the dress over her legs. "You thought Stevie was yours from the beginning, didn't you?"

"No. I didn't know Hank was sterile until later on. You told me the child was Hank's and I believed you. Hell, by then, I couldn't even be sure that it was his."

"You didn't think—" She stopped abruptly. "Oh, dear God, you thought you were one in a line?" she exploded, horrified. "You thought I ran around on Hank with any man who asked me?"

"I knew very little about you except that you knocked me sideways," he said flatly. "I knew Hank ran around on you. I assumed you were allowed the same freedom." He turned away and walked to the window, staring out at the flat horizon. "I asked you to divorce Hank just to see what you'd say. It was exactly what I expected. You had it made—a husband who tolerated your unfaithfulness, and no danger of falling in love."

"I thought I had a good marriage until you came along," she said bitterly.

He turned, his eyes blazing. "Don't make it sound cheap, Jess," he said harshly. "Neither of us could stop that night. Neither of us tried."

She put her face in her hands and shivered. The memory of how it had been could still reduce her to tears. She'd been in love for the first time in her life, but not with her husband. This man had haunted her ever since. Stevie was the mirror image of him.

"I was so ashamed," she choked. "I betrayed Hank. I betrayed everything I believed in about loyalty and duty and honor. I felt like a Saturday night special at the bordello afterward."

He scowled. "I never treated you that way," he said harshly.

"Of course you didn't!" she said miserably, wiping at tears. "But I was raised to believe that people got married and never cheated on each other. I was a virgin when I married Hank, and nobody in my whole family was ever divorced until Sally's father, my brother, was." She shook her head, oblivious to the expression that washed over Dallas's hard, lean face. "My parents were happily married for fifty years before they died."

"Sometimes it doesn't work," he said flatly, but in a less hostile tone. "That's nobody's fault."

She smoothed back her short hair and quickly wiped away the tears. "Maybe not."

He moved back toward her and sat down in a chair across from hers, putting the cane down on the floor. He leaned forward with a hard sigh and looked at Jessica's pale, wan face with bitterness while he tried to find the words.

She heard the cane as he placed it on the floor. "Eb

said you were badly hurt overseas," she said softly, wishing with all her heart that she could see him. "Are you all right?"

That husky softness in her tone, that exquisite concern, was almost too much for him. He grasped her slender hands in his and held them tightly. "I'm better off than you seem to be," he said heavily. "What a hell of a price we paid for that night, Jess."

She felt the hot sting of tears. "It was very high," she had to admit. She reached out hesitantly to find his face. Her fingers traced it gently, finding the new scars, the new hardness of its elegant lines. "Stevie looks like you," she said softly, her unseeing eyes so full of emotion that he couldn't bear to look into them.

"Yes."

She searched her darkness with anguish for a face she would never see again. "Don't be bitter," she pleaded. "Please don't hate me."

He pulled her hand away as if it scalded him. "I've done little else for the past five years," he said flatly. "But maybe you're right. All the rage in the world won't change the past." He let go of her hand. "We have to pick up the pieces and go on."

She hesitated. "Can we at least be friends?"

He laughed coldly. "Is that what you want?"

She nodded. "Eb says you've given up overseas assignments and that you're working for him. I want you to get to know Stevie," she added quietly. "Just in case…"

"Oh, for God's sake, stop it!" he exploded, rising awkwardly from the chair with the help of the cane. "Lopez won't get you. We aren't going to let anything happen to you."

She leaned back in her chair without replying. They

both knew that Lopez had contacts everywhere and that he never gave up. If he wanted her dead, he could get her. She didn't want her child left alone in the world.

"I'm going to make some coffee," Dallas said tautly, refusing to think about the possibility of a world without her in it. "What do you take in yours?"

"I don't care," she said indifferently.

He didn't say another word. He went into the kitchen and made a pot of coffee while Jessica sat stiffly in her own living room and contemplated the direction her life had taken.

"YOU HAVE GOT…to be kidding!" Sally choked as she dragged herself up from the mat for the twentieth time. "You mean I'm going to spend two hours falling down? I thought you were going to teach me self-defense!"

"I am," Eb replied easily. He, too, was wearing sweats now, and he'd been teaching her side breakfalls, first left and then right. "First you learn how to fall properly, so you don't hurt yourself landing. Then we move on to stances, hand positions and kicks. One step at a time."

She swept her arm past her hip and threw herself down on her side, falling with a loud thud but landing neatly. Beside her, Stevie was going at it with a vengeance and laughing gleefully.

"Am I doing it right?" she puffed, already perspiring. She was very much out of condition, despite the work she did around the house.

He nodded. "Very nice. Be careful about falling too close to the edge of the mat, though. The floor's hard."

She moved further onto the mat and did it again.

"If you think these are fun," he mused, "wait until we do forward breakfalls."

She gaped at him. "You mean I'm going to have to fall deliberately on my face? I'll break my nose!"

"No, you won't," he said, moving her aside. "Watch."

He executed the movement to perfection, catching his weight neatly on his hands and forearms. He jumped up again. "See? Simple."

"For you," she agreed, her eyes on the muscular body that was as fit as that of a man half his age. "Do you train all the time?"

"I have to," he said. "If I let myself get out of shape, I won't be of any use to my students. Great job, Stevie," he called to the boy, who beamed at him.

"Of course he's doing a great job," she muttered. "He's so close to the ground already that he doesn't have far to fall!"

"Poor old lady," he chided gently.

She glared in his direction as she swept her arm forward and threw herself down again. "I'm not old. I'm just out of condition."

He looked at her, sprawled there on the mat, and his lips pursed as he sketched every inch of her. "Funny, I'd have said you were in prime condition. And not just for karate."

She cleared her throat and got to her feet again. "When did you start learning this stuff?"

"When I was in grammar school," he said. "My father taught me."

"No wonder it looks so easy when you do it."

"I train hard. It's saved my life a few times."

She studied his scarred face with curiosity. She could see the years in it, and the hardships. She knew very little about military operations, except for what she'd seen in movies and on television. And as Jess had told her, it wasn't like that in real life. She tried to imagine an armed adversary coming at her and she stiffened.

"Something wrong?" he asked gently.

"I was trying to imagine being attacked," she said. "It makes me nervous."

"It won't, when you gain a little confidence. Stand up straight," he said. "Never walk with your head down in a slumped posture. Always look as if you know where you're going, even if you don't. And always, always, run if you can. Never stand and fight unless you're trapped and your life is in danger."

"Run? You're kidding, of course?"

"No," he said. "I'll give you an example. A man of any size and weight on drugs is more than a match for any three other men. What I'm going to teach you might work on an untrained adversary who's sober. But a man who's been drinking, or especially a man who's using drugs, can kill you outright, regardless of what I can teach you. Don't you ever forget that. Overconfidence kills."

"I'll bet you don't teach your men to run," she said accusingly.

His eyes were quiet and full of bad memories. "Sally, a recruit in one of my groups emptied the magazine of his rifle into an enemy soldier on drugs at point-blank range. The enemy kept right on coming. He killed the recruit before he finally fell dead himself."

Her lower jaw fell.

"That was my reaction, too," he informed her. "Absolute disbelief. But it's true. If anyone high on drugs comes at you, don't try to reason with him…you can't. And don't try to fight him. Run like hell. If a full automatic clip won't bring a man down, you certainly can't. Neither can even a combat-hardened man, alone. In that sort of situation, it's just basic common sense to get out of the way as quickly as possible if there's any chance of escape, and pride be damned."

"I'll remember," she said, all her confidence vanishing. She could see in Eb's eyes that he'd watched that recruit die, and had to live with the memory forever in his mind. Probably it was one of many nightmarish episodes he'd like to forget.

"Sometimes retreat really is the better part of valor," he said, smiling.

"You're educational."

He smiled slowly. "Am I, now?" he asked, and the way he looked at her didn't have much to do with teaching her self-defense. "I can think of a few areas where you need...improvement."

She glanced at Stevie, who was still falling on the mat. "You shouldn't try to shoot ducks in a barrel," she told him. "It's unsporting."

"Shooting is not what I have in mind."

She cleared her throat. "I suppose I should try falling some more." She brightened. "Say, if I learn to do this well, I could try falling on an adversary!"

"Ineffective unless you want to gain three hundred pounds," he returned. He grinned. "Although, you could certainly experiment on me, if you want to. It might immobilize me. We won't know until we try it. Want me to lie down and let you practice?" he added with twinkling eyes.

She laughed, but nervously. "I don't think I'm ready to try that right away."

"Suit yourself. No hurry. We've got plenty of time."

She remembered Jess and the drug lord and her eyes grew worried. "Is it really dangerous for us at home...?"

He held up a cautioning hand. "Stevie, how about a soft drink?"

"That would be great!"

"There are some cans of soda in the fridge in the kitchen. How about bringing one for me and your aunt as well?"

"Sure thing!"

Stevie took off like a bullet.

"Yes, it's dangerous," Eb said quietly. "You aren't to go alone, anywhere, at night. I'll always have a man watching the house, but if you have to go to a meeting or some such thing, let me know and I'll go with you."

"Won't that cramp your social life?" she asked without quite meeting his eyes.

"I don't have a social life," he said with a faint smile. "Not of the sort you're talking about."

"Oh."

His face tautened. "Neither do you, if I can believe Jess."

She shifted on the mat. "I haven't really had much time for men."

"You don't have to spare my feelings," he told her quietly. "I know I've caused you some sleepless nights. But you've waited too long to deal with it. The longer you wait, the harder it's going to be to form a relationship with a man."

"I have Jess and Stevie to think about."

"That's an excuse. And not a very good one."

She felt uncomfortable with her memories. She wrapped her arms around her chest and looked at him with shattered dreams in her eyes.

He took a sharp breath. "It will never be like that again," he said curtly. "I promise you it won't."

She averted her eyes to the mat. "Do you think Jess

and Dallas have done each other in by now?" she asked, trying to change the subject.

He moved closer, watching her stiffen, watching her draw away from him mentally. His big, lean hands caught her shoulders and he made her look at him.

"You're older now," he said, his voice steady and low. "You should know more about men than you did, even if you've had to learn it through books and television. I was fiercely aroused that day, it had been a long, dry spell, and you were seventeen years old. Get the picture?"

For the first time, she did. Her eyes searched his, warily, and nodded.

His hands contracted on her soft arms. "You might try it again," he said softly.

"Try what?"

"What you did that afternoon," he murmured, smiling tenderly. "Wearing sexy clothes and perfume and making a beeline for me. Anything could happen."

Her eyes were sadder than she realized as she met his even gaze. "I'm not the same person I was then," she told him. "But you still are."

The light seemed to go out of him. His pale eyes narrowed, fastened to hers. "No," he said after a minute. "I've changed, too. I lost my taste for commando work a long time ago. I teach tactics now. That's all I do."

"You're not a family man," she replied bravely.

Something changed in his face, in his eyes, as he studied her. "I've thought about that a lot recently," he contradicted. "About a home and children. I might have to give up some of the contract work I do, once the kids came along. I won't allow my children anywhere near weapons. But I can always write field manuals and train teachers in tactics and strategy and intelligence-gathering," he added.

"You don't know that you could settle for that," she pointed out.

"Not until I try," he agreed. His gaze fell to her soft mouth and lingered there. "But then, no man really wants to tie himself down. It takes a determined woman to make him want it."

She felt as if he were trying to tell her something, but before she could ask him to clarify what he'd said, Stevie was back with an armful of soft drinks and the moment was lost.

JESS AND DALLAS weren't speaking at all when the others arrived. Dallas was toying with a cup of cold coffee, looking unapproachable. When Eb came in the door, Dallas went out it, without a word or a backward glance.

"I don't need to ask how it went," Eb murmured.

"It would be pretty pointless," Jessica said dully.

"Mama, I learned to do breakfalls! I wish I could show you," Stevie said, climbing into his mother's lap and hugging her.

She fought tears as she cuddled him close and kissed his sweaty forehead. "Good for you! You listen when Eb tells you something. He's very good."

"Stevie's a natural," Eb chuckled. "In fact, so is your niece." He gave Sally a slow going-over with his eyes.

"She's a quick learner," Jessica said. "Like I was, once."

"I have to get back," Eb said. "There's nothing to worry about right now," he added, careful not to speak too bluntly in front of the child. "I have everything in hand. But I have told Sally to let me know if she plans to go out alone at night, for any reason."

"I will," Sally promised. She didn't want to risk her aunt's life, or Stevie's, by being too independent.

Eb nodded. "We'll keep the lessons up at least three times a week," he told Sally. "I want to move you into self-defense pretty quickly."

She understood why and felt uneasy. "Okay."

"Don't worry," he said gently. "Everything's going to be fine. I know exactly what I'm doing."

She managed a smile for him. "I know that."

"Walk me to the door," he coaxed. "See you, Jess."

"Take care, Eb," Jessie replied, her goodbye echoed by her son's.

On the front porch, Eb closed the door and looked down into Sally's wide gray eyes with concern and something more elusive.

"I'll have the house watched," he promised. "But you have to be careful about even normal things like opening the door when someone comes. Always keep the chain lock on until you know who's out there. Another thing, you have to keep your doors and windows locked, curtains drawn and an escape route always in mind."

She bit her lip worriedly. "I've never had to deal with anything like this."

His big, warm hands closed over her shoulders. "I know. I'm sorry that you and Stevie have been put in the line of fire along with Jess. But you can handle this," he said confidently. "You're strong. You can do whatever you have to do."

She searched his hard, lean face, saw the deep lines and scars that the violence of his life had carved into it, and knew that he would never lie to her. Her frown dissolved. His confidence in her made her feel capable of anything. She smiled.

He smiled back and traced a lazy line from her cheek

down to her soft mouth. "If Stevie wasn't so unpredictable, I'd kiss you," he said quietly. "I like your mouth under mine."

Her caught breath was audible. There had never been anyone who could do to her with words what he could.

He traced her lips, entranced. "I used to dream about that afternoon with you," he said in a sensuous tone. "I woke up sweating, swearing, hating myself for what I'd done." He laughed hollowly. "Hating you for what I'd done, too," he added. "I blamed us both. But I couldn't forget how it was."

She colored delicately and lowered her eyes to his broad chest under the shirt he wore. The memories were so close to the surface of her mind that it was impossible not to glimpse them from time to time. Now, they were blatant and embarrassing.

His lean hands moved up to frame her face and force her eyes to meet his. He wasn't smiling.

"No other man will ever have the taste of you that I did, that day," he said roughly. "You were so deliciously innocent."

Her lips parted at the intensity of his tone, at the faint glitter of his green eyes. "That isn't what you said at the time!" she accused.

"At the time," he murmured huskily, watching her mouth, "I was hurting so much that I didn't take time to choose my words. I just wanted you out of the damned truck before I started stripping you out of those tight little shorts you were wearing."

The flush in her cheeks got worse. The image of it was unbelievably shocking. Somehow, it had never occurred to her that at some point he might undress her, to gain access...

"What an expression," he said, chuckling in spite of

himself. "Hadn't you considered what might happen when you came on to me that hard?"

She shook her head.

His fingers slid into the blond hair at her temples where the long braid pulled it away from her face. "Someone should have had a long talk with you."

"You did," she recalled nervously.

"Long and explicit, the day afterward," he said, nodding. "You didn't want to hear it, but I made you. I liked to think that it might have saved you from an even worse experience."

"It wasn't exactly a bad experience," she said, staring at his shirt button. "That was part of the problem."

There was a long, static silence. "Sally," he breathed, and his mouth moved down slowly to cover hers in the silence of the porch.

She stood on tiptoe to coax him closer, lost in the memory of that long-ago afternoon. She felt his hands on her arms, guiding them up around his neck before they fell back to her hips and lifted her into the suddenly swollen contours of his muscular body.

She gasped, giving him the opening he wanted, so that he could deepen the kiss. She felt the warm hardness of his mouth against hers, the soft nip of his teeth, the deep exploration of his tongue. A warm flood of sensation rushed into her lower abdomen and she felt her whole body go tense with it. It was as if her body had become perfectly attuned to this man's years ago, and could never belong to anyone else.

He felt her headlong response and slowly let her back down, lifting his mouth away from hers. He studied her face, her swollen, soft mouth, her wide eyes, her dazed expression.

"Yes," he said huskily.

"Yes?"

He bent and nipped her lower lip sensuously before he pushed her away.

She stared up at him helplessly, feeling as if she'd just been dropped from a great height.

His eyes went to her breasts and lingered on the sharp little points so noticeable at the front of her blouse, the fabric jumping with every hard, quick beat of her heart.

She met that searching gaze and felt the power of it all the way to her toes.

"You know as well as I do that it's only a matter of time," he said softly. "It always has been."

She frowned. Her mind seemed to have shut down. She couldn't quite focus, and her legs felt decidedly weak.

His eyes were back on her breasts, swerving to the closed door, and to both curtained windows before he stepped in close and cupped her blatantly in his warm, sensuous hands.

Sally's mouth opened on a shocked gasp that became suddenly a moan of pleasure.

"I won't hurt you," he whispered, and his mouth covered hers hungrily.

It was the most passionate, adult kiss of her life, even eclipsing what had come before. His hands found their way under her sweatshirt and against lace-covered soft flesh. Her body responded instantly to the slow caresses. She curled into his body, eagerly submissive.

"Lord, what I wouldn't give to unfasten this," he groaned at her mouth as his fingers toyed with the closure at her back. "And sure as hell, Stevie would come outside the minute I did, and show and tell would take on a whole new meaning."

The idea of it amused him and he lifted his head, smiling down into Sally's equally laughing eyes.

"Ah, well," he said, removing his hands with evident reluctance. "All things come to those who wait," he added.

Sally blushed and moved a little away from him.

"Don't be embarrassed," he chided gently, his green eyes sparkling, full of mischief and pleasure. "All of us have a weak spot."

"Not you, man of steel," she teased.

"We'll talk about that next time," he said. "Meanwhile, remember what I said. Especially about night trips."

"Now where would I go alone at night in Jacobsville?" she asked patiently.

He only laughed. But even as she watched him drive away she remembered an upcoming parents and teachers meeting. There would be plenty of time to tell him about that, she reminded herself. She turned back into the house, her mouth and body still tingling pleasantly.

CHAPTER FOUR

JESSICA WAS SUBDUED after the time she'd spent with Dallas. Even Stevie noticed, and became more attentive. Sally cooked her aunt's favorite dishes and did her best to coax Jess into a better frame of mind. But the other woman's sadness was blatant.

With her mind on Jessica and not on time passing, she forgot that she had a parents and teachers meeting the next Tuesday night. She phoned Eb's ranch, as she'd been told to, but all she got was the answering machine and a message that only asked the caller to leave a name and number. She left a message, doubting that he'd hear it before she was safely home. She hadn't really believed him when he'd said the whole family was in danger, especially since nothing out of the ordinary had happened. But even so, surely nothing was going to happen to her on a two-mile drive home!

She sent Stevie home with a fellow teacher. The business meeting was long and explosive, and it was much later than usual when it was finally over. Sally spoke to the parents she knew and left early. She wasn't thinking about anything except her bed as she drove down the long, lonely road toward home. As she passed the large house and accompanying acreage where her three neighbors lived, she felt a chill. Three of them were out on their front porch. The light was on, and it looked as if they were arguing about something. They caught sight of her truck and there was an ominous stillness about them.

Sally drove faster, aware that she drew their attention as she went past them. Only a few more minutes, she thought, and she'd be home...

The steering wheel suddenly became difficult to turn and with horror she heard the sound of a tire going flatter and flatter. Her heart flipped over. She didn't have a spare. She'd rolled it out of the bed to make room for the cattle feed she'd taken home last week, having meant to ask Eb to help her put it back in again. But she'd have to walk the rest of the way, now. Worse, it was dark and those creepy men were still watching the truck.

Well, she told herself as she climbed out of the cab with her purse over her shoulder, they weren't going to give her any trouble. She had a loud whistling device, and she now knew at least enough self-defense to protect herself. Confident, despite Eb's earlier warnings, she locked the truck and started walking.

The sound of running feet came toward her. She looked over her shoulder and stopped, turning, her mouth set in a grim line. Two of the three men were coming down the road toward her in a straight line. Just be calm, she told herself. She was wearing a neat gray pantsuit with a white blouse, her hair was up in a French twist, and she lifted her chin to show that she wasn't afraid of them. Feeling her chances of a physical defense waning rapidly as she saw the size and strength of the two men, her hand went nervously to the whistle in her pocketbook and brought it by her side.

"Hey, there, sweet thing," one of the men called. "Got a flat? We'll help you change it."

The other man, a little taller, untidy, unshaved and

frankly unpleasant-looking, grinned at her. "You bet we will!"

"I don't have a spare, thank you all the same."

"We'll drive you home," the tall one said.

She forced a smile. "No, thanks. I'll enjoy the walk. Good night!"

She started to turn when they pounced. One knocked the whistle out of her hand and caught her arm behind her back, while the other one took her purse off her shoulder and went through it quickly. He pulled out her wallet, looked at everything in it, and finally took out a bill, dropping her self-defense spray with the purse.

"Ten lousy bucks," he muttered, dropping the bag as he stuffed the bill into his pocket. "Pity Lopez don't pay us better. This'll buy us a couple of six-packs, though."

"Let me go," Sally said, incensed. She tried to bring her elbow back into the man's stomach, as she'd seen an instructor on television do, but the man twisted her other arm so harshly that the pain stopped her dead.

The other man came right up to her and looked her up and down. "Not bad," he rasped. "Quick, bring her over here, off the road," he told the other man.

"Lopez won't like this!" The man on the porch came toward them, yelling across the road. "You'll draw attention to us!"

One of them made a rude remark. The third man went back up on the porch, his footsteps sounding unnaturally loud on the wood.

Sally was almost sick with fear, but she fought like a tigress. Her efforts to break free did no good. These men were bigger and stronger than she was, and they had her helpless. She couldn't get to her whistle or spray and every kick, punch she tried was effectively blocked. It occurred to her that these men knew self-defense moves, too, and how to avoid them. Too late, she remembered what Eb had said to her about overconfidence. These men weren't even drunk and they were too much for her.

Her heart beat wildly as she was dragged off the road to the thick grass at the roadside. She would struggle, she would fight, but she was no match for them. She knew she was in a lot of danger and it looked like there was no escape. Tears of impotent fury dripped from her eyes. Helpless while one of the men kept her immobilized, she remembered the sound of her own voice telling her aunt just a few weeks ago that she could handle anything. She'd been overconfident.

A sound buzzed in her head and at first she thought it was the prelude to a dead faint. It wasn't. The sound was growing closer. It was a pickup truck. The headlights illuminated her truck on the roadside, but not the struggle that was going on near it.

It was as if the driver knew what was happening without seeing it. The truck whipped onto the shoulder and was cut off. A man got out, a tall man in a shepherd's coat with a Stetson drawn over his brow. He walked straight toward the two men, who released Sally and turned to face the new threat. Eb!

"Car trouble?" a deep, gravelly voice asked sarcastically.

One of the men pulled a knife, and the other one approached the newcomer. "This ain't none of your business," the taller man said. "Get going."

The newcomer put his hands on his lean hips and stood his ground. "In your dreams."

"You'll wish you had," the taller of them replied harshly. He moved in with the knife close in at his side.

Sally stared in horror at Eb, who was inviting this lunatic to kill him! She knew from television how deadly a knife wound in the stomach could be. Hadn't Eb told her that the best way to survive a knife fight was to never get in one in the first place, to run like hell? And now Eb was going to be killed and it was going to be all her fault for not taking his advice and getting that tire fixed…!

Eb moved unexpectedly, with the speed of a striking cobra. The man with the knife was suddenly writhing on the ground, holding his forearm and sobbing. The other man rushed forward, to be flipped right out into the highway. He got up and rushed again. This time he was met with a violent, sharp movement that sent him to the ground, and he didn't get up.

Eb walked right over the unconscious man, ignoring the groaning man, and picked Sally up right off the ground in his arms. He carried her to his truck, balancing her on one powerful denim-covered thigh while he opened the passenger door and put her inside.

"My…purse," she whispered, giving in to the shock and fear that she'd tried so hard to hide. She was shaking so hard her speech was slurred.

He closed the door, retrieved her purse and wallet from the ground, and handed it in through his open door. "What did they take, baby?" he asked in a soft, comforting tone.

"The tall one…took a ten-dollar bill," she faltered, hating her own cowardice as she sobbed helplessly. "In his pocket…"

Eb retrieved it, tossed it to her and got in beside her.

"But those men," she protested.

"Be still for a minute. It's all right. They look worse than they are." He took a cell phone from his pocket, opened it, and dialed. "Bill? Eb Scott. I left you a couple of assailants on the Simmons Mill Road just past Bell's rental house. That's right, the very one." He glanced at Sally. "Not tonight. I'll tell her to come see you in the morning." There was a pause. "Nothing too bad; a couple of broken bones, that's all, but you might send the ambulance anyway. Sure. Thanks, Bill."

He powered down the phone and stuck it back into his jacket. "Fasten your seat belt. I'll take you home and send one of my men out to fix the truck and drive it back for you."

Her hands were shaking so badly that he had to do it for her. He turned on the light in the cab and looked at her intently. He saw the shock, the fear, the humiliation, the anger, all lying naked in her wide, shimmering gray eyes. Last, his eyes fell to her blouse, where the fabric was torn, and her simple cotton brassiere was showing. She was so upset that she didn't even realize how much bare skin was on display.

He took off the long-sleeved chambray shirt he was wearing over his black T-shirt and put her into it, fastening the buttons with deft, quick hands over the ripped blouse. His face grew hard as he saw the evidence of her ordeal.

"I had a...a...whistle," she choked. "I even remembered what you taught me about how to fight back...!"

He studied her solemnly. "I trained a company of recruits a few years ago," he said evenly. "They'd had hand-to-hand combat training and they knew all the right moves to counter any sort of physical attack. There wasn't one of them that I couldn't drop in less than ten seconds." His pale green eyes searched hers. "Even a martial artist can lose a match. It depends on the skill of his opponent and his ability to keep his head when the attack comes. I've seen karate instructors send advanced students running with nothing more dangerous than the yell, a sudden quick sound that paralyzes."

"Those two men…they couldn't…touch you," she pointed out, amazed.

His pale eyes had an alien coldness that made her shiver. "I told you to get that damned tire fixed, Sally."

She swallowed. Her pride was bruised almost beyond bearing. "I don't take orders," she said, trying to salvage a little self-respect.

"I don't give them anymore," he returned. "But I do give advice, and you've just seen the results of not listening. At least you had the sense to leave a message on my answering machine. But what if I hadn't checked my messages, Sally? Would you like to think where you'd be now? Want me to paint you a picture?"

"Stop!" She put her face in her hands and shivered.

"I won't apologize," he told her abruptly. "You did a damned stupid thing and you got off lucky. Another time, I might not be quick enough."

She swallowed and swallowed again. "The…conquering male," she choked, but she wasn't teasing now, as she had been that afternoon when he'd told her to get the tire fixed.

He drew her hands away from her face and looked into her eyes steadily. "That's right," he said curtly, and he wasn't kidding. "I've been dealing with vermin like that for almost half my life. I told you there was danger in going out alone. Now you understand what I meant. Get that damned tire fixed, and buy a cell phone."

Her head was spinning. "I can't afford one," she said unsteadily.

"You can't afford not to. If you'd had one tonight, this might never have happened," he said forcefully. The heat in his eyes made her shiver. "A man is physically stronger than a woman. There are some exceptions, but for the most part, that's the honest truth. Unless you've trained for years, like a policewoman or a federal agent, you're not going to be the equal of a man who's drunk or on drugs or just bent on assault. Law enforcement people know how to fight. You don't."

She shivered again. Her hair was disheveled. She felt bruises on her arms where she'd been restrained by those men. She was still stunned by the experience, but already a little of the horror of what might have happened was getting to her.

He let her wrists go abruptly. His lean face softened as he studied her. "But I'll say one thing for you. You've got grit."

"Sure. I'm tough," she laughed hollowly, brushing a strand of loose hair out of her eyes. "What a pitiful waste of self-confidence!"

"Who the hell taught you about canned self-defense?" he asked curiously, referring to the can of spray on the ground.

"There was this television self-defense training course for women," she said defensively.

"Anything you spray, pepper or chemical, can rebound on you," he said quietly. "If the wind's blowing the wrong way, you can blind yourself. If you don't hit the attacker squarely in the eyes, you're no better off, either. As for the whistle, tonight there would have been no one close enough to hear it." He sighed at her miserable expression and shook his head. "Didn't I tell you to run?"

She lifted a high-heeled foot eloquently.

He leaned closer. "If you're ever in a similar situation again, kick them off and try for the two-minute mile!"

She managed a smile for him. "Okay."

He touched her wan, drawn face gently. "I wouldn't have had that happen to you for the world," he said bitterly.

"You were right, I brought it on myself. I won't make that mistake again, and at least I got away with everything except my pride intact," she said gamely.

He unfastened her seat belt, aware of a curtain being lifted and then released in the living room. "I sent Dallas straight here as soon as I got the message," he explained, "to watch out for Jess and Stevie. You should have let me know about this night meeting much sooner."

"I know." She was fighting tears. The whole experience had been a shock that she knew she'd never get over. "There was a third man, on the porch. He said that Lopez wouldn't like what they were doing, calling attention to themselves."

He stared at her for a long moment, seeing the fear and terror and revulsion that lingered in her oval face, watching the way her hands clenched at the shirt he'd fastened over her torn bodice. He glanced at the window, where the curtain was in place again, and back to Sally's face.

"Come here, sweetheart," he said tenderly, pulling her into his arms. He cuddled her close, nuzzling his face into her throat, letting her cry.

Her clenched fist rested against his black undershirt and she sobbed with impotent fury. "Oh, I'm so…mad!" she choked. "So mad! I felt like a rag doll."

"You do your best and take what comes," he said at her ear. "Anybody can lose a fight."

"I'll bet you never lost one," she muttered tearfully.

"I got the hell beaten out of me in boot camp by a little guy half my size, who was a hapkido master.

Taught me a valuable lesson about overconfidence," he said deliberately.

She took the handkerchief he placed in her hands and wiped her nose and eyes and mouth. "Okay, I get the message," she said on a broken sigh. "There's always somebody bigger and you can't win every time."

"Nice attitude," he said, approving.

She wiped away the last trace of tears and looked up at him from her comfortable position across his lap. "Thanks for the hero stuff."

He shrugged. "Shucks, ma'am, t'weren't nothin'."

She laughed, as she was meant to. Her eyes adored him. "They say that if you save a life, it becomes yours."

His lips pursed and he looked down at where the jacket barely covered her torn blouse. "Do I get that, too?"

"Too?"

He opened the shirt very slowly and looked at the pale flesh under the torn blouse. There was a lot of it on view. Sally didn't protest, didn't grab at cover. She lay very still in his arms and let him look at her.

His pale eyes met hers in the faint light coming from the house. "No protest?"

"You saved me," she said simply. She sighed and smiled with resignation. "I belonged to you, anyway. There's never been anyone else."

His long, lean fingers touched her collarbone, his eyes narrow and solemn, his expression serious, intent. "That could have changed, tonight," he reminded her quietly. "You have to trust me enough to do what I tell you. I don't want you hurt in this. I'll do anything I have to, to protect you. That includes having a man follow you around like a visible appendage if you push me to it. Think what your principal would make of *that!*"

"I won't make any more stupid mistakes," she promised.

"What would you call this?" he mused, nodding toward the ripped fabric that left one pretty, taut breast completely bare.

"Cover me up if you don't like what you see," she challenged.

He actually laughed. She was constantly surprising him. "I think I'd better," he murmured dryly, and pulled the shirt back over her, leaving her to button it again. "Dallas is at the window getting an education."

"And I can tell how much he needs it," she said with dry humor as Eb helped her back into her own seat.

"That makes two of you," Eb told her. His eyes were kind, and now full of concern. "Will you be all right?"

"Yes." She hesitated with her hand on the doorknob. "Eb, is it always like that?"

He frowned. "What?"

She looked up into his eyes. "Physical violence. Do you ever get to the point that it doesn't make you sick inside?"

"I never have," he said flatly. "I remember every face, every sound, every sick minute of what I've done in my life." He looked at her, but he seemed to go far away. "You'd better go inside. I'll take you and Stevie out to the ranch Thursday and Saturday and we'll put in some more time."

"For all the good it will do me," she managed to say nervously.

"Don't be like that," he chided. "You got overpowered. People do, even 'big, strong' men. There's no shame in losing a fight when you've given it all you've got."

She smiled. "Think so?"

"I know so." He touched her disheveled French knot. "You wore your hair down that spring afternoon," he murmured softly. "I remember how it felt on my bare chest, loose and smelling of flowers."

Her breath seemed to stick in her throat as she recalled the same memory. They had both been bare to the waist. She could close her eyes and feel the hair-roughened muscles of his chest against her own softness as he kissed her and kissed her...

"Sometimes," he continued, "we get second chances."

"Do we?" she whispered.

He touched her mouth gently. "Try not to dwell on what happened tonight," he said. "I won't let anyone hurt you, Sally."

That felt nice. She wished she could give him the same guarantee, but it seemed pretty ridiculous after her poor performance.

He seemed to read the thought right in her mind, and he burst out laughing. "Listen, lady, when I get through with you, you'll be eating bad men raw," he promised. "You're just a beginner."

"You aren't."

"That's true. And not only in self-defense," he added dryly. "You'd better go in."

"I suppose so." She picked at the buttons of the shirt he'd loaned her. "I'll give it back. Eventually."

"You look nice in it," he had to admit. "You can keep it. We'll try some more of my clothes on you and see how they look."

She made a face at him as she opened the door. "Eb, do I have to go and see the sheriff?"

"You do. I'll pick you up after school. Don't worry," he said quietly. "He won't eat you. He's a nice man.

But you must see that we can't let Lopez's people get away with this."

She felt a chill go down her arms as she remembered who Lopez was. "What will he do if I testify against his men?"

"You let me worry about that," Eb told her, and his eyes were like green steel. "Nobody touches you without going through me."

Her heart jumped right up into her throat as she stared at him. She was a modern woman, and she probably shouldn't have enjoyed that passionate remark. But she did. Eb was a strong, assertive man who would want a woman to match him. Sally hadn't been that woman at seventeen. But she was now. She could stand up to him and meet him on his own ground. It gave her a sense of pride.

"Debating if it's proper for a modern woman to like being protected?" he chided with a wicked grin.

"You said yourself that none of us are invincible," she pointed out. "I don't think it's a bad thing to admire a man's strength, especially when it's just saved my neck."

He made her feel confident, he gave her joy. It had been years since she'd laughed so much, enjoyed life so much. Odd that a man whose adult years had been imbued with such violence could be so tender.

"Okay now?" he asked.

She nodded. "I'm okay." She glanced toward the road and shivered a little. "They won't come looking for me?"

"Not in that condition they won't," he said matter-of-factly. "And they're very lucky," he added, his whole face like drawn cord. "Ten years ago, I wouldn't have been so gentle."

Both eyebrows went up at the imagery.

"You know what I was," he said quietly. "Until comparatively recent years, I lived a violent, uncertain life. Part of the man I was is still in me. I won't ever hurt you," he added. "But I have to come to grips with the old life before I can begin a new one. That's going to take time."

"I think you're saying something."

"Why, yes, I am," he mused, watching her. "I'm giving notice of my intentions."

"Intentions?"

"Last time I stopped. Next time I won't."

Her mind wasn't quite grasping what he was telling her. "You mean, with those men...?"

"I mean with you," he said gently. "I want you very badly, and I'm not walking away this time."

"You and what army?" she asked, aghast.

"I won't need an army. But you might." He smiled. "Go on in. I'm having the house watched. You'll be safe, I promise."

She pulled his shirt closer. "Thanks, Eb," she said.

He shrugged. "I have to take care of my own. Try to sleep."

She smiled at him. "Okay. You, too."

He watched her go up onto the porch and into the house, waiting for Dallas, who came out tight-lipped with barely a word to Sally as he passed her.

He got into the truck with Eb and slammed the door.

"What happened to Sally?" he asked, putting his cane aside.

"Lopez's men rushed the truck when she had a flat. I don't know if it was premeditated," he added coldly. "They could have lain in wait for her and caused the flat. The tire was almost bald, but it could have gone another few hundred miles."

"She looked uneasy."

"They assaulted her and may have raped her if I hadn't shown up," Eb said bluntly as he backed the truck and pulled out into the road. "I want to have another look, if the ambulance hasn't picked them up yet."

"You sent for an ambulance?" Dallas asked with mock surprise. "That's new."

"Well, we're trying to blend in, aren't we?" came the terse reply. He glared at the tall blond man. "Difficult to blend in if we let people die on the side of the road."

"If you say so."

They drove to where Sally's pickup truck was still sitting, but there was no sign of the two men. The house nearby was dark. There wasn't a soul in sight.

As Eb digested that, red lights flashed and a big boxy ambulance pulled up behind the pickup truck, followed closely by a deputy sheriff in a patrol car.

Eb pulled off the road and got out. He knew the deputy, Rich Burton, who was one of the department's ablest members. They shook hands.

"Where are the victims?" Rich asked.

Eb grimaced. "Well, they were both lying right there when I took Sally home."

The deputy and the ambulance guys looked toward the flattened grass, but there weren't any men lying there.

"Unless one of you needs medical attention, we'll be on our way," one of the EMTs said with a wry glance.

"Both of the perps did," Eb said quietly. "At least one of them has broken bones."

The EMT gave him a wary look. "Not their legs, by the look of things."

"No. Not their legs."

The EMTs left and Rich joined Eb and Dallas beside the truck.

"Something's going on at that house," Rich said quietly. "I've had total strangers stop me and tell me they've seen suspicious activity, men carrying boxes in and out. That's not all. Some holding company bought a huge tract of land adjoining Cy Parks's place, and it's filling up with building supplies. There's a contractor been hired and a plan has gone to the county commission's planning committee about a business starting up there."

"How much do you know about the men who live here?" Eb asked coolly.

Rich shrugged. "Not as much as I'd like to. But my contacts tell me that there's a drug lord named Manuel Lopez, and the talk is that these guys belong to him. They're mules. They run his narcotics for him."

Eb and Dallas exchanged quiet glances.

"What sort of business are we talking about?" Eb queried.

"Don't know. There's a huge steel warehouse going up behind Parks's place," Rich replied, and he looked worried. "If I were making a guess, and it is just a guess, I'd say somebody had distribution in mind."

CHAPTER FIVE

"A DISTRIBUTION CENTER," Eb said curtly. "With Manuel Lopez, the head of the most violent of the international drug cartels, behind it! That's just what we need in Jacobsville."

"That's right," the younger man replied. He scowled. "How do you know about Lopez?"

Eb didn't answer. "Thanks, Rich," he said. "If I hear anything about the men who attacked Miss Johnson, I'll give you a call."

"Thanks. But I'd bet that they're long gone," he said carelessly. "They'd be crazy to stick around and face charges like attempted rape in a town this size. Lopez wouldn't like the notoriety."

"My guess exactly. So long," Eb said, motioning to Dallas. Rich drove off with a wave of his hand. Eb hesitated, and once Rich was out of sight, he looked for and found a board with new nails sticking through it. It was lying point-side down, now, but the wood was new and there was a long cord attached to it. Evidently it had been placed in the road just as Sally approached, and then jerked away once Sally had run over it. That meant that there had to be a fourth man involved, besides the man on the porch and the two men who'd assaulted Sally. That disturbed Eb.

"They set a trap," Dallas guessed. "She ran over this. That's how she got the flat."

"Exactly." Eb threw the board in the bed of the truck before he climbed in under the wheel. "There were at least four men in on it, and I don't think assault was the sole object of the exercise. I think I'll go over and have a talk with Cy Parks first thing in the morning. He may know something about that new construction behind his place."

CY PARKS WAS GRUMPY. He hadn't been able to sleep the night before, and he was groggy. Even after four years, he still had nightmares about the loss of his wife and five-year-old son in a fire back home in Wyoming. He'd moved here to Jacobsville, where Ebenezer Scott lived, more for someone to talk to than any other reason. Eb was not only a former comrade at arms, but he was also the only man he knew who could listen to the unabridged horror of the fire without losing his supper. It kept him sane, just having someone to talk to. And not only could he talk about the death of his family at Lopez's henchmen's hands but also he had someone to help him exorcise the nightmares of the past that he and Ebenezer shared.

The knock on the door came just as he was pouring his second cup of coffee. It was probably his foreman. Harley Fowler was an adventurer wannabe who fancied himself a mercenary. He was forever reading a magazine for armchair adventurers and once he'd actually answered one of the ads for volunteers and, supposedly, had taken a job during his summer vacation. He'd come back from his vacation two weeks later grinning and bragging about his exploits overseas with a group of world-beaters and lording it over the other ranch hands who worked for Cy. Harley had become the overnight hero of the men. Cy watched him with amused cynicism. None of the men he'd served with had ever returned home strutting and bragging about their exploits. Nor had any of them come home smiling. There was a look about a man who'd seen combat. It was unmistakable to anyone who'd been through it. Harley didn't have the look.

None of the ranch hands knew that Cy Parks hadn't always been a rancher. They knew about the fire that had cost him his family—most people locally did. But they didn't know that he was a former professional mercenary and that Lopez was responsible for the fire. Cy wanted to keep it that way. He was through with the old life.

He opened the front door with a scowl on his lean, tanned face, but it wasn't Harley who was standing on his porch. It was Ebenezer Scott.

Cy's eyes, two shades darker green than Eb's, narrowed. "Lost your way?" he taunted, running a hand through his thick unruly black hair.

Eb chuckled. "Years ago. Got another cup?"

"Sure." He opened the door and let Eb in. The living room, old-fashioned and sparsely furnished, was neat as a pin. So were the formal dining room—never used—and the big, airy kitchen with not a spot of dirt or grime anywhere.

"Tell me you hired a housekeeper," Eb murmured.

Cy got down an extra cup and poured black coffee into it, handing it across the table before he sat down. "I don't need a housekeeper," he replied. "Why are you here?" he added with characteristic bluntness.

"Did you keep in touch with any of your old contacts when you got out of the business?" Eb asked at once.

Cy shook his head. "No need. I gave it up, remember?" He lifted the cup to his wide, chiseled mouth.

Eb sipped coffee, nodded at the strength of it, and put the mug down on the Formica tabletop with a soft thud. "Manuel Lopez is loose," he said without preamble. "We think he's in the vicinity. Certainly some of his henchmen are."

Cy's face hardened. "Are you certain?"

"Yes."

"Why is he here?"

"Because Jessica Myers is here," Eb replied. "She's living with her young son and her niece, Sally Johnson, out at the old Johnson place. She got one of Lopez's accomplices to rat on Lopez without giving himself away. She had access to documents and bank accounts and witnesses willing to testify. Now Lopez is out and he's after Jess. He wants the name of the henchman who sold him out."

Cy made an impatient gesture. "Fighting out in the open isn't Lopez's style. He's the original knife-in-the-back boy."

"I know. It worries me." He sipped more coffee. "He had three, maybe four, of his thugs living in a rental place near Sally's house. Two of them attacked her last night when her truck had a flat tire just down the road from them. It was no accident, either. They've obviously been gathering intelligence, watching her. They knew exactly where she was and exactly when she'd get as far as their place." His face was grim. "I think there are more than four of them. I also think they may have the same sort of surveillance equipment I maintain at the ranch. What I don't know is why. I don't know if it's solely because Lopez wants to get to Jessica."

"Is Sally all right?"

Eb nodded. "I got to her in time, luckily. I broke a couple of bones for her assailants, but they got away and now the house seems to be without tenants— temporarily, of course. Have you noticed any activity on your northern boundary?"

"As a matter of fact, I have," Cy replied, frowning. "All sorts of vehicles are coming and going. They've graded about an acre, and a steel warehouse is going up. The city planning commission chairman says it's going to be some sort of production and distribution center for a honey concern. They even have a building permit." He sighed angrily. "Matt Caldwell has been having hell with the planning commission about a project of his own, yet this gang got what they wanted immediately."

"Honey," Eb mused.

"That isn't all of it," Cy continued. "I investigated the holding company that bought the land behind me. It doesn't belong to anybody local, but I can't find out who's behind it. It belongs to a corporation based in Cancún, Mexico."

Eb's eyes narrowed. "Cancún? Now, that's interesting. The last report I had about Lopez before he was arrested was that he bought property there and was living like a king in a palatial estate just outside Cancún." He stopped dead at the expression on his friend's face. Cy and Eb had once helped put some of Lopez's men away.

Cy's breathing became rough, his green eyes began to glitter like heated emeralds. "Lopez! Now what the hell would he want with a honey business?"

"It's evidently going to be a front for something illegal," Eb assured him. "He may have picked Jacobsville for a distribution center for his 'product' because it's small, isolated, and there are no federal agencies represented near here."

Cy stood up, his whole body rigid with hatred and anger. "He killed my wife and son…!"

"He had Jessica run off the road and almost killed," Eb added coldly. "She lived, but she was blinded. She came back here from Houston, hoping that I could protect her. But it's going to take more than me. I need help. I want to set up a listening post on your back forty and put a man there."

"Done," Cy said at once. "But first I'm going to buy a few claymores…"

It took a minute for the expression on Cy's face, in his eyes, in the set of his lean body to register. Eb had only seen him like that once before, in combat, many years before. Probably that was the way he'd looked when his wife and son died and he was hospitalized with severe burns on one arm, incurred when he'd tried to save them from the raging fire. He hadn't known at the time that Lopez had sent men to kill him. Even in prison, Lopez could put out contracts.

"You can't start setting off land mines. You have to think with your brain, not your guts," Eb said curtly. "If we're going to get Lopez, we have to do it legally."

"Oh, that's new, coming from you," Cy said with biting sarcasm.

Eb's broad shoulders lifted and fell as he sat down again, straddling the chair this time. "I'm reformed," he said. "I want to settle down, but first I have to put Lopez away. I need you."

Cy extended the hand that had been so badly burned.

"I know about the burns," Eb said. "If you recall, most of us went to see you in the hospital afterward."

Cy averted his eyes and pulled the sleeve down over his wrist, holding it there protectively. "I don't remember much of it," he confessed. "They sent me to a burn unit and did what they could. At least I was able to keep the arm, but I'll never be much good in a tight corner again."

"You mean you were before?" Eb asked with howling mockery.

Cy's eyes widened, narrowed and suddenly he burst out laughing. "I'd forgotten what a bunch of sadists you and your men were," he accused. "Before every search and destroy mission, somebody was claiming my gear and asking about my beneficiary." Cy drew in a long breath. "I've been keeping to myself for a long time."

"So we noticed," came the dry reply. "I hear it took a bunch of troubled adolescents to drag you out of your cave."

Cy knew what he meant. Belinda Jessup, a public defender, had bought some of the property on his boundary for a summer camp for youthful offenders on probation. One of the boys, an African-American youth who'd fallen absolutely in love with the cattle business, had gotten through his shell. He'd worked with Luke Craig, another neighbor, to give the boy a head start in cowboying. He was now working for Luke Craig on his ranch and had made a top hand. No more legal troubles for him. He was on his way to being foreman of the whole outfit, and Cy couldn't repress a tingle of pride that he'd had a hand in that.

"Even assuming that we can send Lopez back to prison, that won't stop him from appointing somebody to run his empire. You know how these groups are organized," Cy added, "into cells of ten or more men with their chiefs reporting to a regional manager and those managers reporting to a high-level management designee. The damned cartels operate on a corporate structure these days."

"Yes, I know, and they work complete with pagers, cell phones and faxes, using them just long enough to avoid detection," Eb agreed. "They're efficient and they're merciless. God only knows how many under-cover agents the drug enforcement people have lost, not to mention those from other law enforcement agen-cies. The drug lords make a religion of intimidation, and they have no scruples about killing a man and his entire family. No wonder few of their henchmen ever cross them. But one did, and Jessica knows his name. I don't expect Lopez to give up. Ever."

"Neither do I. But what are we going to do about Lo-pez's planned operation?" Cy wanted to know.

Eb sobered. "I don't have a plan yet. Legally, we can't do anything without hard evidence. Lopez will be extra careful about covering his tracks this time. He won't want anything that will connect him on paper to the drug operation. From what I've been able to learn, Lopez has already skipped town, forfeiting the bond. Believe me, there's no way in hell he'll ever get extra-dited from Mexico. The only way we'll ever get him back behind bars again is to lure him back here and have him nabbed by the U.S. Marshals Service. He's at the top of the DEA's Most Wanted list right now." He finished his second cup of coffee. "If we can get a legal wiretap on the phones in that warehouse once it's operating, we might have something to take to the authorities. I know a DEA agent," Eb said thought-fully. "In fact, he and his wife are neighbors of yours. He's gung-ho at his job, and he's done some undercover work before."

"Most of Lopez's people are Hispanic," Cy pointed out.

"This guy could pass for Hispanic. Good-looking devil, too. His wife's father left her that small ranch…"

"Lisa Monroe," Cy said, and averted his eyes. "Yes, I've seen her around. Yesterday she was heaving bales of hay over the fence to her horse," he added in the coldest tones Eb had ever heard him use. "She's thinner than she should be, and she has no business trying to heft bales of hay!"

"When her husband's not home to do it for her…"

"Not home?" Cy's eyes widened. "Good God, man, he was standing ten feet away talking to a leggy blond girl in an express delivery uniform! He didn't even seem to notice Lisa!"

"It's not our business."

Cy moved abruptly, standing up. "Okay. Point taken. Suppose we ride up to the boundary and take a look at the progress on that warehouse," he said. "We can take horses and pretend we're riding the fence line."

Eb retrieved high-powered binoculars from the truck and by the time he got to the stable, Cy's young foreman had two horses saddled and waiting.

"Mr. Scott!" Harley said with a starstruck grin, running a hand absently through his crew-cut light brown hair. "Nice to see you, sir!" He almost saluted. He knew about Mr. Scott's operation; he'd read all about it in his armchair covert operations magazine, to say nothing of the top secret newsletter to which he subscribed.

Eb gave him a measuring glance and he didn't smile. "Do I know you, son?"

"Oh, no, sir," Harley said quickly. "But I've read about your operation!"

"I can imagine what," Eb chuckled. He stuck a cigar into his mouth and lit it.

Cy mounted offside, from the right, because there wasn't enough strength in his left arm to permit him to grip the saddle horn and help pull himself up. He hated the show of weakness, which was all too visible. Up until the fire, he'd been in superb physical condition.

"We're going to ride up to the northern boundary and check the fence line for breaks," Cy said imperturbably. "Get Jenkins started on the new gate as soon as he's through with breakfast."

"He'll have to go pick it up at the hardware store first," Harley reminded him. "Just came in late yesterday."

Cy gave him a look that would have frozen running water. He didn't say anything. But, then, he didn't have to.

"I'll just go remind him," Harley said at once, and took off toward the bunkhouse.

"Who is he?" Eb asked as they rode out of the yard.

"My new foreman." Cy leaned toward him with mock awe. "He's a real *mercenary,* you know! Actually went on a mission early this summer!"

"My God," Eb drawled. "Fancy that. A real live hero right here in the boonies."

"Some hero," Cy muttered. "Chances are what he really did was to camp out in the woods for two weeks and help protect city campers from bears."

Eb chuckled. "Remember how we were at his age?" he asked reminiscently. "We couldn't wait for people to see us in our gear. And then we found out that the real mercs don't advertise."

"We were like Harley," Cy mused. "All talk and hot air."

"And all smiles." Eb's eyes narrowed with memory. "I hadn't smiled for years by the time I got out. It isn't romantic and no matter how good the pay is, it's never enough for what you have to do for it."

"We did do a little good in the world," came the rejoinder.

"Yes, I guess we did," Eb had to admit. "But our best job was breaking up one of Lopez's cocaine processing plants in Central America and helping put Lopez away. And here he is back, like a bad bouncing ball."

"I knew his father," Cy said unexpectedly. "A good, honest, bighearted man who worked as a janitor just up the road in Victoria and studied English at home every night trying to better himself. He died just after he found out what his only child was doing for a living."

Eb stared off into space. "You never know how kids will turn out."

"I know how mine would have turned out," Cy said heavily. "One of his teachers was in an accident. Not a well-liked teacher, but Alex started a fund for him and gave up a whole month's allowance to start it with." His face corded like wire. He had to swallow, hard, to keep his voice from breaking. The years hadn't made his memories any easier. Perhaps if he could help get Lopez back in prison, it might help.

"We'll get Lopez," the other man said abruptly. "Whatever it takes, if I have to call in markers from all over the world. We'll get him."

Cy came out of his brief torment and glanced at his comrade. "If we do, I get five minutes alone with him."

"Not a chance," Eb said with a grin. "I remember what you can do in five minutes, and I want him tried properly."

"He already was."

"Yes, but he was caught and tried back east. This time we'll manage to apprehend him right here in Texas and we'll stack the legal deck by having the best prosecuting attorney in the state brought in to do the job.

The Hart boys are related to the state attorney general—he's their big brother."

"I'd forgotten." He glanced at Eb. His eyes were briefly less tormented. "Okay. I guess I can give the court a second chance. Not their fault that Lopez can afford defense attorneys in Armani suits, I guess."

"Absolutely. And if we can catch him with enough laundered money in his pockets and invoke the RICO statutes, we can fund some nice improvements for our drug enforcement people."

They'd arrived at the northernmost boundary of Cy's property, and barely in sight across the high-wire fence was a huge construction site. From their concealed position in a small stand of trees near a stream, Eb took his binoculars and gave the area a thorough scrutiny. He handed them to Cy, who looked as well and then handed them back.

"Recognize anybody?" Cy asked.

Eb shook his head. "None of them are familiar. But I'll bet if you looked in the right places, you could find a rap sheet or two. Lopez isn't too picky about pedigrees. He just likes men who don't mind doing whatever the job takes. Last I heard, he had several foreign nationals in his employ." He sighed. "I sure as hell don't want a drug distribution network out here."

"Neither do I. We'd better go have a word with Bill Elliott at the sheriff's office."

Cy shrugged. "You'd better have a word with him by yourself, if you want to get anywhere. I'd jinx you."

"I remember now. You had words with him over Belinda Jessup's summer camp."

"Hard words," Cy agreed uncomfortably. "I've mellowed since, though."

"You and the KGB." He pulled his hat further over his eyes. "We'd better get out of here before they spot us."

"I can see people coming."

"They can see you coming, too."

"That should worry them," Cy agreed, grinning.

Eb chuckled. It was rare these days to see a smile on that hard face. He wheeled his horse, leaving Cy to follow.

THAT AFTERNOON, EB DROVE over to the Johnson place to pick up Sally and Stevie for their self-defense practice.

Sally's eyes lit up when she saw him and he felt his heart jump. She made him feel warm inside, as if he finally belonged somewhere. Stevie ran past his aunt to be caught up and swung around in Eb's muscular arms.

"How's Jess?" Eb asked.

Sally made a face and glanced back toward the house. "Dallas got here just before you did. It's sort of unarmed combat in there. They aren't even speaking to each other."

"Ah, well," he mused. "Things will improve eventually."

"Do you gamble?" she teased. "I feel a lucky streak coming on."

He chuckled as he loaded them into the pickup. No, he wasn't willing to bet on friendlier relations on that front. Not yet, anyway.

"How much do you know about surveillance equipment?" Sally asked unexpectedly.

He gave her a look of exaggerated patience. "With my background, how much do you think I know?"

She laughed. "Sorry. I wasn't thinking. Can a microphone really pick up voices inside the house? Jess tried to convince me that they could hear us through the walls and we had to be very careful what we discussed. I mentioned that Lopez man and she shushed me immediately."

He glanced at her as he drove. "You've got a lot to learn. I suppose now is as good a time as any to teach you."

When he parked the truck at the front door, he led her inside, parking Stevie at the kitchen table with Carl, his cook, who dished up some ice cream for the child while Eb led Sally down the long hall and into a huge room literally crammed with electronic equipment.

He motioned her into a chair and keyed his security camera to a distant view of two cowboys working on a piece of machinery halfway down a rutted path in the meadow.

He flipped a switch and she heard one cowboy muttering to the other about the sorry state of modern tools and how even rusted files were better than what passed for a file today.

They weren't even talking loud, and if there was a microphone, it must be mounted on the barn wall outside. She looked at Eb with wide, frankly disbelieving eyes.

He flipped the switch and the screen was silent again. "Most modern sound equipment can pick up a whisper several hundred yards away." He indicated a shelf upon which sat several pairs of odd-looking binoculars. "Night vision. I can see anything on a moonless night with those, and I've got others that detect heat patterns in the dark."

"You have got to be kidding!"

"We have cameras hidden in books and cigarette packs, we have weapons that can be broken down and hidden in boots," he continued. "Not to mention this."

He indicated his watch, a quite normal looking one with all sorts of dials. Normal until he adjusted it and a nasty-looking little blade popped out. Her gasp was audible.

He could see the realization in her eyes as the purpose of the blade registered there. She looked up at him and saw the past. His past.

His green eyes narrowed as they searched hers. "You hadn't really thought about exactly what sort of work I did, had you?"

She shook her head. She was a little paler now.

"I lived in dangerous places, in dangerous times. It's only in recent years that I've stopped looking over my shoulder and sitting with my back against a wall." He touched her face. "Lopez's men can hear you through a wall, with the television on. Don't ever forget. Say nothing that you don't want recorded for posterity."

"This Lopez man is very dangerous, isn't he?" she asked.

"He's the most dangerous man I know. He hires killers. He has no compassion, no mercy, and he'll do absolutely anything for profit. If his henchman hadn't sold him out, he'd never have been taken into custody in this country. It was a fluke."

She looked around her curiously. "Could he overhear you in here?"

He smiled gently. "Not a chance in hell."

"It looks like something out of *Star Wars*," she mused.

He grinned. "Speaking of movies, how would you and Stevie like to go see a new science fiction flick with me Saturday?"

"Could we?" she asked.

"Sure." His eyes danced wickedly at the idea of sitting in a darkened theater with her...

CHAPTER SIX

SALLY FOUND THE WORKOUTS easier to do as they progressed from falls to defensive moves. Not only was it exciting to learn such skills, but the constant physical contact with Eb was delightful. She couldn't really hide that from him. He saw right through her diversionary tactics, grinning when she asked for short breaks.

Stevie was also taking to the exercise with enthusiasm. It wasn't hard to teach him that such things had no place at school, either. Even at his young age, he seemed to understand that martial arts were for recreation after school and never for the playground.

"It goes with the discipline," Eb informed her when she told him about it. "Most people who watch martial arts films automatically assume that we teach children to hurt each other. It's not like that. What we teach is a way to raise self-esteem and self-confidence. If you know you can handle yourself in a bad situation, you're less likely to go out and try to beat somebody up to prove it. It's lack of self-confidence, lack of self-esteem, that drives a lot of kids to violence."

"That, and a very sad lack of attention by the adults around them," Sally said quietly. "It takes two incomes to run a household these days, but it's the kids who are suffering for it. Any gang member will tell you the reason he joined a gang was because he wanted to be part of a family. But how do we change things so that par-

ents can earn a living and still have enough free time
to raise their children?"

He put both hands on his narrow hips and studied
her closely. "If I could answer that question, I'd run for
public office."

She grinned at him. "I can see you now, mopping the
floor with the criminal element on the streets."

He shrugged. "Piece of cake compared to what I used
to do for a living."

Her pale eyes searched his lean, scarred face while
Stevie fell from one side of the mat to another practic-
ing his technique. "I rented one of those old mercenary
films and watched it. Do you guys really throw gre-
nades and use rocket launchers?"

A dark, odd look came into his pale eyes. "Among
other things," he said.

"Such as?" she prompted.

"High-tech equipment like the stuff you saw in my
office. Plastic explosive charges, small arms, whatever
we had. But most of what we do now is intelligence-
gathering and tactics. And intelligence-gathering," he
told her dryly, "is about as exciting as two-hour-old
cereal in milk."

She was surprised. "I thought it was like war."

He shrugged. "Only if you get caught gathering intelligence," he replied on a laugh. "We were good at
what we did."

"Dallas was one of your guys, wasn't he?"

He nodded. "Dallas, Cy Parks and Callie Kirby's
stepbrother Micah Steele, among others."

Her mouth fell open. "Cy Parks was a mercenary?"

His eyebrows levered up. "You didn't notice that he
has a hard time interacting with other people?"

"It's hard to miss. But in the condition he's in…"

"I know. That's one reason that he isn't in our line of work anymore. He was one of the group that helped put Lopez's organization away a little over two years ago—so was I. It was Jess who got to the man himself. But Lopez appealed the verdict and only went to prison six months ago. As you can see, he's out now," he added dryly.

"Two years ago—that was about the time Cy came to Jacobsville," she recalled.

"Yes. After one of Lopez's goons torched his house in Wyoming. The idea was to kill all three of them, not just Cy's wife and child," he added, seeing the horror in her eyes. "But Cy wasn't asleep, as they'd assumed. He got out."

She grimaced. "But why would Lopez burn his house down?"

"That's how he gets even with people who cross him," he said simply. "He doesn't take out just the person responsible, but the whole family, if he can get to it. There have been slaughters like you wouldn't believe down in Mexico when anyone tried to stand against him. He does usually stop short of children, however; his one virtue."

"I never knew people like him existed," she said sorrowfully.

"I wish I could say the same," he told her. "We don't live in a perfect world. That's why I want you to learn how to defend yourself."

"Fat lot of good it would have done me the night I had the flat tire," she pointed out. "If you hadn't come along when you did…" She shuddered.

"But I did. Don't look back. It's unproductive."

Her soft, worried eyes searched his scarred face quietly.

"What are you thinking?" he asked with a faint smile.

She shrugged. "I was thinking what a false picture I had of you all those years ago," she admitted. "I suppose I was living in a dream world."

"And I was living in a nightmare," he replied. "That unforgettable spring day six years ago, I'd just come home from a bloodbath in Africa, trying to help an incumbent government fight off a military coup by a very nasty native communist general. I lost most of my unit, including several friends, and the incumbent president's office was blown up, with him in it. It wasn't a good time."

She named the country, to his surprise. "We were studying that in a political science class at the time," she said. "I had no idea what you did for a living, or that you were involved. But we all thought it was an idealistic resistance," she added with a smile.

"Idealistic," he agreed. "And very costly, as most ideas are when you try to put them into practice." His eyes were very old as they met hers. "After that, I began to concentrate on intelligence and tactics. War isn't noble. Only the resolution of it is that."

She recalled the fresh scars on his face that day, scars that she'd attributed to ranch work. She studied him with obvious interest, smiling sheepishly when one of his eyebrows levered up.

"Sorry," she murmured.

He moved a step closer to her, forcing her to raise her chin so that she could see his face. The contact, barely perceptible, made her heart race. It wasn't so much the proximity as the way he was looking at her, as if he'd like to press her against him and kiss her until she couldn't stand up.

She moved a step back, her gaze going involuntarily to her cousin, who was giving the punching bag a hard time.

"I hadn't forgotten he was there," Eb said in a velvety tone. His pale eyes fell to her mouth and lingered. Even without makeup and with her long hair disheveled, she was pretty. "One night soon I'm going to take you out to dinner. Dallas can keep an eye on Jess and Stevie while you're away."

Until he said that, she'd actually forgotten the danger for a few delightful minutes. It all came rushing back.

He smoothed out the frown between her thin eyebrows. "Don't brood. I've got everything under control."

"I hope so," she said uneasily. "Does Mr. Parks know that Lopez is out of prison?"

"He knows," Eb replied. He ran a hand through his thick hair. "He's the one loose cannon I'm going to have to watch. Even in the old days, Cy never had much patience. He and his wife weren't much of a pair, but he loved that boy to death. He won't rest until Lopez is caught, and if he gets to him first, we can forget about a trial. You can't ever afford to act in anger," he added quietly. "Anger clouds reason. It can get you killed."

"You can't really blame him for the way he feels. Poor man," she sympathized.

"Pity would be wasted on him," he murmured with a smile. "Even crippled, he's more man than most."

"I don't think of him as crippled," she said genuinely. "He's very attractive."

He glared down at her. "You're off-limits."

Her eyes widened. "What?"

"You heard me."

"I'm not property," she began.

"Neither am I, but don't start thinking about Cy, nevertheless. You can concentrate on me." He took one of her hands in his and looked at it, turning it over gently to study it. "Nice hands," he said. "Short nails, well-kept. No rings."

"I have several of them, mostly silver and turquoise, but I don't wear them very much."

His lean fingers rubbed gently over her ring finger and he looked thoughtful, absorbed.

Her own fingers went to the onyx-and-gold signet ring on the little finger of his left hand with the letter *S* in gold script embossed in the onyx.

"It was my father's," Eb told her solemnly. "He was a hell of a soldier, even if he wasn't the best father in the world."

"Do you miss him?" she asked gently.

He nodded. "I suppose I do, from time to time." He touched the ring. "This will go to my son, if I ever have one."

The thought of having children with Eb made Sally's knees weak, but she didn't speak. Eb seemed about to, when they were interrupted.

"Hey, Sally, look what I can do!" Stevie called, and executed a kick that sent the bag reeling.

"Very nice!" Eb said, grinning. "You're a quick study, young man."

"I got to learn to do it real fast," he murmured, sending another kick at the bag.

"Why?" Eb asked curiously.

"So I can hit that big blond man who makes my mama cry," he said, oblivious to the shocked and then amused looks on the faces of the adults near him.

"Dallas?" Sally asked.

"That's him," Stevie agreed, and his dark eyes glimmered. "Mama was crying last night and I asked her why, and she said that man hates her."

Eb joined the young boy at the bag and went on one knee beside him, his eyes very solemn. "Your mother and Dallas knew each other a long time ago," he told him in an adult way. "They had a fight, and they never made up. That's why she cried. They're both good people, Stevie, but sometimes even good people have arguments."

"Why are they mad at each other?"

"I don't know," Eb replied not quite factually. "That's for them to say, if they want you to know. Dallas isn't a bad man, though."

"He's all banged up," Stevie replied solemnly.

"Yes, he is. He was shot."

"Shot? Really?" Stevie moved closer to Eb and put a small hand on his shoulder. "Who shot him?"

"Some very bad men," Eb told him. "He almost died. That's why he has to use a walking stick now. It's why he has all those scars."

Stevie touched Eb's face. "You got scars, too."

"Yes, I have."

"You ever been shot?" he wanted to know.

"Several times," Eb replied honestly. "Guns can be very dangerous. I suppose you know that."

"I know it," Stevie said. "One of my friends shot himself with his dad's pistol playing war out in the yard. He was hurt pretty bad, but he's okay now. Mama told me that children should *never* touch a gun, even if they think it's not loaded."

"Good for your mom!"

"That man doesn't like my mama," he continued worriedly. "He frowns and frowns at her. She can't see it, but I see it."

"He wouldn't ever hurt her," Eb said firmly. "He's there to protect her when you're away from home," he added wryly.

"That's right, I protect her at home. I'm very strong. See what I did to the bag?"

"I sure did!" Eb grinned at him. "Those were nice kicks, but you need to snap them out from the knee. Here—" he got to his feet "—let me show you."

Sally watched them with lazy pleasure, smiling at the born rapport between them. It was a pity that Stevie didn't like Dallas. That would matter one day. But she had enough problems of her own to worry about.

EB STOPPED BY the local sandwich shop and bought frozen yogurt cones for all three of them, a reward for the physical punishment, he told them dryly.

While the two adults sat at a table and ate their yogurt cones, Stevie became engrossed in some knick-knacks on sale in the same store.

"He's a natural at this," Eb remarked.

"I'll bet I'm not," she mused, having had to repeat several of the moves quite a number of times before she did them well enough to suit her companion.

"You're not his age, either," he pointed out. "Most children learn things faster than adults. That's why they teach foreign languages so early these days."

"Do you speak any other languages?" she asked suddenly.

"Only a handful," he replied. "The romance languages, several dialects of African languages, and Russian."

"My goodness."

"Languages will get you far in intelligence work these days," he told her. "If you're going to work in foreign countries, it's stupid not to speak the language. It can get you killed."

"I had to have a foreign language series as part of my degree," she said. "I chose Spanish, because that's pretty necessary around here, with such a large Hispanic population. I hated it at first, and then I learned how to read in it." Her eyes brightened. "It's the most exciting thing in the world to read something in the language the author created it in. I never dreamed how delightful it would be to read *Don Quixote* as Cervantes actually wrote it!"

"I know what you mean. But the older the novel, the more difficult the translation. Words change meaning. And a good number of the more modern novels are written in the various dialects of Spanish provinces."

She grinned. "Like Blasco-Ibañez, who used a regional dialect for his matador hero, Juan Gallardo, in dialogue."

"Yes."

She finished her cone and wiped her hands. "I became really fascinated with bullfighting after I read the book, so I found a Web site that had biographies of all the matadors. I found the ones mentioned in the book, who fought in the corridas of Spain around the turn of the century."

"Until you read Blasco-Ibañez, you have no idea how dangerous bullfighting really is," Eb agreed. "He must have seen some of the corridas."

"A number of Spanish authors did. Lorca, for example, wrote a famous poem about the death of his friend Sanchez Mejias in the bullring."

He brushed back a strand of gold-streaked brown hair and smiled. "I've missed conversations like this, although a good many of the men I train are well-educated. In fact, Micah Steele, who does consulting work for me, was a resident doctor at one of the bigger Eastern hospitals when he joined my unit."

"Why did he give up a profession that he must have studied very hard for?"

"Nobody knows, and he won't talk. Mostly what we know about him we found out from his father, who used to be a bank president until his heart attack. Micah's stepsister, Callie, looks after old man Steele these days. He and Micah haven't spoken for years, not since he and Callie's mother divorced."

"Do you know why they did?"

He shrugged. "Local gossip had it that Micah's father caught Micah and his stepmother in a compromising position and threw them both out of the house."

"Poor man."

"Poor Callie. She worshipped the ground Micah walked on, but he won't even speak to her these days."

"That name sounds familiar," she commented.

"It should. Callie's a paralegal. She works for Barnes and Kemp, the trial lawyers here in town."

"It's so nice to have a lazy day like this," she murmured, watching Stevie browse among the party decorations on a shelf. "It makes me forget the danger."

"I'm surprised that Lopez hasn't made any more moves lately," he said. "And a little disturbed. It isn't like him to back off."

"Maybe he was afraid those two men who attacked me would be arrested and they'd tell on him," she said.

He laughed mirthlessly. "Dream on. Lopez would have them disposed of before they had time to rat on him." He pursed his lips. "That could be what happened to them. You don't make a mistake when you belong to that particular cartel. No second chances. Ever."

She shivered. "We do keep all the doors locked," she said. "And we're very careful about what we say. Well, Jessica is," she amended sheepishly. "Until you taught me about surveillance equipment, I didn't know that a whisper could be heard half a mile away."

"Never forget it," he told her. "Never drop your guard, either. I'll always have someone close enough to run interference if you get into trouble, but you have to do your part to keep the house secure."

"And let you know when and where I'm going," she agreed. "I won't forget again."

He reached across the table and folded his fingers into hers, liking the way they clung. His thumb smoothed over the soft, moist palm while he searched her eyes.

"You haven't had an easy time of it, have you?" he asked conversationally. "In some ways, your whole life has been in turmoil since you were seventeen."

"In transition, at least," she corrected, smiling gently. "If there's one thing I've learned, it's that everything changes."

"I suppose so." His fingers tightened on hers and the look in his eyes was suddenly dark and mysterious and a little threatening. "I've learned a few things myself," he said quietly.

"Such as?" she whispered daringly.

He glanced down at their entwined fingers. "Such as never taking things for granted."

She frowned, puzzled.

He laughed and let go of her fingers. "I told you that I was engaged once, didn't I?" he asked.

She nodded.

"I never told her what I did for a living. She never questioned where my money came from. In fact, when

I tried to tell her, she stopped me, saying it wouldn't matter, that she loved me and she'd go wherever my job took me." He leaned back in his chair, his expression reflective and solemn. "Her parents were dead. She and an older boy were fostered at the same time to a wealthy woman. They spent years together, but he and Maggie weren't close, so I made all the wedding arrangements and paid for her gown and the rings, everything." His eyes darkened with remembered pain. "I still felt uncomfortable about having secrets between us, though, so the night before the wedding, I told her what I did for a living. She put the rings on the coffee table, got her stuff, and left town that same night. She married two months later…a man twice her age."

She knew about his ex-fiancée, but not how much he'd cared about the woman. The expression in his eyes told her that the pain hadn't gone away. "Didn't she send you a letter, or phone you after she'd had time to think it over?" she asked.

He shook his head. "Until I ran into her in Houston a week ago, I had no idea where she was. Her adoptive mother died just after we broke up. Tough break."

Her heart stopped in her chest. "You…saw her…in Houston?"

He nodded, oblivious to the shock in her eyes. "As luck would have it, she's a new junior partner in an investment firm I use, and widowed."

He stared at her until she looked up, and he wasn't smiling. "You're in a precarious situation, and we've been thrown together in a rather unconventional way. We're friends, but you don't have to live with what I do."

All her hopes and dreams and wild expectations crumbled to dust in her mind. Friends. Good friends. Of course they were! He was teaching her martial arts, he was helping her to survive a potential attack by a ruthless drug lord. That didn't mean he wanted her to share his life. Quite the opposite, it seemed now.

"If a woman cared enough, surely she could give it a chance?" she asked, terrified that her anguish might show.

Apparently it didn't. He leaned back in his chair with a long sigh, reflective and moody. "No. She said she wanted a career, anyway," he replied. "It suited her to have her own money and be independent."

"My parents never shared their paychecks, or anything else," she said carelessly. She glanced at Stevie. "Stevie, we'd better go, sweetheart."

He came running, smiling as he leaned against her and looked across at Eb, who was still brooding. "Can we take Mama a cone?"

"Of course we can," Sally said gently. She dug out two dollars. "Here. Get her a cup of that fat-free Dutch chocolate, okay? And make sure it has a lid."

"Okay!"

He ran off with his grubstake, feeling very adult. Sally watched him, smiling.

"I could have done that," Eb commented.

"Yes, you could, but it wouldn't help teach him responsibility. Six isn't too young to start learning independence. He's going to be a fine man," she added, her voice softer as she watched him.

He didn't comment. He was feeling claustrophobic and he didn't know why. He got up and dealt with the used napkins. By the time he was finished, Stevie came back carrying a small white sack with Jessica's treat inside.

There wasn't much conversation on the way back to the Johnson house, and even then it was completely impersonal. Sally realized that it must have hurt Eb to recall how abruptly his fiancée had rejected him. She might have loved him, but the constant danger of his profession must have been more than she could handle. Now that he was retired from the danger, it might not be such an obstacle.

That was a depressing thought. His ex-fiancée was a widow and he was in a secure profession, and they'd recently seen each other. It was enough to get Sally out of the truck with Stevie and off into the house with only a quick thank-you and a forced smile.

Eb, driving away down the road, felt a vague regret for the loss of the rapport he and Sally had seemed to share. He couldn't understand what had made her so distant this afternoon.

Eb had already contacted a man he knew in the Drug Enforcement Administration on a secure channel and told him what he knew about Lopez and his plans for Jacobsville. He'd also asked about the possibility of having a man go undercover to infiltrate the operation and was told only that the DEA was aware of Lopez's construction project. He wouldn't tell Eb anything more than that.

Understanding government work very well, Eb had assumed that the undercover operation was already underway. He wasn't about to mention that to anyone he knew. Not even Cy.

He had Dallas monitoring some sensitive equipment that gave them direct audio and visual information from Sally's house. Nobody would sneak up on it without being noticed. He'd also had Dallas bug the telephone. That night, he was glad he had.

In the early hours of the morning, Sally was brought wide-awake by the insistent ringing of the telephone.

The number was unlisted, but that didn't stop telemarketers. Ordinarily, though, they didn't call at this hour. It wasn't a good marketing strategy, especially in Sally's case. She'd hardly slept after the discussion with Eb in the yogurt shop. She wasn't in the mood to talk to strangers.

"Hello?" she asked belligerently.

"You'll never see us coming," a slow, ice-cold voice said in her ear. "But unless Jessica gives up the name by midnight Saturday, there will be serious repercussions."

Sally was so shocked that she fumbled with the phone and cut off the caller. She stood holding the receiver, blinking in astonishment. That softly accented tone had chilled her to the bone, despite the flannel gown she was wearing.

No sooner had she righted the telephone than it rang again. This time, she hesitated. Her heart was pounding like mad. She was almost shaking with the force of it. Her mouth was dry. Her palms began to sweat. There was an uncomfortable knot in the pit of her stomach.

She wanted to ignore it. She didn't dare. Quickly, before she lost her nerve, she lifted it.

"She has one last chance," the voice continued, as if the connection hadn't been cut. "She must phone this number Saturday night at midnight exactly and give a name. One minute after midnight, you will all suffer the consequences." He gave the number and hung up. This time the connection was cut even more rapidly. Sally dropped the receiver back into the cradle with icy fingers. She stared down at it with growing horror. Surely Eb and Dallas and the others would be watching. But were they listening as well?

The phone rang a third time, but now she was angry and she didn't hesitate. She jerked it up. "Hello...?"

"We couldn't get a trace," Eb said angrily. "Are you all right?"

She swallowed, closed her eyes, took a deep breath, and swallowed again. "Yes," she said calmly. "I'm all right. You heard what he said?"

"I heard. Don't worry."

"Don't worry?" she parroted. "When a man's just threatened to kill everyone in my house?"

"He won't kill anybody," he assured her. "And he's through making threats for tonight. I'm going to find out where that phone is. Go to sleep. It's all right."

The receiver went dead. "I am sick and tired of men throwing out orders and hanging up on me!" she told the telephone earpiece.

It did no good, of course, except that voicing her irritation made her feel a little better. She climbed back into bed and lay awake, wide-eyed and nervous, until dawn. Just before she and Stevie left for school, out of the child's hearing range, she told Jessica what had happened.

"Eb and the others are watching us," Sally assured her quickly. "But be careful about answering the door."

"No need," Jessica said. "Lopez may be certifiable, but he's predictable. He never takes action until his demands haven't been met. We have until midnight Saturday to think of something."

"Wonderful," Sally said on a sigh. "We have today and tomorrow. I'm sure we'll have Lopez and all his cohorts in jail by then."

"Sarcasm doesn't suit you, dear," Jessica said with a smile. "Go to work. I'll be fine."

"I wish I could guarantee that all of us would be fine," Sally murmured to herself as she went out the door behind Stevie.

Somehow she knew that life would never be the same again. It had been bad enough hearing Eb talk about the woman he'd loved who had rejected him at the altar, and knowing from the way he spoke of it that he hadn't gotten over her. But now, she had drug dealers threatening to kill Jessica and Stevie as well as herself. She wondered how in the world she'd ended up in such a nightmare.

It didn't help when Eb phoned again and told her that the phone number she'd been given was that of a stolen cell phone, untraceable until it was answered, and it rang and rang unnoticed now. There would be no time to run a trace precisely at midnight. It was the most disheartening news Sally had received in a long time.

CHAPTER SEVEN

EB WAS DISTURBED by the message he'd intercepted from Lopez. He knew, even better than Sally did, that it wasn't an idle threat. The drug lord, like his minions, was merciless. He'd had countless enemies neutralized, and he wouldn't hesitate because Jessica was a woman. Just the month before his arrest, he'd had the leader of a drug-dealing gang disposed of for cheating him. It was chilling even for a professional soldier to know what depths a human being could sink to in the name of greed.

He and Dallas started planning for the certainty of an attack. The Johnson homeplace was isolated, but it had plenty of cover where men could hide. Eb intended having people in place long before Lopez's hired goons could find a safe passage to the house to carry out the madman's orders. Anything else would be impossible, since he knew Jessica would never sacrifice her informant's life, even to save herself and her family.

"I think we can safely assume that these men aren't professionals," Dallas said quietly. "Their way will be to wade in shooting."

Eb's pale eyes narrowed. "I wouldn't bet the lives of two women and a child on that," he replied. "Lopez knows I'm here, and that I have trained professionals working for me. He also knows that I'm why Jessica talked Sally into moving back here in the first place.

He's ruthless, but he isn't stupid. When he comes after Jessica, he'll send the best people he's got."

"Point taken," Dallas said heavily. "I suppose it was wishful thinking." He glanced worriedly at Eb. "We could bring all three of them over here."

"Sure we could. But it would only postpone the inevitable. Lopez doesn't quit. He'll look on it as a setback and find another way to get to them. Besides, they can't stay here indefinitely. Sally has a job and Stevie has to go to school."

Dallas stared into the distance, quiet and thoughtful. "Stevie doesn't like me," he murmured. "He told his mother he was learning karate so that he could work me over." He shot a half-amused glance in Eb's direction. "Spunky kid."

"Yes, he is," Eb agreed. "Pity he has to grow up without a father. And before you fly at me," he interrupted Dallas's exclamation, "I know Jessica didn't tell you whose child he was. But you know now."

"I know," Dallas muttered irritably, "for all the good it does me. She won't even discuss it. The minute I walk in the door, she clams up and stays that way until I leave. I can barely get her to say hello and goodbye!"

"Then she cries herself to sleep at night because you hate her."

The blond man's dark eyes widened. *"What?"*

"That's why Stevie wants to deck you," Eb said simply. "He's very protective of his mother."

Dallas seemed to calm down a little. "Imagine that," he mused. "Well, well. So she isn't quite as disinterested as she pretends." He stuck his hands into his pockets and leaned back against the wall. "No chance she'll turn in the guy who ratted on Lopez, I gather?"

"Not one in a million." He studied the other man for a moment. "You're really worried."

"Of course I am. I've seen the aftermath of Lopez's vendettas," Dallas said curtly. "What worries me most is that if someone's willing to trade his life or his freedom to get you, he can. No protection is adequate against a determined killer."

"Then ours will make history," Eb promised him. "Let's go over to Cy Parks's place. I want to see if he's got a way to contact that guy in Mexico who used to work as a mercenary with Dutch Van Meer and Diego Laremos back in the eighties. He went on to do work infiltrating drug cartels."

"J.D. Brettman led that mercenary group," Dallas recalled, grinning. "He's a superior court judge in Chicago these days. Imagine that!"

"I heard that Van Meer lives with his wife and kids in the northwestern Rocky Mountains on a ranch. What about Laremos?" Eb asked.

"He and his family live in the Yucatán. He's given up soldiering, too." He shook his head. "Those guys were younger than us when they started and they made fortunes."

"It was a different game back then. Times have changed. So have the rules. We'd never get away with some of the stunts those guys pulled." Eb felt in his pocket for his truck keys. "All of us met them, but Cy and Diego Laremos got to know each other well several years back when Cy was doing a little job down around Cancún for a wealthy yachtsman. He may know the professional soldier who helped a friend of Laremos's escape some nasty pothunters and a kidnapper."

"Do I know this friend?" Dallas wanted to know as they headed out the door.

"You probably know *of* him—Canton Rourke."

"Good Lord, Mr. Software?" Dallas exclaimed. "The guy who lost everything and then regrouped and now has a corporation in the Fortune 500?"

"That's him." Eb nodded. "Turns out the new Mrs. Rourke's parents are university professors who devote summers to Mayan digs in the Yucatán. It's a long story, but this Mexican agent does a little freelance work. He'd be an asset in this sort of operation."

"He might even have some contacts we could use?"

"That's so." Eb got in and started the truck. He glanced at Dallas. "Besides that, he's done undercover work on narcotics smuggling for the Mexican government and lived to tell about it. That proves how good he is. A lot of undercover people get killed."

"He'd be just what we need, if we can get him. I don't imagine the DEA is going to tell us who their undercover guy is, or what he finds out."

"Exactly. That's where I hope Cy's going to come in. He doesn't like any of the old associations very much anymore, but considering the danger Lopez poses, he might be willing to help us."

"Pity about his arm."

Eb shot him a wry glance. "Yes, but it's a lucky break it wasn't the arm he uses."

They drove over to Cy Parks's ranch, and found him watching his young foreman, Harley, doctoring a sick bull yearling in the barn. He was lounging against one of the posts that supported the imposing structure, his hat low over his eyes, his arms folded over a broad chest, one booted foot resting on a rail of the gate that enclosed the stall where his man was busy.

He turned as Eb and Dallas strode down the neat chipped bark covered floor to join him.

"You two out sightseeing?" Cy drawled without smiling, his green eyes narrowed and curious.

"Not today. We need a name."

"Whose?"

"The guy who worked with your friend Diego Laremos out near Chichén Itzá. I think he might be just what we need to infiltrate Lopez's cartel."

Cy's eyebrows lifted. "Rodrigo? You must be out of your mind!" he said at once.

"Why?"

"Good God," Cy burst out, "Diego says that he's such a renegade, nobody will hire him anymore, not even for black ops!"

"What did he do?" Dallas asked, aware that the young man in the stall had perked up and was suddenly listening unashamedly.

"For a start, he crashed a Huey out in the Yucatán last year," Cy said. "That didn't endear him to a certain government agency which was running him. Then he blew up an entire boatload of powder cocaine off Cozumel that the authorities were trying to confiscate—millions' worth. In between he wrecked a few hired cars in various chases, hijacked a plane, and broke into a government field office. He walked off with a couple of classified files and several thousand dollars' worth of high-tech listening devices that you can't even buy unless you're in law enforcement. After that, he went berserk in a bar down in Panama and put two men in the hospital, just before he absconded with a suitcase full of unlaundered drug money that belonged to Manuel Lopez..."

"Are we talking about the same Rodrigo that the feds used to call 'Mr. Cool'?" Eb asked with evident surprise.

"That isn't what they call him these days," Cy said flatly. "Mr. Liability would be more like it."

"He was with Laremos and Van Meer in Africa back in the early eighties," Eb recalled. "They left, but he signed on with another outfit and kept going."

"That's when he started working freelance for the feds," Cy continued. "At least, that's what Diego said," he added for Harley's benefit. He didn't want his young employee to know about his past.

"Anybody know why Rodrigo went bananas in Panama?" Dallas asked.

Cy shrugged. "There are a lot of rumors—but nothing concrete." He studied the other two with pursed lips. "If you want him for undercover work to indict Lopez, he'd probably pay you to hire him on. He hates Lopez."

Eb glanced past Cy at Harley, whose mouth was hanging open.

"Don't mind him," Cy told his companions with a mocking smile. "He's a mercenary, too," he added dryly.

Harley scrambled to his feet. "Can't I hire on?" he burst out. "Listen, I know those names—Van Meer and Brettman and Laremos. They were legends!"

"Put the top back on the medicine before you spill it," Cy told the young man calmly. "As for the other, that's up to Eb. It's his party."

Harley fumbled the lid back on the bottle. "Mr. Scott?" he asked, pleading.

"I guess we could find you something to do," Eb said, amused. Then the smile faded, and his whole look was threatening. "But this is strictly on the QT. You breathe one word of it locally and you're out on your ear. Got that?"

Harley nodded eagerly. "Sure!"

"And you'll work for him only after you do your

chores here," Cy said firmly. "I run cattle, not commandos."

"Yes, sir!"

Cy exchanged a complicated glance with Eb. "I've got the last number I had for Rodrigo in my office. I'll go get it."

He left the other three men in the barn. Harley was almost dancing with excitement.

"I'll be an asset, sir, honestly," he told Eb. "I can shoot anything that has bullets, and use a knife, and I know a little martial arts…!"

Eb chuckled. "Son, we don't need an assassin. We're collecting intelligence."

The boy's face fell. "Oh."

"Running gun battles aren't a big part of the business," Dallas said without cracking a smile. "You shoot anybody these days, even a criminal, and you could find yourself behind bars."

Harley looked shocked. "But…but I read about it all the time; those exciting battles in Africa…"

"Exciting?" Eb's eyes were steady and quiet.

"Why, sure!" Harley's eyes lit up. "You know, testing your courage under fire."

The boy's eyes were gleaming with excitement, and Eb knew then for certain that he'd never seen anyone shot. Probably the closest he'd come to it was listening to an instructor—probably a retired mercenary—talking about combat.

Harley noticed his employer coming out of the house and he grimaced. "I hope Mr. Parks meant what he said. He's not much on adventure, you see. He's sort of sarcastic when I mention where I went on my vacation, out in the field in Central America with a group of mercenaries. It was great!"

"Cy wasn't enthusiastic, I gather?" Eb probed.

"Naw," Harley said heavily. "He's just a rancher. Even if he knows Mr. Laremos, he sure doesn't know what it's like to really be a soldier of fortune. But we do, don't we?" he asked the other two with a grin.

Eb and Dallas glanced at each other and managed not to laugh. Quite obviously, Harley believed that Cy's information about Rodrigo was secondhand and had no idea what Cy did before he became a rancher.

Cy joined them, presenting a slip of paper with a number on it to Eb. "That's the last number I have, but they'll relay it, I'm sure."

"You still hear from Laremos?" Eb asked his friend.

"Every year, at Christmas," Cy told him. "They've got three kids now and the eldest is in high school." He shook his head. "I'm getting old."

"Not you," Eb chuckled.

"We'd better go," Dallas said, checking his watch.

"So we had."

"What about me?" Harley asked excitedly.

"We'll be in touch, when the time comes," Eb promised him, and, oddly, it sounded more like a threat.

Cy saw them off and came back to take one last look at the bull. "Good job, Harley," he said, approving the treatment. "You'll make a rancher yet."

Harley closed the bull in his stall and latched the gate. "How do you know Mr. Laremos, sir?" he asked curiously.

"Oh, we had a mutual acquaintance," he said without meeting the other man's eyes. "Diego still keeps in touch with the old group, so he knows what's going on in the intelligence field," he added deliberately.

"I see. I thought it was probably something like that," Harley said absently and went to work on the calf with scours in the next stall, reaching for the pills that were commonly called "eggs" to dose it with.

Cy looked after the smug younger man with amusement. Harley had his boss pegged as a retiring, staid rancher with no backbone and only an outsider's familiarity with the world of covert operations. He'd think that Cy had gotten all that information from Laremos, and, for the present, it suited Cy very well to let him think so. But if Harley had in mind an adventure with Eb and the others, he was in for a real shock. In the company of those men, he was going to be more uncomfortable than he dreamed right now. Some lessons, he told himself, were better learned through experience.

WHEN THEY GOT back to the ranch, Eb phoned the number Cy had given him. There was a long pause and then a quick, deep voice giving instructions. Eb was to leave his name and number and hang up immediately. He did. Seconds later, his phone rang.

"You run that strategy and tactics school in Texas," the deep voice said evenly.

"Yes."

"I read about it in one of the intelligence sitreps," he returned, shortening the name for situation reports. "I thought you were one of those vacation mercs who sat at a desk all week and liked to play at war a couple of weeks a year, until I spoke to Laremos. He remembers you, along with another Jacobsville resident named Parks."

"Cy and I used to work together, with Dallas Kirk and Micah Steele," Eb replied quietly.

"I don't know them, but I know Parks. If you're looking for someone to do black ops, I'm not available," he said curtly, with only a trace of an accent. "I don't do overseas work anymore, either. There's a fairly large price on my head in certain Latin American circles."

"It isn't a foreign job. I want someone to go under-cover here in Texas and relay intelligence from a drug cartel," Eb said flatly.

There was a long pause. "I'd find someone with a terminal illness for that sort of work," Rodrigo replied. "It's usually fatal."

"Cy Parks told me you'd probably jump at the chance to do this job."

"Oh, that's rich. And what job would that be?"

"The drug lord I want intelligence on is Manuel Lopez. I'm trying to put him back in prison perma-nently."

The intake of breath on the other end was audible, followed by a description of Lopez that questioned his ancestry, his paternity, his morals, and various other facets of his life in both Spanish and English.

"That's the very Lopez I'm talking about," Eb re-plied dryly. "Interested?"

"In killing him, yes. Putting him back in prison... well, he can still run the cartel from there."

"While he's in there, his organization could be suc-cessfully infiltrated and destroyed from within," Eb suggested, dangling the idea like a carrot on a string. "In fact, the reason we're under the gun in Jacobsville right now is because a friend of our group is protect-ing the identity of an intimate of Lopez who sold him out to the DEA."

"Keep talking," Rodrigo said at once.

"Lopez is trying to kill a former government agent who coaxed one of his intimate friends to help her get the hard evidence to put him in prison. He's only out on a legal technicality and he's apparently using his temporary freedom to dispose of her and her informant."

"What about the so-called hard evidence?" Rodrigo asked.

"My guess is that it'll disappear before the retrial. If he manages to get rid of the witnesses and destroy the evidence, he'll never go back to prison. In fact, he's already skipped bond."

"Don't tell me. They set bail at a million dollars and he paid it out of petty cash," came the sarcastic reply.

"Exactly."

There was a brief hesitation and a sigh. "Well, in that case, I suppose I'm working for you."

Eb smiled. "I'll put you on the payroll."

"Fine, but you can forget about retirement benefits if I go undercover."

Eb chuckled softly. "There's just one thing. We've heard that you and Lopez had a common interest at one time," he said, putting it as delicately as he could. "Does he know what you look like?"

There was another pause and when the voice came back, it was strained. "No, you can be sure of that."

"This won't be easy," Eb told him. "Be sure you're willing to take the risk before you agree."

"I'm quite sure. I'll see you tomorrow." The line went dead.

EB TOOK SALLY out to dinner that night, driving the sleek new black Jaguar S that he liked to use when he went to town.

"We'll go to Houston, if that suits you?"

She agreed. He looked devastating in a dinner jacket, and she was shy and uneasy with him, after what she'd learned about his fiancée. In fact, she'd told herself she wasn't going to be alone with him ever again. Yet here she sat. Resolve was hard when emotions were involved. His feelings for the woman he'd planned to marry were unmistakable in his voice when he talked about her, and now that she was free, he might have a second chance. Knowing that part of him had never gotten over his fiancée's defection, Sally was reluctant to risk her heart on him again. She kept a smiling, pleasant, but determined distance between them.

Eb noticed the reticence, but didn't understand its purpose. He could hardly take his eyes off her tonight. His green eyes kept returning to linger on her pretty black cocktail dress under the long red-lined black velvet coat she wore with it. Her hair was in a neat chignon at her nape, and she looked lovely.

"Are you sure this is a good idea?" Sally asked him. "I know Dallas will take care of Jess and Stevie, but it seems risky to go out at night with Lopez and his men around."

"He's a vicious devil," he replied, "but he is absolutely predictable. He'll give Jessica until exactly midnight Saturday. He won't do one thing until the deadline. At one minute past midnight," he added curtly, "there will be an assault."

Sally wrapped her arms closer around her body. "How do we end up with people like that in the world?"

"We forget that all lives are interconnected in some way, and that selfishness and greed are not desirable traits."

"What good will it do Lopez to kill Jessica and us?" she asked curiously. "I know he's angry at her, but if she's dead, she can't tell him anything!"

"He's going to be setting an example," he said. "Of

course, he probably thinks she'll give up the name to save her child." He glanced at Sally. "Would you?"

"I wouldn't have a hard time choosing between my child and someone who's already turned against his own people," she admitted.

"Jessica says there are extenuating circumstances," he told her.

She stared at her fingers. "I know. She won't even tell me who the person was." She glanced at him. "She's probably covering all her bases. If I knew who it was…"

He made a sound deep in his throat. "You'd turn the person over to Lopez?"

She shifted restlessly. "I might."

"Cows might fly."

He knew her too well. She laughed softly. "I wish there was another way out of this, that's all. I don't want Stevie hurt."

"He won't be." He reached across to clasp her cool hand gently in hers and press it. "I'm putting together a network. Lopez isn't going to be able to move without being in someone's line of sight from now on."

"I wish…" she began.

"Don't wish your life away. You have to take the bad with the good—that's what life is. Good times don't make us strong."

She grimaced. "No. I guess they don't." She leaned her head back against the headrest and drank in the smell of the leather. "I love the way new cars smell," she said conversationally. "And this one is just super."

"It has a few minor modifications," he said absently.

She turned her head toward him with a wicked grin. "Don't tell me—the headlights retract and become machine gun ports, the tailpipe leaves oil slicks, and the passenger seat is really an ejectable projectile!"

He laughed. "Not quite."

"Spoilsport."

"You need to stop watching old James Bond movies," he pointed out. "The world has changed since the sixties."

Her eyes studied his profile quietly. He was still handsome well into his thirties, and he glorified evening clothes. She knew that she couldn't look forward to anything permanent with him, but sometimes just looking at him was almost enough. He was devastating.

He caught that scrutiny and glanced at her, enjoying the shy admiration in her gray eyes. "Can you dance?" he asked.

"I'm not in the class with Matt Caldwell on a dance floor," she teased, "but I can hold my own, I suppose. Are we going dancing?"

"We're going to a supper club where they have an orchestra and a dance floor," he said. "A sophisticated place with a few carefully placed friends of mine."

"I should have known."

"You'll like it," he promised. "You'll never spot them. They blend in."

"You don't blend," she murmured dryly.

He chuckled. "If that's a compliment, thank you," he said.

"It was."

"You won't blend, either," he said in a low, soft tone.

She clutched her small bag tightly in her lap, feeling the softness right through her body. It made her giddy to think of being held in his arms on a dance floor. It was something she'd dreamed about in her senior year of high school, but it had never happened. As if it would have. She couldn't really picture Eb at a high school prom.

"You're sure Jess and Stevie will be okay?" she asked as he pulled off the main highway and onto a Houston city street.

"I'm sure. Dallas is inside and I have a few people outside. But I meant what I said," he added solemnly. "Lopez won't do a thing until midnight tomorrow."

She supposed that was a sort of knowledge of the enemy that came from long experience in a dangerous profession. But she couldn't help worrying about her family. If anything happened while she was away, she'd never forgive herself.

THE CLUB WAS just off a main thoroughfare, and so discreet that it wouldn't have drawn attention to itself. The luxury cars in the parking lot were an intimation of what was inside.

Inside, the sounds of music came from a room off the main hallway. There was a bar and a small coffee shop, apart from the restaurant. Inside, an employee in a dinner jacket led them into the restaurant, which ringed a central dance floor, where a small jazz ensemble played lazy blues tunes for several couples who were dancing.

"This is really spectacular," she told Eb when they were seated near a small indoor waterfall with tropical plants blooming around it.

"It is, isn't it?" he asked, leaning back to study her with a warm smile. "I have to admit, it's one of my favorite haunts when I'm in Houston."

"I can see why." She searched his eyes in a long, tense silence.

He didn't smile. His eyes narrowed as they locked into hers. She could almost hear her own heart beating, beating, beating...!

"Why, Eb!" came a soft voice from behind Sally.

"What a coincidence to find you here, at one of our favorite night spots."

Without another word being spoken, Sally knew the identity of the newcomer. It couldn't be anyone except Eb's ex-fiancée.

CHAPTER EIGHT

"HELLO, MAGGIE," EB SAID, standing up to greet the pretty green-eyed brunette who took possession of his arm and smiled up at him.

"It's good to see you again so soon!" she said with obvious pleasure. "You remember Cord Romero, don't you?" She indicated a tall, dark-haired, dark-eyed man beside her without meeting his eyes. "He and I were fostered together by Mrs. Amy Barton, the Houston socialite."

"Sure. How are you, Cord?" Eb asked.

The other man, his equal in height and build, nodded. Sally was curious about Maggie's obvious uneasiness around the other man.

"Sally, this is Maggie Barton and Cord Romero. Sally Johnson." They all acknowledged the introductions, and Eb added, "Won't you join us?"

Sally's heart plummeted as she saw Maggie's eyes light up at the invitation and knew she wouldn't refuse.

"We may be intruding," Cord said with a pointed look at Sally.

"Oh, not at all," Sally said at once.

"I thought Sally needed a night out," Eb said easily and with a warm smile in Sally's direction. "She's an elementary schoolteacher."

The man, Cord, studied her with open curiosity while Eb seated Maggie.

"Allow me," Cord said smoothly, standing behind Sally's chair.

Sally smiled at the old-world courtesy. "Thank you."

Eb glanced at them with unreadable eyes before he turned back to Maggie, who was flushed and avoided looking at the other couple. "Quite a coincidence, running into you here," he said in a neutral tone.

"It was Cord's idea," Maggie said. "He felt like a night on the town and he doesn't date these days. Better your foster sister than nobody, right, Cord?" she added with a nervous laugh and a smile that didn't touch her eyes.

Cord shrugged broad shoulders indolently and didn't say a word, but his distaste for her reference was there, in those unblinking dark eyes.

Sally was curious about him. She wondered what he did for a living. He was very fit for a man his age, which she judged to be about the same as Eb's. His hands were rough and callused, as if he worked physically rather than sat behind a desk. He had the same odd stare that she'd noticed in Eb and Dallas and even Cy Parks, a probing but unfocused distant stare that held a strange hollowness.

"How are things going at the ranch?" Maggie asked gently. "I heard that you had Dallas out there with you."

"Yes," he replied. "He's doing some consulting work for me."

"Shot to pieces, wasn't he?" Cord asked abruptly, his eyes on Sally's face.

"That happens when a man doesn't keep his mind on his work," Eb said with a pointed glance at Cord, who averted his eyes.

"One of my friends is hosting a huge party down in Cancún for Christmas," Maggie murmured, drawing a lazy polished nail across the back of Eb's hand. "Why don't you take some time off and go with me?"

"No time," Eb said with a smile to soften the words. "I'm not a man of leisure."

"Baloney," she replied. "You could retire on what you've got squirreled away."

"And do what?" came the dry response. "Do I look like a lounge lizard to you?"

"I didn't mean that," she said, and her eyes searched his face for a long moment. "I meant that you could give up walking into danger if you wanted to."

"That's an old argument and you know what the answer is," Eb told her bluntly.

She withdrew her hand from his with a sad little sigh. "Yes, I know," she said wearily. "It's in your blood and you can't stop." Involuntarily she glanced at Cord.

Eb frowned a little as he watched her wilt. Sally saw it and knew at once that he and Maggie had gone through that very argument years ago when she'd broken their engagement. It wasn't their emotions that had split them up. It was his job that he wouldn't quit, not even for a woman he'd loved enough to marry.

She felt helpless. She'd known at some level that he was carrying a torch for Maggie. She stared at her own short, unpolished nails and compared them with Maggie's long, red-stained, beautiful ones. The difference was like the women themselves—one colorful and flamboyant and drawing attention, the other reclusive and practical and…dull. No wonder Eb hadn't wanted her all those years ago. Beside the exotic Maggie, she was insignificant.

"What subject is your specialty, Miss Johnson?" Cord asked curiously.

"History, actually," she said. "But I teach second grade, so I'm not really using it."

"No ambition to teach higher grades?" he persisted.

She shook her head and smiled wryly. "I tried it when I did my practice-teaching," she confessed. "And by the end of the day, my classroom was more like a zoo than a regimented place of learning. I'm afraid I don't have the facility to handle discipline at a higher level."

Cord's lean face lightened just a little as he studied her. "I had the facility, but the principal and the school board didn't like my methods," he replied.

"You teach?" she asked, enthused to find a colleague in such an unlikely place.

"I taught high school science for a year after I got out of college," he said. "But it wasn't a profession I could love enough to continue." He shrugged. "I found I had an aptitude in a totally unrelated area."

Maggie's hand clenched on her water glass and she took a quick sip.

"What do you do?" she asked, fascinated.

He glanced at Eb, who was openly glaring at him. "Ask Eb," he said on a brief, deep laugh, with a cold glance in Maggie's direction. "Can we order now?" he asked, lifting the menu. "I haven't even had lunch today."

Eb signaled a waiter and brought Sally's conversation with Cord to an end.

It was the longest and most tense meal Sally could remember having sat through. Maggie and Eb talked about places and people that they shared in memory while Sally concentrated on her food.

Cord was polite, but he made no further attempt at conversation. At the end of the evening, as the two couples parted outside the restaurant, Maggie held on to Eb's hand until he had to forcibly draw it away from her.

"Can't you come up and have dinner with us again one evening?" Maggie asked plaintively.

"Perhaps," Eb said with a careless smile. He glanced at Cord. "Good to see you."

Cord nodded. He glanced down at Sally. "Nice to have met you, Miss Johnson."

"Same here," she said with a smile.

Maggie hesitated and looked uneasy as Cord deliberately took her arm and propelled her away. She went with him, but her back was arrow-straight and she looked as if she was walking on hot coals and on the way to her own execution.

Eb stared after them for a long moment before he put Sally into the sleek Jaguar and climbed in under the wheel. He gave her a look that could have curdled milk.

"Don't encourage him," he said at once.

Her mouth fell open. "Wh...what?"

"You heard me." He started the car, and turned toward Sally. His eyes went over her like sensual fingers, brushing her throat, her bare shoulders under the coat, the shadowy hollow in her breasts revealed by the low-cut dress. "He has a weakness for blondes. He was ravishing you with his eyes."

She didn't know how to respond. While Sally was trying to come up with a response, he moved closer and slid a hand under her nape, under the heavy coil of hair, and pulled her face up toward his.

"So was I," he whispered roughly, and his mouth went down on her lips, burrowing beneath them, pressing them apart, devouring them. At the same time, his free hand slid right down into the low bodice of her dress and curved around her warm, bare breast.

"Eb!" she choked, stiffening.

He was undeterred. He groaned, overcome with desire, and his fingers contracted in a slow, heated, sensual rhythm that brought Sally's mouth open in a tiny gasp. His tongue found the unprotected heat of it and moved inside, in lazy, teasing motions that made her whole body clench.

He felt her nervous fingers fumble against the front of his dress shirt. Impatiently, he unfastened three buttons and dragged her hand inside the shirt, over hair-roughened muscles down to a nipple as hard as the one pressing feverishly into the palm of his hand.

She was devastated by the passion that had kindled so unexpectedly. She couldn't find the strength or the voice to protest the liberties he was taking, or to care that they were in a public parking lot. She didn't care about anything except making sure that he didn't stop. He couldn't stop. He mustn't stop, he mustn't…!

But he did, suddenly. He held her hands together tightly as he moved a little away from her, painfully aware that she was trying to get back into his arms.

"No," he said curtly, and shook her clenched hands.

She stared into his blazing eyes, her breath rustling in her throat, her heartbeat visible at the twin points so blatantly obvious against the bodice of her dress.

He glanced down at her and his jaw clenched. His own body was in agony, and this would only get worse if he didn't stop them now. She was too responsive, too tempting. He was going to have to make sure that he didn't touch her that way when they were completely alone. The consequences could be devastating. It was the wrong time for a torrid relationship. If he let himself lose his head over Sally right now, it could cost all of them their lives.

Forcefully, he put her back into her own seat and fastened the seat belt around her.

She just stared at him with those huge, soulful gray eyes that made him feel hungry and guilt-ridden all at the same time.

"I have to get you home," he said tersely.

She nodded. Her throat was too tight for words to get out. She clutched her small purse in her hands and stared out the window as he put the car into gear and pulled out into traffic.

It was a long, and very silent, drive back to her house. He was preoccupied, as distant as she remembered him from her teens. She wondered if he was thinking about Maggie and regretting the decision he'd made that put her out of his life. She was mature now, but beautiful as well, and it didn't take a mind reader to know that she was still attracted to Eb. How he felt was less obvious. He was a man who knew how to hide what he felt, and that skill was working overtime tonight.

"Why did Maggie introduce Cord as a foster child at first and then refer to him as her brother? Are they related?" she asked.

"They are not," he returned flatly. "His parents died in a fire, and she came from a severely dysfunctional family. Mrs. Barton adopted both of them. Maggie took her name, but Cord kept his own. His father was a rather famous matador in Spain until his death. Maggie does usually try to present Cord as her brother. She's scared to death of him, despite the fact that they've kept in close touch all these years."

That was a surprise. "But why is she scared of him?"

He chuckled. "Because she wants him, although she's apparently never realized it," he returned with a quick glance. "He's been a colleague of mine for a long time, and I always thought that Maggie got engaged to me to put Cord out of the reach of temptation."

She pondered that. "A colleague?"

"That's right. He still works with Micah Steele," he said. "He's a demolitions expert."

"Isn't that dangerous?"

"Very," he replied. "His wife died four years ago. Committed suicide," he added shockingly. "He never got over it."

"Why did she do something so drastic?" she asked.

"Because he was working for the FBI when they married and he got shot a few months after the wedding. She hadn't realized his work would be so dangerous. He was in the hospital for weeks and she went haywire. He wouldn't give up a job he loved, and she found that she couldn't live with the knowledge that he might end up dead. She couldn't give him up, either, so she took what she considered the easy way out." His face set grimly. "Easy for her. Hell on him."

She drew in a sharp breath. "I suppose he felt guilty."

"Yes. That was about the time Maggie broke up with me," he added. "She said she didn't want to end up like Patricia."

"She knew Cord's wife?"

"They were best friends," he said shortly. "And something happened between Cord and Maggie just after Mrs. Barton's funeral. I never knew what, but it ended in Maggie's sudden marriage to a man old enough to be her father. I don't know why, but I think it had something to do with Cord."

"He's unique."

He glared at her. "Yes. He's a hardened mercenary now. He gave up law enforcement when Patricia died and took a job with an ex-special forces unit that went into freelance work. He started doing demolition work and now it's all he does."

Her eyes softened. "He wants to die."

"You're perceptive," he mused. "That's what I think, too. Hell of a pity that he and Maggie don't see each other. They're a lot alike."

She looked at her purse. "You aren't still carrying a torch for her?"

He chuckled. "No. She's a kind, sweet woman and I probably would have married her if things had been different. But I don't think she could have lived with me. She takes things too much to heart."

"Don't I?" she fished.

He smiled. "At times. But you're spunky, Miss Johnson, and despite the scare you had with your two neighbors, you don't balk at fighting back. I like your spirit. When I lose my temper, and I do occasionally, you won't be looking for a closet to hide in."

"That might be true," she confessed. "But if you were into demolition work, I think I'd run in the opposite direction when I saw you coming."

He nodded. "Which is exactly what Maggie did," he replied. "She ran from Cord and got engaged to me."

That was heartening. If the woman was carrying a torch for another man, it might stop Eb from falling back into his old relationship with her.

"Jealous?" he murmured with a sensuous glance.

Her heart raced. She moved one shoulder a little and avoided his eyes. Then she sighed and said, "Yes."

He chuckled. "Now that really is flattering," he said. "Maggie is part of the past. I have no hidden desire to rekindle old flames. Except the one you and I shared," he qualified.

Sally turned her head and met his searching gaze.

Her breath caught in her throat as she stared back at him hungrily.

"Watch it," he said, not quite jokingly. "When we drive up in your yard, we'll be under surveillance. I don't want an audience for what we were doing in the parking lot at that restaurant."

She laughed delightedly. "Okay."

"On the other hand," he added, "we could find a deserted road."

She hesitated. It was one thing for it to happen spontaneously, but quite another to plan such a sensual interlude. And she wasn't sure of her own protective instincts. Around Eb, she didn't seem to have any.

"Don't make such heavy weather of it," he said after a minute. "There's no hurry. We've got all the time in the world."

"Have we?" she wondered, remembering Lopez and his threats.

"Don't gulp down your life, Sally," he said. "Take it one minute at a time. I'm not going to let anything happen to you or Jessica or Stevie. Okay?"

She swallowed. "Sorry. I panic when I think about how dangerous it is."

"I've been handling danger for a long time," he reminded her. "I have a state-of-the-art surveillance system. Nothing is going to get past it."

She managed a weak smile. "He's very ruthless."

"He's been getting away with murder," he said simply. "He doesn't think the justice system can touch him. We're going to prove to him that it can."

"How do you bring a man to justice when he's rich enough to buy a country?"

"You cut off the source of his wealth," he said simply. "Without its head, the snake can't go far."

"Good point."

"Now stop worrying."

"I'll try."

He reached across the seat for her hand and locked it into his big, warm one. "I enjoyed tonight."

"So did I," she said gently.

"Maggie isn't my future, in case you were wondering," he added in a soft tone.

Sally hoped fervently that it was true. She wanted Eb with all her heart.

His fingers tightened on hers. "I think it might be a good idea if I start driving you and Stevie to school and picking you up in the afternoons."

Her heart leaped. "Why?"

He glanced at her. "Because Lopez wouldn't hesitate to kidnap either or both of you to further his own ends. Even two miles is a long distance when you don't have any sort of protection."

She stared at him worriedly. "Why didn't Jess leave well enough alone?" she asked miserably. "If she hadn't gotten that person to talk…"

"Hindsight is wonderful," he told her. "But try to remember that Lopez's operation supplies about a quarter of all narcotics sold in the States. That's a lot of addicted kids and a fair number of dead ones."

She grimaced. "Sorry. I was being selfish."

"It isn't selfish to be concerned for the welfare of people you love," he told her. "But getting Lopez behind bars, and cutting his connections, will help make the world a better place. A little worry isn't such a bad trade-off, considering."

"I guess not."

He brought the back of her hand to his mouth and

kissed it warmly. "You looked lovely tonight," he said. "I was proud of you."

Her face flushed at the rare compliment. "I'm always proud of you," she replied softly.

He chuckled. "You're good for my ego."

"You're good for mine."

He kept his eyes on the road with an effort. He wanted to pull the car onto a side road and make passionate love to her, but that was impractical, given the circumstances. All Lopez's men needed was an opportunity. He wasn't going to give them one, despite his teasing comment to Sally about it.

When they pulled up in her driveway, the lights were all on in the house and Dallas was sitting in the front porch swing, smoking like a furnace.

"Have a nice time?" he asked as Eb and Sally came up the steps.

"Very nice," Eb replied. "I ran into Cord Romero."

"I thought he was overseas, helping detonate unexploded land mines?"

"Not now," Eb told him. "He's in Houston. Between jobs, maybe. Why are you sitting out here?"

Dallas stared at the red tip of his cigarette. "Jessica has a cough," he replied. "I didn't want to aggravate it."

"Are the two of you speaking?" Eb drawled.

Dallas laughed softly. "Well, she's stopped trying to throw things at me, at least."

Sally's eyes went enormous. That didn't sound like her staid aunt.

"What was she throwing?" Eb asked.

"Anything within reach that felt expendable," came the dry reply. "Stevie thought it was great fun, but she wouldn't let him play. He's gone to bed. She's pretending to watch television."

"You might talk to her," Eb suggested.

"Chance," Dallas replied, "would be a fine thing. She doesn't want to talk, thank you." He finished the cigarette. "I'll be out in the woods with Smith."

"Watch where you walk," Eb cautioned.

"Mined the forest, did we?" Dallas murmured wickedly.

Eb grinned. "Not with explosives, at least."

Dallas shook his head and went down the steps, to vanish in the direction of the woods at the edge of the yard.

Sally rubbed her arms through the coat, shivering, and it wasn't even that cold. She felt the danger of her predicament keenly and wished that she could have done something to prevent the desperate situation.

"You're doing it again," Eb murmured, drawing her against him. "You have to trust me. I won't let anything happen to any of you."

She looked up at him with wide, soft eyes. "I'll try not to worry. I've never been in such a mess before."

"Hopefully you never will again," he said. He bent and kissed her very gently, nipping her lower lip before he lifted his head. "I'll be somewhere nearby, or my men will be. Try to get some sleep."

"Okay." She touched her fingers to his mouth and smiled wanly before she turned and walked to the door. "Thanks for supper," she added. "It was delicious."

"It would have been better without the company," he said, "but that was unavoidable. Next time I'll plan better."

She smiled at him. "That's a deal."

He watched her walk inside the house and lock the door behind her before he turned and got back into his truck. Less than twenty-four hours remained before

Lopez would make good his threat. He had to make sure that everyone was prepared for a siege.

SALLY PAUSED IN the doorway of the living room with her eyes wide as she saw the damage Jessica had inflicted with her missiles.

"Good Lord!" she exclaimed.

Jess grimaced. "Well, he provoked me," she muttered. "He said that I'd gotten lazy in my old age, just lying around the house like a garden slug. I do not lie around like a garden slug!"

"No, of course you don't," Sally said, placating her while she bent to pick up pieces of broken pottery and various other objects from the floor.

"Besides, what does he expect me to do without my eyesight, drive the car?"

Sally was trying not to smile. She'd never seen her aunt in such a tizzy before.

"He actually accused me of insanity because I won't give up the name to Lopez," she added harshly. "He said that a good mother wouldn't have withheld a name and put her child in danger. That's when I threw the flowerpot, dear. I'm sorry. I do hope it hit him."

Sally made a clucking sound. "You're not yourself, Jess."

"Yes, I am! I'm the result of all his sarcasm! He can't find one thing about me that he likes anymore. Everything I do and say is wrong!"

"He doesn't seem like a bad man," Sally ventured.

"I didn't say he was bad, I said he was obnoxious and condescending and conceited." She pushed back a strand of hair. "He was laughing the whole time."

Which surely made things worse, Sally mused silently. "I expect it was wails of pain, Jess."

"You couldn't hurt him," she scoffed. "You'd have to stick a bomb up his shirt."

"Drastic surely?"

Jess sighed and leaned back in the chair, looking drained. "I hate arguments. He seems to thrive on them." She hesitated. "He taught Stevie how to braid a rope," she added unexpectedly.

"That's odd. I thought Stevie wanted to beat him up."

"They had a talk outside the room. I don't know what was said," Jess confessed. "But when they came back in here, Dallas had several lengths of rawhide and he taught Stevie how to braid them. He was having the time of his life."

"Then what?"

"Then," she said, her lips compressing briefly, "he just happened to mention that I could have taught him how to braid rope and a lot of other things if I'd exert myself occasionally instead of vegetating in front of a television that I can't see anyway."

"I see."

"Pity I ran out of things to throw," she muttered. "I was reaching for the lamp when he called a draw and said he was going to sit on the front porch. Then Stevie decided to go to bed." She gripped the arms of her chair hard. "Everybody ran for cover. You'd think I was a Chinese rocket or something."

"In a temper, there is something of a comparison," Sally chuckled.

The older woman drew in a long breath. "Anyway, how was your date?"

"Not bad. We ran into his ex-fiancée at the restaurant."

"Maggie?" Jess asked, wide-eyed. "How is she?"

"She's very pretty and still crazy about Eb, from

all indications. I think she'd have followed us home if her dark and handsome escort hadn't half dragged her away."

"Cord was there?"

"You know him?" Sally asked curiously.

Jess nodded. "He was a handsome devil. I had a yen for him once myself, but he married Patricia instead. She was a little Dresden china doll, blonde and absolutely gorgeous. She worshipped Cord. They'd only been married a few months when he was involved in a shoot-out with a narcotics dealer. She couldn't take it. When Cord came home from the hospital, she was several days dead, with a suicide note clutched in her fingers. He found her. He was like a madman after that, looking for every dangerous job he could find. I don't suppose he's over her yet. He loved her desperately."

"Eb says he works with Micah Steele."

"He does, and there's a real coincidence. Micah also has a stepsister, Callie. You know her, she works in Mr. Kemp's law office."

"Yes. We went to school together. But Micah doesn't have anything to do with her or his father since his father divorced Callie's mother. They say," she murmured, "that old Mr. Steele caught Micah with his new wife in a very compromising position and tossed them both out on their ears."

"That's the obvious story," Jessie said dryly. "But there's more to it than that."

"How does Callie feel about Micah's work, do you think?"

"The way any woman would feel," Jessie replied gently. "Afraid."

Sally knew that Jess was talking about Dallas, and how she'd regarded his work as a soldier of fortune.

She stared at the darkened window, wondering how she'd feel under the same circumstances. At least Eb wasn't involved in demolition work or actively working as a mercenary. She knew that she could adjust to Eb's lifestyle. But the trick was going to be convincing Eb that she could—and that he needed her, as much as she needed him.

CHAPTER NINE

SALLY FOUND HERSELF jumping at every odd noise all day Saturday. Jessica could feel the tension that she couldn't see.

"You have to trust Eb," she told her niece while Stevie was watching cartoons in the living room. "He knows what he's doing. Lopez won't succeed."

Sally grimaced over her second cup of coffee. Across the kitchen table from her, Jess looked serene. She wished she could feel the same way.

"I'm not worried about us," she pointed out. "It's Stevie…"

"Dallas won't let anything happen to Stevie," came the quiet reply.

Sally smiled, remembering the broken objects in the living room the night before. She drew a lazy circle around the lip of her coffee cup while she searched for the right words. "At least, the two of you are speaking."

"Yes. Barely," her aunt acknowledged wryly. "But Stevie likes him now. They started comparing statistics on wrestlers. They both like wrestling, you see. Dallas knows all sorts of holds. He wrestled on his college team."

"Wrestling!" Sally chuckled.

"Apparently there's a lot more to the professional matches than just acting ability," Jessica said dryly. "I'm finding it rather interesting, even if I can't see what they're doing. They explained the holds to me."

"Common threads," Sally murmured.

"And one stitch at a time. What did you think of Cord Romero?"

"He's the strangest ex-schoolteacher I've ever met," Sally said flatly.

"He was never cut out for that line of work," Jessica said, sipping black coffee. "But demolition work isn't much of a profession, either. Pity. He'll be two lines of type on the obituary page one day, and it's such a waste."

"Eb says Maggie's running from him."

"Relentlessly," Jess said dryly. "I always thought she got engaged to Eb just to shake Cord up, but it didn't work. He doesn't see her."

"He's in the same line of work Eb was," Sally pointed out, "and Eb said that his job was why she called off the wedding."

"I think she just came to her senses. If you love a man, you don't have a lot to say about his profession if it's a long-standing one. Cord's wife was never cut out for life on the edge. Maggie, now, once had a serious run-in with a couple of would-be muggers. She had a big flashlight in her purse and she used it like a mace." She laughed softly. "They both had to have stitches before they went off to jail. Cord laughed about it for weeks afterward. No, she had the strength to marry Eb—she simply didn't love him."

Sally traced the handle of her cup. "Eb says he isn't carrying a torch for her."

"Why should he be?" she asked. "She's a nice woman, but he never really loved her. He wanted stability and he thought marriage would give it to him. As it turned out, he found his stability after a bloody fire-fight in Africa, and it was right here in Jacobsville."

"Do you think he'll ever marry?" she fished.

"When he's ready," Jess replied. "But I don't think it will be Maggie. Just in case you wondered," she teased.

Sally pushed back a wisp of hair from her eyes. "Jess, do you know where your informant is now, the one that Lopez wants you to name?"

She shook her head. "We lost touch just after Lopez was arrested. I understand that my informant went back to Mexico. I haven't tried to contact...the person."

"What if the informant betrays himself?"

"You're clutching at straws, dear," Jessica said gently. "That isn't going to happen. And I'm not giving a witness up to the executioner in cold blood even to save myself and my family."

Sally smiled. "No. I know you wouldn't. I wouldn't, either. But it's scary to be in this situation."

"It is. But it will be over one day, and we'll get back to normal. Whatever happens, happens." Jess reminded her niece, "It's like that old saying, when your time's up, it's up. We may not know what we're doing, but God always does. And He doesn't have tunnel vision."

"Point taken. I'll try to stop worrying."

"You should. Eb is one of the best in the world at what he does. Lopez knows it, too. He won't rush in headfirst, despite his threat."

"What if he has a missile launcher?" Sally asked with sudden fear.

Miles away in a communications hot room, a man with green eyes nodded his head and shot an order to a subordinate. It wouldn't hurt one bit to check out the intelligence for that possibility. Sally might be nervous, but she had good instincts. And a guardian angel in cowboy boots.

MANUEL LOPEZ WAS a small man with big ambition. He was nearing forty, balding, cynical and mercenary to the soles of his feet. He stared out the top floor picture window of his four-story mansion at the Gulf of Mexico and cursed. One of his subordinates, shifting nervously from one foot to the other, had just brought him some unwelcome news and he was livid.

"There are only a handful of men," the subordinate said in quiet Spanish. "Not a problem if we send a large force against them."

Lopez turned and glared at the man from yellow-brown eyes. "Yes, and if we send a large force, the FBI and the DEA will also send a large force!"

"It would be too late by then," the man replied with a shrug.

"I have enough federal problems in the United States as it is," Lopez growled. "I do not anticipate giving them an even better reason to send an undercover unit after me here! Scott has influence with his government. I want the name of the informant, not to wade in and kill the woman and her protectors."

The other man stared at the spotless white carpet. "She will never give up the name of her informant," he said simply. "Not even for the sake of her child."

Lopez turned fully to look at the man. "Because now it is only words, the threat. We must make it very real, you understand? At midnight tonight in Jacobsville, precisely at midnight, you will have a helicopter fly over the house and drop a smoke bomb. A big one." His eyes narrowed and he smiled. "This will be the attack they anticipate. But not the real one, you understand?"

"They will probably have missiles," the man said quietly.

"And they are far too soft to use them," came the sneering reply. "This is why we will ultimately win. I have no scruples. Now, listen. I will want a man to remove one of the elementary school janitors. He can be drugged or threatened, I have no interest in the method, just get him out of the way for one day. Then you will have one of our men take his place. The substitute must know what the child looks like and which class he is in. He is to be taken very covertly, so that nothing out of the way is projected until it is too late and we have him. You understand?"

"Yes," the man replied respectfully. "Where is he to be held?"

Lopez smiled coldly. "At the rental house near the Johnson home," he said. "Will that not be an irony to end all ironies?" His eyes darkened. "But he is not to be harmed. That must be made very clear," he added in tones that chilled. "You remember what happened to the man who went against my orders and set fire to my enemy's house in Wyoming without waiting for the man to be alone, and a five-year-old boy was killed?"

The other man swallowed and nodded quickly.

"If one hair on this boy's head is harmed," he added, "I will see to it that the man responsible fares even worse than his predecessor. I am a violent man, but I do not kill children. It is, perhaps, my only virtue." He waved his hand. "Let me know when my orders have been carried out."

"Yes. At once."

He watched the man go and his odd yellow-brown

eyes narrowed. He had watched his mother and siblings die at the hands of a guerrilla leader at the age of four. His father had been a poor laborer who could barely earn enough to provide one meal a day for the two of them, so his childhood had been spent scavenging for food like an animal, hiding in the shadows to avoid being tortured by the invaders. His father had not been as fortunate, but the two of them had managed to work their way to the States, to Victoria, Texas, when he was ten. He watched his father scrape and bow as a janitor and hated the sight. He had vowed that when he was a man, he would never know poverty again, regardless of what it cost him. And despite his father's anguish, he had embarked very quickly on a path to easy money.

He looked down at the white carpet, a dream of his from youth, and at the wealth with which he surrounded himself. He dealt in drugs and death. He was wealthy and immensely powerful. A word from him could topple heads of state. But it was an empty, cold, bitter existence. He had lived at first only for vengeance, for the ability and the means to avenge his mother and his baby brother and sister. That accomplished, he wanted wealth and power. One step led to another, until he was in over his head, first as a murderer, then as a thief, and finally, as a drug lord. He was ruthless and he knew that one day his sins would catch up with him, but first he was going to know who had sold him out to the authorities two years before. What irony that vengeance had led him to power, and now it was vengeance that had almost brought him down. He cursed the woman Jessica for refusing to give him the name. He had only discovered her part in his arrest six months before. She would pay now. He would have the name of his betrayer, whatever the cost!

He stared down at the rocks and winced as he saw once again, in his memory, the floating white dress and the equally white face and open, dead eyes of the woman he'd wanted even more than the name of the person who had betrayed him. Isabella, he thought with anguish. He had never loved, not until Isabella came into his home as a housekeeper, the sister of one of his lieutenants' friends. She had talked to him, admired him, teased him as if he were a boy. She had made herself so necessary to him that he told her things that he told no one else. She had made him want to be clean, to give up his decadent life, to have a family, a home. But when he had approached her ardently, she had suddenly wanted no part of him. In a fit of rage when she pushed him away at a party on his yacht, he hit her. She went over the rails and into the ocean, vanishing abruptly under the keel of the boat.

He had immediately regretted the act, but it was too late. His men had searched for her in the water until daybreak before he let them give up the search, only to find her washed up on the beach, dead, when he arrived back at his mansion. Her death had cheapened him, cheapened his life. He was deeply sorry that his temper had pushed him to such an act, that he cost himself the most precious thing in his life. He had killed her. He was damned, he thought. Damned eternally. And probably he deserved to be.

Since that night, two years ago, just before his arrest in the United States for narcotic trafficking, he had no other thought than to find the man who had betrayed him. Nothing made him happy since her loss, not even the pretty young woman who sang at a club in Cancún just recently. He had taken a fancy to her because she reminded him of Isabella. He had ordered his henchmen to bring her to him one night after her performance. He had enjoyed her, but her violent revulsion had angered him and she, too, had felt his wrath. She had taken her own life, jumped from a high balcony rather than submit to him a second time. Her death had wounded him, but not as deeply as the loss of Isabella. Nothing, he was certain, would ever give him such anguish and remorse again. He thought of the woman Jessica and her son, of the fear she would experience when he had her child. Then, he thought angrily, she would give him the name of her informant. She would have to. And, at last, he would have his vengeance for the betrayal that had sent him to an American prison.

EB HADN'T COME near the house all day. After Stevie was tucked up in bed, Jessica and Sally sat together in the dimly lit living room and watched the clock strike midnight.

"It's time," Sally said huskily, stiff with nerves.

Jessica only nodded. Like Sally, her frame was rigid. She had made her decision, the only decision possible. Now they were all going to pay the consequences for it.

Even as the thought crawled through her mind, she heard the sudden whir of a helicopter closing in.

"Get down!" Jessica called to Sally, sliding onto the big throw rug full-length. She felt Sally beside her as the helicopter came even closer and a flash, followed by an explosion, shook the roof.

Smoke came down the chimney, filling the room. Outside, the whir of the helicopter was accompanied by small arms fire and the sounds of bullets hitting something hard. Then that sound was abruptly interrupted by a sudden whooshing sound. Right on the heels of that came a violent explosion that lit up the whole sky and then the unmistakable sound of falling debris.

"There went the chopper," Jessica said huskily. "Sally, are you all right?"

"Yes. We have to get out," she said, coughing. "The smoke is going to choke us!"

She helped Jessica to her feet and started her down the hall to the front door while she went to grab Stevie up out of his bed and rush down the same hall with him in her arms. It was like a nightmare, but she didn't have time to count the cost or worry about the outcome. She was doing what was necessary to save them, in the quickest possible time. She could only pray that they wouldn't run out right into the arms of Lopez's men.

She caught up with Jess, who was feeling her way along the wall. Taking her by the arm, with Stevie close, she propelled them to the front door, unlocked it, and rushed out onto the porch.

Eb was running toward them, but an Eb that Sally didn't recognize at first. He was dressed completely in black with a face mask on, carrying a small automatic weapon. Other men, similarly dressed, were already going around the back of the house.

"Come with me," Eb called, herding them into the forest and into a four-wheel-drive vehicle. "Lock the doors and stay put until we check out the house," he said.

He was gone even as the words died on the air. Stevie huddled close to his mother while Sally watched Eb's stealthy but rapid approach toward the house, her heart racing madly. Even though the attack had been expected, it was frightening.

A tap on the window next to Jessica on the passenger side made them all jump. Dallas pulled off his face mask, smiling as he replaced a walkie-talkie in his belt. "Open the window," he said.

Sally fumbled with the key in the ignition and powered the passenger side window down.

"We got the chopper," he said. "But it's only a smoke bomb in the house, irritating but not deadly. Lopez is a man of his word. He did attack at midnight. Pity about the chopper," he added with glittery eyes. "That will set him back a little small change."

Sally didn't ask the obvious question, but she knew that somebody had to be piloting that helicopter. She felt sick inside, now that the danger was past.

"Is everyone all right?" Jessica asked. "We heard shots."

"The chopper was well-equipped with weapons," Dallas said. "But he wasn't a very good shot."

"Thank God," Jessica said heavily.

Dallas reached in and touched her face gently, pausing to run a rough hand over Stevie's tousled hair. "Don't be afraid," he said softly. "I won't let anything happen to you."

Jessica held his hand to her cheek and choked back a sob. Dallas bent to touch his mouth to her wet eyes.

Impulsively Stevie leaned across his mother to hug the big blond man, too. Watching them, Sally felt empty and alone. They were already a family, even if they hadn't realized it.

Dallas's walkie-talkie erupted in a burst of static. "All clear," Eb's voice came back to them. "I'm phoning the sheriff while the others open the windows and turn on the attic fan to get this smoke out of here. Then I'll lock up."

"What about…" Dallas began.

"We'll take the women and Stevie home with us,"

he said. "No sense in leaving them here for the rest of the night. Sally?"

Dallas moved the walkie-talkie to her mouth. "Yes?" she said, shaken.

"Come in and help me find what you need in the way of clothes for all three of you. Dallas, take Jess and Stevie back to the house. We'll catch up."

"Sure thing."

Sally got out of the vehicle, still in her jeans and sneakers and sweatshirt, her long hair falling out of its braid. Dallas got in under the wheel as she walked back to the house. She heard the engine roar and glanced back to see the utility vehicle pull out of the yard. At least Jess and Stevie were safe. But she felt shaken to the soles of her sneakers.

Eb was in the smoky living room, having just hung up the phone. His mask was in one hand, dangling along with the small machine gun. He looked tough and angry as he glanced at Sally's white face. He didn't say a word. He just held out his arm.

Sally ran to him, and he gathered her up in his arms and held her tight while she shivered from the shock of it all.

"I'm no wimp, honest," she whispered in a choked attempt at humor. "But I'm not used to people bombing my house."

He chuckled deeply and hugged her close. "Only a smoke bomb, baby," he said gently. "Noisy and frightening, but not dangerous unless it set fire to something. He had to make a statement, you see. Lopez is a man of his word."

"Damn Lopez," she muttered.

"Amen."

Around them, men were pouring over the house. Eb escorted Sally down the hall to her bedroom.

"Get what you need together," he said, "but only essentials. I'd like to get you out of here very soon after the sheriff arrives."

"The sheriff...?"

"It's his jurisdiction," he told her, "I'm sanctioned, if that's what the worried look is about," he added when he saw her face. He smiled. "I wouldn't take the law into my own hands. Not in this country, anyway," he added with a grin.

"Thank goodness," she said heavily. "I had visions of trying to bail you out of jail."

"Would you?" he teased.

"Of course."

She looked so solemn that the smile faded from his lips. He gathered a handful of her thick blond hair and pulled her wan face under his. His grip was a little tight, and the look in his green eyes was glittery. "Danger is an aphrodisiac, did you know?" he whispered roughly, and bent to her mouth.

He hadn't kissed her that way before. His mouth was hard and demanding on her lips, parting them ruthlessly as his body shifted and one arm pushed her hips deliberately into the changing contours of his own.

She felt helpless. Her mouth opened for him. Her body arched up, taut and hot, in the grip of madness. She returned his kiss ardently, moaning when his legs parted so that he could maneuver her hips between them, letting her feel the power of his arousal.

His tall, fit body shuddered and she could feel the sharp indrawn breath he took.

After a few wild seconds, he dragged his mouth away from hers without letting her move away even a fraction of an inch. He looked down at her with intent, searching her wide, soft gray eyes hungrily. The arm that was holding her was like a steel rod at her back, but against her legs, she felt the faintest tremor in his.

"I've gone hungry for a long time," he whispered gruffly.

She didn't know how to reply to such a blatant statement. Her eyes searched his in an odd silence, broken only by the whir of the attic fan in the hall and the muffled sound of voices as Eb's men searched the house. She reached up and touched his hard mouth tenderly, loving the immediate response of his lips to the caress.

He bent, nuzzling his face against hers to find her mouth. He kissed her urgently, but with restraint, nibbling her lower lip sensuously. Both arms went around her, riveting her to him. Her own slid under his arms and around his hard waist, holding him close. She closed her eyes, savoring the wondrous contact. The fierce hunger he felt was quite obvious in the embrace, but it didn't frighten her. She wanted him, too.

"When I heard the explosion," he said at her ear, his voice tight with tension, "I didn't know what we were going to find when I ran toward the house. We'd planned for any eventuality, but the chopper came in under radar. We didn't even hear the damned thing until we could see it, and then the launcher jammed...!"

She hadn't imagined that Eb would be afraid for her. It was wonderful. She hugged him closer and felt him shiver.

"We were a little shaken," Sally whispered. "But we're all okay."

"I didn't expect to feel like this," he said through his teeth.

She lifted her head and looked up at his strained face. "Like…this?"

His green gaze met her soft gray one and then fell to her mouth, to her soft breasts flattened against him. "Like this," he whispered and moved deliberately against her while he held her eyes.

She blushed, because it was blatant.

But he didn't smile. "I knew you were going to be trouble six years ago," he said through his teeth. He bent and kissed her again, fiercely, before he put her away from him and stood trying to get his breath.

She was shivering a little in the aftermath of the most explosive sensuality she'd ever felt. She searched his face quietly, despite the turmoil inside her awakened body.

"You've never felt like that before, have you?" he asked in a hushed tone.

She shook her head, still too shaken for words.

"If it's any consolation, it gets steadily worse," he continued. "Think about that."

He turned and went out into the hall with her puzzled eyes following him. She touched her swollen lips gingerly and wondered what he meant.

THE SHERIFF, BILL ELLIOTT, and two deputies pulled up in the yard, took statements and looked around with Eb and the other men. Sally was questioned briefly, and when the house was secure, Eb drove her back to his house with the rest of his men remaining in the woods.

"I don't think Lopez has any idea of trying again tonight," he said, "but I'm not taking any chances. I've already underestimated him once."

"He does keep his word," she said huskily.

"Yes."

"What do we do now?"

"I take you and Stevie to school and Jess stays at my house. In fact, you all stay at my house," he said curtly. "I'm not putting you at risk a second time."

She was stunned at the emotion in his voice. He was really concerned about her. She felt a warm glow all the way to her toes.

He glanced at her with slow, sensuous eyes. "At least at my own house, I can find one room with no bugs." His eyes went to her breasts and back to her face. "I'm starving."

She knew he wasn't talking about food, and her heart began racing madly.

He caught her hand in his free one and worked his fingers slowly between hers, pressing her palm to his. "Don't worry. I won't let things go too far, Sally."

She wasn't worried about that. She was wondering how she was going to go on living if he made love to her and then walked away.

WHEN THEY GOT to the house, Jessica and Dallas were in the small bedroom Eb's male housekeeper had given Stevie, tucking him in.

Eb had his housekeeper show the others to their rooms and he excused himself, tugging Sally along with him, to Dallas's obvious amusement.

"Where are we going?" Sally asked.

"To bed. I'm tired. Aren't you?"

"Yes."

She supposed he was giving her a room further down the hall, but he didn't stop at any of the closed doors. He led her around a corner and through two double doors into a huge room with Mediterranean furnishings and green and gold and brown accessories. He closed the double doors, locking them, before he turned to the dresser and pulled out a pair of blue silk pajamas.

"You can wear the pajama top and I'll wear the bottoms," he said matter-of-factly.

Her breath escaped in a rush. "Eb..."

He drew her into his arms and kissed her slowly, with deliberate sensuality, making nonsense of her protests with his hands as they skimmed under the sweatshirt and up to find her taut breasts.

She moaned, feeling the fever rise in her as he unfastened the bra and touched her hungrily. Her body arched, helping him, inviting him. Her hands gripped hard against the powerful muscles of his upper arms, drowning in waves of pleasure.

His mouth lifted fractionally. "I won't hurt you," he breathed. "Not in any way. But you're sleeping in my arms tonight."

She started to protest, but his mouth was already covering hers, muffling the words, muffling her brain.

His hands removed the sweatshirt and the bra and he looked at her with quiet, possessive eyes, drinking in the soft textures, the smooth skin, the beauty of her. He touched her gently, smiling as her body reacted to his skilled hands.

His mouth slid down to her breasts and kissed them slowly, each caress more ardent than the one before. He had her out of her jeans and sneakers and down to her briefs before she realized what was happening.

He moved away just long enough to pick up the pajama top and slip it over her head, still buttoned. He lifted her, dazed, in his arms and paused, balancing her on one knee, to pull the covers back so that he could tuck her into bed. He leaned over her, balancing on his hands, and searched her flushed, fascinated face.

"I'll be in after I've talked to Dallas and reset the monitors."

She didn't bother to protest. Her gray eyes searched his and she sighed a little unsteadily. "All right."

His eyes kindled with pleasure. He smiled, because he knew she was accepting anything he proposed. It was humbling. He kissed her eyelids closed. "Sleep well."

She watched him go, uncertain if that meant he was sleeping elsewhere. She was so tired that she fell asleep almost as soon as the doors closed behind him, wrapped in sensuous dreams.

CHAPTER TEN

SALLY HAD VIOLENT, passionate dreams that night. She moved helplessly under invisible caressing hands, moaning, arching up to prolong their warm, sweet contact. Her body burned, swelled, ached. She whispered to some faceless phantom, pleading with it not to stop.

There was soft, deep laughter at her ear and the rough warmth of an unshaven face moving against her skin, where her heart beat frantically. Slowly it occurred to her that it felt just a little too vivid to be a dream…

Her eyes flew open and blond-streaked brown hair came into focus under them in the pale dawn light filtering in through the window curtains. Her hands were enmeshed in its thick, cool strands and when she looked down, she realized that her pajama top was open, baring her to a marauding mouth.

"Eb!" she exclaimed huskily.

"It's all right. You're only dreaming," he whispered, and his mouth slid up to cover her lips as the hair-roughened skin of his muscular chest slid over her bare breasts. She felt his legs entwining with her own, felt the throb of his body, the tenderness of his hands, his mouth, as he learned her by touch and taste.

"Dreaming?"

"That's right." He lifted his lips from hers and looked down into misty gray eyes. He smiled. "And a lovely dream it is," he added in a whisper as he lifted away enough to give his eyes a stark view of everything the pajama top no longer covered. "Lovelier than I ever imagined."

"What time is it?" she asked, dazed.

"Dawn," he told her, smoothing her long hair back away from her flushed face. "Everyone else is still asleep. And there are no bugs, of any sort, in here with us," he added meaningfully.

She touched his rough cheek gently, studying him as he'd studied her. He was still wearing the pajama trousers, but his broad chest was bare. Like her own.

He rolled over onto his back, taking her with him. He guided her hands to his chest with a quiet smile. "I was going to let you wake up alone," he murmured. "But I didn't have enough willpower. There you lay, blond hair scattered over my pillows, the pajama top half off." He shook his head. "You can't imagine how lovely you look in the dawn light. Like a fairy, all creamy and gold. Irresistible," he added, "to a man who's abstained as long as I have."

She traced the pattern of hair over his breastbone. "How long have you abstained?"

"Years too long," he whispered, searching her eyes. "And that's why I set the alarm in Dallas's room to go off five minutes from now. It will wake him and he'll wake Jess and Stevie. Stevie will come looking for you." He grinned. "See how carefully I look after your virtue, Miss Johnson?"

She gave her own bare torso a poignant glance and met his eyes again.

He lifted an eyebrow. "Virtue," he emphasized, "not modesty. I don't seduce virgins, in case you forgot."

She couldn't quite decide whether he was playing or serious.

He saw that in her face and smiled gently. "Sally, the hardest thing I ever did in my life was to push you away one spring afternoon six years ago," he said softly. "I had passionate, vivid dreams about you in some of the wildest places on earth. I'm still having them." His hand swept slowly down her body, watching it lift helplessly to his touch. "So are you, judging by the sounds you were making in your sleep when I came to bed about ten minutes ago. I crawled in beside you and you came right up against me and touched me in a way I won't tell you about."

She searched his eyes blankly. "I did what?"

"Want to know?" he asked with an outrageous grin. "Okay." He leaned close and whispered it in her ear and she cried out, horrified.

"No need to feel embarrassed," he chided. "I loved it."

She knew her face was scarlet, but he looked far more pleased than teasing.

He traced her lower lip lazily. "For a few tempestuous seconds I forgot Lopez and last night, and just about everything else of any immediate importance." His eyes darkened as he held her poised above him. "I've lived on dreams for a long time. The reality is pretty shattering."

"Dreams?"

He nodded. He wasn't smiling. "I wanted you six years ago. I still do, more than ever." He brushed back her disheveled hair and looked at her with eyes that were tender and possessive. "I'm your home. Wherever I go, you go."

She didn't understand what he meant. Her face was troubled.

He rolled her over onto her back and propped himself above her. "From what I know of you, my lifestyle isn't going to break you. You've got spirit and courage, and you're not afraid to speak your mind. I think you'll adjust very well, especially if I give up any work that takes me out of the country. I can still teach tactics, although I'll cut down my contract jobs when the babies start coming along."

"Babies?" She looked completely blank.

"Listen, kid," he murmured dryly, "what we're doing causes them." He frowned. "Well, not exactly what we're doing. But if we were wearing less, and doing a little more than we're doing, we'd be causing them."

Her whole body tingled. She searched his eyes with a feeling of unreality. "You want to have a child with me?" she asked, awed.

"Oh, yes. I want to have a lot of children with you," he whispered solemnly.

She laid her hands flat on his broad chest, savoring its muscular warmth as she considered what he was saying. She frowned, because he hadn't mentioned love or marriage.

"What's missing?" he asked.

"I teach school," she said worriedly. "My reputation…"

Now he was frowning. "God Almighty, do you think I'm asking you to live in sin with me, in Jacobsville, Texas?" he asked, with exaggerated horror.

"You didn't say anything about marriage," she began defensively.

He grinned wickedly. "Do you really think I spent so much time on you just to give you karate lessons?" he drawled. "Darlin', it would take years of them to make you proficient enough to protect yourself from even a weak adversary. I brought you over here for practice so that I could get my arms around you."

Her eyes brightened. "Did you, really?"

He chuckled. "See what depths I've sunk to?" he murmured. He shook his head. "I had to give you enough time to grow up. I didn't want a teenager who was hero worshipping me. I wanted a woman, a strong woman, who could stand up to me."

She smoothed her hands up to his broad shoulders. "I think I can do that," she mused.

He nodded. "I think you can, too. Can you live with what I do?"

She smiled. "Of course."

He drew in a slow breath and his eyes were more possessive than ever. "Then we'll get Jess out of harm's way and then we'll get married."

She pulled him down to her. "Yes," she whispered against his hard mouth.

Seconds later, they were so close that she wasn't certain he'd be able to draw back at all, when there was a loud knock at the door and the knob rattled.

"Aunt Sally!" came a plaintive little voice. "I want some cereal and they haven't got any that's in shapes and colors. It's such boring cereal!"

Sally laughed even as Eb managed to drag himself away from the tangle of their legs with a groan that was half amusement and half agony.

"I'll be right there, Stevie!"

"Why's the door locked?" he called loudly.

"Come on here, youngster, and let's see if we can find something you'd like to eat," came a deep, amused adult voice.

"Okay, Dallas!"

The voices retreated. Eb lay shivering a little with reaction, but he grinned when Sally sat up and looked down at him with love glowing in her eyes.

"Close call," he whispered.

"Very," she agreed.

He took a long, hungry last look at her breasts and resolutely sat up and fastened her buttons again with a rueful smile. "Maybe food is a bearable substitute for what I really want," he mused.

She leaned forward and kissed him gently. "I'll make you glad we waited," she whispered against his mouth.

Several heated minutes later, they joined the others at the breakfast table, but Eb didn't mention future plans. He was laying down ground rules for the following week, starting with the very necessary trip Sally and Stevie must take to school the next day.

"We could keep him out of school until this is over," Dallas said tersely, glancing at the child who was sitting between himself and Jessica. "I don't like having him at risk."

"Neither do I," Jessica said heavily. "But it's possible that he won't be. Lopez has a weakness for children," she said. "It's the only virtue he possesses, but he's a maniac about abusive adults. He'd never hurt Stevie, no matter what."

"I'd have to agree with that," Eb said surprisingly.

"Then life goes on as usual," Jessica said. "And maybe Lopez will make a mistake and we'll have him. Or at least," she added, "a way of getting at him."

"What about Rodrigo?" Dallas asked abruptly.

"He phoned me late last night," Eb told him. "He's already in town, in place. Fast worker. It seems he has a relative, a 'mule' who works for Lopez in Houston, a distant relative who doesn't know what Rodrigo really does for a living. He got Rodrigo a job driving a truck for the new operation here." He let out a breath through his teeth. "Once we get Lopez's attention away from Jess," he added, "that operation is going to be our next priority."

"Can't you just send the sheriff over there to arrest them?" Sally asked.

"It's inside the city limits. Chief Chet Blake has jurisdiction there, and, of course, he'd help if he could," Eb told her. "But so far, all we have on Lopez's employees is a distant connection to a drug lord. Unless we can catch them in the act of receiving or shipping cocaine, what would we charge them with? Building a warehouse is legal, especially when you have all the easements and permission from the planning commission."

"That's why we're going to stake out the place, once this is over," Dallas added. He glanced from Jessica to Stevie with worried eyes. "But first we have to solve the more immediate problem."

Jess felt for his hand on the table beside her and tangled her fingers into it. "We'll get through this," she said in a soft tone. "I can't cold-bloodedly give a human being's life up to Lopez, no matter what the cost. The person involved risked everything to put him away. And even then, his attorneys found a loophole."

"Don't forget that it took them a couple of years to do that," Eb reminded her. "He won't be easy to catch a second time. He has enough pull with the Mexican government to keep them from extraditing him back here for trial."

"I hear DEA's going to put him on their top ten Most Wanted list," Dallas said. "That will turn up the heat a little, especially with a fifty-thousand dollar reward to sweeten the deal."

"Lopez would double their bounty out of his pocket change to get them off his tail, even if we could find someone crazy enough to go down to Cancún after him," Eb said.

"Micah Steele would, in a second," Dallas replied.

Eb chuckled. "I imagine he would. But he's been working on a case overseas with Cord Romero and Bojo Luciene."

"Bojo, the Moroccan," Dallas recalled. "Now there's a character."

Eb was immediately somber. "Okay, tomorrow morning I'll follow Sally and Stevie in to school. Dallas can tail them on the way home. We'll stay in constant contact and hope for the best."

"The best," Dallas replied, "would be that Lopez would give up."

"It won't happen," Eb assured him.

"Have you considered contacting your informant?" Dallas asked Jessica. "If we could get him back to the States, we could arrange around-the-clock protection and get him into the witness protection program, where even Lopez couldn't find him."

She grimaced. "I thought of that, but I honestly don't know how to locate my informant," she said sadly. "The people who could have helped me do it are dead."

Eb scowled. "All of them?"

Jessica nodded with a sigh. "All of them. About six months ago. Just before my accident."

"Rodrigo might be able to dig something up," Dallas said.

"That's very possible," Eb agreed. "Jessica, you could trust him with the name. I know, you don't want to put your informant in danger. But if we can't find him, how can we protect him?"

She hesitated. Then she shifted in her chair, clinging even more tightly to Dallas's big hand. "Okay," she said finally. "But he has to promise to keep the information to himself. Can I trust him to do that?"

"Yes," Eb said with certainty.

"All right, then. When can we do it?"

"Tomorrow after school," Eb said. "I'll get Cy Parks to run into him 'accidentally' and slip him a note, so that Lopez won't get suspicious."

Jessica's head moved to rest on Dallas's shoulder. "I wish I'd done things differently. So many people at risk, all because I didn't do my job properly."

"But you did," Dallas said at once, sliding a protective arm around her. "You did what any one of us would do. And you did put Lopez away. It's not your fault that he slipped out of the country."

Jessica smiled. "Thanks."

"You going to marry my mama, Dallas?" Stevie piped up.

"Stevie!" Jessica exclaimed.

"Yes, I am," Dallas said, chuckling at Jessica's red face. "She just doesn't know it yet. How do you feel about that, Stevie?"

"That would be great!" he said enthusiastically. "You and me can watch wrestling together!"

"Yes, we can." Dallas kissed Jess's hair gently and looked at his son with proud, possessive eyes.

Sally, watching them, knew that everything was going to be all right for Jessica, once they were out of this mess. She'd be free to marry Eb and she'd never have to worry about her aunt or her cousin again. Even more important, Jessica would be loved. That meant everything to Sally.

EB FOLLOWED THEM to school the next morning, keeping a safe distance. But there were no attempts on them along the way, and once they were inside the building, Sally felt safe. She and Stevie went right along to her class, smiling and greeting teachers and other children they knew.

"It's gonna be all right, isn't it, Aunt Sally?" Stevie asked at the door to her classroom.

"Yes, I think it is," she said with a warm smile.

She checked her lesson plan while the students filed into the classroom. A boy at the back of the room made a face and caught Sally's attention.

"Miss Johnson, there's a puddle of something that smells horrible back here!"

She got up from her desk and went to see. There was, indeed, a puddle. "I'll just go and get one of the janitors," she said with a smile.

But as she started out the door, a tall, quiet man appeared with a mop and pail.

"Hi, Harry," she said to him.

"Hard to be inside today when it's so nice outside," he said with a rueful smile. "I should be sitting on the river in my boat right now."

She smiled. "I'm sorry. But it's a good thing for us that you're here."

He started to wheel the bucket and mop away when one of the wheels came off the bucket. He muttered something and bent to look.

"I'll have to carry it. Can I get one of these youngsters to help me carry the mop?" he asked.

"I'll go!" Stevie volunteered at once.

"Yes, of course," Sally said. "Would you rather I went with you?"

He shook his head. "No need. This strong young man can manage a mop, can't you, son?" he asked with a big grin.

"Sure can!" Stevie said, hefting the mop over one shoulder.

"Let's away then, my lad," the man joked. "I'll send him right back, so he won't miss any class," he promised.

"Okay."

She watched Stevie go down the crowded hall behind Harry. It wasn't quite time for class to start, and she didn't think anything of the incident. Until five minutes later, when Stevie hadn't reappeared.

She left a monitor in charge of her class and went down the hall to the janitor's closet. There was the broken bucket, and the mop, but Stevie was nowhere in sight. But the janitor was. He'd been knocked out. She went straight to the office to phone Eb and call the paramedics. Fortunately Harry only had a slight concussion. To be safe, he was taken to the hospital for observation. Sally felt sick. She should have realized that Lopez might send someone to the school. Why had she been so gullible?

Eb arrived at the front office with the police chief, Chet Blake, and two of his officers. They went from door to door, combing the school. But Stevie was no longer there. One of the other janitors remembered seeing a stranger leave the building with the little boy and get into a brown pickup truck in the parking lot.

With that information, the police put out a bulletin. But it was too late. They found the pickup truck minutes later, abandoned in another parking lot, at a grocery store. Stevie was nowhere to be seen.

THEY WAITED BY the telephone that afternoon for the call that was sure to come. When it did, Eb had to bite down hard on what he wanted to say. Jessica and Sally had been in tears ever since he brought Sally home to the ranch.

"Now," the voice came in a slow, accented drawl, "Stevie's mother will give me the name I want. Or her son will never come home."

"She had to be sedated," Eb said, thinking fast. "She's out cold."

"You have one hour. Not a second longer." The line went dead.

Eb cursed roundly.

"Now what do we do?" Sally asked.

He phoned Cy Parks. "Did you get that message sent for me?" he asked.

"Yes. Scramble the signal."

Eb touched a button on the phone. "Shoot."

Cy gave him a telephone number. "He should be there by now. What can I do to help?"

Eb didn't have to be told that the news about Stevie's abduction was all over town. "Nothing. Wish me luck."

"You know it."

He hung up. Eb dialed the other number and waited. It rang once. Twice. Three times. Four times.

"Come on!" Eb growled impatiently.

On the fifth ring, the receiver was lifted.

"Rodrigo?" Eb asked at once.

"Yes."

"I'm going to put Jessica on the line, and leave the room. She'll give you a name. You know what to do with it."

"Okay."

Eb gave the receiver to Jessica and motioned everybody out of the communications room. He closed the door.

Jessica felt the receiver in her hands and took a deep

breath. "The name of my informant was Isabella Medina," she said quietly. "She worked as a housekeeper for…"

There was an intake of breath on the other end of the line. "But surely you knew?" he asked at once.

"Knew what?" Jessica stammered.

"Isabella was found washed up on the rocks in Cancún, just before Lopez's capture," Rodrigo said abruptly. "She is long dead."

"Oh, good Lord," Jessica gasped.

"How could you not know?" he demanded.

Jessica wiped her forehead with a shaking hand. "I lost touch with her just before the trial. I assumed that she'd gone undercover to escape vengeance from Lopez. She wasn't going to testify, after all. She only gave me sources of hard information that I could use to prosecute him. Afterward, there were only three people who knew about her involvement, and they died under rather…mysterious circumstances."

"This is the name Lopez wants?" he asked.

"Yes," she said miserably. "He's got my son!"

"Then you lose nothing by giving him the name," he said quietly. "Do you?"

"No. But he may not even remember her…"

"He was in love with her," Rodrigo said coldly. "His women have a habit of washing up on beaches. The last, a young singer in a Cancún nightclub, died only weeks ago at his hands. There is no proof, of course," he added coldly. "The official cause of death was suicide."

He sounded as though the matter was personal. She hesitated to ask. "You knew the singer?" she ventured.

There was a pause. "Yes. She was…my sister."

"I'm very sorry."

"So am I. Give Lopez the name. It will pacify him

and spare your son any more adventures. He will not harm the boy," he added at once. "I think you must know this already."

"I do. At least he has one virtue among so many vices. But it doesn't ease the fear."

"Of course not. Tell Scott I'll be in touch, and not to contact me again. When I have something concrete, I'll call him."

"I'll tell him. Thank you."

"De nada." He hung up.

She went into the other room, feeling her way along the wall.

"Well?" Sally asked.

"My informant is dead," Jessica said sadly. "Lopez killed her, and I never knew. I thought she'd escaped and maybe changed her name."

"What now?" Sally asked miserably.

"I give Lopez the name," Jessica replied. "It will harm no one now. She was so brave. She actually worked in his house and pretended to care about him, just so that she could find enough evidence to convict him. Her father and mother, and her sister, had been gunned down in their village by his men, because they spoke to a government unit about the drug smuggling. She was sick with fear and grief, but she was willing to do anything to stop him." She shook her head. "Poor woman."

"A brave soul," Eb said quietly. "I'm sorry."

"Me, too," Jessica said. She wrapped her arms around herself, feeling chilled. "What if Lopez won't believe me?"

"You know," Eb said quietly, "I think he will."

"Let's hope so," Dallas agreed, his eyes narrow and dark with worry.

Sally put a loving arm around her aunt. "We'll get Stevie back," she said gently. "Everything's going to be okay."

Jessica hugged her back tearfully. "What would I do without you?" she whispered huskily.

Sally exchanged a long look with Dallas. She smiled. "I think you're going to find out very soon," she teased. "And I'll be your bridesmaid."

"Matron of honor," Eb corrected with soft, tender eyes.

"What?" Jessica exclaimed.

"I'm going to marry your niece, Jess," Eb said gently. "I always meant to, you know. And," he added with mock solemnity, "it does seem the least I can do, considering that she's saved herself for me all these years, despite the blatant temptations of college life…"

"Temptations," Sally chuckled. "If you only knew!"

"Explain that," Eb challenged.

She let go of Jessica and went close to him, sliding her arms naturally around his hard waist. "As if there's a man on the planet who could compare with you," she murmured, and reached up to kiss his chin. Her eyes literally glowed with love. "There never was any competition. There never could be."

Eb lifted an eyebrow. "I could return the compliment," he said in a deep, quiet tone. "You're in a class all your own, Sally mine."

She laid her cheek against his hard chest. "They'll give Stevie back, won't they?" she asked after a minute.

"Yes," he said, utterly certain.

Sally glanced at Jessica, who was close beside Dallas now, leaning against him. They looked as if they'd always belonged together. Things had to turn out all right for them. They just had to. Lopez might have one virtue, but Sally wasn't at all sure that Eb was right. She only prayed that Stevie would be returned when Jess gave up the informant's name. If Lopez did keep his word, and that seemed certain, there was a chance. She had to hope it was a good one.

CHAPTER ELEVEN

IN EXACTLY AN HOUR from the time Lopez hung up, the phone rang again. Eb let Jessica answer it.

"Hello," she said quietly.

"The name," Lopez replied tersely.

She took a slow breath. "I want you to understand that I would never have given up my informant under ordinary circumstances. But nothing I say can harm her now. I only found out today that she's beyond your vengeance. So it doesn't matter anymore if you know who she was."

"Who…she was?" Lopez asked, his voice hesitant.

"Yes. Was. Her name was Isabella…"

His indrawn breath was so harsh that Jessica almost felt it. "Isabella," he bit off. There was a tense pause. "Isabella."

"I lost touch with her before your trial," Jessica said curtly. "I assumed that she'd gone away and taken on another identity to escape being found out. I didn't know that she was dead already."

Still, Lopez said nothing. The silence went on for so long that Jessica thought the connection was cut.

"Hello?" she asked.

There was another intake of breath. "I loved her," he spat. "In my life, there was no other woman I trusted so much. But she wanted nothing to do with me. I should have known. I should have realized!"

"You killed her, didn't you?" Jessica said coldly.

"Yes," he said, and he didn't sound violent. He sounded oddly subdued. "I never meant to. But I lashed out in a moment's rage, and then it was too late, and all my regrets would not bring her back to life." He drew another breath. "She was close enough to me that she knew things no one else was permitted to know. It occurred to me that she was asking far too many questions, but I was conceited enough to believe she cared for me." There was another brief pause. "The boy will be returned at once. You will find him at the strip mall in the toy store in five minutes. He will not be harmed. You have my word. Nor will you ever be threatened by me again. I…regret…many things," he added in an odd tone, and the line went dead abruptly.

Jessica caught her breath, still holding the receiver in her hand, as if it had life.

"Well?" Dallas asked impatiently.

She felt for the instrument and replaced the receiver with slow deliberation. "He said that Stevie would be in the toy store in the strip mall, in five minutes, unharmed." Her eyes closed. "Unharmed."

Eb motioned Dallas toward Jessica.

"Let's go," he said tersely.

"What if he lied?" Jessica asked as Dallas escorted her out to the big sports utility vehicle Eb drove.

"We both know that Lopez is a man of his word, regardless of his bloody reputation," Dallas said tersely. "We have to hope that he told the truth."

Jessica nibbled on her fingernails all the way to the mall, which was only about six minutes away from Eb's ranch. She sat close beside Dallas in the back seat, holding his hand tightly. Sally glanced back at them, silently praying all the way, worried for all of them, but especially for little Stevie. Her hand felt for Eb's and he grasped it tightly, sparing her a reassuring smile.

The minutes seemed like hours as they sped into town. Eb had no sooner parked the vehicle in the parking lot than Jessica was out the door, hurrying with Dallas right beside her to guide her steps.

Eb and Sally followed the couple into the small toy store, and there was Stevie, sitting on the floor, playing with a mechanical elephant that walked and lifted its trunk and trumpeted.

"It's Stevie," Dallas said huskily. "He's...fine!"

"Where? Stevie!" Jessica called brokenly, holding out her arms.

"Hi, Mom!" Stevie exclaimed, leaving the toy to run into her arms. "Gosh, I was scared, but the man taught me how to play poker and gave me a soda! He said I was brave and he admired my courage! Were you scared, Mom?"

Jessica was crying so hard that she could barely speak at all. She hugged her child close and couldn't seem to let him go, even when he wiggled.

"Let his dad have a little of this joyful reunion," Dallas murmured dryly, holding out his arms.

Stevie went right into them and hugged him hard. "I don't have a real dad now," he said, "but you're going to be a great dad, Dallas! You and me will go to all the wrestling matches and take Mom and describe everything to her, won't we?"

"Yes," Dallas said, his voice husky, his eyes bright as he rocked his child in his arms with mingled relief and affection. "We'll do that."

Jessica felt her way into Dallas's arms with Stevie and pressed there for a long moment. Beside them, Sally held tight to Eb's hand and smiled with pure relief.

"I had an adventure," Stevie said when his parents let go of him. "But it's nice to be home again. Can I have that elephant? He sure is neat!"

"You can have a whole circus if I can find one for sale," Dallas laughed huskily. "But for now, I think we'll go back to the ranch."

They paid for the elephant and got into the truck with Eb and Sally.

"Can you drop us off at our house?" Jessica asked Eb.

There was a hesitation. She heard it and smiled.

"Lopez said that he had no more business with me," Jessica told him. "He didn't even question what I told him," she added. "He said that Isabella was always asking him questions and pretending to care about him. He knew she didn't. He did sound very sorry that he killed her. Perhaps the small part of him that's still human can feel remorse. Who knows?"

"One day," Dallas said curtly, "we'll catch up with him. This isn't over, you know, even if he is through making threats toward you and Stevie. He's going to pay for this. And, somehow, we're going to stop him from setting up business in Jacobsville."

"We have Rodrigo in place," Eb agreed, "and Cy watching the progress of the warehouse. It won't be easy, but if we're careful, we may cut his source of supply and his distribution network right in half. Cut off the head and the snake dies."

"Amen," Dallas replied.

DALLAS GOT OUT of the sports utility vehicle with Jessica and Stevie, waving the other couple off with a big smile.

"You really believe Lopez meant it when he said he was quits with Jessica?" Sally asked, still not quite convinced of the outlaw's sincerity.

"Yes, I do," Eb replied, glancing at her with a smile. "He's a snake, but his word is worth something."

Sally turned her head toward Eb and studied his profile warmly, with soft, covetous eyes.

He glanced over and met that look. His own eyes narrowed. "A lot has happened since last night," he said quietly. "Do you still mean what you told me at dawn?"

"That I'd marry you?" she asked.

He nodded.

"Oh, yes," she said, "I meant every word. I want to live with you all my life."

"It won't bother you to have professional mercenaries running around the place at all hours for a while?" he teased.

She grinned. "Why should it? I am, after all, a mercenary's woman."

"Not quite yet," he murmured with a wry glance. "And very soon, a mercenary's wife."

"That sounds very respectable," she commented.

"I'm glad you waited for me, Sally," he said seriously.

"So am I." She slid her hand into his big one and held on tight. It tingled all the way up her arm.

"We've had enough excitement for today," he said. "But tomorrow we'll see about getting the license. Do you want a justice of the peace or a minister to marry us?"

"A minister," she said at once. "I want a permanent marriage."

He nodded. "So do I. And you have to have a white gown with a veil."

Her eyebrows arched.

"You're not just a mercenary's woman, you're a virtuous mercenary's woman. I want to watch you float down the aisle to me covered in silk and satin and lace, and with a veil for me to lift after we've said our vows."

She smiled with her whole heart. "That would be nice. There's a little boutique…"

"We'll fly up to Dallas and get one at Neiman Marcus."

She gasped.

"You're marrying a rich man," he pointed out. "Humor me. It's going to be a social event. Let me deck you out like a comet."

She laughed. "All right. I'd really love a white wedding, if you don't mind."

"And we'll both wear rings," he added. "We'll get those in Dallas, too."

Her eyes were full of dreams as she looked at her future husband hungrily. There was only one small worry. "Eb, about Maggie…"

"Maggie is a closed chapter," he told her. "I adored her, in my way, but she was never in love with me. I stood in Cord's shadow even then, and she never realized it. She still hasn't." He glanced at her and smiled. "I love you, you know," he murmured, watching her eyes light up. "I'd never have proposed if I hadn't."

"I love you, too, Eb," she said solemnly. "I always will."

His fingers curled tighter into hers. "Dreams really do come true."

She wouldn't have argued with that statement to save her life, and she said so.

It was the society event of the year in Jacobsville, eclipsed only by Simon Hart's wedding with the governor giving Tira away. There were no major celebrities at Eb and Sally's wedding, but Eb did have a conglom-

eration of mercenaries and government agents the like
of which Jacobsville had never seen. Cord Romero was
sitting with Maggie on the groom's side of the church,
along with a tall, striking dark-haired man with a small
mustache and neat brief beard. Beside him was a big
blond man who made even Dallas look shorter. On the
pew across from him, on Sally's side of the church, was
a blue-eyed brunette who avoided looking at the big
blond man. Sally recognized her as Callie, the stepsister
of the big blond man, who was Eb's friend Micah Steele.

A number of men in suits filled the rest of the
groom's pews. Some were wearing sunglasses inside.
Others were watching the people on the bride's side of
the church, which wasn't packed, since Sally hadn't
been back in Jacobsville long enough to make close
friends in the community. Jessica was there with Stevie and Dallas, of course.

Sally walked down the aisle all by herself, since she
hadn't contacted either of her parents about her wedding. They had their own lives now, and neither of them
had written to Sally since the breakup of their family
when she moved in with Jessica. She didn't really mind
going it alone. Somehow, under the circumstances, it
even seemed appropriate. She wore a dream of a wedding gown, with yards and yards of delicate lace and
a train, and a veil that accentuated her blond beauty.

Eb stood at the altar waiting for her, in a gray vested
suit with a white rose in his lapel. He turned as she
joined him, and looked down at her with eyes that made
her knees weak.

The ceremony was brief, but poignant, and when
Eb lifted the veil to kiss her for the first time as her
husband, tears welled up in her eyes as his mouth tenderly claimed hers. They held hands going back down

the aisle, wearing matching simple gold bands. Outside the church, they were pelted with rice and good wishes. Laughing, Sally tossed her bouquet and Dallas intercepted it to make sure it landed in Jessica's hands.

They climbed into the rented limousine and minutes later, they were at Eb's ranch, pausing just long enough to change into traveling clothes and rush to the private airstrip to board a loaned Learjet for the trip to Puerto Vallarta, Mexico, for their brief honeymoon.

The trip was tiring, and so was the aftermath of the day's excitement. Sally climbed into the huge whirlpool bath while Eb made dinner reservations for that evening.

She didn't realize that she wasn't alone until Eb climbed down into the water with her. He chuckled at her expression and then he kissed her. Very soon, she forgot all about her shock at the first sight of her unclothed bridegroom in the joy of an embrace that knew no obstacles.

He kissed her until she was clinging, gasping for breath and shivering with pleasure.

"Where?" he whispered, stroking her tenderly, enjoying her reactions to her first real intimacy. "Here, or in the bed?"

She could barely speak. "In bed," she said huskily.

"That suits me."

He got out and turned off the jets, lifting her clear of the water to towel them both dry. He picked her up and carried her quickly into the bedroom, barely taking time to strip down the covers before he fell with her onto crisp, clean sheets.

She knew that first times were notoriously painful, embarrassing, and uncomfortable, but hers was a notable exception. Eb was skillful and slow, arousing her to a hot frenzy of response before he even began to touch her intimately. By the time his body slid down against hers in stark possession, she was lifting toward him and pleading for an end to the violent tension of pleasure he'd aroused in her.

Her breath jerked out at his ear at the slow, steady invasion of her most private place in a silence that magnified the least little sound. She heard his heartbeat, and her own, increase with every careful thrust of his hips. She heard his breathing, erratic, rough, mingling with her own excited little moans.

She felt one lean hand sliding up her bare leg as he turned and shifted his weight against her, and when he touched her high on her inner thigh in a rhythm like the descent of his body, she arched up toward him and groaned in anguish.

He laughed softly at her temple while he increased the rhythm and caressed her in the most outrageous ways, all the while whispering things so shocking that she gasped. Tossed between waves of pleasure that grew with each passing second, she found herself suddenly suspended somewhere high above reality as she went over some intangible cliff and fell shuddering with ecstasy into a white-hot oblivion.

She felt him there with her, felt his pleasure in her body, felt his own release even as hers threatened to last forever. She wondered dimly if she was going to survive the incredible delight of it. She shivered helplessly as pleasure washed over her and she clung harder to the source of it, pleading for him not to stop.

When she was finally exhausted and barely able to catch her breath, he tucked her close in his arms and pulled the sheet over them.

"Sleep now," he whispered, kissing her forehead.

"Like this?" she asked unsteadily.

"Just like this." He wrapped her closer. "We'll sleep a little. And then…"

"And then."

The dinner reservations went unclaimed. Through the long night, she learned more than she'd ever dreamed about men and bodies and lovemaking. For a first time, she told her delighted husband, it was quite extraordinary.

They had breakfast in bed and then set out to explore the old city. But by evening, they were exploring each other again.

A WEEK LATER, they arrived back home at Eb's ranch, to find a flurry of new activity. A local undercover DEA agent, whose wife Lisa Monroe lived on a ranch next door to Cy Parks, had been found murdered. Apparently he'd infiltrated Lopez's organization and been discovered. Rodrigo was still undercover, and Eb was concerned for him. The warehouse next door to Cy was in the final stages of construction. Things were heating up in Jacobsville.

"At least we had a honeymoon," Eb murmured dryly, hugging his new wife close.

"So we did," she agreed. She looked up at him lovingly. "And now you're back off adventuring."

"Well, so are you," he pointed out. "After all, isn't teaching second-graders a daily adventure as well?"

She hugged him close. "Being married to you is the biggest adventure, but you have to promise not to ever get shot at again."

"I give you my word as a Girl Scout," he murmured dryly.

She punched him in the stomach. "And if you wade

into battle, I'll be right there beside you holding spare cartridges."

He searched her eyes. "You really are a hell of a woman," he murmured.

She grinned. "I'm glad you noticed."

"Lucky me," he said only half facetiously, and bent to kiss her with unbridled passion. "Lucky, lucky me!" he added while he could manage speech.

Sally wrapped her arms around him and held on tight, as intoxicated with pleasure as he was. There would always be the threat of danger, but nothing that the mercenary and his woman couldn't handle. But for the moment, she had her soldier of fortune right where she wanted him—in her gentle, loving arms.

* * * * *

Books by Lee Tobin McClain

HQN Books

Safe Haven
Low Country Hero

Love Inspired

Redemption Ranch
The Soldier's Redemption
The Twins' Family Christmas

Rescue River
Engaged to the Single Mom
His Secret Child
Small-Town Nanny
The Soldier and the Single Mom
The Soldier's Secret Child
A Family for Easter

Christmas Twins
Secret Christmas Twins

Lone Star Cowboy League: Boys Ranch
The Nanny's Texas Christmas

Don't miss *Low Country Dreams,* the next book
in the Safe Haven series from HQN!

HIS SECRET CHILD

Lee Tobin McClain

Then he said to them, "Whoever welcomes this little child in my name welcomes me; and whoever welcomes me welcomes the one who sent me. For it is the one who is least among you all who is the greatest."
—*Luke* 9:48

For my daughter, Grace

CHAPTER ONE

FERN EASTON LOOKED at the fire she'd just built, then out the window at the driving snow, dim in the late-afternoon light. She shivered, but not because she was cold.

No, she was happy.

Two whole weeks to herself. Two whole weeks to work on her children's book in blessed peace.

As soon as she'd gotten home from the library, she'd shucked her sensible slacks and professional shirt and let her hair out of its usual tidy bun. Threw on her softest jeans and a comfortable fleece top. Next, she'd set up her drawing table in the living room of her friends' house.

House-sitting was awesome, because out here on the farm, no one would bother her.

Out here, she had a chance to fulfill her dream.

From the back room, her four-year-old daughter crowed with laughter over the antics of the animated mice and squirrels on the TV screen. Her *daughter*. Some days, Fern couldn't believe her good fortune.

She'd fed Bull, the ancient, three-legged bulldog she was babysitting as a part of the house-sitting deal. Puttering around like this, feeding an animal, taking care of her sweet child, was what she wanted, and determination rose in her to make it happen full-time.

She'd create a fantasy world with her books, and in

her life, too. She wouldn't have to deal with the public or trust people who'd inevitably let her down. She wouldn't have to come out of her shell, listen to people telling her to smile and speak up. She wasn't really shy, she was just quiet, because there was a whole world in her head that needed attention and expression. And now, for two weeks, she got to live in that world, with a wonderful little girl and a loving old dog to keep her company.

She practically rubbed her hands together with glee as she poured herself a cup of herbal tea and headed toward her paints.

Knock, knock, knock.

She jerked at the unexpected sound, and worry flashed through her.

"Hey, Angie, I know you're in there!"

Fern felt her nose wrinkle with distaste. Some friend of the homeowners. Some male friend. Should she answer it?

More knocking, another shout.

Yeah, she had to answer. Anyone who'd driven all the way out here in a snowstorm deserved at least a polite word from her before she sent them away.

She opened the door to a giant.

He wore a heavy jacket and cargo pants. His face was made of hard lines and planes, only partly masked by heavy stubble. Intense, unsmiling, bloodshot eyes stared her down. "Who are you?"

Whoa! She took a step backward and was about to slam the door in this unkempt muscleman's face—she had her daughter's safety to think about, as well as her own—when Bull, the dog, launched his barrel-shaped body at the door, barking joyously, his stub of a tail wagging.

"Hey, old guy, you're getting around pretty good!" The man opened the door, leaned down.

"Hey!" Fern stepped back, then put her hands on her hips. "You can't come in here!"

The guy didn't listen; he was squatting down just inside the door to pet the thrilled bulldog.

Fern's heart pounded as she realized just how isolated she was. Never taking her eyes off him, she backed over to her phone and turned it on.

"Where's Troy and Angelica?" The man looked up at her. "And who're you?" His voice was raspy. Dark lines under his eyes.

"Who are *you*?"

He cocked his head to one side, frowning. "I'm Carlo. Angie's brother?"

Her jaw about dropped, because she'd heard the stories. "You're the missionary soldier guy!" She set her phone back down. "Really? What are you doing here?"

His eyes grew hooded. "Got some business to conduct here in the States. And I'm sick."

"Oh." She studied him. Maybe illness was the reason for his disheveled look.

"Your turn. Who are you? You supposed to be here?"

"My name's Fern. I'm house-sitting."

"Okay." He nodded and flashed an unexpected smile. "I didn't think you looked real dangerous."

The appeal of a smile on that rugged face left Fern momentarily speechless, warming her heart toward the big man.

"Thought I could bed down with my sister and get myself together before I get started with my…legal work. Where is she?"

"She's at Disneyland Paris." She said it reluctantly. "For two weeks."

"She's in Paris?" His face fell. "You've gotta be kidding."

She studied him. "Didn't you think to, like, call and check with her? When did you last talk?"

"It's been months. I don't…live a normal life. And like I said, I've been sick." He swayed slightly and unzipped his jacket. "Still have a little fever, but it's not catching."

"Hey. You don't look so good." In fact, he looked as though he was going to pass out, and then how would she ever get him out of here? She took his arm gingerly and guided him toward the couch. "You'd better sit down." She helped him out of his heavy, hooded, military-style jacket.

"I don't want to bother you…" He swayed again and sat down abruptly.

So now she had some giant guy who claimed to be Angelica's brother, smack dab in the middle of her living room. She studied him skeptically as she picked up her phone again. Dark gray sweater that didn't look any too new, heavy combat boots melting snow on the floor. Hmm.

Could he be acting this whole thing out in order to get in here and…what? Steal everything Troy and Angelica had? They were plenty comfortable, as evidenced by the Euro-Disney vacation, but they didn't put their money on display in expensive possessions, at least as far as she'd been able to tell in the few months she'd known Angelica.

What else could he want? Had someone told him she was going to be out here alone? She normally wasn't a skittish person, but this was different. This wasn't safe.

She was about to dial 911 when he said, "Let me call Ang. I have to figure out what to do next."

He reached in his pocket and pulled out an ancient-looking flip phone.

Fern walked to the back room to glance in on Mercedes. The child was fully immersed in her princess movie, a Friday-night treat Fern allowed reluctantly. For one thing, she wasn't overly fond of the princess phenomenon for little girls, and for another, she'd rather read Mercy storybooks than have her watch TV.

But those were preferences. Mercedes had watched princess movies with her mom, and it comforted her to watch them now.

Even one day with Mercedes was a blessing, but now she had the potential, even the likelihood, of adopting her permanently and for real. That was truly exciting. That was a dream much bigger than her dream of writing and illustrating children's books.

If she could create a nest for herself and a child—or six—who needed a home, and write on the side, she'd be the happiest woman on earth.

And maybe, just maybe, that was what God had in mind for her. Because she obviously wasn't suited to relating to other people, right? She wasn't cut out for marriage, nor couples' entertaining, nor a single's life with a big close-knit group of friends.

But kids! Kids and books. And a dog or two, she thought, walking back out to the front room followed by the loyal Bull. She rubbed his graying head and let him give her a sloppy kiss. This was the life.

Or it would be, once she got rid of her uninvited guest.

"Stupid phone." Carlo shook his head and stared at the shiny black object in his hand. "It's not doing anything. I can't reach her."

"We can try my phone," Fern offered. She picked

hers up and clicked through her few contacts, watching as the man removed his boots and set them on a newspaper beside the couch. Despite his size, he seemed very weak. Fern wasn't as afraid as she'd been before.

She put in the call. Felt a little bad about it—she couldn't remember exactly what time it was in Paris, and she hated to wake up her friends.

No answer.

"Did you get a connection?" Carlo asked.

She shook her head. "Angelica bought some special plan to be able to talk over there. I should be able to get hold of her, but it might take a while."

The guy, Carlo, stared down at his hands. "I guess I'll be on my way, then."

"Where will you go?" she blurted out against her own will.

"I'll figure it out."

"Do you have friends in town? You grew up here, right?"

He nodded slowly, putting a forefinger and thumb on his forehead and massaging, as though it hurt. "I did grow up here. Unfortunately, I wasn't the most upright kid. So a lot of people have a bad impression of me."

"That's too bad. I don't think it's a judgmental town these days—at least, I haven't felt it to be—but maybe it was different in the past."

Carlo shrugged. "We were a pretty offbeat family. My parents made some enemies and I just added to the number. It's not Rescue River's fault."

That made her almost like him, that he admitted his own culpability rather than blaming everyone else but himself. A disease so many people seemed to have these days.

"Do you…would you like something to drink?"

"Yes, thank you." His face had taken on a greenish cast. "My head hurts pretty bad."

"Of course. Tea and aspirin?"

"Tea sounds good. I've got medicine."

Fern hurried into the kitchen and turned on the gas under her kettle to bring it back to a boil. It was so rare for her to have someone over, she barely knew how to handle it. But Carlo looked as though he was about to pass out.

What was she going to do? She couldn't have him stay. Oh, the place was plenty big, but she couldn't house a giant man who seemed to take up all the air in a room. She couldn't deal with company full-time.

Being solitary, living in her own head, was what had saved her as a foster child, shuttled from house to house, never fitting in, never really wanted. It had become a habit and a way of life. Nowadays, she preferred being alone. She thought longingly of her paints, of the children's story she was working on.

The water boiled and she fumbled through the cupboards, finding a mug and tea bag. Carried it out to the living room.

"Do you like milk and sugar... Oh. No, you don't."

He'd fallen asleep.

He'd tipped over right there on the couch and was breathing heavily, regularly.

No! That wouldn't do. She didn't want a stranger sleeping on the couch. She had to get him out of here. "Hey," she said, nudging him with her knee as she set the tea down beside him.

He leaped to his feet and grabbed her instantly in a choke hold, pulling her against his chest.

"Aaah! Hey!" she screamed, which made Bull start barking.

Carlo dropped his arms immediately and side-stepped away from her, lifting his hands to shoulder level. "Sorry. Sorry."

She backed halfway across the room and eyed him accusingly. "What was that for?"

"Jungle instinct," he said. "Sorry. I…don't do well when I'm startled. Did I hurt you?"

She rubbed her neck and stretched it from side to side as her heartbeat slowed back down to normal. "I'm fine." The truth be told, his closeness had had a very weird effect on her. She didn't like being grabbed, of course, but being forced to lean against that broad chest had given her a strange feeling of being…protected. Of being safe.

Which was ridiculous, because obviously, having him here was putting her and Mercedes at risk, not keeping her safe.

"Mama Fern? You okay?" The little-girl voice behind her was wary.

She turned, squatted down and smiled reassuringly. "Yeah, honey, I'm fine. C'mere." She held out her arms, and the little girl ran into them, nuzzling against her.

"I didn't know you had a child here." Carlo stood as if to come over toward them, and then swayed.

Fern wrapped her arms tighter around Mercedes. "Sit down and drink your tea," she ordered, gesturing toward it on the end table. "You look terrible. Do you know what's wrong? Have you seen a doctor?" She sat cross-legged and settled Mercedes in her lap.

"You ever hear of dengue fever?"

"Dengue! You have it?" The mother in her was glad it was indeed noncontagious.

He nodded. "You know what it is?"

"I'm a reference librarian, so I learn about all kinds of things like that. Do you have a bad case?"

"I hope not." He was rubbing the back of his neck again, as if it hurt. "It's been a couple of weeks and I thought I was better, but I'm weak. And apparently, it's possible to relapse, and if you do, it's pretty serious."

"Fatal sometimes."

"Thanks for reminding me."

"Sorry. Sit down."

He did, and drank the tea, and she watched him and stroked Mercy's hair and wondered how on earth she could get rid of him.

CARLO STARED AT the blurry woman and child across the room and wondered what to do.

His head was pounding and the pain behind his eyes was getting worse.

He reached out and brought the teacup to his lips, trying hard to hold it steady. Forced himself to drink. Staying hydrated was key.

"So you don't know anyone in town you could stay with?" she asked skeptically. "From growing up here, I mean?"

Well, let's see. He could stay with the family he'd bummed off when his parents had been too drunk or stoned to unlock the trailer door. Or maybe the teacher he'd lifted money from when his little sister had needed medicine they couldn't afford.

Or, who knew? Maybe some of the guys with whom he'd chugged six-packs in the woods had made good and would take him in. Trouble was, he'd lost touch during his years in the jungle.

"I'm not sure. I can work something out. Stay with my grandfather, maybe." Although Angelica had said something about new rules at the Senior Towers, maybe they'd make an exception for an ailing veteran, if he and Gramps could resolve their differences long enough for him to ask nicely.

He tried to stand and the world spun.

"Sit down!" She sounded alarmed.

He did, wishing for a cold cloth to cover his eyes.

"Let me call the emergency room in Mansfield. You need a doctor."

He waved a hand. "Not really. All they can do is tell me to rest and wait it out."

"Oh." She bit at her lower lip. Whoever she was, she was real pretty. Long brown hair and fine bones and big eyes behind those glasses. The kind of woman he'd like to sit down and have a conversation with, sometime when he wasn't delirious. "Well," she continued, "do you think some food would make you feel better? Chicken soup?"

Something hot and salty sounded delicious. He'd slept through the meals on the plane and hadn't stopped for food on the drive from the airport. Maybe that was why he felt so low. "Yeah, food would be great."

"Be right back. C'mon, Mercy."

"Is he staying all night, Mama Fern?" The little girl didn't sound worried about it.

Somehow this Fern didn't strike him as the type who'd have men overnight casually. She looked way too guarded and buttoned up. But her little girl seemed perfectly comfortable with the notion of a man spending the night.

"No, he's not staying. But we're going to fix him a snack before he goes. Come on, you can help."

"Yay!" The little girl followed her mother and Carlo watched them go, feeling bemused.

How old was this little girl—maybe three or four?

Not far off from his own daughter's age, so he ought to pay attention, see what she did, what she liked. He needed to make a good first impression on the child he was coming to raise.

More than that, for now, he needed to figure out what to do. It was a blow that his sister wasn't here, and of course he should have called, had tried to call, but when he hadn't reached them, he'd figured she and her new husband would be here. They were newly-weds, practically, though Angelica's last note had let him know she was expecting a baby. And they also had a kid who was in full recovery from leukemia, his beloved nephew, Xavier. Not to mention that they ran a dog rescue. Shouldn't they be staying close to home?

It wasn't the first time he'd miscalculated. He seemed to be doing that a lot lately. So he'd eat whatever this pretty lady brought him, drink a lot of water. He'd hold off on those pain pills the doctor had given him, the ones with the mild narcotic, until he'd bedded down for the night. After his years in South and Central America, Carlo wasn't a fan of drugs in any form, and the last thing he needed was to feel any foggier. He needed to get himself strong enough to leave and find a place to stay. Tomorrow he'd talk to the lawyers and to his daughter's social worker and soon, very soon, he'd have his daughter. And he could start making amends for not trying hard enough to make his marriage work and for not considering that Kath could've been pregnant when she kicked him out that last time.

The woman—what had she said her name was? Fern?—came back out carrying a crockery bowl. She set it on a tray beside him, and the smell of soup tickled his nose, made him hungry for the first time in days.

Behind her, the little girl carefully carried a plastic plate with a couple of buttered rolls on it.

It all looked delicious.

"I'll eat up and then be on my way," he promised, tasting the soup. *Wow. Perfect.* "This is fantastic," he said as he scooped another spoonful.

"Mama Fern always has good food."

Something about the way the little girl talked about her mother was off, but Carlo was too ecstatic about the chicken soup to figure out what it was.

"So…" The woman, Fern, perched on the other edge of the couch, watching him eat. "What are you going to do?"

He swallowed another spoonful. "As soon as I finish this soup—which is amazing—I'm going to head into Rescue River and see if I can find a place to stay."

"There's that little motel right on the edge of town. It tends to fill up during storms, though. Travelers coming through don't have a lot of choices."

"There's a few doors I can knock on." Not really, but she didn't need to know that. He could sleep in his truck. He'd slept in worse places.

Although usually, the problem was being too hot, not too cold. He'd have to find an all-night store and buy a couple of blankets.

"So what brought you out of the jungle?"

He paused in the act of lifting a spoon to his mouth. She was being nosy and he hated that. But on the other hand, she was providing him with soup and bread and a place to sit down.

"You're nicer than my mommy's boyfriends." The little girl leaned on the couch and stared up at him.

He couldn't help raising an eyebrow at Fern.

Fern's cheeks turned a pretty shade of pink. "She's not talking about me. I'm kind of her foster mom."

"And she's gonna 'dopt me!"

"After all the grown-up stuff gets done, sweets."

They went on talking while Carlo slowly put down his spoon into his almost empty bowl of soup and stared at the two of them.

It couldn't be.

Could it?

It had to be a coincidence. Except, how many four-year-old girls were in need of being adopted in Rescue River, Ohio?

Could Fern have changed her name from Mercedes to Mercy?

No, not likely, but he'd learned during battle to consider all possibilities, however remote.

He rubbed his hand over his suddenly feverish face and tried to think. If this girl, by some weird set of circumstances, was Mercedes—his own kid, whom he hadn't known about until two weeks ago—then he needed to get out of here right away. He was making a terrible impression on someone who'd be sure to report every detail to the social workers.

Not only that, but his lawyer friend had advised him not to contact the child himself.

The child. Surely she wasn't his? The hair color was his own, but light brown hair was common. He studied her, amazed at her beauty, her curls hanging down her back, at her round, dark eyes. She was gorgeous. And obviously smart.

And obviously close with this woman who wanted to adopt her.

If this was foster care, then it was different from anything he'd imagined. He'd expected to find his daughter staying in a dirty old house filled to the brim with kids. No doubt that stereotype was from his own single bad experience years ago, but it was the reason he'd dropped everything, not waited to recover from his illness, and hopped a plane as soon as he realized he was a father and that his child's mother was dead.

He didn't want a child of his to suffer in foster care. He wanted to take care of her. And he would, because surely this beautiful child in this idyllic life was no relation to him.

When he did find his own daughter, he'd find a way to make up for some of the mistakes of his past.

Maybe redeem himself.

"Are you finished?"

The pair had stopped talking and were staring at him. Oh, great. He was breathing hard and sweating, probably pale as paper.

"I'm done," he said, handing her the plate and bowl. "Thank you."

She carried them into the kitchen and he took the opportunity to study the child.

"How do you like it here?" he asked her.

"I like Bull," she said, "but home is nicer."

"Home with Mommy Fern?"

"Mama Fern. Yes."

"I guess you miss your mommy."

She looked at him. "Do you know her?"

He settled for "I don't think so." Because almost certainly, this wasn't his own child, whose mother, Kath, he had indeed known quite well. Theirs had been a mistaken marriage, born of lust and bad judgment. Soon after the wedding, they'd started having serious problems. Her drinking and drugs and promiscuous behavior had led to them breaking up, not once, but twice.

What he hadn't known was that the last time she'd kicked him out, he'd left her pregnant.

Fern walked back into the room and squatted down beside the child with a natural grace. "Half an hour till your bedtime, sweets. Want to have your snack in front of the TV? Finish your movie?"

"Yeah." The little girl hugged Fern. "Thanks for letting me."

"Fridays only. Let's get you set up."

Carlo's head was spinning so badly with questions and fever that he had to stay seated, but he forced himself to keep his eyes open and take deep breaths. Not only was he sick, but he was dizzy with confusion.

Could God have arranged it that he'd meet his child this way, rather than wearing nice clothes in a social worker's office?

Was that beautiful little girl his daughter?

Fern came back in. "She loves her princess movies," she said apologetically. "I'm not real big on TV for little kids, but it comforts her."

Carlo lifted his hands. "I'm not judging. Don't most kids watch TV?"

"Yeah, but… I want to do better."

She was a good, caring foster mom. And he had to find out the truth. "How old did you say she is?"

"She's four, going on five."

He nodded. "Now, did you name her Mercy or was that already her name?"

She looked at him as if he had lost his mind. "You can't change a four-year-old's name. She's been Mercy all her life."

Relief poured over him. He hadn't messed up the all-important moment of meeting his own daughter. To be polite, he tried to keep the conversation going. "And you're...hoping to adopt her?"

"I'm planning on it," she said with satisfaction. "Everything's looking great. As long as the birth father doesn't show up, I'm golden."

He cocked his head to one side. "You don't want her father to find her?"

She shook her head impatiently. "It's not like that. He's shown no interest in her for four years, so it's hardly likely he'll show up now. Typical deadbeat dad, but we had to publish announcements for a few weeks to make sure he doesn't want her."

Carlo's head spun at her casual dismissal. He wanted to argue that just because a dad wasn't around, that didn't mean he was a deadbeat. Some dads didn't even know they had a child. But there was no need to argue with the woman who'd treated a stranger so kindly. "Mercy's kind of an old-fashioned name," he said instead.

She smiled. "Oh, that's just what I call her sometimes. Her mom did, too. Her full name is actually Mercedes."

The name slammed into his aching head with the force of a sledgehammer's blow. He had indeed blundered into the home of his own child.

CHAPTER TWO

Fern frowned at the man on her couch. He was pale, his forehead covered in a fine sheen of sweat. Great, just great. The poor man was deathly ill.

Maybe he should go to the hospital. Didn't the ER have to take everyone, regardless of their ability to pay? Although the nearest ER was quite a ways off…

She walked over to the window, flipped on an outdoor light and gasped. Huge snowflakes fell so thickly that it was hard to see anything, but she could make out thigh-high drifts next to the porch.

"What's wrong?" She heard his slow footsteps as he came over to stand behind her.

His looming presence made her uncomfortable. "It's getting worse out there."

"I should go." He turned, swayed and grabbed the back of a chair with one hand and her shoulder with another. "Whoa. Sorry."

Compassion warred with worry in her heart. "Why don't you at least take a little nap? You're not looking so good."

"I… Maybe I will. Don't know if I can make it to my truck."

She helped him to the couch, even though having his arm draped over her shoulder felt strange. The few guys she'd dated had been closer to her own small size, not like this hulking giant, and they tended not to snuggle up. Something about her demeanor didn't invite that.

She helped him down onto the couch and noticed he was shivering. Finding a quilt, she brought it over and spread it out across his body. Located a more comfortable pillow and helped him lift his head to slide it underneath.

His hair felt soft, and he smelled clean, like soap.

"Thanks, I really appreciate...this." His blue eyes drifted shut.

Fern watched him for a few minutes to make sure he was really out. Then she watched the end of the princess movie cuddling with Mercedes, and then carried her up to bed on her back, cautioning her to be quiet because of the man sleeping in the living room.

"Who is he, Mama Fern?"

"He's our friend Angelica's brother. You know Xavier? This man is his uncle."

"I like Xavier," Mercedes said with a little hero worship in her voice. "He's in first grade."

"That's right."

Fern read two picture books and then, firmly denying the request for a third, turned off the light.

She grabbed a novel and sat down on the floor outside the child's bedroom.

Sometimes nights were hard for Mercedes. She still missed her mom.

But tonight was a good night. Within minutes, Mercedes had drifted off and was breathing the heavy, steady breath of a child in sleep.

Fern went back downstairs quietly, picked up her phone and headed to the kitchen where her sleeping housemates couldn't hear her.

This time, the call went through and a couple of minutes later, she was talking to her yawning friend Angelica. "What? Carlo's there?"

"He's asleep on the couch even as we speak."

"Let me go out in the hall so I don't wake my boys. I can't believe this!" Angelica's voice proved that she'd come wide-awake. "I haven't seen him for a couple of years, except for a few minutes at our wedding. Why'd he have to show up now, instead of last week?"

"He didn't even stay for the whole wedding?"

"No, he stayed. And at our house after for a night, but I was with my husband." Her voice went rich and happy.

Sudden hot jealousy flashed through Fern. Why couldn't *she* ever feel that joy that seemed to come so readily to other fortunate women?

She got a grip on herself. What was wrong with her? She was truly happy for her friend. She explained about Carlo's fever. "He's pretty sick, and he said that's why he hadn't called first. I just wanted to touch base with you because…well, he's a stranger and I don't know if it's safe to have him here. I mean, I know you and I'd trust you with my life, and Mercedes's, but…"

"I totally understand." Angelica paused, obviously thinking. "I wonder who he could stay with. We could call Troy's brother, Sam, and see if he could stay out there. Or Gramps. He could bunk down at the Senior Towers. They have a new rule about no guests staying overnight, but maybe they'll bend it for Carlo, at least for one night." She sounded doubtful.

"I hate to make him go," Fern said. "It's snowing something awful."

"Carlo's been in much worse places. He's very tough. He can handle a little drive in the snow."

"I don't know. He's pretty shaky."

"Let me make a few calls," Angelica said with a huge

yawn. "I'm sure I can get hold of somebody who'll take him in, if this phone doesn't glitch again."

"It's okay, you go back to sleep. I can call Sam or your grandpa." Fern's shy side cringed at the notion of talking to men she barely knew, but it would be worth it to get the disconcerting Carlo out of her house.

"Oh, could you? That would be so wonderful. We had a long day, and Xavier didn't want to go to sleep, and…"

"And you're frazzled. Go back to bed. I'll deal with Carlo."

"Thanks so much! And, Fern, he's a totally trustworthy guy, okay? A real hero. He took incredible care of me when I was a kid. He managed everything when our parents couldn't, and got Gramps to take me in. Plus, he's done all kinds of top-secret military stuff. Has a security clearance that's a mile high. And he's served as a missionary in all kinds of super-dangerous places. So you're safe with him, whatever happens."

They said their goodbyes and Fern stared at the man on the couch. A military hero, huh? And a missionary to boot.

But as she studied him, another thought crossed her mind: What if he wasn't Carlo? What if he was a criminal who'd just assumed that name and identity? Sure, Bull had acted friendly, but maybe the guy had a pocket full of good-smelling dog treats.

How could she verify that this guy on her couch was in fact Carlo, Angelica's brother, the war hero?

She walked around the house, looking at the photo groupings, but she didn't see any that included Angelica's brother. Of course, he hadn't been around lately, but you'd think she would have old pictures of him…

Except that the two of them had grown up in chaos, and Angelica had struggled, really, right up until she'd reconnected with Troy. So there were no pictures of Xavier and his uncle Carlo; Angelica probably hadn't even had a phone.

She saw a khaki-colored duffel bag by the door, next to his jacket, and an idea crossed her mind.

She looked back at the stranger, watching the steady rise and fall of his chest.

Then she walked over toward his things. Surely he'd have identification there, or at least something to verify his identity. To put her mind at ease. Searching the man's belongings wasn't the most ethical thing to do, but she had a child to protect.

And if she was going to search, she needed to do it now, while he slept.

A quick check of his jacket pockets revealed nothing, so she undid the knots that tied the duffel shut, moving slowly and carefully. Given how he'd jumped up and grabbed her, he was obviously pretty sensitive to noise. She had to be utterly silent.

She eased the bag open and then tensed as his breathing changed. He shifted over to his side while she sat, frozen, watching him.

As soon as he breathed steadily again, she parted the edges of the bag.

The first thing she saw was an eight-inch hunting-type knife, in an old-looking leather case that would go on a belt.

Well, okay, then. He hadn't taken *that* through airport security, no way.

She picked it up with the tips of two fingers, pulled it out of the duffel, and set it beside her on the floor.

Digging on through, she found some trail mix, a thriller paperback and a Bible that had seen hard use.

She took the risk of flipping through it and saw underlining, highlighting, turned-down pages.

Wow. He took his faith seriously. What would that be like? Since being saved, Fern attended church most Sundays and read a devotional book every night before she went to sleep, but she'd never gone so far as to study the Bible on her own.

He certainly didn't fit the stereotype of a Bible scholar, but Angelica had said he was a missionary. And anyway, who was she to judge? The fact that he had books, especially a Bible, was a point in his favor. Not quite enough to counteract that deadly looking knife, though.

Next, she found a vest. Camo colored, made of heavy nylon, with pouches that held hard plates. She pulled it out a little, making a slight clatter, and her heart pounded as she went still, turning her gaze to the man on the couch.

He shifted but didn't open his eyes.

Whew. He was really out. She studied the vest more closely. A bulletproof, military-style vest? But why?

She put the vest down, thinking through the few facts she knew about Angelica's brother. He'd been a good uncle to Xavier, a male influence who'd gotten him into sports when he was little. He'd been in the military, and right before Xavier became sick, Carlo had gotten the call to the missionary field. Come to think of it, she didn't know whether the call was from a person or from God. Why hadn't she listened more closely?

And if he'd gone into the missionary field more than two years ago, why were a bulletproof vest and hunting knife in the top of his overnight bag?

She rummaged underneath the vest and pulled out a photo in a metal frame, of Carlo squatting down in the midst of a group of ragged, dark-skinned boys. In the background was jungle-type vegetation and a leaf-covered hut. All of them, Carlo and the boys, were smiling broadly. The younger ones were pressed close to Carlo and he had his arms around them.

So he liked kids. Reassuring.

She wasn't finding the ID she wanted, but she was finding evidence of a man with a complicated life.

She fumbled further and found a piece of notebook paper, folded over twice and much crumpled. She opened it up.

"Dear Uncle Carlo, I miss yu pls come hom."

The signature was a scrawled XAVIER.

Fern drew in a deep breath and let it out, some of her fears abating.

She hadn't found an ID, but she believed in the man now. He was Angelica's brother, and if his possessions were any indication, he cared about kids, especially his nephew. Why else would he keep the letter from Xavier?

Carefully, she replaced all the items in the bag and closed it up. Then she sat back on her heels and studied the man.

He was breathing evenly, now lying on his side. He had short hair and his skin was bronzed, and there were creases at the corners of his eyes. Obviously a guy who spent most of his time outside.

She tried to remember what Angelica had told her about him. Their friendship had started at church, so it wasn't that old. It was natural that Angelica had talked about her brother's missionary work, but hadn't she also mentioned something about a marriage that hadn't worked out, somewhere out West? If she remembered right, Angelica hadn't even had the chance to meet Carlo's wife—the marriage had been too brief and chaotic.

His arms bulged out the edges of the T-shirt he was wearing, but his face had relaxed in sleep, erasing most of the harshness.

Here was a soldier, but also a missionary. With a well-worn Bible. Who cared about kids.

As she watched him, she was aware of a soft feeling inside that she rarely felt. Aware that her heart was beating a little bit faster.

How ridiculous. He was nothing like the few guys she'd gone out with before—mostly pale, video-gaming types. If he'd ever set foot in the children's room of a library, she'd be surprised.

And there was no way he'd look at the likes of her! She only attracted supernerds. She was a boring librarian who never left Ohio. She couldn't keep up with him.

"Quit staring."

"What?" She jumped about six feet in the air.

"Did you like what you found?" he asked lazily.

"What I… What do you mean?" Fern felt her face flashing hot.

"In my bag."

"You were awake!" She felt totally embarrassed because of her thoughts, because of how long she'd sat staring at him. Had he been watching her, too? What had he been thinking?

"I'm a trained soldier. I wake up when you blink. So don't try to pull one over on me." He was half smiling, but there was wariness in his eyes. "What were you looking for?"

"Um, an ID? I wanted to see if you were really Angelica's brother. I talked to her, but then I thought you might not be Carlo at all."

"You didn't find an ID in there," he said flatly, "so why aren't you calling the police?"

"Or pulling your own nasty-looking knife on you? Because of your letter from Xavier."

"What?"

"You had a letter from Xavier. And it was folded and refolded, almost to where it's tearing at the creases. So that means you looked at it a bunch of times. You really care about your nephew, don't you?"

A flush crept up his cheeks. "Yeah. He's a good kid."

"And maybe you're not a terrible guy. Or at least, maybe you're who you say you are." Awkward, awkward. Fern was way too awkward with people, especially men. Being alone was way more comfortable and safe.

CARLO TRIED TO sit up, pulling on the back of the couch to shift his weight to a sitting position. The room only spun for a minute.

He had to get out of here before his pretty hostess dug deeper into his stuff or his psyche and found out something he didn't want known.

Bad enough that she'd found a hunting knife in his bag. He checked his ankle holster reflexively, even though he knew his weapon was safe there.

Her phone buzzed and she checked the front of it. Worry creased her face as she punched a message back. Then she got up and turned on the TV.

The weather analysts were in their glory as she flipped from station to station.

"It's being called the storm of the century!"

"If you don't have to go out, don't go out!"

"Stay tuned for a list of closings!"

Finally, she settled on the local station he remembered from his childhood. A reporter stood in front of an overturned tractor trailer on the interstate as snow blew his lacquered hair out of control. "Folks, it looks as if things are only going to get worse for the next couple of days. All nonemergency vehicles are advised to stay off the roads, and several of our rural counties have just issued complete road closings…"

Great. He needed to get out while he could. He stood to go and her phone buzzed again. She answered and as he chugged the rest of his tea and reached for his boots, he heard one side of an intense conversation that seemed to be about dogs.

When she clicked off the phone, she looked worried.

"What's going on?" he asked. "I mean, besides the snowstorm. I need to get out of here while I can."

"They've actually closed the roads between here and town," she said. "And the people Troy and Angelica hired to take care of the dogs can't get out here."

"How many dogs?"

"Something like forty."

"That's a lot. Where?"

She walked to the window that faced the back of the house and gestured out. When he put his face to the glass and looked, he saw the vague outline of a barn about a football field's distance away. It came back to him then, from Angie's wedding: the size of the barn, the number of dogs Troy and Angelica housed inside.

When he walked to the other window and looked out toward his truck, it was completely obscured. As was that path that had led to it.

He rubbed the back of his neck, thinking. He really, really wanted to get out of here, and he was sure he could make it in his truck.

On the other hand, he hated to leave a woman and child alone out here. "How are you going to take care of the dogs?"

"I'll get it done." She straightened her shoulders as worry creased her forehead. "How hard can it be?"

"Pretty hard. You've never done it before?"

"No, but one of their usual helpers can coach me through it by phone."

He studied the storm, then turned back to look at the petite woman in front of him. Taking care of forty dogs meant a lot of messy kennels to clean. There'd be heavy bags of food to carry, water to fetch, medications to dispense if any of them were sick. And from what his sister had told him, they weren't the easiest dogs.

He made a snap decision. "I'd better stay and help you." Even as he said it, his heart sank. That was the last thing he wanted to do.

"Excuse me? I'll be the one issuing invitations. Which I didn't do."

"Sorry to be rude. But there's no way you can manage all those dogs alone. What will you do with your daughter?"

"I don't know, but I'll figure it out, okay? Look, I don't even know you."

He nodded. "I know. It's not exactly comfortable, is it? I can sleep in my truck or in the barn."

She tossed her head back, looking at the sky. "There's no way that will work! The barn and the bunkhouse aren't winterized, not well enough for a person to stay, and you'll freeze to death in your truck. And you're sick!" She bit her lip and looked around, struggle evident on her face.

"I assume you'll give me a blanket if I'm extranice?" He meant to lighten her mood, but the line came out sounding flirtatious. *Great move, Camden.*

She ignored him. "I guess," she said slowly, "you can stay in the TV room. And I'll lock the doors upstairs."

"If you're sure, that would be fantastic." It was a shame that women had to be so careful, but they did. And he was glad his daughter—his *daughter*, he could still barely wrap his mind around that concept—was safe with someone like stern, protective, beautiful Fern.

She was worrying her lower lip. "For now, I'd better check on Mercy and then go out and make sure the dogs are okay. They got their dinner, but I want to make sure they're warm enough. Let them out into their runs one last time."

"I'll go with you." He stood and got his feet under him.

"No! You don't need to come." Then she bit her lip, and he couldn't help thinking how cute she was. Not a stereotypical librarian at all, despite the thick glasses.

"What?"

"I… I guess I don't want you to stay here alone with Mercy, either."

"Then, you'll have to accept my help. As much as I can do anyway. Bull can watch over…your little girl." Whoa, he had to be careful what he said until he decided how he was going to punt.

She let out a sigh and he recognized it. "Not a people person, eh? Me, either. We don't have to talk."

She stared at him. "You get that?"

"I get that. I've got an introverted side myself."

She raised an eyebrow and then put on her coat and sat down to pull furry boots over her skinny jeans. "I guess I could use some help, come to think of it. It's like a *Little House on the Prairie* storm. Wonder if we should tie a line from the house to the barn."

"Not a bad idea," he said. "But I think we'll be able to see our way back. The structures are bigger than in Laura Ingalls Wilder's day."

She stared at him again. "Why do you know about Laura Ingalls Wilder?"

"Because I have a little sister," he said. "I used to get books at the library for her all the time. Those were some of her favorites. Mine, too, if you want to know the truth."

"You're a sensitive soldier?"

"More like a desperate big brother." He chuckled. "It was either books or playing with her one and only Barbie doll. I couldn't stomach that."

She opened the door and cold wind cut into Carlo's body like a frigid knife. He wasn't used to this, not after years in the tropics. "You ready?" he asked, shrugging into his jacket.

"I guess. But if you collapse out there, I don't think I can drag you back."

"I won't collapse." In truth, he felt better after the meal and the bit of a nap. Strong enough to make it out to the barn, which he could barely see through the whiteout conditions. Maybe a rope wasn't a bad idea, at that.

He broke a path all the way to where the dogs were, checking back frequently to make sure she still followed. She was small boned and thin, and the cold and wind had to affect her more than it did him, but she pushed on without complaining.

When they got to the kennels, she took the lead, unlocking the gate and then the barn door, letting herself in to a chorus of barking. She approached each dog, touching them, clucking at them, and they calmed down quickly.

Okay, so on top of being cute and maternal, she was a dog whisperer.

And she was raising his daughter and hoping to keep

the child away from her worthless birth father, he reminded himself. She was his enemy, not his friend. He was here to learn more about her, not admire her looks or skills.

"If you start at that end, we can let out whoever wants out," she said, nodding toward the kennels closest to the door.

He knew from his sister's notes that most of the dogs were bully breeds because Troy, who owned the rescue, took in dogs that wouldn't otherwise find a home. As he started opening kennels, he could see that some were scarred, probably from abuse or neglect. But their rough background didn't mean they were stupid; most elected not to go out in the storm. When he finished his side, he checked the heating unit.

Fern was taking twice as long as he was to work with the dogs, and he realized she was patting and playing a little with each one. She was obviously unafraid of them, even though several stood as tall as her waist.

Carlo started letting out the dogs on her side, this time taking a little more energy to pat and talk to them.

By the time they met in the middle, he was feeling feverish again, but he still needed to keep the energy to get back to the house. "Ready to go back?"

"Sure. You look done in."

"I am. But I'll do my best not to collapse on you." He tried to smile.

"At least let me lead this time."

"No, it's…"

But she was already out the door. She obviously was a woman who did what she wanted to do, who, despite appearing shy, was very independent. Okay, then. He could respect that.

The storm had grown even worse. His breath froze

and the wind whipped his face, and despite the fact that he'd broken a path and had someone walking in front of him, Carlo came close to losing his footing several times. His head was swimming.

Then Fern stumbled and fell into a thigh-deep snowdrift.

He reached for her, braced himself and pulled her out, and as he steadied her, he felt a sudden stunning awareness of her as a woman.

She looked up into his eyes and drew in a sharp breath.

Did she feel what he felt, or was the closeness a distinct displeasure?

Wind squealed around the fence posts, and whiteness was all he could see. Whiteness and her face. "Come on," he said into her ear. "We've got to get inside."

She pulled away from him and soldiered on toward the house, tossing a mistrustful look over her shoulder.

It was going to be a long night.

CHAPTER THREE

FERN WOKE UP to silence, utter silence. The light in the room was amazing. She walked to the window and gazed out into a world of soft white mounds overlaid with a crystalline sparkle. Sunlight peeked through a gap in heavy clouds that suggested the snowstorm wasn't done with them yet.

When you see the wonder of God's creation, how can you doubt Him? She smiled as her friend Kath's words came back to her, even as she marveled at her friend's faith. Despite Kath's horrendous past and her illness, she'd been able to praise God and had taught Fern to do the same.

She slipped out of bed and went to her bedroom door. Locked.

Oh, yeah. The stranger.

As if a locked door could stop a man of Carlo's skills. But it had made her rest a little easier.

Her feeling of peace shaken, she took a deep breath and headed down the hall into Mercedes's room. Maybe the stranger would sleep for a long time. He certainly needed to; by the end of the evening last night, he'd looked awful.

She frowned at the intrusion into her safe world. She'd wanted to be out here alone, not hosting a stranger. A disturbing stranger.

Why was he so disturbing?

Because you're attracted to him, an inner voice said.

She shook her head. She didn't want to be attracted to him. To anyone, really, but especially to this jock type who was so handsome, so far out of her league. She didn't need to get her heart broken. She needed to protect it, because she needed to stay sane for Mercedes. Opening herself up to feelings would make all the bad stuff come back in, and she just wasn't ready for that.

She opened Mercy's door and walked over to the child's bed. She was staying in Xavier's room, so the surroundings were pure boy: race-car sheets, soccer trophies, toy trains and a big container of LEGO blocks.

Even in that setting, Mercedes glowed with girliness in her pink nightgown, her long curls spread across the pillow.

Fern's heart caught inside her. She'd never loved anyone so much in her life. And if she could save one child, maybe more, from the pain she'd been put through as a ward of the state, she'd have done a lot.

Mercedes was sleeping hard. For better or worse, she was a late riser. Well, Fern would take advantage of the time and the light to do some artwork.

She grabbed a diet soda out of the refrigerator, not wanting to take the time to make coffee, and headed right toward her worktable. Sat down, got out her paints and immersed herself in capturing the snowy scene out the window.

A while later—minutes? Hours? She couldn't tell— she smelled something that plunged her straight back to her own childhood. The memory was mixed, and she painted awhile longer, taking advantage of her own heightened emotions to evoke more feelings with her art.

"Breakfast's ready!"

The deep voice startled her, making her smear a stroke of paint. She jumped up and turned around. The sight of Carlo with a spatula in hand disoriented her.

"Whoa," he said, approaching her with concern. "I didn't mean to scare you."

Fern pressed a hand to her chest. "It's fine. What's that smell?"

"Bacon. I hope it's okay…"

"You got in the fridge and took out bacon and cooked it?" Her voice rose to a squeak. "Really?"

"Yeah, well, I figured Angelica would have some. Actually, it was in the freezer. But I also stole some eggs, which may have been yours. And they're getting cold. Where's Mercedes?"

Fern was still trying to wrap her mind around the fact that this…this man was cooking in her kitchen. Well, her friend's kitchen, but still. She'd never had a man in her home. She didn't know how to handle it. Didn't want to know.

"Mama Fern?" Mercedes's plaintive voice from the top of the stairs gave Fern a welcome focus.

She hurried up and wrapped her arms around the child. "Hey there, sleepyhead. What's going on?"

"What's cooking? It smells yummy."

"Um…bacon." Up until this moment, Fern hadn't intended to eat any; she wanted to get this man out of the house quickly, not break bread with him.

But if Mercedes liked bacon, then bacon it would be. "Our guest cooked breakfast," she explained. "Let's wash your face and hands and you can come on down and eat."

Minutes later, the three of them sat around the wooden table. Carlo had served up plates of bacon, eggs and toast, and he'd even poured orange juice and set out fruit on the side.

"This is good," Mercedes said, her mouth full, jam on the side of her face.

"It sure is good, Mercy-Mercedes." He made a funny face at the little girl, and she burst out in a torrent of giggles.

Fern's breath caught.

Amazing that Mercedes could still be so happy and trusting, given the difficulties of life with her mother and then the loss of her. Amazing that she, Fern, got to raise this incredible child.

And it was amazing to be sitting here around the table with a child and a handsome, manly man who knew his way around the kitchen and could joke around with a child.

Thing was, Carlo was trouble.

Oh, he'd been questionable when he showed up here on her doorstep, sick and wild looking. But that man, that kind of trouble, she'd been able to handle.

Now, seeing him feeling better and being charming and domestic, she felt the twin weights of longing and despair pressing down on her heart.

She wanted a family.

She'd always wanted a family, wanted it more than anything. She hadn't had one, even as a child.

But there was no way she could form a family with any man worth the having. She just wasn't the type. She was shy, and awkward, and unappealing. She wore thick glasses and read books all the time and didn't know how to flirt or giggle.

So the part of her that looked around the table and wished for something like this, forever, just needed to be tamped down.

She couldn't have it and she needed to stop wanting it.

Abruptly, she stood up. "I've got to go feed the dogs."

"But, Mama Fern, *I* want to come see the dogs."

Fern hesitated. The animals were generally good, but they were just so big and strong. The idea of having a four-year-old—her own precious four-year-old—in their vicinity was a little too scary.

Carlo put a hand on her arm and she jerked away at the burn of it, staring at him.

His eyebrows went up and he studied her. "Sorry."

"It's okay. I'm jumpy." Awkward, awkward.

"Let's finish breakfast, and then we can all go out together."

"Yeah!" Mercedes shouted.

Oh, great. More pseudo–family togetherness. "That's fine," Fern said. "I'm going to start the dishes."

"But you haven't finished your—"

"I'm not hungry," she interrupted, and it was true. Her appetite had departed the moment those feelings of inadequacy and awkwardness and unlovableness arose in her.

She carried her dishes to the counter, fuming. Why had he shown up? Why hadn't he left her there in peace, to do her art and create some kind of family, even if not the real or the best kind?

You couldn't have handled the dogs alone, a voice of logic inside her said. *Maybe God's looking out for you. Maybe He sent a helper.*

But did He have to send a helper who was so handsome, who woke those desires for something she could never have?

She scrubbed hard at the pan that had held the bacon

and eggs. Looked out the window toward the kennels, and breathed, and tried to stuff her feelings back down.

"What were you working on in there?" Carlo asked.

"What do you mean?" On the defensive.

"Your easel. Your art."

"I... I do some writing and illustrating."

"Really? Can I see?"

"No!" She grabbed a towel to dry her hands and hurried toward the easel, bent on covering her work.

Carlo scooted his chair back to watch her from the kitchen. "Hey, it's okay. I wouldn't have looked without your permission."

"I'm just... It's silly. I... I don't like to show anyone my work before it's done." Truth to tell, her stories and illustrations were the one place she felt safe to delve into her own issues, to the challenges of her past. Sometimes, she felt it was all too revealing, but she was so driven to do it.

She could do her children's books and raise a family just fine. But to have a handsome man looking through her stuff, making fun of it maybe, asking questions— that she couldn't deal with. No way.

The wall phone's ringing was a welcome respite. She tucked the cover over her easel and hurried over to it.

"Hello?"

"Fern, it's Lou Ann Miller. From church?"

Fern vaguely remembered a tart, smiling, gray-haired woman who often sat with Troy and Angelica. "Hi, Lou Ann."

"Listen, I had an email from Angelica waiting for me this morning, and she let me know you have some unexpected company. Are you all right? How's Mercy?"

"We're doing fine." Fern looked at Mercedes. Carlo had found a clean dishcloth, wetted it and was washing off the child's messy face and hands, making silly faces to keep her from fussing about it.

"That's great. And don't worry about your new helper. He has a good heart."

"You know him?" She heard her own voice squeak.

"Oh, yes. I've known that boy most of his life." Lou Ann chuckled. "Pretty rough around the edges, isn't he?"

Fern looked at the man who'd invaded her safe haven. Even playing with an innocent little child in front of the fire, he looked every inch a mercenary: thick stubble, bulging biceps, shadowy, watchful eyes. "Yes," she said, swallowing. "Yes, he is."

CARLO SAT ON the floor building a block tower with the child he was almost certain was his daughter. He studied her small hands, her messy curls, her sweet, round cheeks.

His daughter's foster mother was talking to someone named Lou Ann on the phone. Probably Lou Ann Miller, who had to be getting old these days. He remembered stealing pumpkins from her front porch with a big gang of his friends. She'd chased after them and called all of their parents.

All the other boys had gotten punished. Not him, though. His parents had thought it was funny.

As he'd grown up, he'd realized that their neglect wasn't a good thing, especially when he'd seen how it affected his younger sister. When he'd had to take up their slack. He'd judged his folks pretty harshly.

But they'd been there at least some of the time. Unlike him, for his own daughter. How had it never occurred to him that Kath could have gotten pregnant during their brief reconciliation?

He wanted to clasp Mercedes tight and make up for the previous four years of her life. He wished he could rewind time and see her first smile, her first step.

But no. He left his wife pregnant and alone, and even though she'd kicked him out without telling him the truth about the baby she carried, had pressured him into signing the divorce papers, he should have tried harder. A lot harder.

Kath's letter, which had apparently languished for a couple of months before reaching him, had just about broken his heart. She'd found the Lord, and moved to Rescue River because she'd liked the way he'd described it and wanted to raise their daughter there.

Apparently, she'd even thought there was a chance they could remarry and raise Mercedes together. Sometime later, after he'd sown his wild oats and come back home to the States.

But it had turned out they didn't have the time for that. Kath had found out she was dying, and that was when she'd written to him, telling him about Mercedes and urging him to come home and take care of his daughter. She'd kept his identity secret from her social worker in case he wasn't able to come home—warped Kath logic if he'd ever heard of it. So until the social worker received the copy of Kath's letter he'd mailed and verified the information, even she wouldn't know there was an interested, responsible father in the picture.

Which was how Mercedes had ended up with Fern, apparently.

Carlo ran his hand through his hair and almost groaned aloud. He shouldn't have given up on their marriage so readily, but the truth was, he'd realized there was no more love or connection between them. Kath had been deep into a partying lifestyle she hadn't wanted to change. Reuniting would have been such an uphill battle that he hadn't minded when she'd kicked him out after just a week.

He was no good at relationships, never had been. But he hated that he'd left her to struggle alone. And even more, he hated that he'd left this innocent child to be raised by an unstable mother.

So now he was going to try to fix what had gone wrong. Maybe he'd failed as a husband. He'd failed at getting Kath into rehab. Failed as a father, so far.

But now that he knew about her existence, he was determined not to fail Mercedes. No, sir, never again. Though he was horrible at intimate relationships, he got along okay with kids. Even had a gift for working with them, according to his friends in the missionary field. Ironic that he, the guy who scared off most women and a lot of men, seemed to connect effortlessly with kids.

When Fern got off the phone, he stuffed down his feelings and made his face and voice bland. The first step in getting his daughter back was to find out what had been going on in her life. "Everything okay?"

Fern nodded, biting her lip. That was a habit of hers, he noticed. And it was really distracting, because she had full, pretty lips.

"Who was that?"

She gave him a look that said he'd overstepped his boundaries.

"Miss Lou Ann, from church," Mercedes said. "She gave me a toothbrush. Want to see?"

"Sure," Carlo said, and watched the child run toward the stairs, his heart squeezing in his chest.

"Lou Ann Miller gives all the children toothbrushes. Musical ones. She doesn't believe in candy."

"That figures. I remember her."

Fern cocked her head to one side. "She remembers you, too."

"I don't doubt it." He studied Fern and risked a question. "How'd you end up taking care of Mercedes anyway?"

She hesitated.

Easy, easy. "No need to tell me if you don't want to. I'm just curious."

Fern perched on the hearth and started stacking blocks absently. "It's okay. I need to get used to talking about it. But it's a sad story."

Carlo's stomach twisted with shame. He was, at least in part, responsible for the sadness.

"She's my friend Kath's little girl. Kath wasn't in town that long, but she made a huge difference in my life. We got...super close. And then she died." Fern's voice cracked just as Mercedes came trotting back down the stairs, musical toothbrush in hand.

"Look, mister! It makes a song!" She shook it vigorously and then looked up and touched Fern's face. "Why you sad, Mama Fern?"

"Just thinking about your mama."

"Oh." Mercedes nodded. "Bye!" she said suddenly, and ran across the room to a pink case full of dolls and doll clothes.

Fern chuckled. "Kids. When they don't want to talk about something, you know it."

Carlo had to know. "What...what did she say about Mercedes's dad? Was he ever in the picture?"

"She didn't talk much about him. Said he had issues. But what kind of guy would leave a terminally ill woman to cope with their little daughter alone?"

That was the question.

He had a lot to make up for, and it started with helping his daughter right now, stranded in the storm.

Given how fiercely protective Fern seemed, he didn't think he could explain his role in the situation without arousing her ire and getting kicked out. And then how would the pair cope, given that the snow was starting up again?

No, better to wait out the storm without revealing his identity. Once it was over, he could see about paternity tests and get advice from a lawyer about how to proceed.

Meanwhile, he could help out a vulnerable child and foster mom. Maybe start to absolve himself of some of his misdeeds. Get to know little Mercedes.

Redeem himself. If that was even possible.

CHAPTER FOUR

FOR CARLO THE late-morning trip out to the kennels was completely different from the night before.

It was daylight, and snowing hard.

And he was carrying Mercedes.

Just the feel of those little arms curled trustingly around his neck as he fought his way through thigh-high snowdrifts made his heart swell. He wasn't worthy, he didn't deserve it, but God had given him this moment, a blessing to cherish.

"You doing okay, sweets?" came Fern's voice from behind him.

Was she calling *him* sweets?

"I'm fine, Mama Fern," Mercedes piped up, and Carlo realized his mistake. Oh, well, it had felt nice for that one second. He shook his head and kept moving steadily toward the barns.

As soon as they got inside, Mercedes struggled to get down and ran to see the dogs. Carlo sank down on the bench beside the door, panting. Mercedes was tiny, but carrying her while breaking a trail had just about done him in.

"You're still sick," Fern scolded, standing in front of him. "You should probably be resting, not working."

"I'm fine, I just need a minute." Carlo wiped perspiration from his brow and staggered to his feet, calling to mind all the time he'd spent in battle under less than ideal physical circumstances. "What's the drill? Same as last night?"

Fern put a hand on her hip. Man, was she cute! "The drill is, you sit there and rest. Mercedes and I will feed the dogs."

"I'm a good helper," Mercedes called over from where she was squatting in front of a kennel, fingers poking in at the puppies inside.

"That's right, honey. But we never put our fingers in unless we're sure of our welcome."

Mercedes's lower lip poked out. "These ones are fine. You said."

"That's right. You're doing it just right."

Sunshine returned to the little girl's face and Carlo marveled at her mood shifts. Was that normal, or a product of losing her mom and changing homes? Or of whatever lifestyle Kath had put her through?

In any case, Fern seemed to handle his daughter beautifully. He wondered if he could do half as well.

"Oh, before I forget." Fern snapped her fingers and hurried over to the cage just next to the one where Mercedes was squatting. "We're supposed to check on this one mama dog. I got a text this morning."

"Pregnant?" Carlo asked. He was starting to catch his breath. Man, his stamina was totally gone after just a couple of weeks of this wretched tropical fever. But he needed to pull himself together and show he was a hard worker, a man who could protect and care for others. That was how he'd get custody of his daughter, not by wheezing on a bench like a ninety-year-old with lung disease.

"No, she's not pregnant. She had puppies and all but one died, so they put the one in with another litter to socialize it and...aw, Mama, you're lonely, aren't you?"

Carlo walked over to where Fern was kneeling and peered into the kennel. A large chocolate-brown dog lay in the back corner, head on paws.

"C'mere, come on, Brownie, I'll give you a biscuit," Fern coaxed, but the dog stayed down, emitting a low whine.

"That's not good. They said she needs to eat." Fern frowned. "I wonder if it's good for her to be right next to her puppy like this. Where she can see her, but not be with her. That would be hard."

No kidding. Carlo found himself identifying with the mama dog. "Is she feeding the pup?"

"Apparently not." Fern nodded toward the next kennel, where five or six puppies played and rolled and nipped each other. "I guess that mama dog over there is feeding all of them. And they say it's better for a puppy to be with other pups, but I feel bad for poor Brownie."

"Mama Fern, look! The little one is hurt!" Mercedes's voice sounded distressed.

Both Fern and Carlo stepped over to where Mercedes knelt by the cage full of puppies. "Over there, Mama! Help him!"

In the corner of the cage, a small brown-and-white-spotted puppy lay alone. Carlo felt his heart constricting, looking at Mercedes's face, wondering if the little guy was dead and if so, how that would affect Mercedes. "Is there a flashlight?"

"Mercedes, run and get our flashlight from the desk," Fern urged, kneeling to see the little dog. "He's not moving," she said to Carlo in a low voice.

"Here, Mama!" Mercedes handed the flashlight to Fern and she shone it on the puppy. Its eyes were closed, its breathing rapid, but at least there was breathing.

There were also a couple of open wounds on his side and back.

"Oh, wow, I don't know what to do," Fern said. "That's the one that doesn't belong. It looks like either the mama dog or the other pups have turned on him."

As if on cue, the chocolate-colored dog began to whine from the next kennel.

"Should we put him back with his mama?" Carlo asked.

"I don't know. Let me text the people who normally take care of them," Fern said. "And meanwhile, I'll get the others fed."

"I'll stay and watch over him," Mercedes offered.

"Okay, that will be great. I think Carlo will stay with you and help. Right?" Fern gave him a stern, meaningful stare.

"Um…okay." Man, this diminutive, shy librarian had a spine of steel. There was no disagreeing with her.

This time, Fern didn't linger with each dog, but moved rapidly from kennel to kennel, letting dogs out into the runs if they'd go, pouring food from large canisters. Carlo marveled at how hard she was capable of working, and he handled the dogs two or three kennels to either side of the problem dogs, trying to lighten her load while also keeping an eye on Mercedes, making sure she wasn't seeing something upsetting.

When Mercedes cried out, he was glad he'd stuck close. He rushed back over in time to see one of the other puppies jump on top of the spotted pup and nip at it. "He's hurting the little puppy," Mercedes cried. "Stop him!"

Carlo didn't know if it was normal puppy play or something more aggressive, but he could see that the little guy wasn't in any shape to play rough. "Step back, and I'll pull him out," he told Mercedes, and then he went in and picked up the puppy.

"Oh, no, oh, no, is he okay?"

"I don't know." He needed to keep Mercedes calm as well as help the pup. Which meant keeping her busy. "Can you find a towel we can wrap him in?"

Fern was all the way down at the other end of the kennel, so Carlo got Mercedes to help him wrap the puppy in the towel she'd found. "We'll be really careful," he said, watching Mercedes. His daughter. Wow.

"Mama Fern said kids can only touch a dog with two fingers, so you better hold him," Mercedes told Carlo gravely.

So he sat cross-legged on the floor and held the dog, and Mercedes petted the pup with two fingers, and somehow she ended up sitting in his lap, leaning her head against his chest and chattering every thought that came into her four-year-old brain.

Just keep breathing, Carlo told himself.

No matter what happened, he'd have these moments with his daughter to cherish forever. He could enjoy the fruity smell of her hair and the pink of her cheeks and the confiding, sweet tone of her voice. He could look at her dark eyes and realize that those came from Kath, but her strong chin probably came from his side of the family. He got a sudden memory of his sister, Angelica, when she was small, and realized that Mercedes had her flat cheekbones and cute nose.

Fern came up behind them, a heavy bag of dog food in her arms, breathing hard. "Oh, man," she said, "you took him out. Is he okay?"

"I think he's going to be." Carlo looked up and tried to communicate with his eyes that he had no idea, but was putting a positive spin on things for Mercedes's sake. He felt like a cad for just sitting here while she worked, but on the other hand, he could clearly see that Mercedes needed nurturing. So maybe this was how you managed it with two parents—you dumped gender stereotypes and played whichever role needed playing at the time.

Fern was studying her phone. "They said to take him out if he's being bullied, that sometimes the rest of the litter turns on a puppy."

The sad mama dog came up to the front of the cage and sniffed and whined her agitation.

"Do you think she knows it's hers?" Fern asked.

"Sure looks that way. What else did your friends say?"

"Oh, they're not my friends, they're just people who help out here. I don't..." She trailed off, waved a hand, leaving Carlo curious about what she'd been about to say. "Anyway, they said maybe we should take the mama and the pup up to the house, and see if she could still feed him some. Apparently, they just moved him over a day or two ago. She might still have her milk."

"We can have them at the house?" Mercedes jumped out of Carlo's lap and threw her arms around Fern. "I always wanted a puppy! What's his name, Mama Fern?"

"I don't think he has one yet." Fern stroked Mercedes's hair and there was such happiness and tenderness in her face that Carlo had to look away. "We'll think of something to call him, at least for now."

"His name is Spots," Mercedes announced. "'Cause he has spots!"

"Makes sense to me." Carlo got to his feet, bringing the pup with him. "If you carry the little one and I carry the mama..."

"Can you? She's huge."

He gave her a look and then opened the cage. "I can, unless she wants to walk. I don't know how her health is."

"And you hafta carry me," Mercedes reminded him.

"That's right." He patted her messy hair as warmth spread through his chest.

So they made their way back to the house in stages. Carlo carried the big dog while Mercedes and Fern worked in the kennel and watched the puppy. Then he went back to carry Mercedes while Fern brought the puppy and a bag of supplies.

By the time they got settled in the house again, he was sweating and dizzy, but he kept it together and brought in a bunch of wood and built a fire. Made sure the mama and puppy were settled, along with Fern and Mercedes. And then he collapsed onto the sofa.

He must have dozed off or even passed out, because Fern touched him and he jerked and then relaxed. Something in her touch was soothing.

"You made yourself sick again, didn't you?" she scolded. "I heated up more soup. Sit up and eat it."

Carlo couldn't let her do this. Couldn't let himself accept the caretaking, especially when he knew that his only shot at Mercedes was being superman here. If he couldn't be superman, if he had to be weak, then he needed to hide it away. Along with his strange desire to reach up and touch Fern's cheek. "I'll just sleep it off in the den," he growled, and slunk away from the vulnerability and the weakness and the worry.

FERN WATCHED HIM go, and the sense of rejection was enormous. Just like her to mess things up with Carlo. Of course he didn't want to spend time around her. She'd come on too strong with the nurturing, but what was she supposed to do? She was more used to being around kids and animals than adults. Kids and animals loved being taken care of.

A big manly man like Carlo was different, she supposed, and it was just her own awkwardness that had made her think she could take care of him, or that he'd want her to.

"Mama? What are we gonna do now?"

The plaintive voice pulled Fern out of her funk. It didn't matter what some strange man thought of her. She squatted down beside Mercedes, who was sitting cross-legged petting the little puppy. "You're doing just the right thing. I'm proud of you for being so gentle. You just keep doing that while I text the caretakers and find out what to do next."

Although Fern could see now that Brownie's ribs showed, her demeanor was much happier. She wasn't whining anymore, just licking her puppy as if to make up for the time apart.

Minutes later Fern's phone buzzed and she read the instructions, still sitting with her arm around Mercedes. "Okay, they say we're supposed to get the mama dog something to eat. Even if she's nursing, we should put some soft food nearby so she can eat whenever she needs to and get her milk back up."

"What's the puppy doing?"

Fern watched as the puppy nuzzled at the mama dog's teats and took a deep breath. Okay, time for a new mothering challenge. "Mama dogs feed their pups from their bodies. The dog has a nipple like a baby bottle, and milk comes out of it."

"That's silly! That's not where milk comes from."

"Nope, but our milk comes from cows."

Mercedes's nose wrinkled. "I don't drink from a cow!"

Fern chuckled. "No, but the cow gets milked by the farmer, and then the milk gets sent to the grocery store, and then we buy it and drink it." She hesitated. "When you were a baby, you drank from your mama just like that little puppy." She didn't want to upset Mercedes, but the social worker had told her it was good to refer to her biological mother naturally, in conversation. That way, Mercedes would know that her mother and her experiences with her mother weren't a taboo subject.

"I drank from my mommy?" Mercedes asked wonderingly.

"Yes, your mommy told me she breast-fed you for a whole year. She loved you so much."

"Yeah." Mercedes looked thoughtful for a minute. "Hey, the puppy is biting the mommy!"

Fern was watching, too. The puppy was obviously getting some sustenance, but even to her inexperienced eye, it looked like a struggle. "Tell you what, let's get Brownie that food. Maybe she needs more to eat before she can feed her pup." She sincerely hoped Brownie could feed the pup entirely, both because it was better for the little guy, and because she didn't know exactly how they'd manage the frequent feedings a little puppy would need.

"What will she eat?"

"I guess she'll eat Bull's food." Suddenly, Fern realized she hadn't seen the old bulldog. "Where is Bull anyway?"

"Mr. Carlo took him in the den. He said it was better if they didn't meet yet, because they might fight."

"Okay." She had to appreciate Carlo's practical help.

The man was just…capable, and it was a relief to have him here even though he made her uncomfortable.

After Brownie had eaten and settled down with a big doggy sigh, her pup beside her, Fern and Mercedes played board games in front of the fire. Mercedes had a snack and took a short nap, and Fern seized the opportunity to work a little on her picture book.

When Mercedes got up, she distracted her with half an hour of television so she could work a little more and finish her ideas. A small flash of guilt about that, but after all, it was a snow day and half an hour of TV wasn't too bad. Mercedes normally went to day care while Fern worked, and she was used to structure and varied activities in her day.

What else was she going to do with little Mercy? She put her paints away and then wandered into the kitchen. Outside the windows, the sun peeked through clouds on its way to a beautiful sunset, all pink and peachy and orange and purple. Snow was heaped high against the fence line and the barn. Trees raised spidery arms into the sky, and the beauty was breathtaking. Yes, she had to do a winter story soon just so she could capture some of this in her art.

She daydreamed of Ezra Scott Keats and *The Snowy Day*. They didn't own the picture book, but she'd checked it out several times from the library. She looked through Angelica's various shelves of picture books and found that one, along with several others related to snow.

She and Mercedes lay down by the fire for a little while, reading, but it was clearly not active enough for the little girl and she got fidgety. So Fern pulled out her big guns. "Want to bake cookies?"

"Yeah!" Mercedes's eyes glowed. "Can we really?"

"Sure. Let's go find all the ingredients. I'm sure Angelica has everything basic." It was true; as the mother of a first-grader, Angelica kept her kitchen well stocked in chocolate chips.

As they mixed together the dough, as she showed Mercedes what to do and let her help, Fern flashed back to one memorable day in her favorite foster home, where Granny Jentis had let two of the girls help her bake cookies. It had been just such a snowy day. They'd baked batch after batch of sugar cookies and Fern remembered the thrill of licking the spoon and of watching the sticky dough turn into delicious warm cookies.

If she had her way, Mercedes would have many, many days like that: homey, family days.

Sudden fear flashed through her. What if things didn't work out? What if something happened in the adoption process and Mercedes couldn't stay?

She drew in a deep breath. Glanced over reflexively at the verse Angelica had hung on the kitchen wall: "There is no fear in love; but perfect love casts out fear."

Angelica was a good Christian. The whole family was. And the thought of enough love to rid yourself of fear was amazing.

Fern didn't have that. She wished she did, and she knew from church that many believers had such faith that fear was gone or greatly diminished. That would be wonderful. Now, with so much more than she'd ever had to lose, Fern wished fervently that she had that safe, loving, loved feeling.

She didn't. And with her background, she didn't know if she ever would.

But she loved Mercedes with all her heart, and all she could do was to focus on that love.

They were pulling the first batch of cookies out of

the oven when Carlo came in, rubbing his stubbly face. In his faded jeans and loose sweater, sleeves pushed up to reveal brawny forearms, he looked impossibly handsome, and Fern's heart rate shot up just looking at him.

Which was weird, because she *never* went mushy and boy-crazy like other women.

"Smells great in here," he said, sounding calmer and more cheerful than before. "What's going on?"

"We baked cookies!" Mercedes shouted, her voice joyous. "I never did it before, and Mama Fern says I'm really good at it."

"Hmm." Carlo bent over the cookie tray Fern was holding, pretending to sniff the cookies. His nearness just about took Fern's breath away, weirdly enough. "I'm not sure. Would you like me to be a cookie tester for you?"

Fern whirled away and set the cookies down on a pot holder on the counter. "He's trying to fool us, Mercy. He wants the first taste of a cookie, but you're the one who gets that."

Mercedes studied him carefully. "He can try it," she said finally. "I like him."

Carlo took a hot cookie, bit into it and licked the crumb off his lip. His eyes sparkled at Fern. "Hmm," he said. "That was…" He knelt in front of Mercedes. "The very best cookie I ever tasted!"

"I know, and this is the very best day I ever had!" Mercedes's eyes widened then. "Except I wish Mommy was here."

Fern squatted down and hugged the little girl. "Your mama would be so proud of you for all your hard work today," she said.

There was a yip from the corner, sounding as if one

of the dogs was barking approval, and Carlo looked over. "How are they doing?"

When they all went over to check, the puppy was nursing contentedly while the older dog lay on her side.

"Mama Fern, she's smiling!" Mercedes cried.

"It looks that way. I think she's happy to be with her pup."

Indignant yowling came from the room where Carlo had been sleeping. "Sounds like old Bull isn't happy to be left out," Carlo said.

"Do you think we should put them together?"

"Not yet, but maybe later tonight. Bull seems like a nice guy, but this is his territory and—"

A loud *pop* interrupted him.

All the lights went out.

CHAPTER FIVE

"WHOA!" CARLO TENSED instantly and reached for the spot where he'd last seen Mercedes, but his hand brushed Fern's hip instead and he jerked it back.

"Mama!" Mercedes cried, and he sensed rather than saw Fern kneeling beside her.

"Shh, sweets, it's okay. Mama Fern's here." She directed her voice toward him. "What happened?"

"Must be from the storm." He had pretty good night vision and spatial memory, so he made his way across the room and opened the window shades.

Sunset had turned the sky purple and orange and pink, but he couldn't see any electrical lights outside, not even way in the distance where another farm was usually visible. The outage must be widespread.

Behind him, Mercedes's scared sniffling turned into a wail.

"I'm right here, Mercy." Fern's voice was calm, even upbeat. "Looks as if we're going to have a little adventure."

"I don't like dark," the child cried.

Carlo fumbled in his pocket for the flashlight that was always on his key chain. In a minute, its feeble beam was joined by a stronger one from Fern's phone. "There we go," he said. "Light and an adventure."

As had become automatic in his missionary work,

he sent up a quick prayer. *Unexpected stuff here, Lord, but not to You. Help us.*

"Wonder where Troy and Angelica keep the candles," Fern mused. She'd stood and was cuddling Mercedes on her hip.

"No dark," the little girl sobbed.

"Shh, it's going to be okay. We'll have fun."

"No, 'cause lights cost money. And we can't get them back for a long time."

Her words smote Carlo. Kath and Mercedes must have gone without electricity. Without intending to, he'd neglected his own child to the point where she'd lacked the physical necessities of life.

He'd lived up to every bad expectation he'd heard growing up. That Camden boy. Always in trouble. Won't amount to anything.

Fern's voice, sweet and calm, brought him back to the present. "Oh, no, Mercy, the reason the power went out is the storm. No big deal. The lights will come back on as soon as the workers can fix the electrical lines."

Mercedes lifted her head. "Can we still make the cookies?" she asked plaintively.

"Um…no. The oven won't work without power."

"But I want to bake the cookies!"

"Shh!" Fern sounded frustrated and a little scared. "We've got a lot to think about."

Hearing the anxiety in Fern's voice made Carlo's training snap into place. *Take charge.* "First thing, we're all okay." He injected total confidence into the words as he put a hand on Fern's shoulder and a hand on Mercedes's. "That's most important. Next issue is the dogs. How are our guys in here?"

As he'd hoped, the thought of the dogs stopped Mercedes's crying, which had to take a load of stress off Fern.

He was rewarded by her grateful smile. "Can you help me check them out, Mercy?" she asked, and they all walked over to examine the mama and puppy.

True to canine form, the two appeared to be completely relaxed. But when Carlo shone his light on the pup, he noticed that its sores looked raw. "Did your friends say what to do about these?"

"They said they'd heal unless the pup or mama get obsessive about licking them."

Just then, Brownie lifted her head and started licking her puppy's back.

"Hmm." To Carlo, the wounds looked worse, and then a memory came back to him. "I have an idea about how to stop her from licking. Mind if I try?"

Even in the dim light he could see Fern's concerned frown. "How much do you know about dogs?"

Good for her. The dogs were her responsibility and she couldn't let just anyone take charge of them. He lifted his hands. "Believe me, I'm no veterinarian. But I did spend a week on a farm one time and something similar was going on with a mama cow and a calf."

"And you fixed it?"

"No, I watched a very experienced farmer fix it, and it worked."

She scratched behind the mama dog's ears and looked up at him. "In Central America? And if it was a farm, must've been during the missionary years?"

He stared at her. "You really pay attention."

"That's the benefit of us quiet types." Her slow smile made his heart skip a beat.

They were all kneeling around the sleepy pair of dogs. Carlo could see the furniture as dark shapes, and outside the window, the moon was just starting to rise.

When he leaned away from the dogs and toward Fern, he noticed her light floral perfume.

"As long as it doesn't hurt the dogs." She bit her lip, her face suddenly scrunched with worry, and he couldn't help it—he reached out a hand and smoothed the lines from her forehead.

Which made her go very, very still.

"Hey," he said to calm the fear in those huge eyes. And to calm his own suddenly racing heart. "I want the dogs to stay safe, too. I don't want to hurt them, okay? You can trust me."

Even as he said it, his stomach turned over. Because yeah, she could trust him about the dogs, but what about her and Mercedes? Wasn't he keeping the biggest secret of all from them?

She blinked behind those glasses, smiled and nodded. "Okay, farmer Carlo. Do your stuff."

Man, was she cute when she tried to be funny. Apparently, Mercedes thought so, too, because she chortled with laughter. "He's not a farmer, Mama Fern! He's a soldier!"

Carlo was standing up to get what he needed from the kitchen, but at those words, he stiffened. "Who told her that?"

Fern lifted her hands, palms up. "Not me. How'd you know, Mercy?"

"I guessed a secret!" Mercedes crowed. "'Cause he's like the movies Mommy watched at night."

"There you go, Rambo," Fern said drily.

He turned away, using his flashlight to guide him toward the kitchen. He was trying to leave his mercenary days behind, trying to atone for them, actually, but it seemed he couldn't shed the stink of war. Nor the things he'd done there.

Oh, he'd been on the right side, fighting for the common people against dictators who committed atrocities and ruined lives. But you couldn't help getting some blood on your hands, and as time had gone by, it had haunted him more, not less.

He shook off the thoughts and found lemon and red pepper and salt. Mixed them into a paste in a bowl, making sure the amount of red pepper was much less than his farmer friend would have used, figuring a puppy's skin was more tender than a calf's. And then he carried it out and spread a little near the cut.

The mama dog was curious, but even one whiff of his concoction made her turn away, snorting.

"Hey," Fern protested. "What if she rejects the puppy now?"

"Let's just watch. Mamas are protective. They'll go against their best interest to take care of their young."

Boy, did he hope he was right! He'd gotten attached to the little pup, and he felt responsible for it. Not only that, but he wanted to shove the skepticism off Fern's face, to replace it with admiration. Fortunately, for now at least, the dog kept the puppy close to her side and allowed him to nurse.

Carlo did the evening feed of the kennel dogs himself, brushing aside Fern's offer to go out with him. He needed a few minutes away. He needed to think.

Was he doing the right thing, not telling Fern the truth about his connection to Mercedes?

She'd be angry if he told her now, that was for sure. She might kick him right out into the snowstorm.

If she did that, he'd be fine, he'd manage, but what would happen to her and Mercedes? With shaky electricity and phone service and a barn full of dogs to take care of, they needed help. He was more and more impressed with Fern's self-reliance and independent spirit, but even she had her limits. Taking care of a farm and a bunch of dogs and a little girl in these conditions was much more than a one-woman job.

When he went back inside, the relief on her face made him feel ten feet tall, and more certain that he was right to keep things calm, keep controversial stuff to himself, while they needed him.

He noticed that the floor was strewn with toys, mostly action figures and little plastic soldiers and dinosaurs. A box of juice lay on its side next to a dark, damp spot on the carpet. "You okay?"

"I'm okay," she said, pushing her glasses up her nose, "but Mercy's got issues. She's still a little scared of the dark, and after you left, it got worse. It's because of stuff she went through with her mom. And to top that off, she's easily frustrated, and I… Well, I caved and let her watch a video on my phone. It's stupid, because we need to save the charge, since the landline gets glitchy in storms, but I didn't know what else to do."

"She had a meltdown?"

She nodded. "They can come on suddenly. Again, it's a function of her background. Kath was honest with me about how she wasn't the best at parenting throughout Mercedes's younger years. There was poverty and some drug use, and Mercedes didn't always get comforted right away. That affects a kid."

Once again, guilt washed over Carlo. He should have been there, helping, maybe even taking custody of Mercedes if Kath wasn't able to handle her care. If only he'd known.

"So anyway, she's upset right now because she never made cookies before, if you can believe it, and now we can't because of the stove."

He took a breath and did what he'd been trained to do: let the past go, focus on now. There was a lot in Mercedes's history he couldn't fix, but this was one thing he could. "I have an idea," he said. "We can rig something up to bake cookies using the fireplace. Want to help me try?"

She cocked her head to one side, a slight smile making her look flirtatious. "Are you really that handy?"

"Let's just say I've spent a lot of time improvising. Do you have any tinfoil?"

They used his flashlight to go through the dark kitchen cupboards, finding what they needed. They were fortunate to stumble onto an oil lamp, too, half-full. Once that was lit, Carlo carried it out to where Mercedes huddled under a blanket on the couch, clutching Fern's phone. He set the oil lamp on the hearth above, well out of the child's reach—you couldn't be too careful with kids and fire.

"Okay," Fern said, carrying the rest of the supplies out to the fireplace. "Do your best."

"Hey, Mercy, want to stop watching the video and help me build an oven?" He needed to save the charge on that phone. His own phone was next to worthless, and they had to be able to get in touch with the outside world for emergency purposes. The landline had been out when he'd checked.

Carlo fooled around with baking sheets and tinfoil while Mercedes watched. Finally, he had something he thought would work. "Bring those cookies, women!" he jokingly commanded.

Fern flashed him a fake scowl. "Neanderthal," she shot at him before rising effortlessly to her feet from a cross-legged position and taking Mercedes to the kitchen.

Mercedes seemed to have forgotten her fear of the dark, and the dogs slept peacefully, and Carlo felt calm descend over him. *Thank You, Lord*, he whispered as he looked around the lamp-lit room.

So many times he'd been in places where weather and illness and violence had made life awful. Here was the softer side, the reason he'd fought for his country. Here was the home that he'd not had while growing up.

Angelica had done herself proud, creating such a wonderful environment for herself and her child, pushing through all the barriers to a relationship that came from the way they'd been raised. He was proud of his little sister, and happy for her, too. She practically glowed through the phone when she talked about her new husband. And as Fern and Mercedes came back into the room, Mercedes carefully carrying a tray of cookies to bake, he had a moment of wishing he might get some of that glow, that joy, for himself.

This won't last. Fern will be furious when she finds out.

But just for this one night, he was going to pretend.

So they put the cookies in the makeshift convection oven. Carlo had no clue about how long it would take—he was anything but a chef—but whatever the baking time, he figured it would be too long for a four-year-old. "Want to let Bull out?" he asked Mercedes. "The old guy's got to be lonely in there."

"Yeah!" she yelled, and ran to the door.

"Hold on." He raised a hand, his voice automatically taking on the tone of command, and she turned around, eyes wide. "Don't touch that door. We want to get the mama and pup ready."

"You guard them while I help Mercedes get Bull," Fern said. She was lifting an eyebrow at him, her expression cool, and suddenly he knew she was thinking he'd overstepped his bounds, that he shouldn't think he could tell everyone what to do.

"Hey, I'm used to being in charge, what can I say?" He spread his hands and grinned at her.

"I noticed." One hand on her hip, she lifted her chin. Yeah, a woman to be reckoned with.

"I'm keeping her entertained, right?" he challenged her.

She frowned another second, considering, and then chuckled. "Yes, you are, and I'm grateful. Just…not used to sharing the spotlight." As she said it, a surprised expression crossed her face.

"What's wrong?"

"I normally hate having other people around!" Then she clapped a hand to her mouth. "That came out wrong. It's just that, I'm an introvert. Kids and animals I can hang with all day, but I usually find adults to be pretty exhausting."

"But not me?" He kept his eyes locked on hers.

"You can be…annoying, but not exhausting." She said the words slowly, and her eyes widened, and she blew out a breath. "This is freaking me out." And she turned around to where Mercedes was waiting at the living room door.

She wasn't the only one freaked out. Carlo hadn't ever been this comfortable around a woman. Or actually, his agitated inability to take his eyes off Fern wasn't what he'd call comfortable. But he wanted to stick with her. Wanted to protect and help her. Didn't want this private interlude to end.

"Here he comes! Look out!" Mercedes cried as Bull raced into the room, moving with surprising agility on his three legs.

He saw the other two dogs and skidded to a halt.

A low growl came from Brownie's chest, and her hackles rose.

Bull lumbered toward the pair and Carlo watched the dogs closely. In battle, he'd learned to trust his instincts, and he was relying on them now. If a fight started, he'd have to move fast.

Bull reached the mother dog and she stood, moving in front of the puppy. There was still that little growl, maybe a whine, coming from her chest.

And then Bull's stub of a tail started to wag. He sniffed the mama dog and then pushed past her to the pup, and she let him. He sniffed the little one and then jerked his head away from the ointment on the pup's back. Then the old bulldog plopped down on the floor beside their bed, letting out a massive doggy sigh.

"He likes them!" Mercedes said. "Oh, Bull, you're such a good dog! I wish we could have a dog, Mama Fern," she added as a calculating expression came into her eyes.

"That's something to think about." Fern winked at Carlo and he about melted.

"The cookies!" Mercedes cried, and Fern hurried over to check. They pulled them out just in time.

And for all their half burned, half baked gooiness, they were the best cookies Carlo had ever had.

The house got progressively colder—even a gas furnace wouldn't operate without electricity—so they stuck close to the fire. After they'd scrounged for a little dinner and read several storybooks, Fern went upstairs and came down with an armload of blankets. "It's warmest here, so we'll kind of camp out like a pioneer family," she explained to Mercedes as she spread blankets out on the floor.

"And he's like the daddy!" Mercedes pointed at Carlo.

Fern laughed. "Yes, he's like the daddy."

Carlo's conscience nudged him. *Like* nothing. He *was* the daddy.

And here was maybe the only time he'd get to spend with his daughter, so he was going to make the best of it. He got up and helped Fern create a giant nest on the hearth rug. Soon, Mercedes, safe in between the two grown-ups, was yawning in the glow of the fire.

"Tell me the story about the princess," she begged Fern.

"But you've heard it a thousand times. And Carlo doesn't want to hear it."

"Oh, yes, I do." Anything to keep her talking in that quiet, slightly husky voice, and to watch the lamplight glow golden on the hair of his little girl.

It was like something right out of Laura Ingalls Wilder. It was them against nature, their little family against the world. He listened to Fern's story of a princess who had one mama watching over her in heaven and one taking care of her on earth, and marveled at how she nurtured his little girl. Marveled that God had worked so much for good.

He didn't want the moment to stop. And when Mercedes's eyes closed, her lashes dark against flushed cheeks, he wanted to lean over and kiss her forehead, but that might be too weird.

And who was he kidding? He wanted to kiss Fern, too. But that, for sure, he didn't dare to do. "Sleep tight, you two," he said, and made his way to the cold, lonely couch in the next room.

CHAPTER SIX

THE NEXT DAY Fern got out her watercolors and sat at her easel in front of the big picture window. But her eyes couldn't stay on her work. She kept getting distracted by the scene outside.

The day had dawned bright and sunny, but not as cold, and blessedly, the electricity had come back on sometime during the night. There was snow everywhere, and it was above her knees when they'd gone out to feed the dogs at sunrise.

And now Carlo had taken Mercedes outside to build a snowman. "Mama Fern needs some time to herself," he'd said cheerfully after breakfast.

How had he known that?

"So," he'd continued, looking only at Mercedes, "you and I are going to build the biggest snowman in the state of Ohio."

"Yay!"

Fern had felt a moment's hesitation, letting him take Mercedes out. Caring for the child was *her* job. But somehow, the situation felt right, if very strange. Her, Fern Easton, nerd extraordinaire, stranded here with a beautiful little girl and a giant, attractive soldier who normally wouldn't give her the time of day. Stranded, and spending time together like a family.

She'd never in her life felt part of a family. As early as she could remember, she'd known she was the extra, the foster kid, the one on the outside. Even in families that had lots of foster kids, she'd been the quiet one nobody had chosen to play with.

Now she knew it made sense; she'd gone into foster care grieving the loss of her parents, and so any ability she had to attach would have needed to be gently drawn out. She could hear echoes of her own history in Mercedes sometimes, how touchy grief was when the loss of a mother was involved, how it kept reemerging with different events and reminders. From her reading, she knew that the cycle would continue throughout Mercedes's childhood: good months, and then plunging back into sadness again as she reached a new developmental stage.

Fern hadn't had a consistent, understanding caregiver in childhood, so she'd gone inside herself. And yeah, it had damaged her, to the point where she was terminally awkward with people and had only a few friends. Though some part of her longed for love and connection, she knew a warm family life wasn't in the cards for her.

Books had been her consolation and her friends, sometimes her only friends. They still were.

And thinking of books, she needed to concentrate on hers, she scolded herself. She'd been looking forward to this vacation time for ages, as an opportunity to work on the book she was contracted to do. Things hadn't gone as planned, at all, but right at this moment, she had a caregiver for her child and she had time to work. She'd best take advantage of it.

But the scene outside kept tugging at her.

Carlo and Mercedes were working together to lift the second giant snowball on top of the first one. Actually, Carlo was working and Mercedes was being more of a hindrance than a help, like any self-respecting four-year-old. She grabbed the snowball too tight and a big chunk broke off.

But Carlo didn't get mad. He laughed, set what remained of the snowball on top of the first and showed Mercedes how to pack extra snow into the hole she'd created.

He was a patient man, surprisingly patient. In her experience, most dads couldn't handle the antics and illogic and roller-coaster emotions of a preschooler, not as well as moms could. And someone like Carlo, obviously accustomed to the world of men, should have been totally out of his element.

Instead, he seemed amazingly comfortable with Mercedes. He seemed to truly care about her.

Watching them together, seeing their laughing faces, Fern frowned. There was something…some connection…

She shook off the thought, forced her attention back to her work and managed to get an illustration finished. And then, when her thoughts drifted once more to the scene outside the window, she gave up. Gathering a few supplies, she pulled on her warm jacket and went out to help them with the snowman.

"Mama!" Mercedes screamed when she saw Fern. "Look what we did! He's the biggest snowman in the whole state!"

"I think you might be right," Fern said, because the snow giant did indeed stand as tall as Carlo. "But I think he needs eyes and a nose, don't you?"

When she produced a carrot for a nose and chocolate sandwich cookies for eyes, Mercedes was ecstatic and of course, she had to place them herself. So Fern lifted her up while Carlo steadied the snowman. "How about a scarf?" he offered, and removed the plaid one he'd taken from the closet.

His coat was open and his head bare, and he wasn't shivering; he looked white toothed and handsome, and Fern's heart gave a little lurch. This was dangerous stuff. Dangerous, and not for her. She couldn't trust a man like that, and she certainly couldn't interest him. She turned away, feeling suddenly awkward.

And was rewarded with a snowball smacking her in the leg.

"Mama Fern, he threw a snowball at you!" Mercedes cried. "I want to do that, too!"

"No way!" She spun, not wanting…something. For Mercedes to play rough. For Carlo to tease. For them to have fun together as the family that they weren't.

"C'mon, Mercy, I'll help you," Carlo offered.

Fern opened her mouth to protest, but Carlo silenced her with a look. Which was a great trait for a military commander, but supremely annoying in a houseguest.

"But," he continued, "you have to follow the rules of snowballs. Do you know what they are?"

"I didn't know there were rules," Mercedes said, wide-eyed.

"There are. You can't throw a snowball at a person's head or face. And when they say stop, you have to stop."

Yeah, yeah, Mr. Controlling. Fern took advantage of his distraction to land a snowball in the middle of Carlo's back.

"Hey!" In a flash he'd leaned down, scooped and formed a snowball and lobbed it at her. "Don't mess with a soldier, lady!"

"Me, me, I want to do it!" Mercedes cried, jumping up and down, and Carlo helped her form a snowball and throw it.

In for a penny, in for a pound. Fern wasn't going to be able to stop the battle, so she worked out her mixed feelings toward Carlo with a fierce barrage of snowballs, tossing the occasional lob in Mercedes's direction to keep the child happy. And she *was* happy; Fern loved the pink of Mercedes's cheeks and the sparkle in her eyes.

Mercedes hadn't had a man in her life, not much. According to Kath, there had been a few boyfriends, but no one who'd lived in or stuck around.

Seeing the way Mercedes acted with Carlo, her excitement, her tiny flirtations—and seeing the confident, physical way he played with her—Fern realized the benefits a male influence could provide.

Unfortunately, it wasn't in the cards for her to marry and provide that influence. She was just too shy with men.

Unless… Except…

No. This was temporary. God had provided her with so much, giving her Mercedes. She couldn't expect, didn't deserve, any more. She'd have to solve the problem of a male influence for Mercedes another way.

CARLO HATED TO do it, but he turned on the television when they got inside. They'd been out of touch with the outside world for the better part of the day, but it was only right that he check and find out the weather forecast. They needed to know how long they'd be stranded and, if necessary, ration the supplies that were starting to run low.

"Looks as if we'll get some winds and drifting tonight," the local weatherman was saying, "but the winter storm itself seems to be over. And around Ohio, the hardest-hit rural communities are starting to dig themselves out."

"Good news," Carlo made himself say to Fern. "Looks as if we may have one more night, max, before the plows get through."

"That's...great," she said with enthusiasm that sounded forced. Making him wonder if she was enjoying their isolation, at least the slightest little bit.

"Can we have hot chocolate?" Mercedes asked. "And more cookies?"

"Sure," Fern said, smiling at Mercedes.

Trust a kid to stay in the present and remember what was important: hot chocolate after a stint of playing outdoors.

And trust a woman like Fern to know how to do hot chocolate right: in big mugs, with leftover Christmas candy canes for stirrers and big dollops of marshmallow crème.

"Let's watch TV!" Mercedes cried as Fern carried the mugs toward the front room, where the fireplace was.

Fern narrowed her eyes. "Let's read a book *and* watch TV," she proposed. "Which do you want to do first?"

"TV, TV," Mercedes begged, and Fern frowned, cocking her head to one side.

"You can take the woman out of her library, but you can't really take the library out of the woman," Carlo said.

A smile tugged at the corners of her mouth. "Showing my true colors."

"You're good for her," Carlo said. "But there's nothing wrong with a movie now and then."

"Not if we all watch together," Fern said. "And not if

it's—" she studied the shelf of DVDs "—*March of the Penguins*!" She held up the case triumphantly.

"Not a documentary!" Carlo scanned the shelf, knowing his sister would have his favorite movie. "How about *A Christmas Story*? I always wanted a Red Ryder BB gun!"

"Let me see that. A gun? And a PG rating? I don't think so."

And though he fake begged and pleaded, Fern wouldn't back down. And she got Mercedes to vote with her by challenging her to walk like a penguin. And pretty soon they were all doing it, and laughing, and Carlo was giving in.

Truthfully, he didn't much care what movie it was, when he could watch it with this woman and this child and a delicious mug of hot chocolate.

And pretend the world outside wasn't really waiting for them.

CHAPTER SEVEN

HOURS LATER, FERN came downstairs after putting Mercedes to bed. It was dark outside, but way too early to fall asleep, and she felt a sudden sense of trepidation.

The scene in front of her felt scarily intimate. Like one of a million old movies she'd seen.

Slowly, she walked into the room. Fireplace…check. Furry hearth rug…check. Low light…check. Snowstorm outside…check. Handsome man smiling at her…check.

It was a setting for romance, and she knew exactly what was supposed to happen next. Even she herself was a stereotype: the shy librarian who'd take her glasses off and let her hair down and become a beautiful, passionate, at-ease woman.

Except that was where the movie shut down; that was the page missing from the romance novel. She *wasn't* a secretly passionate and beautiful woman waiting to be unleashed.

She stomped in and sat down on the fur rug. It was itchy, and the fire felt hot. She couldn't see anything in the low light. "I can't wait to get out of here," she said, and looked at Carlo defiantly. If he had some other expectation, just because there'd been a few sparks between them, he was going to be disappointed.

Carlo looked at her strangely. "Really?"

"Yeah, really." She knew she sounded hostile, but

it was better than pathetic. "Don't you want to leave?" She figured he was dying to. He'd been kind to stay, but a man like Carlo had a million more exciting things to do than hang with the likes of her.

"No, I don't." He shifted onto his side and propped his head on his elbow. "I'm in no hurry at all for the plows to get through." He leaned back on his elbows and smiled at her.

That smile warmed her face and chest, making her wish for things that women like her never got. She looked away. "I can't wait," she repeated. "I'm going crazy stuck in here."

"Because…"

"It's too hot!" She scooted away from the fire.

Carlo raised an eyebrow. "Take something off."

"Oh, please." She tried to sound casual, sophisticated, like the women he must be used to. Inside, his suggestion made her heart flutter like a caged bird.

He reached out and touched her arm and she jerked violently away.

"I just meant you have about six layers on." He regarded her with a cryptic expression.

Heat rose in her cheeks. She'd misinterpreted his remark as flirting, thinking he might be a little bit attracted to her, especially since there was no one else around.

She reached for safer ground, a change of subject. "So since we have some time," she said, "why don't you tell me about your adventures in Central America?"

His eyebrows lifted, and he looked surprised and a little uncomfortable. *So there, buddy, I'm turning the tables on you.*

"That's not very good entertainment." He sat forward and poked at the fire. "Maybe we should just turn on the game."

As if to disallow that possibility, at that moment the power snapped off again. The room, suddenly dark, seemed to shrink to the circle of two in the fire's low light.

"Must be the rising temperatures," Carlo said. "Makes for heavy snow on trees and power lines." He stood and fumbled for the matches and lit the lamp, which cast its soft glow over the room.

"Hopefully, it won't stay off for as long this time," she said. In reality, she welcomed the dim light, where Carlo couldn't see her embarrassment, or whatever other feelings he stirred in her. "Guess that rules out TV, and you'll have to entertain me."

"Oh, really?"

"By telling me about your adventures." She was back on steady ground now; she'd turned the tables and felt in control. The romantic situation was firmly squashed down, and she could do what she did best: listening.

"Why don't you tell me about you?" he asked, flopping down on his back with a kind of pleading in his voice.

"Nope. Nothing ever happens to me. How come you decided to go to Central America?"

He was silent for a minute, but she let him be, sensing the reason was complicated. Finally, he spoke. "I was looking for a way to use what I'd learned in the army, and make money, and get away from Rescue River. And I was kind of an adrenaline junkie."

"Why doesn't that surprise me?" But she smiled. She could imagine a younger Carlo, restless, wanting to do big things.

"I heard about an outfit that was helping out down

there. Found out I had some sharpshooter skills they needed. The rest…" Through the dim room, she could see him lift his hands. "The rest just played out."

"Did you like it?"

"What, Central America?"

"Fighting. Being a soldier."

Firelight flickered across his face, and a log shifted and burst, sending out sparks and a crackling sound. Fern grabbed a pillow from the couch and put it under her head. Now the fur rug didn't feel scratchy to her, just soft and warm. "Was it…fun? Exciting?"

He let out a dry laugh. "Aah. No. Nobody really likes being a soldier."

"But that's not true. A lot of people are proud of being in the military. Or…paramilitary, whatever it was with you."

"It was both, and being proud of it and liking it are two different things. I'm proud of some of the things we were able to accomplish, but…" He shook his head and shifted, a rustling movement in the dark room. "There's a lot you don't want to know about."

"People do want to know. At the library, military memoirs are getting more popular all the time."

"Especially if they sugarcoat the truth. The only audience that can take the true story are other vets."

"Maybe." She waited, but he obviously wasn't going to talk any more about that. And as a sheltered American who'd benefitted immensely from all that the armed forces had done for her, who was she to argue?

On the other hand, she did want to keep him talking, so things wouldn't go all romantic. So she could stay in control. And most guys loved to talk about themselves. Carlo didn't seem to be fitting that stereotype, but maybe she just hadn't found the right topic. "So why did you become a missionary?"

"Can't we talk about something else? Why did you become a librarian?"

"Because I love books. Why'd you become a missionary?"

He lifted himself up onto his side again and even in the dim light of the fire, she knew he was looking at her. "You're a persistent little thing, aren't you?"

"I've been called…stubborn. Why don't you want to talk about it?" Oh, she was on a roll now. If she could just keep him on edge and talking about himself, he wouldn't try to make some horribly awkward or obligatory move on her. They could both be spared that.

"I can talk about it," he said, "if you're really interested."

"I am."

"Okay, then," he said. "I found Jesus, or rather, He found me."

She leaned toward him, curious. "No atheists in foxholes? Or was it more than that?" She'd had her own, quiet moment of conversion, but a part of her wished for fireworks.

He gave her a wry smile. "I'm sure that's part of it, but no. I think God chases us all our lives. I think He wants us to live His way."

Had God sought her? Fern tucked that away for further consideration. "And being a soldier wasn't His way?"

"Well." He sighed. "Let's just say there was a better way."

He was glossing over the story, she could tell. "I don't believe you."

He sat up straighter. "What?"

"You make it sound all pretty," she said, "but I suspect there's a lot more to the story. And that it's not all cut-and-dried."

"You calling me a liar?"

"No, no. Just a...a whitewasher. Like, why'd you have a knife and practically battle armor in your bag if you're just a sweet innocent missionary now?"

His eyes narrowed just a little. "Being a missionary doesn't mean having life easy. I've probably been in more dangerous situations as a missionary than I was as a soldier. But as long as we're making accusations... I think you're a distractor. I think you want to keep me talking so I don't think about and talk about you."

She picked at a spot on the wooden floor, not looking at him. "What do you mean?"

"I mean," he said, "that you sit over there on the other side of the fireplace with your arms wrapped around your knees, telling me I'm not truthful enough. It keeps the focus off you, and you like it that way."

She couldn't help smiling at how well he'd read her. "Touché. It's working, isn't it?"

His eyes glowed in the firelight, holding hers, and suddenly there was a whole lot more tension in the room. So much so that it felt overwhelming.

"Tell me about your call to be a missionary," she said.

"Why?"

She shrugged. "I'm curious, that's all."

"Why?"

"Because..." She thought about it. "Because God hasn't called me and I want to know what it's like."

"Okay." Apparently satisfied by her answer, he leaned back and cradled his head in his arms, staring up at the ceiling. "It was as if... I couldn't get away. I didn't have peace. I felt Him telling me He wanted to use me. Not in words, but…in thoughts. It was weird."

Fern felt oddly jealous. "Yeah?"

"Yeah. So I'd go into the next village and do what my job required, and I kept thinking, do they know Jesus, have they had the chance? It got to be an obsession. The first thing I'd do is look around, see if anyone had a cross hanging on the wall or a Bible beside their bed."

"And if they didn't?"

"If they didn't, well, no matter how horrible they were being, I couldn't do anything to put them at risk of death. I couldn't contribute to anyone dying unsaved."

"Must have cramped your style as a mercenary."

"Exactly!" He chuckled. "I don't think anyone's ever asked me about this stuff before. It was as if God was pushing me out of fighting for justice and into saving souls."

Fern turned over on her side to see him better and her heart fluttered again. Man, she'd better look out, because she could really fall for this guy. He was good and sincere and manly, not to mention super handsome. His words mesmerized her. A scene from her favorite Shakespeare play flashed into her mind: Othello, the older war general, explaining how Desdemona had fallen in love with him.

"She loved me for the dangers I had passed. And I loved her that she did pity them."

"What?"

Had she said that out loud? She felt her cheeks burning. "Nothing, just thinking."

"About what?"

"About Shakespeare, if you must know." And she wasn't saying any more than that. Wasn't going to tell him she was dreaming about love stories and wishing someone like her could experience romance, too, even if just for the duration of a winter storm.

CARLO LOOKED AT Fern's face, so pretty in the flickering firelight, and drew in his breath. He felt so drawn to her. On a physical level, definitely. Behind those glasses, her eyes were huge. Her hair shone as glossy as polished mahogany around her shoulders, and her petite figure was the perfect slender hourglass. Half the town's library patrons probably came in just to get a glimpse of her.

But her appeal went beyond the physical. She'd drawn him out into talking about things he never talked about, and she really listened, unlike a lot of people for whom conversation was an opportunity to talk about their own issues and lives. She seemed really interested, and she'd made him think.

She was quite a woman, and with the way she was looking at him right now, he was in real danger of losing his heart. But the problem was, it was all going to blow up, and soon. Once the plows came through and they all rejoined the real world, it was just a matter of days until the truth came out about him being Mercedes's father.

Now he wished he'd told her right away. What would have been the harm? He should have announced his suspicions that first night, despite being sick as a dog and dizzy and unsure.

Yeah, he'd had his reasons. He hadn't wanted her to get mad and kick him out and then be stuck here alone. Before that, he remembered, he'd wanted to investigate the situation and pick up clues about how to approach getting custody of Mercedes.

He'd never dreamed he'd get to feel so close to her.

That he'd care what she thought of him, or that it would matter if she hated him.

Because she would hate him, he was pretty sure of that. No matter how he tried to explain it, the reality was that he'd withheld the truth. And Fern, who was stubborn and upright and moral in addition to being cute and a very good mother, wouldn't stand for that.

So he needed to do everything he could now to convince her he was a good guy. And although he really wanted to drag her into his arms and kiss the shadows away from her eyes, he needed to resist the temptation of those full, pretty lips.

He sat up and moved a little back and rubbed his hands together. "Enough about me. What about you, Fern? Don't you feel called to what you do?"

She cocked her head to one side. "I'm not sure."

"Being a librarian is doing good in the world, right? And if the Rescue River library is anything like it used to be, it does a lot for the poorer people in the community."

"Yes, I remember you said you used to take your sister there."

He held up a hand. "Stop trying to turn the tables. I want to hear about you, not talk more about myself."

She stuck out her lower lip in an unconsciously pretty pout. "I don't like talking about myself."

"Talk about the library, then. Do you still have programs for the poor and rural kids?"

She hesitated, then nodded. "Yes. We just started a new one, in fact. Some of the migrant kids can't get library cards because they don't have a permanent address. So we started the friendly sponsor program. People in the community can offer their address to a migrant family, sort of guaranteeing that the books will come back. It ends up building some nice connections, in addition to making sure the kids can have plenty of books to read."

"Folks will do that?"

"The response has been amazing." In the dim light, her eyes glowed. "We thought we'd have a waiting list for the migrant kids, but instead, we have a waiting list of families wanting to sponsor them. I love Rescue River."

"Pretty impressive," he said. "And that was probably all your idea."

She looked down, then met his eyes, a smile tugging at the corners of her mouth. "Yeah. It was."

"And you don't think God has anything to do with your being in Rescue River and working at the library?"

Her brow wrinkled as she stared into the fire. "I don't know, maybe He does. I like my job and I've been able to help with some good things."

He noticed her modesty, her humility, and liked it. "But..."

"But what I really want to do is write and illustrate children's books. I could reach even more people that way. And it's as if there's something tugging at me all the time, pulling me into myself, into my...my dreamworld. I have so many ideas I want to share."

"Now that sounds like God."

"Is it? I can't tell. I feel selfish for even wanting to write."

"Selfish?" It was the last word he'd associate with someone who'd just taken in her friend's kid to raise. "How come?"

"Because it's so much fun!" She leaned back and looked up at the ceiling. "I have to kind of steel myself to go to work at the library every day, because it means so much time interacting with people. I'm an introvert, and it tires me out."

"I can relate," he said. "I need time to recharge myself."

"But when I'm writing and illustrating my children's books, I feel as if I could work all through the night and never stop. I have endless energy for it."

"And your work in the library has helped you, I'm sure. But maybe God's telling you it's time to go in a different direction."

Her eyes widened as she looked up at him. "Do you think so?"

His breath caught. Something about this pretty, passionate woman confiding in him and asking his advice took him to a place he'd never gone before. "Yeah," he said, reaching out to touch her chin with one finger. "Yeah, I think so."

Her eyes went wide and conscious then, and her tongue flicked across her lips. Sudden awareness of him as a man, he could guess that much, and he didn't know what to do about it.

Back in his previous life, he'd have known exactly what to do. With his wife, they'd been on the same page. Marriage had been more of an impulse than a true commitment.

He hadn't understood true commitment back then, and his actions had shown it. His choice of a wife had shown it.

But now it was different. He'd found Christ and realized the error of his ways. He'd learned what God wanted for a man and a woman, and it wasn't a one-night stand or even a short, intense relationship.

It was for life.

And he wasn't good for life. Not now, maybe not

ever. He was still feeling his way with God, trying to understand where his work was supposed to go and who was supposed to be a part of it. So far, the only message he'd gotten clearly was that he needed to try to take care of his daughter.

Which he'd assumed would mean sweeping her away from an unsuitable and neglectful foster family and raising her himself.

He hadn't guessed he'd end up half falling in love with the wonderful woman who was already doing a pretty fine job raising his daughter.

He couldn't help it; he leaned in closer. Those full lips were so pretty and her eyes soft and questioning. He reached out and ran a hand along her hair, and it was just as soft and silky as it looked.

She opened her mouth and started to speak, then closed it.

He let his fingers tangle in her hair, just a little. "Is this okay?"

She bit her lip. "I… I don't know."

"How come?" She was as jumpy and nervous as a fawn and he needed to tread carefully here. His hormones were leading, for sure, but he needed to follow his heart and soul, as well.

She shook her head rapidly and looked away. "I just don't do this kind of thing," she said to the wall, her voice so soft he could barely hear it.

"Because…because why?"

She shook her head hard again and looked down. Were those tears in her eyes?

"Hey," he said, "we're not doing any particular kind of thing right now, okay? No need to be worried."

Her face went pink. "I didn't mean… I didn't expect you to…" She met his eyes, her face miserable. "I'm not the kind of woman men make passes at. Especially men like you."

He felt his eyebrows lift almost into his hairline. "That's hard to believe."

"No, it's true," she said. "I don't really date."

"Do you...have some kind of belief against it?" He knew she was a Christian, a fairly new one, and sometimes people put tight limits on themselves as new Christians. Though he couldn't imagine that Fern needed them. She seemed like such a balanced, thinking woman.

"No. I just don't get asked out."

"You're kidding."

"Not kidding." She tossed her hair out of her eyes and looked at him with a touch of defiance. "Guys just don't see me that way."

"You sure you're not putting up some kind of vibe against being approached?"

She cocked her head, then nodded decisively. "That, too."

"You're not putting out that vibe with me." He let his hand curl into her hair again, and a whiff of flowery shampoo floated his way.

Lord, help! He wasn't going to be able to stop if he started kissing her.

"I'm not putting out that vibe because... I'm drawn to you." Her words were so quiet that Carlo had to lean in to hear them.

He shut his eyes, still holding on to her. *Lord, what do I do now?*

But he already knew the answer: back off. Fern was an amazing woman, one of a kind, and she deserved much better than someone as damaged and bad at relationships as he was. Someone who was, even now, withholding the truth from her. She deserved a real chance at love.

He slid his hand out of her hair reluctantly, and put it on her shoulder. There, that was good. That was friendly and impersonal. "We're both vulnerable. It's been a long couple of days." He swallowed hard and let his hand drop. Made himself lean back away from her.

Her eyes widened with an expression of utter betrayal. "You made me tell you I'm attracted and then... Really, Carlo?"

"I'm sorry." His body was still at a fever pitch and he'd used up every ounce of his store of human kindness and patience and self-control. "I just don't think it's a good idea."

"You've got that right." She scrambled to her feet and spun around. "I can trust you to watch the fire, at least?" Her cheeks held high spots of color and her voice sounded shaky.

"Um, sure." Clearly, he'd done something wrong. He'd been trying to do the right thing, and he'd screwed up. At least with her, but maybe not with God, because backing off from romance, given the major secret he was keeping, was definitely the right thing to do.

But keeping his emotional distance wasn't easy, and he needed physical distance to do it. "I'll handle the fire," he said more gruffly than he'd intended. "Go on up to bed."

CHAPTER EIGHT

"MAMA FERN, MAMA Fern, there's trucks outside! And it's sunshining!" Forty pounds of excited four-year-old landed on Fern's stomach.

Fern squeezed her eyes against the bright light and wrapped her arms around Mercedes, turning on her side to snuggle the child close. "You're *my* sunshine, sweets."

But inside, she felt as if one of those snowplows—which she could now hear scraping and grinding gears out on the road—had run right over her.

After Carlo's abrupt rejection, she'd tossed and turned much of the night. She'd replayed it over and over in her mind: the way he'd gotten her talking, the things he'd shared, how close she'd felt to him, how comfortable. Had that been false?

She'd actually told him she was attracted to him. Hot embarrassment flooded her chest and neck and face even now.

"Let's go tell Mr. Carlo!" Mercedes wiggled in her arms and, when Fern let her go, bounced upright.

Fern couldn't face him, not yet. "Mama needs to shower and get dressed. You can go tell him."

"Okay!" The child jumped down to the floor and ran out, yelling, "Mr. Carlo! Mr. Carlo! There's trucks!"

It was just another stab, how quickly Mercedes had gotten attached to Carlo. She'd expect them to stay friends, would want to see him.

Fern drew in deep breaths, a calming strategy she'd learned from a social worker way back when she was a kid and something awful happened. *Just get through the next hour, the next week.* Pretty soon the snowplows would break through, and they wouldn't have to see each other every hour of every day.

After that, Angelica would come home and Fern's vacation would be over. She could go back to her small life in her little house down the street from the library. She could focus on Mercedes and her job and her children's books. No more pretending that she could make it in the normal adult world of happy, promising relationships.

She wrapped her arms around her hollow-feeling stomach and trudged to the bathroom, but even a long, hot shower didn't lift her spirits.

Breakfast felt strained, even punctuated by Mercedes's happy talk and the sound of the plows and a few other vehicles driving by outside. Apparently, the county had gotten the road clear. Fern broke her own rule about keeping her phone away from the table and texted John Allen Bunting, who plowed the farm roads and driveways. From him she learned it would be another hour or two before they were fully out.

Before Carlo could leave.

Oh, she wanted him gone. It hurt to look at him. Because like a fool, she'd gone further than getting attracted to him. Somewhere during the past three days of snowbound privacy, she'd lost a piece of her heart to the man.

To avoid him, she washed the breakfast dishes by hand, looking out the window into the blindingly sunny, snowy world. When would John Allen and his plow come? When could she escape this torture of being stuck in the house with the man who'd broken through the walls around her heart just so he could crush it?

"Hey." He touched her shoulder, a tiny taste of the fruit forbidden to her. "You okay?"

"Fine." That came out harsh, so she tossed him a fake smile to soften it. Trying to be subtle, she eased her shoulder out from under his hand.

Instead of letting her go, he clamped his hand down tighter. "No. Uh-uh. What's wrong?"

"Nothing's wrong!" She spun hard away from his hand and from that patient, patronizing tone in his voice. As if she were Mercedes's age. *Come on, John Allen, get your plow out here.*

He took a step backward, hands up. "Whoa. What's going on? Are you upset about last night?"

"Just…leave…me…alone." She ground out the words through clenched teeth and turned back to the sink, plunging her hands into the warm, soapy water.

He started to walk away and then turned back. "No. No, I'm not willing to leave it like that. The plows will be here soon and I—"

"Let's hope," she interrupted and then stared down at the suds, taking deep breaths. "Where's Mercedes? Would you mind keeping her busy for a little while?"

"She's playing with her dolls. She's fine."

And indeed Fern could hear the chirp of Mercedes's pretend voices from the living room.

Get a grip on yourself. At all costs, she had to avoid letting him see into her soul again. Had to protect herself from more of the hurt that had kept her awake all night. Staying inside herself was safer.

No fighting. That was too passionate. "Did you sleep okay?" she asked brightly, grabbing a cup and plunging it into the soapy water.

"Fern. That's already clean." He reached in and pulled the cup away from her, and their hands touched in the soapy water, slippery and warm.

Something like electricity shot through Fern's hand, up her arm and straight to her heart. Carlo's spicy aftershave tickled her nose.

He sucked in his breath. "Talk to me. What's going on?"

She pulled away from all the feelings and shook her head.

"Last night, I felt we were getting so close. And now you've shut me off."

"You shut *me* off!" The words burst from her and she clenched her jaw to keep from saying more.

He was still standing so close, half behind her, and he leaned sideways to see her face.

She tucked her head down, but heard his soft exclamation.

He moved away and the space where he'd been felt cold, as cold as the icicles that hung outside the windows, sparkling and dripping in the sunlight.

And then he was back with a dish towel. He took her ever so gently by the elbows and pulled her away from the sink. Turned her around as if she were a child—and she was, size-wise, compared to him—and dried her hands. "Come on," he said, pulling her toward the table. "Sit down. I have to talk to you."

She didn't want this, didn't want to get into some long discussion of her own inadequacies. Clearly, he felt bad. "It's… I have a lot to do before the plows come. And you do, too. You have to get your stuff together."

A muscle twitched in his jaw. "I know, but I think we've got ten minutes for a conversation, right?"

She looked at the clock on the wall, an absurd teakettle with a face. "I'm not going to get out of this, am I?"

"No, Fern. We need to talk."

She jerked out a kitchen chair and sat down. "So talk." She was behaving like a sulky teenager, but it was better than being a lovesick idiot.

He raised an eyebrow and spun another chair around so he could straddle it, leaning his arms on the chair's back as he faced her. "I'm sorry I let those romantic feelings build last night. Is that what you're upset about?"

Let him think so. Let him think the mousy librarian was offended by his miserable joke of a pass. "Sure."

"I… I try to live a good Christian life, but of course I fail a lot, like every other human. You're pretty and real and warm. I got attracted to you, and I let it show."

She nodded without looking at him. He hadn't gotten all that attracted, apparently; he hadn't even kissed her.

He ran a hand over his hair. "In that kind of situation, when I'm feeling stressed or pressured or tempted, I try to grab on to God. He helps me, but it's not always pretty."

"Oh, yeah, I'm sure you've been in that kind of situation a lot."

He cocked his head to one side. "Lots of emergencies, yeah."

"Lots of women, too, I'm sure." Why was she talking about this? She sounded like a jealous fool.

He shook his head slowly. "Not so many women. I was thinking more of other kinds of danger. You get good at those battlefield prayers." He studied her. "No, I haven't felt like that about a woman in… Well, ever."

"Right."

"It's true. There's a, I don't know, some kind of spiritual dimension to what I—"

"Look, why are you trying to flatter me? It was crystal clear that you didn't want to kiss me, and I understand that. There's no need to pretend otherwise. In fact, it's kind of insulting."

He reached out and put a hand on either side of her face, forcing her to look at him. "I'm not lying. I really wanted to kiss you."

Was it true? Could it be true?

"I wish…" He broke off, shaking his head.

"What?" He looked so concerned and so vulnerable that her hurt feelings floated away. Borne by that line he'd started to say… What was it? That there was a spiritual dimension to what he felt for her?

Could a librarian and a mercenary be soul mates?

He flashed a smile that just about devastated her. "I wish we could stay here awhile longer. Just the three of us."

And then he unstraddled the chair, stood and pulled her into a hug.

She wanted to protest. Needed to protest, needed to stop this. But the truth was his touch felt wonderful. The careful and respectful way he cradled her against his chest made her feel safe, safe in a way she never had felt before in her life.

She remembered seeing other kids held by their parents like this, cuddled lovingly but with nothing malicious in the intention, no worries that things were going to go in a wrong direction. The only times she'd been hugged or held, that she could remember anyway, there'd been an accompanying smell of liquor on the breath and hands where they shouldn't have been. Those times, she'd struggled to get away.

And she'd learned to cross her arms and look away and keep her distance. She'd learned that getting close only led to something that felt ugly, a mockery of closeness. With a flash she understood why nobody ever asked her out: she'd learned to put out the "go away" signal, and she'd forgotten to let go of it after she was an adult and safe.

Only Carlo had cared enough to push past that barrier, and he'd done it last night. He'd gotten her to talk, and touch, and feel. He'd told her of his admiration for her and he'd listened closely to how she felt.

And when the time came for them to make a decision about where to go next, he'd backed off respectfully, choosing the wiser route for both of them.

Fern was an independent woman and she never, ever relied on anyone except herself. But maybe, just maybe, Carlo was someone else she could rely on a little bit.

He brushed back her hair and touched the corner of her mouth and looked into her eyes without smiling. "I still want to kiss you."

From a place inside her that she hadn't known existed came a half smile and a warm feeling. "Why don't you do it, then?" The words came out in a husky whisper, not sounding like a prim, shy librarian at all.

His eyes went dark and he looked at her lips, then back at her eyes. "You're sure?"

She only nodded, staring at him.

"Whatever else happens," he said, "whatever you see or hear or think in the future, just remember one thing."

"What's that?" Her voice came out a breathy whisper and she was warm, so warm. She leaned toward him, her tongue wetting her dry lips. She'd never kissed anyone before, not except for a quick peck at the end of a bad date, but for some reason she had no fear at all. She knew Carlo could guide her through this.

She let her hand tighten on his arm, feeling the muscle bulge beneath his thermal shirt, and drew in her breath with a gasp.

"I want you to remember, this is what's real." He touched her cheek with the tenderness she'd longed for her whole life.

And then he proceeded to kiss her thoroughly.

Now, WHY HAD he done that? As soon as Fern got up and walked wobbly across the room, leaned back against the counter and stared at him, hand to her mouth, Carlo started yelling at himself inside his head.

You're an idiot!

She's gonna be even more upset when she finds out the truth!

Should have stuck with the program from last night!

But kissing her had felt so very good. So perfectly *right*, and that was something he'd never experienced before. Kissing her, and not just that, but being here with her, felt like coming home. To a home he'd never had.

He was feeling an urge to pull Fern and Mercedes to him and never let go, to stay on a snowy farm with them forever.

And to do that, he needed to tell her the truth before the plows broke through. The idea of letting her know that he was almost for sure Mercedes's father made him break out sweating.

"We need to talk," he said before he could chicken out. "There's something I—"

"Let's play a game!" Mercedes came racing in, her hair a messy tangle of curls, still in her princess nightgown. She flung herself against Fern, looking up. "Please?"

So adorable, and Carlo felt a surge of love for her that was qualitatively different from anything he'd ever felt in his life. He'd lived to protect kids—that was half of what he'd been doing, fighting in Central America—but his own child multiplied anything he'd ever felt before by a number too big to name.

Even more important that he tell Fern, so that the two of them could work it out and figure it out, could do this right, in a way that made it good for Mercedes. "We'll play in a minute, honey," he said as Fern scooped the child up. "I have to talk to Mama Fern first."

Fern snuggled her face into Mercedes's hair and then cut her eyes at him. "But sometimes Mama Fern doesn't like to talk. Right, Mercedes?"

"That's right," Mercedes explained to Carlo, her face serious. "Sometimes Mama Fern's ears hurt from listening and her mouth hurts from talking, and we have to be quiet."

Fern's cheeks went the most perfect shade of pink. "And that's because…" she prompted.

"It's not anything bad about you," Mercedes said, reaching out to pat Carlo's arm reassuringly. "It's just the way Mama is made."

Carlo's heart expanded enough to hold a little more love. God bless a woman who could explain instead of yelling or shutting down, who could make a talkative little girl feel supportive and understanding about her mama's need for quiet time.

Fern was an amazing mother. And an amazing woman. And he really, really needed to find a way to tell her the truth.

"What game should we play, sweets?" she asked.

"I'll go get one of Xavier's!" Mercedes ran into the living room. He heard cupboard doors flung open, boxes rattling as they crashed to the ground. "Sorry," Mercedes sang as she banged the boxes around.

"Fern—"

"Looks as if John Allen just started on the farm road," she said, flitting away from him, hurrying through the door and into the living room to peer out the picture window. "It'll be a while until he digs our vehicles out."

He followed. "But just real quick—"

"It's an introvert thing." She put a hand on her hip and mock glared up at him. "Don't you get it? I need time to process things before I can talk about them."

"Let's play this one!" Mercedes produced a game from the stack and hurried to the fire. "You come sit here," she ordered, tugging at Carlo until he caved in and sat where she was pointing. "And, Mama, you sit here."

She'd positioned the adults on either side of herself, and they formed a little semicircle facing the fire. Facing away from the window, from the outside world.

Carlo drew in a breath and tasted a mix of happiness and fear, more intense than anything he'd felt in the worst jungle firefight.

"Come on, let's play!"

Obviously, Fern wasn't going to let him have the conversation he needed to have right now. And obviously, they couldn't have that conversation in front of Mercedes. So he did what he'd done in battle: forced himself to stay in the moment.

You did that by focusing on sensations, not thoughts. So Carlo took deep breaths, catching the whiff of baby shampoo from Mercedes's hair and something muskier from Fern's. He looked at the colorful children's game and stretched out his hand to the warmth of the flickering fire. Felt the soft fur of the rug beneath them, their little island.

"Your turn!" Mercedes nudged him, and he tried to understand the game. "What do I do?" he asked.

Fern chuckled. "It's for ages three and up," she said, holding up the box lid to show him. "It's not that complicated."

"You have to take your guy through the maze without waking up the daddy," Mercedes explained. "If you land on the ones where you have to push the button, you might wake him up."

Carlo obediently rolled the dice and took a card.

When Mercedes was done with her turn and Fern was taking hers, Mercedes looked at him seriously. "I don't have this game at home," she explained, "because I don't have a daddy."

"Oh, really?" His heart thudded in a sick way.

"Xavier has a daddy," she said thoughtfully. "So he has this game about daddies."

"I see." He glanced over at Fern, feeling that his guilt was written all over his face. But she was checking her texts, not paying any attention to their conversation.

"Xavier *got* a daddy," Mercedes said, studying him. "He didn't have one, but then he got one."

Was this his cue to speak? He stared into the brown eyes so like his little sister's. *Lord? A little help here?*

"Right, Mama?" Mercedes leaned against Fern.

"What, sweets?"

"Xavier didn't have a daddy, but he got one," Mercedes explained patiently. "Maybe he—" she pointed at Carlo "—maybe *he* could be my daddy."

Carlo's heart just about exploded out of his chest, worse than that time a land mine had gone off six paces away from him and his buddy.

And just like then, he had the urge to preserve the person at risk. Had to protect Mercedes from finding out wrong, had to keep Fern from saying something negative about Mercedes's absentee daddy that would come back to haunt him.

He opened his mouth and closed it again. What could he say? Where did he start?

"Every family is different, honey," Fern said, stroking Mercedes's hair. She didn't look at Carlo, and he saw that her cheeks were pink. "It's hard not to have a daddy sometimes, isn't it?"

"Yeah." Mercedes scrunched her nose. "It would be fun to have a real daddy to wake up for real, not just in a game. And for Donuts with Dad at school."

Relief flooded him, a cowardly relief as he realized the moment of absolutely having to tell Mercedes the truth was passing, thanks to Fern's tactful words.

Right behind the relief, the enormity of what he'd done by not being there crashed into Carlo all over again. Mercedes had been going through life without a dad. Seeing other kids whose dads were there for them and knowing she wasn't protected like that. Of thinking her daddy knew about her and didn't care enough to show up.

"I know. Donuts with Dad was hard." Fern side hugged Mercedes and nuzzled her hair. "I didn't look much like a dad, did I?"

The pressure on him averted, Carlo stared at Fern. "You went to her Donuts with Dad day?"

"Well, yeah. She didn't have anyone else."

"There weren't any other single moms there?"

"Tommy Tremain had his grandpa there, because his dad's in a war," Mercedes explained. "And Sierra doesn't have a daddy, but her uncle came, and he's a fireman. Chief…" She looked over at Fern for help.

"Chief Kenny. Kenny Snyder," she added for Carlo's

benefit. "Most people around here have extended families who can step in and help at times like that," Fern explained to Carlo. "But I… Well, I don't. And Kath's family isn't anywhere nearby."

"So that left you." His heart hurt, a little bit for Fern and a lot for Mercedes. And for himself, because he'd have loved to be there, but he hadn't even known he'd had a child.

"Yeah, I was the only woman." Fern wrinkled her nose. "A bit awkward. I'm not too good at talking sports with the daddies, but I can eat doughnuts really well, huh?" She ruffled Mercedes's hair.

"And Sierra's uncle sat by you the whole time!" Mercedes proclaimed. She cocked her head to one side. "Maybe *he* could be my daddy. Then I'd have a fireman. A chief!"

"Um, no." Fern was blushing now, and she snuck a glance at Carlo through her hair.

Carlo guessed all the dads had liked having Fern there. Especially Kenny Snyder, whom Carlo had known as a kid. Somehow Fern had gotten the idea that she wasn't attractive, but that was a bunch of hooey. Even her shyness was just…cute. The men had probably fallen all over each other to make her feel comfortable.

And that was a picture he needed to get out of his head, because it made him want to storm in and claim her in front of the whole town.

As they turned their attention back to the game, Carlo studied Fern. In all that conversation about fathers—which sounded as though Fern and Mercedes had been over before—Fern hadn't said one negative word about Mercedes's missing biological dad. He was grateful for that. And he could see, too, that telling Mercedes the truth about his own identity as her father would have to be handled delicately. She was of an age where she was noticing things, noticing how she fit into the world and how her own family compared with others.

He needed to get Fern aside and tell her the truth about his connection to Mercedes, but it might not happen today. Even now he could hear the snowplows scraping on the road, bringing the outside world closer.

He looked at the two heads bent over the game. Both with shiny brown hair, lit by sun, they looked like mother and daughter.

They looked beautiful, and he wanted to wrap his arms around both of them and protect them from a world that was all too cold and dangerous.

Treasure this moment. Because everything was going to change all too soon.

Could they just have one more hot chocolate? One more laugh over a silly mistake Mercedes made in the game? One more shy exchange of glances in front of a roaring fire?

But now the scraping sound was right outside the door, as if someone was shoveling the sidewalk, and Bull started to bark while the mama dog, Brownie, gave a low-keyed woof, as well.

When the knock came, Mercedes jumped up while Fern held on to Bull. "Don't ever open the door without an adult to help you check who's there," Fern warned. "Could you get that?" she asked Carlo.

He strode to the door right behind Mercedes. "Lift me up," she ordered, and he swung her into his arms so she could look out the high windows on the door.

And who was he kidding? So he'd get another chance to hold his daughter.

He looked out, too, and saw a smiling, bundled-up

stranger with a shovel in hand. Drew in a breath, took one glance back at their warm, private haven.

Then he opened the door with his daughter in his arms and a sense of impending doom.

CHAPTER NINE

As THE DOOR opened, Fern took one last look around the room where they'd spent much of the past three days. With game boxes scattered across the floor, it looked a little messy, but the fire and the lamp and the mugs they'd used for hot chocolate brought back memories already.

It had been an unforgettable bonding time for her and Mercedes. And Carlo had been a huge part of that. Unexpectedly, he'd woven his way into the world she was building with herself and her child...and she hadn't minded one bit.

"Hey, hey!" It was Kenny Snyder, the fire chief, coming inside, stomping the snow off his boots. He was a warm, caring man, a deacon at their church. And so big and blustery and loud that she always found him a bit overwhelming.

"Sierra!" Mercedes shouted, and Fern realized that Chief Kenny had his niece, just a little older than Mercedes, with him. "I built a snowman, did you see?"

"I did, too." Sierra surveyed the room and then looked up at her uncle, shrugging off her coat. "Can I play with Mercedes?"

"Sure. That's why I brought you." He bent down to help her take off her snowy boots, talking to Fern and Carlo at the same time. "Everyone from the congregation knew you were stranded out here and we were all concerned. Since I'm a deacon, I got elected to come and check on you. And since little miss here was driving her mom crazy at home, I decided to bring her along to see her friend Mercedes."

"That was nice of you," Fern said. "Come on in, Sierra. You can pet Bull, just be gentle. He's an older gentleman." She made sure the child knew how to interact with a dog and then loosened her grip on Bull, who proceeded to lick Sierra's hands.

Mercedes was still up in Carlo's arms, and Chief Kenny cocked his head to one side and looked at both of them, a puzzled expression on his face.

"This is Carlo Camden. Angelica's brother?" She hurried to introduce the two men as Mercedes struggled to get out of Carlo's arms. "He showed up unexpectedly to visit his sister just as the storm was started, so he's been here with us."

"We knew each other in school, but it's been a while." Carlo put Mercedes down and held out his hand to shake with Kenny, who was still studying him with some puzzlement. "We made it through the storm just fine. Fern and Mercedes were troupers, even when the power went out. But it'll be good to get some help with the dogs again."

As if on cue, Bull barked once and that roused Brownie and her puppy. Once little Sierra saw them, there was no question about where the girls would play. "Explain to Sierra how to be gentle with Spots," Fern called over the children's excited shrieks, knowing Mercedes would love to be the authority figure to the other girl.

Their little private world had been invaded, and Fern couldn't help regretting it. Spending time with Carlo had been surprisingly peaceful—well, mostly—but

Chief Kenny and his niece were loud and energetic and it was already giving her a headache.

As was the fact that he kept staring at Carlo. What was that all about?

And then she realized that he was probably thinking they'd spent the nights together. Her face heated, not only because of the inference but because it had a tiny basis in truth. An attraction *had* grown between them, culminating in some romantic moments last night and a very sweet kiss this morning. One that had left her feeling full of promise.

Still, she needed to do damage control, because Chief Kenny was a big talker and knew everyone in town. "Um, Carlo, when you go out to your truck, I can help carry your stuff. From the TV room. Where you slept."

Carlo looked at her blankly. "Okay."

She shot him a "help me out here" look and went past the girls into the TV room, returning with a pile of blankets and pillows. "Carlo slept in there," she said pointedly to Chief Kenny.

"Oh!" Light dawned on the man's face. "Well, of course he did! It's great you had some help." He kept looking at Carlo. "I just can't shake this weird idea... Mercedes, honey, come over here a minute."

Always eager to please, Mercedes ran over.

"Stand right there."

"Uncle Kenny!" Sierra complained. "We want to play with the puppy."

Carlo rubbed the back of his neck. His face had gone pale and he opened his mouth as though he wanted to say something. But no words came out.

"Can I go back and play with Sierra now?" Mercedes asked politely, and Fern smiled at her daughter's good manners.

The chief nodded. "Sure, of course." After she was safely occupied with Sierra, over in the corner where the dogs were, he turned to Carlo again. "Mercedes looks exactly like you used to look as a kid," he said. "I just can't shake the idea that you're somehow related. You look as alike as father and daughter! Of course that couldn't be." He looked from Carlo to Mercedes and back again. "Could it?"

Fern looked at Carlo, waiting for him to laugh off the fire chief's odd notion.

But Carlo's face was still and sad and solid. "It's possible, but Mercedes doesn't know," he said quietly. He shot her a quick glance, then looked back at Kenny. "Neither does Fern. There are a lot of steps to take, so I'd prefer you keep that speculation to yourself."

Chief Kenny lifted his hands like stop signs. "Of course! Of course! Sorry." He went on talking while Fern's world whirled into a faster and faster rhythm until she thought she might pass out from the dizzy feelings.

Chief Kenny had asked if Carlo was Mercedes's father.

And rather than denying it, he'd said, "Mercedes doesn't know."

She reached for a chair arm and sank slowly onto the edge of the chair, because her legs felt so shaky. "You said Mercedes didn't know," she said to Carlo, her brow furrowing. "And that I didn't. Does that mean… you did?"

He squeezed his eyes shut for a moment and then came over to squat in front of her. Chief Kenny was still talking, backing away, going across the room to kneel down by the girls and the dogs.

"Fern… I—"

"You *did* know. Is it true? Are you Mercedes's father?"

"I—"

"Don't you dare lie to me." She kept her voice soft so Mercedes wouldn't hear, but the fury she felt had to be coming through. "Anymore. Don't lie anymore."

"Fern. When I got here, I was sick. Practically delirious. I had no idea of finding...of finding my daughter in this house. I came to see Angelica."

She couldn't even process his words, because the enormity of what she'd just learned was pressing down on her. *Carlo was Mercedes's father.*

If it was true, if he was Mercedes's father, then all his kindness was false. Mercedes's father had left her, abandoned her, left her to live with Kath when she was deep into drugs. He'd let Mercedes be neglected and scared and alone all those years, put her at risk.

"You're a big military hero, but you couldn't take care of your own child?" The words burst out of her.

He blinked and shook his head back and forth, slowly. "I didn't know about her, Fern. I didn't even know she existed until a few weeks ago."

"How can that be?" Her voice had a little hitch in it, and she took a couple of deep, gasping breaths to calm down. "How could you not know?"

"Kathy kicked me out and I went back to the jungle." His voice was patient, calm. Infuriatingly so.

"Doing your important missionary work?" He was still squatting in front of her chair, trapping her, and she couldn't bear it. She nudged at him with the side of her foot. "Could you...move?"

He shuffled over to the side, still on his knees and too close. "I wanted to try to work things out with her, Fern. That's why I came home, after I found the Lord."

She waved her hand. "You keep talking and talking. You're full of excuses. But a little girl has suffered. Your own child."

Suddenly, Mercedes was there, looking worried, putting a hand on each of them. "Stop fighting! Kind words and inside voices."

"Sorry, Mercy." She kept the words in a whisper to hide her near hysteria. And she looked: from Carlo to Mercedes, from Mercedes to Carlo.

How had she not noticed what Chief Kenny had seen instantly? What kind of idiot was she?

She drew in another breath and forced calm into her voice. "Run and play with Sierra, honey. Look, she's holding Spots!"

Mercedes turned. "No, not like that, two fingers!" she cried, and ran toward Sierra. Chief Kenny was beside her, looking their way with concern.

"Let's go in the kitchen and talk," Carlo suggested, and even though she didn't want to do anything the man said, she recognized that he was right. She wasn't going to get any less upset. And she didn't need Mercedes seeing that.

God had chosen *this* man to do missionary work? Really?

She got to her feet, shaking off Carlo's helpful touch at her elbow, and walked to the kitchen on stiff, old-lady legs. She felt as if she'd been hit by a sledgehammer. She felt as if she were going to die.

"Are you here to take her from me?" she demanded as soon as they were in the kitchen.

He pulled out a chair for her. "Fern, there's so much we need to talk through. And I can't tell you how sorry I am to upset you like this."

"You *are* here to take her away. You tricked me on

purpose, to get her to like you, and it worked, and now you're going to take her away." At the idea of losing Mercedes, a huge dark gulf opened inside her. She wrapped her arms around herself and stared down at the floor, trying to hold herself together.

She'd tried so hard to give Mercedes everything she needed, and it had brought her so much joy to do it. And Mercedes was making progress, feeling more secure by the day. To change things now, to have her go live with her father...with Carlo... She lifted her eyes to look at him. "I'm not letting you have her."

"Look, Fern, I know you're angry. We can talk this through."

His kind, understanding tone lit a fire in her. *He* wasn't upset. *He* wasn't angry.

Because he was the one who had just calmly ruined her life and that of the little girl she loved.

"You can talk all you want." She stood up then, poked him in the chest. "You can tell me all your excuses. But here's what I know. You've neglected this child for her whole life, the whole time she needed you, and now you've come in and messed her up again. She thinks you're just some nice man, and now she'll have to find out you're her father, and you were lying to her!"

The calm expression was gone from Carlo's face now. He'd gone white, and now he took a step back, his fists clenching at his sides.

"What?" she taunted. "Nothing to say now? Why don't you try sweet-talking me? It worked to distract me from the truth before."

"I've got plenty to say." His voice sounded stiff, guarded. "But I'd better not say it."

"Go ahead," she challenged. This anger felt way better than despair.

"Fern, you're not thinking of that little girl in there. You're thinking of yourself and your own hurt feelings."

She narrowed her eyes at him. "You have no idea what's going on in my head."

"All I know," he said, "is that Mercedes wants a daddy. And now that I know about her, I'm here to be one. I think you're mad because it interferes with your neat little plan to have complete control of her."

"Oh, that's nice." She put her hands on her hips. "Start accusing me, will you? Take the spotlight off yourself. Maybe I *am* mad that you lied to me. That you…that you kissed me, just to get close to me so you could take Mercedes!" Was that true? Had his advances toward her been just about trying to get his daughter back?

She'd thought it was weird that a big, handsome, charismatic man like him was attracted to a mousy little librarian like her, but somehow, this morning, he'd made it seem believable. She'd gotten all happy. She'd even started imagining a future with him. But it was a big lie. "I need a moment," she said, and went into the pantry and slammed the door behind her, taking deep, gulping breaths, trying to regain control. Because if she didn't, if she really let go, she might never pull herself together again.

As soon as Fern left the room, Carlo sank down at the kitchen table and let his head fall into his hands.

How had everything gone so terribly wrong?

The pain on Fern's face was the worst thing. He'd gotten past some of those walls she'd built around her heart, he'd started to connect with her and then he'd caused her pain. He'd never regain her trust.

And maybe he'd never be able to have access to his daughter.

Lord, help. It was his simplest prayer, the one he used when he was too weary and discouraged for words. The one he'd used in the POW camp. The one he'd used when his best buddy had died in his arms.

He counted on the fact that God could fill in the blanks. But how God could help with or fix this, he honestly didn't know.

Fern came out of the pantry, grabbed a paper towel and blew her nose. Then she turned to face him. "It's best that you go now." Her voice was completely, dangerously calm.

But Carlo didn't want to go. Didn't want to leave this place that had held such happiness, however brief. "We need to set up a time to talk, figure some things out," he said. "Obviously, this was a shock, and I'm sorry—"

"Stop. Now."

The abrupt words surprised him into silence.

"I don't want to meet with you. I don't ever want to see you again. You betrayed me, which I obviously don't like, but you also betrayed Mercedes, and that's unforgivable."

The words dug at his shaky self-confidence. She was right. What had he been thinking, coming back here?

"What kind of person does that? What kind of person are you?" She shook her head, raising her hands like barriers. "Never mind. Just go."

Inside, the part of him that had been a bad kid, the talk of the town for it, came kicking and screaming to life. The way that hurt boy had reacted followed close behind the feelings, but Carlo was older now, wiser, could stifle the automatic flash of defensive rage.

"You're angry. With good reason. But we still have to talk."

"I'm not talking to you!" Her voice was loud, sharp and a little scratchy, as though she wasn't used to yelling. Well, of course she wasn't. Fern was a quiet librarian.

Except when she wasn't.

The door to the kitchen burst open. "Hey, did you get things worked out?" The fire chief, whom Carlo couldn't like, not when he'd accidentally shoved Carlo under a bus, sounded booming and jovial.

Fern swallowed, the muscles working in her neck, and her fingers gripping the countertop turned white. "Carlo had just decided to leave."

"Not exactly right," Carlo said. "You'd decided I should leave. Which I'll do, as soon as we set up another time to talk."

"Hey, hey, I feel responsible," Chief Kenny said. "I… I maybe shouldn't have said anything."

"You were right to speak up," Fern said, her voice dripping icicles. "Otherwise, I don't know when the truth would have come out."

"Hey." Chief Kenny came up and put an arm around Fern, who cringed a little. "I'd like to help."

"I'd like some time alone," she said firmly.

The man looked startled, then nodded. "Yes, of course, I understand. Would you like someone from the congregation come to visit you? Maybe a woman."

"Who'd tell the world our troubles? I don't think so."

He patted her shoulder. "Not everyone's a gossip. I'll see if Lou Ann Miller can come over here. Won't tell her anything except that you could use the company, and you can talk or not, as you like. Okay?"

Carlo saw Fern fight the urge to wither the jovial,

clueless fire chief with a choice putdown, saw the muscles in her throat move as she swallowed. "All right," she said in a resigned voice.

"And as for you," Kenny said, turning to Carlo, "I'd be glad to get together, talk over old times. Do you have a church home?"

"Oh, he's super religious," Fern interjected sarcastically. "He's a missionary. A real hero!"

"Is that so?" Kenny smiled hesitantly. He seemed to realize he was out of his element.

"I've been working as a missionary, yes," Carlo said. "And I'd be happy to get together sometime, but right now we need to set up a joint appointment with the social worker. Daisy Hinton?"

"Fine," Fern said. "Now get out." She waved a hand at Carlo and then turned to the fire chief. "I mean him, not you. Although—"

"Mama!" Mercedes stepped through the doorway, eyes wide, one finger in her mouth. "Why did you tell Mr. Carlo to leave? Stop fighting!"

Fern squatted down and held out her arms, and the little girl ran to her. Fern hugged her tight, tears running down her face like a stream over stone.

After a minute, Mercedes struggled free. "You're crying, Mama," she said, reaching out to touch Fern's face. "What's the matter?"

"Nothing you need to worry about, sweets." Fern's voice broke on the pet name.

Mercedes turned to Carlo and put her hands on her hips. "Were you mean to Mama Fern?" she asked him reproachfully.

"Not on purpose, but yeah. I hurt her feelings." Carlo was starting to think it was definitely a good idea to leave now. He'd gotten what he needed, a plan to meet with Fern and the social worker. Now he needed to get out before he blurted the whole truth to a four-year-old.

The trouble was, if he left, he wasn't sure when he'd ever see his child again.

He squatted down to Mercedes's level. "I'm going to go," he said, his throat tight. "Give me a hug?"

"Don't you dare." Fern moved to put herself between Mercedes and him. "Mercedes, go in the other room."

Mercedes started to cry. "Mama, he just wants a hug!"

"He wants a lot more than that," she said, her voice low and furious. "But he's not going to get it."

"Come on, my man," Chief Kenny said, clapping an arm around his shoulders. "Probably best to leave."

Carlo could tell from the fire chief's watchful expression that the man thought he was going to do something dangerous. Carlo was the bad kid by reputation, and maybe that wasn't just in the past. No one trusted him, and why should they? He hadn't exactly earned anyone's trust.

TWO HOURS LATER, Carlo had gotten a room at the cheap hotel at the edge of Rescue River and was kicking himself for not doing that in the first place. Better to have braved an accident than to have ruined everything with his daughter.

But the roads were closed. And they needed your help.

When he thought of Fern and Mercedes out there alone at the rescue, what it would have been like for them to take care of the dogs and deal with the electricity going out, he had to be glad he'd been there.

He should have told the truth as soon as he'd realized it, that was all. He'd been an idiot.

After an hour of beating himself up, he pulled himself together, as he'd done so many times before. He called the social worker, Daisy Hinton—Sam Hinton's little sister, whom he remembered vaguely from his school years, and had seen most recently at his sister's wedding—and made an appointment to see her the next Monday. And then he took a shower and shaved and put on clean clothes. He had to get out of his miserable state of mind so that he could function, could get on his game and figure out how to play this right.

Somehow he'd envisioned returning to Rescue River a little differently. He'd thought he would come stay with Angelica and Troy, get his feet under him and get their take on the situation. When he was ready, he'd go to work on getting his daughter back.

His illness and the snowstorm and Angelica's absence had wrecked his plans. Not to mention that he'd met a woman who'd softened his jaded heart, who touched him in a way no one ever had...and then hurt her terribly. Now he had total chaos on his hands.

He tried to pray, but his thoughts kept circling back to all the ways he'd screwed up. He kept picturing Fern's hurt eyes and Mercedes's worried expression. He had a whole weekend to get through before he could move on this and fix things, and if he spent it in this tiny motel room, he was going to be in no shape to stand up and fight for his child.

Air, he needed air. He pulled on the down coat he'd picked up at the discount store on the way into town and headed out on foot into the little town where he'd grown up.

It wasn't five minutes until he ran into someone who knew him.

"Well, as I live and breathe, it's Carlo Camden," said

a woman with gray hair peeking out from a furry hat. She wore a fur coat that reached to the top of her boots and she walked with one of those rolling walkers.

He squinted at her. "Miss Minnie Falcon?" Automatically, he straightened his shoulders and stuck out a hand to his old Sunday-school teacher. "How are you, ma'am?"

"Doing well for eighty-nine. What are you doing back in town?"

Of course she'd ask that, and of course he didn't have a ready answer and couldn't find one, not in the sharp light of those piercing blue eyes.

"I'm, uh, just visiting." He stuck his hands into his pockets, feeling as if he were fourteen.

"Visiting whom?" Her eyes were sharp with curiosity.

Did he have to answer her out of respect for her age? "A few people," he said vaguely, and turned the tables. "How about you? Are you still living in the same big place on Maple Street?" He remembered being invited to Miss Minnie's home as a Sunday-school kid, dragging Angelica along because there was no one else to care for her, and being petrified with fear that she'd put a dirty hand on the wallpaper or break a china figurine. But to his surprise, tart Miss Minnie, who'd seemed ancient even back then, had been kind. She'd taken one look at the rapid pace with which Carlo and Angelica were eating her cookies and made them sit down in her kitchen for a full lunch—sandwiches and fruit and milk.

"I sold my home to Lacey Armstrong two years ago. She's making a guesthouse out of it, although why she would do that, I don't know. She wants to redecorate it in all kinds of modern styles, make it artsy, whatever that means."

In his old teacher's voice Carlo heard sadness and loss. "Where are you living now?" he asked gently.

Her mouth twisted a little. "I'm in prison over at the Senior Towers. My nieces and nephews insisted."

"Accepting visitors?"

She looked surprised. "Why would you want to visit an old lady like me?"

"Because," he said, "I learned about missionaries in your Sunday-school class, and now I've become one. I remember how you made missionary life sound so exciting. Thought you might want to hear a bit about mine, see a few pictures."

"Are you trying to raise money?" she asked, her eyes narrowing.

He laughed outright. "No. I'm not sure what's next for me."

"All right, then. You come and see me, and we'll talk."

She turned toward the Chatterbox Café, and when Carlo saw the table of gray-haired ladies waving, he figured the place was aptly named. The story of his being back in town, a missionary and planning to visit her, would give his old teacher a little bit of news to share.

He continued on down the street with a marginally better attitude toward the town of his youth.

He passed the bar where his parents had spent a fair amount of time. He was familiar with the place, having gone in to find his folks multiple times, especially when they were neglecting Angelica. On occasional visits back to town, he'd stopped in and seen some of his old high school cronies. But he'd given up drinking, not liking what it did to him or to others.

Across the street was his brother-in-law's veterinarian's office, and he wondered who was staffing it while

Troy was traveling. An answer came when a man in scrubs walked out, helping an older woman carry a large dog crate. It looked like Buck Armstrong, a guy Carlo vaguely remembered as being in Angelica's class at school. He stopped and watched the pair walking toward the lone SUV parked in front of the clinic as he remembered what Angelica had said about Buck's struggles with alcoholism.

Apparently, before Troy and Angelica had gotten back together, Buck had asked Angelica out and then showed up too drunk to drive. He was a veteran, so Angelica said, and as he watched the man hoist the crate into an SUV, speak briefly to the owner and then stride back into the vet clinic, Carlo figured he might like to get to know him. Nobody understood a vet like a vet, and if the guy was drying out, he might welcome a friend who didn't socialize exclusively at bars.

Up ahead was the church. Carlo noted it for future reference and then turned down Maple Avenue.

Inside a building that he remembered as a dress shop, he saw decorations and renovations going on for what looked like a restaurant. Past that, he could see the Senior Towers, so named because, at six stories, they were the tallest buildings in town. Just visible was Miss Minnie's massive old Victorian, which apparently was being renovated, as well. What must that be like, for the old woman to look out the windows of her Senior Towers apartment and watch the innards of her old home being ripped out?

Yes, he'd visit her soon.

He turned the corner and there was the library, a squat brick building that had been something of a haven for him and Angelica growing up. Fern's workplace now.

Fern. He drew in a breath and let it out in a sigh,

wondering how she was doing, whether she and Mercedes were enjoying some solitude or had gotten out for shopping or visiting.

Funny how a few days together had let him in on their routine. It was late afternoon, so Fern was probably fixing dinner, letting Mercedes help her, talking to the child in her serious way about measurements and kitchen safety.

He missed them with an awful, achy, scraped-raw feeling. Before he could sink into more sadness, he hurried past the library and came upon the park.

Every kid in town was there, it seemed, sledding on the small hill, enjoying what was left of a Friday's daylight. Whoops and shouts came from bigger boys on saucer sleds. He looked more closely when he noticed that several kids were sliding on cardboard, just as he and Angelica had done. Worked almost as well as a sled, maybe a little more adventurous.

He walked closer and noticed a couple of parents watching the sledding hill, calling out cautions to their kids in Spanish. On impulse, he greeted them in their native tongue, asking about their kids. It turned into a conversation, and Carlo learned that they were new in town, living on the same so-called Rental Row where Carlo had lived as a kid. They were from Guatemala, where he'd spent some time, and they shared a few stories. By the time he left, he had an invitation to their home for enchiladas—real ones, not the taco-joint kind.

He headed back toward the motel in a thoughtful frame of mind. There'd been a time when he wanted to run as far as possible away from Rescue River. The place held too many bad memories.

What he hadn't counted on was that he himself had changed. He'd grown up. And the town was changing, too, getting some new business, opening to some new kinds of people. Given its background on the Underground Railroad, it had always been a little more diverse than the average midwestern farm town, but it looked as though that diversity was increasing. The family he'd just met had said there were a number of people from Mexico and Central America in their neighborhood.

All of a sudden, Rescue River didn't look half bad. The problem was that his own ineptness had probably ruined his chances of building a home here.

CHAPTER TEN

ON SUNDAY MORNING, Fern was dishing scrambled eggs onto Mercedes's plate when the farmhouse doorbell rang.

Her whole body tensed. Was he back?

Friday had been a rough day, with her own emotions so raw and Mercedes upset about how she'd kicked Carlo out. Yesterday, she'd managed to cocoon with Mercedes all day, reading stories, watching movies and playing in the snowy yard. Through it all, she'd tried to convey all the love and caring she felt for the little girl, sick at heart that their time together might come to an end soon.

She just hadn't wanted to face the world, not with her own humiliation about Carlo's betrayal so raw, and her fears about losing Mercedes so intense. But now Mercedes scooted out of her chair and ran to the door, clearly joyous about company.

"Wait, don't open it without Mama," she called, setting the egg pan down on the stove and hurrying after Mercedes. For all she knew, Carlo could have come to sweep the child away, legally or not.

He wouldn't do that, said a voice inside her. The voice that knew Carlo as an honorable, even heroic man.

You don't know him as well as you thought you did, said a rival voice. *He might.*

But when she opened the door, slender, silver-haired

Lou Ann Miller stood there with a napkin-covered basket in hand. "Hello! I tried to call but couldn't get through."

"Spotty reception," Fern apologized. No need to mention she'd turned her phone off.

"Anyway, I made way too many of these rolls, and I wanted to share them with you and Mercedes. You like cinnamon rolls, honey?"

Mercedes squealed. "Mommy used to cook them. She let me pop the can and it made a bang!"

Lou Ann chuckled. "These are made the old-fashioned way, but they'll be almost as good as the canned ones. May I come in a minute, Fern?"

At that, Fern realized then that she was keeping a seventysomething woman on the porch in the cold. "Of course! We were just sitting down to breakfast. Would… would you like to join us?"

"Now, that's an offer I can't refuse," Lou Ann said. She handed her big puffy coat to Mercedes. "You find a place to put that, dear. Maybe right over there on the banister. No need to hang it up."

As she led the well-dressed woman toward the kitchen, Fern resigned herself to a lecture, probably an effort to get her to attend church. After all, it was Sunday morning, and only nine o'clock. There was plenty of time to get there for the ten-thirty service.

Normally, she would go. She'd been extra meticulous about churchgoing since she had Mercedes to care for, a young soul to raise up right. Today, though, she felt hopeless about that and unable to face the friendly, curious, small-town congregation.

"What a good breakfast you cook for that child," Lou Ann said as they approached the table, and the older woman's approval warmed her. She was glad she'd fixed a big pan of eggs, plenty to share.

She finished dishing them up, took the plastic wrap off the fruit she'd cut up earlier and whisked away the loaf of raisin bread, replacing it with Lou Ann's rolls. They all sat down, and Mercedes reached her hands out trustingly. "Can we sing my prayer, Mama Fern?"

"Of course." But Fern's own voice broke a little as Mercedes belted out the preschool blessing, backed by Lou Ann's deep alto. How long until she lost custody of Mercedes?

"You know the prayer!" Mercedes said to Lou Ann as she grabbed for a cinnamon roll.

Lou Ann helped her to serve herself. "Of course. I learned it from Xavier, right here in this kitchen."

So they chatted about Xavier and Angelica and Troy, how Lou Ann had helped Troy around the house when he'd broken his leg, how she'd watched them become a family. "There's something about this place," Lou Ann said, looking around the cheerful kitchen. "It just seems to lend itself to people coming together."

Fern kept her eyes on her plate. It hadn't worked in her case, though for a brief, unrealistic moment, she'd thought it had.

"Mr. Carlo stayed here with us during the blizzard," Mercedes announced. "And I asked if I could get him for a daddy, like Xavier got Mr. Troy, but…" She shook her head, her face worried. "Him and Mama Fern had a fight."

"Mercedes!" Fern looked quickly at Lou Ann, expecting harshness and judgment.

But the older woman just nodded and helped herself to more fruit without looking at Fern. "Sometimes that happens."

"Uh-huh." Mercedes seemed to take Lou Ann's calm reaction as evidence that nothing was wrong.

Fern got a tiny flash of the same feeling herself. Maybe this was just a fight. Maybe there was still a chance.

Mercedes lifted her hands in a comical, palms-up gesture. "Whatever."

Both women laughed, Fern blushing a little, and Lou Ann patted Mercedes's shoulder. "As far as having a daddy goes, any man would feel blessed to have you for his little girl."

The child's expression faltered. "I'm probably not gonna get one. Can I go watch TV?" Without waiting for an answer, she darted from the table and into the TV room.

"Mercedes!" Fern started to stand up.

Lou Ann touched her hand. "Let her go. You have to choose your battles with little ones, and I must have upset her with my comment. I'm sorry."

Fern sighed. "She's sensitive about her lack of a father, and I think her mom told her some negative things before she turned her life around."

"That's tough. Plus, she's recently lost her mother. And she may not feel quite secure with you. It's only been a few months, isn't that right?"

"Yes, and the adoption isn't finalized." Fern felt an uncharacteristic urge to pour her heart out to Lou Ann, but she stopped herself. "There's a lot of uncertainty. A lot to worry about."

"I'm sure." Lou Ann stood up and started carrying dishes to the counter before Fern could stop her. "You sit. I know this kitchen better than you do, and a single mom doesn't get many breaks."

The unexpected kindness warmed Fern, giving her

a safe, cared-for feeling she wasn't used to. "But you're a guest."

"My offer comes with a price. I want you and Mercedes to come to church with me."

Of course. That was why she'd come. Fern had guessed as much. "Did Chief Kenny put you up to this?"

"Kenny told me you could use a visit," Lou Ann admitted. "It was my idea to do it Sunday morning. You could ride in to church with me."

"And be trapped into staying for the social hour, too?" Fern blurted out the words before she thought and then clapped her hand to her mouth. "I'm so sorry! It's a generous offer and I really appreciate it. I'm just... having some trouble right now, and I don't think I can face everyone."

"Then, drive yourself and sit in the back. You need the message," Lou Ann said bluntly. "And so does that little girl."

Mercedes came in then, carrying the puppy, with Brownie trailing close behind. Fern opened her mouth to scold Mercedes for picking up the puppy without an adult present, but she clamped her mouth shut. *Choose your battles*, Lou Ann had said, and she was right.

"Well, isn't that a little cutie!" Lou Ann bent over to pat the puppy's head.

Brownie let out a low growl.

"Brownie, it's okay." Fern moved to comfort the mama dog and make sure she didn't lunge at Lou Ann. "She was separated from her pup for a while, and she's protective."

"That's how mothers are," the older woman said comfortably before turning back to load dishes into the dishwasher.

Feeling a sudden rush of sympathy for Brownie, Fern

knelt beside the big dog and wrapped an arm around her, rubbing her ears. Mercedes set the puppy down beside Brownie and they all laughed as its legs splayed out on the slippery floor. For the first time since Carlo had dropped his bombshell, the pressure in Fern's chest eased a little.

Lou Ann was kind. And she was also right. Both Fern and Mercedes needed to get out, and they needed a good dose of spiritual comfort. "I think we'll take your advice and go to church," she said to Lou Ann. "I'll drive so you don't have to come back out here, but thanks for the push. We needed it."

That was how Fern and Mercedes ended up sliding into the back row of the little white clapboard church a minute after the service started. Just hearing the praise music made Fern let out her tight-held breath in a sigh.

There was a force in the universe bigger than she was. There was a God who cared, not just about her, but about Mercedes. Which meant she could rest a little, could put at least some of the weight of the child's future into the Lord's capable hands.

Mercedes ran happily up to the front during the children's sermon and then went off to children's church. Fern breathed slowly in and out and watched the sunlight turn the stained-glass windows into jewels. The scripture passages and the sermon washed over her, providing a sense of comfort, a hint of peace…at least until the pastor started talking forgiveness and reconciliation.

Hearing it in the abstract made excellent sense.

Thinking about actually doing it, especially where Carlo was concerned… That was another matter.

Oh, there was a part of her that wanted to forgive him. To tell him what he'd done was fine, to try to recapture that sweet, sweet hope that somehow her solitary life could expand into something bigger, that love could heal her lonely heart.

But that was wishful thinking.

After church she edged toward the door, hoping to slip down the back stairs to the children's wing, pick up Mercedes and escape. But everyone, it seemed, knew she and Mercedes had been stranded out at the dog rescue, and the kind expressions of concern trapped her.

And then she heard Mercedes's voice coming from the front of the sanctuary. "Mama Fern, Mama Fern! Look who found me!"

Carlo.

Heads turned at the sound of the happy, excited, little-girl voice, and everyone smiled and cooed at the sight of the handsome man carrying the adorable child.

Fern's own heart hitched, then pounded hard. Carlo was amazing. Glorious. Protective. A hero.

Yeah, and how many of the friendly, admiring congregation were noticing what Chief Kenny had noticed, the strong familial resemblance between Carlo and Mercedes? What was Carlo thinking?

Fern marched over, took Mercedes from Carlo's arms and set the child down. "You do *not* have the right to pick her up from Sunday school," she whispered hotly.

Mercedes stuck her finger in her mouth, looking worried, and Fern's stomach lurched. She squatted down to comfort her, but just then Mercedes caught sight of one of her Sunday-school friends opening a sparkly pink purse a couple of pews down. "Can I go play with Addison?" she begged.

Addison was a godsend. "Sure," she said, standing up. As soon as Mercedes was out of earshot, she turned on Carlo, ignoring the way her heart raced just at his nearness. "Picking her up from Sunday school was totally out of line."

"I'm sorry. I was down there helping move some props for the puppet show and she saw me. The teacher let her come with me after I explained our connection."

Her eyebrows lifted practically into her hairline. "You explained your connection?"

"The blizzard," he said patiently. "Give me a little credit, Fern."

She couldn't match his calm tone, so she settled for keeping her voice low. "Chief Kenny recognized your relationship the moment he saw you with Mercedes. What makes you think everyone else in the church won't?"

"Would that be such a disaster? Everyone will know soon."

Fern looked over at Mercedes, now engaged in a game of pretend with Addison's plastic ponies. The church was emptying out. Fern leaned back against the side of a pew, frowning up at Carlo. "Yes, it would be a disaster! What if Mercedes finds out?"

He drew in a breath and let it out in a sigh. "I'd like to talk to you about how to tell her. I tried texting and calling, but I couldn't get through."

Yeah. That. "I did turn my phone off," she admitted.

"Hiding?"

"Would you blame me?"

He leaned toward her a little, and his hand lifted as if to touch her hair.

She sucked in a breath, shook her head.

His hand dropped. "Hiding is understandable. But, Fern, I want you to know I made an appointment with the social worker for Monday. It would be nice if you could be there. Maybe that's a way for us to talk calmly about this."

Fern felt as if the world was closing in on her way too quickly. She bit her lip and looked away.

"We can't delay on this," Carlo said. "Like it or not, it's a small, gossipy town. News travels fast. I'd like to figure out how to tell Mercedes, as well as how to proceed from here. Daisy agreed."

"You *told* Daisy?"

His brow wrinkled. "Of course I told her. She's the social worker. As soon as I got Kath's letter, I mailed her a copy and let her know I wanted to take care of Mercedes. When I talked to her yesterday, she was supportive."

Fern lifted her eyes to the church rafters, trying to breathe calmly. Daisy was supportive.

Fern was going to lose Mercedes.

"Oh, Fern!" A woman Fern had met a few times at the elementary school, whose pretty Asian features contrasted with her church-unconventional leather jacket and jeans, came up behind them. "Good, you're here. I wanted to suggest that you come ice-skating with the church group. It's a singles event, but kids are welcome, so you could bring Mercedes." She paused and then looked up at Carlo. "Hey… Carlo? You're Angelica's brother, right?"

"That's right," he said. "Susan. I remember you from my sister's wedding. Good to see you."

"You should come, too, if you're going to be in town," Susan said, and Fern felt a burn of jealousy so intense she had to put her hands behind her back to hide their clenching. Who did this woman think she was, horning in on Fern's man?

And where had *that* ridiculous thought come from?

"Think about it. Info's on the church website." Susan gave Fern another smile and then headed off toward another group of people talking.

Fern had to deal with this and she had to work with him and she had to quit acting as if she were the center of the universe. For Mercedes's sake, they had to work together. "All right," she said. "I'll come to meet with you and Daisy. But I warn you, I'm going to fight to keep custody of her with everything I have."

"Of course. You're a considerable adversary, and I do respect that." He turned abruptly and walked away.

A considerable adversary? Fern thought about the term and wondered. Was that what she wanted to be?

On Monday morning, Carlo arrived at Daisy Hinton's office half an hour early, hoping to catch the social worker before the official appointment and plead his case. He figured the deck was stacked against him, but he had to try everything he could to get at least some chance to be a father to Mercedes.

He entered the front door of the quaint brick building and passed a small, glassed-in playroom where a man sat cross-legged on the floor, playing trucks with a toddler.

Carlo clenched his jaw. That would be his fate if he didn't get Daisy on his side. Supervised visits in a little room.

He wanted so much more.

He wanted what they'd had during the storm. A cozy family life. But he'd ruined that possibility by his own stupid actions.

He reached Daisy's office. The door was open, so he tapped on the door frame as he looked in.

The short, well-rounded young woman with reddish

curls tumbling down her back and rings on every finger bore a slight resemblance to the girl he'd seen around Rescue River growing up, not that his ragtag family had run in the same circles as the wealthy Hintons. She'd been at Angelica's wedding, but then she'd been friendly and smiling. Today her expression was all business as she turned away from her computer. "Yes? Oh, hey. You must be Carlo." She frowned. "I thought our appointment was at ten."

"You're right. I came early, hoping to chat for a minute."

She gave one last longing look at the screen, cast a glance at the folders on her desk and then nodded reluctantly. Clearly, she was a busy woman.

Carlo waved a hand. "Go ahead, finish what you were doing. I'm sorry to intrude. Do you want me to wait outside?"

"No. Just give me a minute."

While she tapped on her keyboard, Carlo looked around the office, trying to get a bead on the woman who had control of his future and his happiness. A fountain bubbled in the corner, and paintings of large, bright flowers covered the walls. The couch and chairs and coffee table looked like somebody's living room—an artist's, maybe—and the subtle scent of vanilla added to the hominess. A big basket held a variety of children's toys. For Mercedes's sake, he was glad that if she'd had to spend time in a social worker's office, it was a cozy one.

"Okay, that's that." Daisy turned her chair to face him, and despite her colorful appearance, her level gaze told him she was the no-nonsense type.

He decided that total honesty was his best policy. "I think I really messed up by meeting Mercedes before

I was supposed to. We got to know each other and got friendly, but she has no idea I'm her father."

"So you mentioned on the phone." Daisy fumbled through the stacks of file folders on her desk, finally coming up with one that, he figured, must be Mercedes's. "She's four, right?" She scanned the file with practiced eyes. "Four, going on five. So she's young enough not to do a lot of logical questioning. We might be okay, if you and Fern handle the telling with sensitivity."

"I screwed up with Fern, too, by not telling her the truth as soon as I suspected Mercedes might be my child. She's not happy with me now."

"Oh, really?" Daisy studied him, her gaze cool. "It definitely would have made more sense to build from a foundation of honesty. Why didn't you tell her?"

He stared at her wooden desk. "Aside from the fact that I was half-delirious with dengue fever... I didn't know her at all. And I'm not a real trusting guy."

He suspected that would be the end of his credibility with Daisy, but he'd prayed about it and he was committed to being truthful now. He could only hope that would lead him back to the right path.

To his surprise, she sounded sympathetic. "I understand that. I'm friends with your sister after all, so I know how you guys grew up. But if you're not trusting, then why are you being up-front with me now?"

"Well..." Should he tell her he'd prayed about it?

"Is it to try to get me on your side before Fern comes in?"

"No!" He paused. *Tell the truth.* "Well, maybe a little. I just know Fern's dead set against me, and I really want the chance to parent Mercedes. To do a better job with her than my dad did with me and Angelica."

That admission seemed to soften Daisy. She nodded slowly. "I had a chance to verify the unusual circumstances between you and Mercedes's mom."

"Yeah?"

Daisy tapped her pen on the desk, looking out the window at the town's main street, and then seemed to reach a decision. "When she spoke to me, she'd told me Mercedes's dad didn't want any involvement. But that letter she sent you, the one you mailed to me, clarified that *she* was the one who'd hidden Mercedes's existence from you."

Carlo's heart jumped with hope. "So you don't hold me responsible for neglect?"

"No. And more important, the court won't, either, since we'll have her letter on record."

"Do I have a chance to get custody of Mercedes?" Even as he said it, an uncomfortable, guilty feeling rose in him.

The reason was Fern. Fern, and the important attachment she'd built with Mercedes. Fern, whose determination and beauty and strength had captivated him. He had opened his mouth to say so when Daisy raised a hand. "I'd like to hold off on discussing anything more until every participant of the meeting is here, for the sake of fairness."

"I wondered when that was going to occur to someone." The voice—Fern's voice—came from directly outside the office door.

Carlo jerked back to see Fern, hands on hips, jaw set.

"Fern! Come on in." A crease appeared between Daisy's eyebrows. "Did you hear what we were talking about?"

"I didn't mean to eavesdrop, but I'm upset you started the meeting without me." She cast a frown at Carlo.

She had a point, and guilt chomped at his gut.

Fern sat down in the chair Daisy was waving toward, her back straight, shoulders squared. "I think we should talk about what's best for Mercedes."

"Exactly," Daisy said. "Fern, I assume you now know that Carlo is very likely to be Mercedes's father. He's willing to take a paternity test—" She glanced over at Carlo. "Right?"

"Ready anytime."

"So we'll need to get Mercedes in for samples."

"Blood samples?" Fern squeaked.

"No. A simple cheek swab. We can have a tester come here."

Fern gave a short nod, but Carlo, watching her closely, saw her hands clench into fists, balling the material of her plain dark skirt.

He reached out to touch her arm, wanting to reassure her, but she jerked away. Daisy put her chin on her clasped hands, watching the two of them, obviously assessing.

Carlo felt that things were spinning out of control. "Look, I don't want to break the attachment Mercedes has with Fern. At the same time, as her father, I want to raise her."

"Looks as if you want two incompatible things," Fern said. Her voice was absolutely cool, absolutely level. Her hands clenched and unclenched on her skirt.

"Let's don't rush into anything until we have the results of the paternity test," Daisy advised. "I see that the two of you have some issues. We might need to go to court, but I'd like to work it out here if we could. Court battles are expensive and hard on kids."

Fern's face went pale. "I don't want to put Mercedes through that."

"Nor do I." Carlo leaned forward, elbows on knees. "Seems to me that we adults need to make sure we keep talking and try to figure it out. We all want what's best for Mercedes."

"I hope so," Fern murmured. Her voice was low, but it cut Carlo that she seemed to suspect he wasn't putting Mercedes first.

"It's always better for a child to have contact with her biological parents, as long as they're not abusive," Daisy said.

"I suppose," Fern said guardedly, and Carlo frowned, suddenly wondering about Fern's background. What had her family of origin been like? She'd mentioned something about foster care. If her own background was rough, that would be a factor in how she approached this situation. Just as his own background, having a mom and dad who couldn't parent well, had affected him.

"If the test comes back positive, which seems likely," Daisy said, "the first order of business will be to tell Mercedes about it. It's a small town and from what I understand, someone has already recognized some physical similarities."

"That's right," Carlo said. "It's urgent that we tell her rather than having someone ask Mercedes an awkward question. Can we talk about how to do that?"

Fern stared at him, and Carlo, knowing her as well as he'd come to, saw the moment when the walls went up inside her. She stood, knocking her leg against the coffee table and wincing, clenching her fists. "Look," she said, "it's obvious what's going to happen. You're her dad, and you're going to get custody of her. Excuse me if I need…a moment…to deal with that."

She spun away and ran from the room.

Carlo and Daisy stood at the same moment. "I'll

go after her," Carlo said. "Please. Let me handle this."
Though he had no idea how to make things right, his
aching heart told him he had to try.

CHAPTER ELEVEN

FERN SPEED-WALKED PAST the Senior Towers and the library and the park and somehow ended up by the elementary school.

She stood outside the fence, looking in at a noisy crowd of children in winter coats and snow boots, black and brown and white kids all together, the sounds of English mingling with Spanish and what sounded like Vietnamese. She had to look pathetic, but she couldn't seem to move.

She loved Rescue River's little primary school, had been doing programs here regularly since she'd gotten the job at the library. After she'd taken Mercedes in, her visits gained new meaning. Soon, she'd be the mother of a child at this school.

Or so she'd thought. Not anymore.

Tears burned her eyes, blurring the lively playground in front of her, and she dug in her purse for a tissue. Thankfully, as the mother of a four-year-old, she was well stocked. She blew her nose and wiped her eyes and took slow, deep breaths. She had to pull herself together, at least for long enough to get home to cry in privacy.

"Hey, you look pretty bad." The blunt voice belonged to Susan, the woman from her church who'd invited her to the singles event.

Oh, great. A teacher she knew *would* have to be on playground duty on the day Fern showed up crying.

"Anything I can do? Only catch is, I have to keep an eye on these little sweethearts, as well."

Fern shook her head, wiped her eyes and blew her nose. "Thanks. I... I'm having a few problems, that's all."

"Come on in. You can watch the kids with me and pull yourself together before everyone in Rescue River starts to gossip."

Fern didn't really want to socialize, but Susan had a point. "Okay."

"Gate's right over here." Susan walked with her on the other side of the fence until a couple of upset-sounding kid shouts distracted her. "Sorry, I've got to deal with this before it escalates. Hey, Mindy, what's wrong?" Susan headed toward the sliding board to mediate a very loud argument.

Fern was opening the gate herself when a large, male hand clapped down on her shoulder, sending what felt like tiny electrical shocks right to her heart. "There you are!"

Carlo.

Half inside the gate, she turned to face him. "What?"

He produced her coat and wrapped it around her shivering shoulders. "You left this at Daisy's office." Then he leaned closer. "You've been crying."

"Thank you, Captain Obvious," Susan said from behind Fern, and then stepped between her and Carlo. "What did you do to her?"

Carlo took a step back. "Hi, Susan. I'm afraid it's private."

"No problem, but we don't need any extra drama here at the school. Fern's welcome, she has her clearances, but you need to stay outside the fence."

The unfamiliar feeling of having another woman protect her gave Fern a tiny boost. She couldn't remember the last time that had happened. If ever. It helped that Susan showed no sign of romantic interest in Carlo.

A muscle in Carlo's jaw tightened. "Of course." He took a couple more steps back.

"Up to you," Susan said to Fern. "Come with me when I take the kids inside in, let's see…" She consulted her phone. "In three minutes. Or stay out with him. Either way, we need to close the gate. Mindy!" With the teacher's eyes in the back of her head, Susan must have noticed that a new circle of kids was gathering around the little girl who'd been involved in the fight a minute ago. "Be right back. I hope."

Carlo studied Fern through the fence. "Come walk with me. We need to talk."

She shook her head. "I can't. I… I just can't."

"Look, I know this is hard and awful. It is for me, too."

Fern opened her mouth to snap at him, but the defeated look in his eyes tugged at her heart. For the first time, she tried to look at the whole situation from his point of view.

He'd been rejected by his wife, not once, but twice. Then he'd gotten notice that she'd died and that he had a child, and he'd come rushing back to fulfill his duties, disregarding deathly illness to do so.

He'd met his daughter unprepared, had spent time getting close to her and now couldn't see her except under the care of a social worker.

The pain and conflict of all of it showed in his haunted eyes.

She lifted her hands, palms up. "I'm really sorry, Carlo. I just don't see how one of us can win without the other one losing." And she couldn't sacrifice her stake in Mercy's future, because she knew she was an important part of the child's stability.

She put a hand up to the tall chain-link fence at the same time he did. They pressed their hands together, staring at each other, neither of them smiling. Fern's heart pounded out of control.

Finally, he spoke. "We need to figure out how to tell Mercedes the truth. That takes priority. After that…" He paused a moment, as if considering how to say something difficult.

"What?" Her voice came out as a feathery whisper she didn't recognize. "What after that?"

"After that," he said, looking hard into her eyes, "maybe we can figure out this thing between us."

Hope and panic rose in her. Hope—and surprise, really—that he thought there was a thing between them. But panic, too, because it was all happening way too fast. "I don't feel as if I can figure anything out just now."

He pressed his hand against hers through the fence, curling large, blunt fingers through the chain links to clasp the tips of hers. "You're cold."

She couldn't look away. She'd been cold, too cold, for too long.

"You should go inside."

"I should." She licked suddenly dry lips.

One eyebrow lifted, quizzical.

How could she be feeling such wildly contradictory emotions toward this complicated, infuriating man?

Her confusion must have shown on her face, because he nodded once. "I'll be quick, then. After you left, Daisy told me option B. Which is having her tell Mercedes with the two of us, or just me, standing by."

"No!"

"Right. To me, that's not ideal. So let's have dinner tomorrow night and we'll talk it through, figure it out."

"Tomorrow?" She had no plans, but she needed time to pull herself together. Carlo's intensity scared her, plain and simple. "I can't find a sitter for Mercedes that fast."

"Then, Wednesday? We need to do this soon, Fern, before the cat gets out of the bag some other way."

It wasn't that she didn't want to see him. It was that she was desperate to see him. It was that his hand, gripping at hers, felt way too right for something that was totally wrong. "Okay, Wednesday," she said, then pushed off the fence, turned away from his too-perceptive eyes and hurried toward the school.

The sound of children yelling pulled her out of her own concerns. There was Mindy, the little girl who'd been fighting, struggling as Susan carried her inside. Other children were tugging at Susan's leg, trying to tell their side of the story. Fern looked around—surely there was another adult out here?—but the only aide was kneeling down beside a child who'd apparently fallen off the swings.

Fern quickened her step. "Hey," she said to the most persistent of the kids who was tugging at Susan. "Why don't you tell me what happened? And we'll see if we can find some answers in books next time I come for library reading time, okay?"

As she'd hoped, the offer of adult attention and a listening ear drew the clamoring kids away from Susan. She nodded sympathetically at the childhood tale of a push, the seizing of a ball and some name-calling, and promised to bring a book that told a similar story the next time. "Now, looks as if everyone's lining up to go inside," she said. "Show me how fast you can line up without talking."

As the kids lined up, Susan, still carrying the sobbing Mindy, cast her a grateful smile. "I need to take her to the nurse," she told Fern. "Meet me in the teachers' lounge."

Because she didn't have anything else to do and no ideas about how to solve her problems, she did as Susan suggested. Every step through the school reminded her that she wouldn't have a child here after all. Carlo was trying to get along with her, doing better than she was. That would make him look wonderful to Daisy, the social worker, whom Fern had undoubtedly alienated by abruptly running away from her office.

She sank into a battered chair in the teachers' lounge and looked around, trying to keep from crying. The lounge clearly saw heavy use. Job-safety notices and motivational posters filled the pale green walls, and stacks of education-related magazines spilled off a table beside a worn vinyl couch. The sink was full of coffee cups and the window shade was tilted askew.

Fern grabbed a magazine and opened it, but tears kept leaking out of her eyes, blurring her vision. She grabbed a handful of tissues from the jumbo-size box on the desk, listening to the shouts of children and the remonstrating voices of adults, rising and falling as children headed to their classrooms.

Susan charged through the door, all energy, and perched on the edge of a chair beside Fern. "Hey, you okay? I'm the only teacher with this planning time, so we should have the place to ourselves. Though no guarantees."

Fern wiped her eyes. "You probably have so much work to do."

"Nothing I don't want to procrastinate about," Susan said with a philosophical shrug. "Besides, I need to rest from carrying Mindy. She's not a small kid." She shook out her arms and rotated her shoulders, grimacing.

A bell sounded and the noise of children's voices faded. Class time again.

Fern wasn't quite ready to spill her secrets to a woman she didn't know all that well. "Yeah, what happened out there on the playground? Looked as if some kids have a history."

Susan nodded, "Yeah, you could say that. Mindy kind of has a double problem. You saw how she's missing a hand, right? But much worse than that, she also lost her mom a couple of years ago. She's one angry little girl, and she doesn't turn it inward."

"She fights?"

Susan nodded. "She isn't usually the instigator, but let anyone make a remark about her hand or her mom and she slugs them. No impulse control." Susan slapped a hand over her mouth. "Sorry. I shouldn't be running off at the mouth about a kid. Especially to a parent, or a future parent at least. Your daughter will be here next year, right?"

"If I get to keep her," Fern said. "It's…a question." Her throat closed on the last words and she stared down at her lap, trying to stop the tears.

"Wow, really? I'm so sorry, that's got to be hard." She paused. "Speaking of Mercedes, she probably has some issues similar to Mindy's. She just lost her mom as well, correct? And Dad's nowhere in the picture in her case. At least Mindy has her father."

"Well…" Fern met Susan's eyes. "Mercedes doesn't know her dad. But he *is* back in the picture."

Susan's eyes widened. "Wait a minute. Is Carlo Camden her dad?"

Fern looked away. "I... Look, Susan, he may be, but she doesn't know, so cone of silence, okay?"

"Totally!" Susan stared at her. "Oh, my gosh. Does Angelica know Carlo has a child?"

"If Carlo hasn't told her yet, I'm sure he will soon." She shook her head. "Even Carlo didn't know about Mercedes until a few weeks ago. Or so he says."

"Wow." Susan leaned back in her chair, staring at Fern. "So that's why he showed up in town. Every red-blooded woman in Rescue River is aware of his presence, but I don't think anyone has guessed that much."

Fern looked sharply at Susan, noticing anew how beautiful she was. And she was so much more outgoing and friendly than Fern. A lively woman who could hold her own with Carlo, much better than Fern could herself. "So everyone's noticing Carlo?"

Susan lifted her hands, palms out. "Not me. I'm an anomaly. I'm not looking to date anyone."

"Oh? Why's that?" Susan would surely have her choice of men. Susan wouldn't have any problem getting what Fern herself, face it, wasn't ever going to have: a husband, a home, children.

Susan laughed. "I'm totally undomestic and I'm too sarcastic and blunt. Men are terrified of me. They want kinder, gentler ladies. Like you, Fern."

Fern shook her head. "I'm hardly a hit with guys."

"Really?" Susan looked skeptical, then shrugged. "Well, then that makes two of us. God didn't make everyone to be married. I'm finally getting comfortable with that notion, after a pretty unhappy experience being engaged."

Susan sounded vehement, and Fern looked at her in

surprise, startled out of her own troubles. "Wow, I never would have guessed. Especially since you run the singles group at church. I thought you were, well, looking."

"Anything but," Susan said, "but when you're single, friends are even more important. Which is why you should come ice-skating. We strong single women have to stick together."

Fern's tight muscles relaxed just a little. "Maybe I will."

"And listen," Susan said. "Just because Carlo showed up doesn't mean all hope is lost. I mean, didn't Mercedes's mom specifically want you for a guardian? That should carry some weight."

"Not much, from the look of things." Misery washed over Fern again.

Susan took her hand. "I'll pray for you, okay? You and Mercedes."

"Thanks." And as she got up to leave, she blinked wonderingly. She did feel the tiniest bit better after talking to Susan. And maybe, just maybe, she'd started to make a friend.

WITH A DAY to kill before he could see Fern and figure out how to tell Mercedes the truth, Carlo decided to stop at the Senior Towers on Tuesday morning. He'd promised Miss Minnie Falcon he'd come visit, but even more important, his grandfather lived there, and Carlo had avoided the man since arriving in town the week before. Okay, the blizzard was a decent excuse, but that had been over for several days and he still hadn't connected with Gramps.

They didn't always get along. Carlo had been harsh to the old man in his teenage years, insisting that he drop everything to take care of Angelica when their parents had dropped the ball. In turn, Gramps had been loudly critical of his own teenage misbehavior. When they saw each other, which was rare, they tended to grapple and circle like a couple of pit bulls.

Still, they were family.

As Carlo walked into the Senior Towers, he was surprised to see that the front lobby had plenty of people in it, enjoying the sun that poured through the windows. The repurposed apartment building had to be close to a hundred years old, but it felt a lot more homelike than more modern senior communities. The entryway had gleaming woodwork and high, old-fashioned tin ceilings. There were real plants in every nook and cranny, a colorful fish tank and lace curtains at the windows.

"There you are," Miss Minnie called, and extricated herself from a cluster of women to hobble toward a pair of chairs. "I've just been talking to the ladies about how you spent the weekend with that librarian who visits here, Fern Easton."

Whoa! She still had that Sunday-school teacher's voice that could silence a room. Time for damage control. "Yes," he said, giving Miss Minnie a kiss on the cheek and sitting down beside her. "I did end up staying out at my sister's place. When I got to town, I didn't know Angelica was away."

"You hadn't heard that she and that veterinarian husband went all the way to Europe to go to Disneyland?"

"Nope. But the roads were closed and the people Troy and Angelica had hired to care for the dogs couldn't get out there, so I was glad I could help Fern out."

"Mmm," Miss Minnie said, "I'm sure Fern was glad, too."

"Maybe," he said. "Although she was reluctant to have a stranger stay, the house is big enough that she was able to offer me a downstairs couch to sleep on." He wanted to be crystal clear that nothing untoward had gone on, knowing the likelihood that Miss Minnie would gossip. "Look," he said, "I brought some pictures from the missionary field for you to have. Thought you'd like to share your influence as a Sunday-school teacher."

The murmur of voices rose around them as people returned to their conversations. Good.

At the sight of the photos he'd brought, her eyes brightened with interest, and she asked a lot of questions about his missionary work. Carlo was just congratulating himself on how he'd turned the tables when Miss Minnie waved to a man who'd emerged from the small library adjacent to the lobby.

"Bob, come meet another veteran," Miss Minnie said. She turned to Carlo. "Bob Eakin was a glider man in World War Two."

Automatically, Carlo stood, greeting the leather-faced man and meeting his piercing blue eyes. "Thank you for your service."

"And you as well, young man."

"Carlo knows your favorite librarian," Miss Minnie said to the older man.

"You know our Fern?" The man looked him up and down and then gave a slow nod. "She'll be here today, matter of fact. Comes every Tuesday."

Carlo's heart thumped with a mixture of emotions. He wanted to see Fern, sure, but he also knew that she wouldn't be expecting him here today. Better to wait and not see her. That way he wouldn't nix his chances of getting on her good side tomorrow night. Someone like Fern didn't appreciate surprises.

"I thought Fern was on vacation," Miss Minnie said. "She's not been at the library, from what I heard."

"She'll be here anyway." Bob turned to Carlo and explained, "She stops in with new books. She knows we have a line of folks waiting to check them out."

"Leads a book discussion group for us ladies, too," Miss Minnie said.

"That one is smart. Reads everything in sight. Even knows a little military history." Bob nudged Carlo. "You could do worse. She took in that little gal when her friend passed on, no questions asked."

The last thing Carlo needed was a ninetysomething matchmaker trying to push him and Fern together. She would hate that.

Which meant that Carlo needed to get on with visiting his grandfather and then get out of here. He said goodbye to Bob and Miss Minnie and, one short elevator ride later, was knocking on his grandfather's door.

"It's about time you got here." Gramps opened the door and then turned and headed back to his small living room.

Carlo followed him. "How you doing, Gramps?"

"I've been better. Heard you've been in town awhile. Glad you finally stopped by."

"I had some business to take care of, I've been sick and I got stranded in a blizzard. Is that enough excuses, or do you want more?"

"I heard about all that," Gramps said. "Ain't nothing to do around here except gossip, especially since your sister took her trip."

Hearing the loneliness behind his grandfather's words, Carlo felt his automatic defensiveness fade away. Gramps was feeling neglected and lacking his normal visits from Angelica, who'd always gotten along with the old man much better than Carlo had. "Sounds as if they're having fun over there," he said, keeping his tone mild.

"I don't see why anyone needs to go to Europe when we've got a perfectly good Disney World right here in the USA. Two, in fact."

Carlo chuckled. "There might be a few other appealing things about Paris."

"You're not staying for lunch, are you?"

Carlo hesitated.

"Don't bother if it's too much trouble."

"It's not trouble. It's just that..." He decided to be honest. If you couldn't tell the truth to family, who could you tell it to? "I'd like to stay, but I'm trying not to antagonize Fern. The librarian lady I met staying at Angelica's place? Heard she's coming to the Senior Towers today."

"About her." The old man's hand clamped down on Carlo's forearm. "Want to ask you something."

"Yeah?"

"Do I have a great-granddaughter I don't know about?"

The question hung in the air of the quiet apartment while Carlo's mind spun. He looked into his grandfather's eyes and realized he had the right to know.

He shifted in his chair until he was facing Gramps. "I think so. We went for a paternity test yesterday and should get the results back soon."

Gramps's eyes widened. "I've been hearing whispers, past couple of days, but I didn't believe it was true." His bushy eyebrows came together and he glared. "Why've you been so scarce, such that a stranger had to take in one of ours?"

"I just found out." He filled in his grandfather on

Kath's letter and how he'd rushed home. "And the thing is, Mercedes—that's her name—doesn't know yet. Fern and I want to tell her ourselves, so please put a stop to any rumors you hear."

Gramps shook his head, his eyes on Carlo's. "Don't you remember how a small town works, boy? There's no stopping rumors. If you try, you only make 'em spread faster."

"What am I supposed to do, then?" He hadn't anticipated leaning on his grandfather when he came in here, but he was at the end of his rope. Fern didn't want anything to do with him, but his daughter stood to be hurt if they couldn't work out the adult problems.

"Back when I was young," Gramps said, "you'd do the right thing."

"What's that?"

Gramps looked at him as if he were a particularly dense specimen. "Marry her."

Carlo stared, then laughed. "You've missed a vital step. Fern isn't Mercedes's mother. She—"

"She is now," Gramps interrupted.

Carlo shook his head. "Kath was her mother, and I was married to Kath until she kicked me out. Fern is just…" He trailed off, because he knew that, in every way that mattered, Fern *was* Mercedes's mother now.

"Not trying to buck responsibility, are ya? That never was your way."

"No! I'm not…" He trailed off as he realized that he was trying to convince Gramps that he'd done his best, trying to gain absolution.

"Do you like her?"

"Who, Mercedes? Of course!"

"No, idiot. Fern. You like Fern?"

Carlo leaned away from the harsh voice and scrutinizing eyes, suddenly feeling about twelve. "I like her plenty. She's a great person."

"And you're at loose ends. Looking for a purpose, far as I can see. You've always wanted to help the underdog, probably because of how you grew up. Well, here's an underdog, and she just happens to be your daughter. How about marrying her mom?"

Carlo opened his mouth and then shut it as the possible solution coursed through his body and soul.

Marry Fern? Could he do it? Should he do it?

Would she have him?

He focused on the probably negative answer to that question. "Not likely she'd have me if I asked."

Gramps crinkled his eyes shrewdly. "Scared?"

The word hung between them.

Slowly, Carlo nodded. "You know how I grew up. You know I haven't had a good example of marriage set before me, and I wasn't a good husband the first time. Why would it be any different with someone I'm marrying just for the sake of the child?" Although he knew in his heart that marrying Fern wouldn't be just about Mercedes.

"Ah, but—" Gramps wagged his finger at Carlo. "Now you've got religion. With the Lord on your side, you can do a whole lot more than you can without Him."

Gramps got to his feet, leaning heavily on the arm of the chair but waving away Carlo's offer of support. "You better go on, now. Think about what I said. And make sure you tell that little one fast, because I got the feeling the rumors ain't gonna die down."

Carlo gave the old man an impulsive shoulder hug that had him waving Carlo away but looking just a little pleased. Carlo went down the elevator and headed toward the exit, his mind spinning. He needed some time to figure all this out. But he didn't have time, because the wagging tongues of Rescue River—not ill intentioned, but wagging nonetheless—were going to say something that would filter back to Mercedes. And he couldn't stand the thought of his daughter hurting that way.

She *was* his daughter, he was sure of it. And he needed to do the right thing, but...marry Fern? Could the solution really be that simple? And that...exciting?

He was just about to the door when he glanced to the right, into the little library. There was Fern, talking to the veteran Bob Eakin with animation, a book in her hand.

He could sneak past her and leave. Or he could do the right thing.

She'd probably be glad if he didn't stop in. She wouldn't want to see him before their prearranged time. If then. She had no interest in seeing him anytime, really.

So he should go.

Instead, he turned and walked into the library.

Bob gave him a knowing look. "I'd better get down to the cafeteria if I want to hold my table," he said, winking at Carlo as he headed out the door. "That Minnie Falcon is always trying to steal my window seat."

"But... Oh." Fern watched the old man's surprisingly rapid exit and then looked at Carlo without the faintest hint of happiness. More like resignation. "What are you doing here?"

"Visiting my grandpa. And Miss Minnie Falcon." He looked around to make sure no one else was in the room, then closed the little library's door. "Fern, we need to talk, and soon. Rumors are spreading."

Her lips tightened. "I said I'd meet you for dinner. Tomorrow."

"I'm worried it's not soon enough. Where's Mercedes?"

"She's at her day care program. I wanted to keep her in her routine, so she's still going part days even though I'm on vacation." She sounded defensive.

"Good," he said. "Would you want to go have lunch and talk about it now? Because I'm worried she'll hear something soon."

Fern looked at him and he read the struggle on her face. "I have to finish up here," she said. "I handpick books for a few of the residents."

"That's fine, I can wait. Or I can read. Or I can help."

"Fine," she said, stress evident in her voice. "Wait here." She turned on her heel and spun out of the library.

Leaving Carlo to stare down unseeingly at the stack of books in front of him and wonder just what he was going to propose during the lunch to come.

CHAPTER TWELVE

An hour later, Fern sat across from Carlo at the back of the Chatterbox Café, feeling incredibly awkward.

Why was he treating her so gently, as if she was about to shatter? Did he think she wasn't strong enough to face the truth of the situation, the fact that she might very well lose Mercedes?

Well, he might have a point. She *wasn't* strong enough for that.

The café was bustling, full of moms with children, the police chief and one of the officers, some workmen from down at the pretzel factory. Waitresses in pink shirts rushed around with trays and pots of coffee. Through the large windows at the front of the restaurant, Rescue River's main street was visible, picturesque with snow.

Fern could smell burgers and fries, which she normally loved. Now the greasy odor turned her stomach. She grabbed a plastic-coated menu from the stand on the table and stared at it, barely seeing it.

But it beat staring at Carlo, who was even more handsome now that he was clean shaven. He'd hung up their winter coats, and his short sleeves revealed his massive soldier arms. Without the beard stubble, his jaw looked even more square, and his eyes, as he watched her, shone dark blue and honest.

She had to keep reminding herself that he'd misled

her and Mercedes, not letting them know his beliefs about being Mercedes's father.

She pinched the back of her hand, hard, to distract herself from the emotional pain of Carlo's betrayal and of losing Mercedes.

"Thank you for coming," Carlo said, still sounding cautious.

"Sure. We have to talk. It's just…hard."

"I know, and I'm sorry. How do you think we should tell her?"

She shook her head. "I'm worried she'll be upset. Especially if she thinks there's going to be a change in her living situation. Which…there will be." Her stomach lurched as she said the words, and her eyes filled with tears.

"Um, about that." Carlo reached across the table and took her hand. "I have an idea." He ran his thumb over her knuckles in a back-and-forth motion.

Even that light touch took her breath away. She tugged her hand back. "What's your idea?"

He took a deep breath and then blew it out. "This is going to sound crazy, but…we could get married."

Fern's heartbeat accelerated as everything around them seemed to fade away.

Marriage. To Carlo. A real family. Fun and caring and sweet, sweet togetherness. Her heart seemed to expand in her chest.

When she didn't answer, he continued talking. "I don't mean a regular marriage. I wouldn't expect that. It would be for Mercy's sake."

She stared at him. His mouth kept moving, but she'd stopped processing the words.

She'd gotten stuck on two particular phrases.

We could get married, which had made her heart soar.

I don't mean a regular marriage, which had brought her right back down to earth with a crashing thud. Of course someone like Carlo wouldn't be able to really love someone like her.

"Can I take your order?" came a perky voice. It was Lindy Thompson, who'd just graduated from high school last spring. She was a sweet and pretty girl, and Fern liked her because she was a reader who made regular appearances in the library.

"Hey," Lindy said, staring at Carlo. "You're that big war hero, right?"

A flush of color crossed Carlo's face. "I'm a veteran, but no big hero."

"No, I remember hearing about you in town. I was telling my brother he should meet you. Didn't you get a whole bunch of medals?"

He rubbed the back of his neck. "I may have a few. Who's your brother? Is he a vet, too?"

"Yeah, and he's not doing so well." Lindy's mouth turned downward. "He's got to go have some more surgeries just as soon as he's up for it, but we don't know when that will be."

"I'm sorry. You give him my best, will you?"

"Oh, thank you, I will! That's really nice of you!"

Okay, enough. The girl's eyes held the kind of hero worship that was pretty much irresistible to men. Great.

"Hey, maybe you could meet him sometime," Lindy suggested. "It would mean a lot to him. Sometimes he and Mom come in for lunch."

"Sure," Carlo said easily. "I'm in town for a while."

Lindy took their orders and Fern struggled with an absurd sense of jealousy.

Carlo didn't really want to marry her. Much more suited to him would be someone like pretty, young, outgoing Lindy. Just look at him, how handsome he was, how modest about his war achievements, how kind to a young waitress. He was a catch, all right, and in a little town like Rescue River, he'd be snatched up immediately. By someone much more fun and lively than Fern.

"So," Carlo said after Lindy walked away, "guess my suggestion fell flat."

She bit her lip. *No, it sounded wonderful!*

"I mean that we should get married."

This was the moment. She could agree to a marriage and have the wonderful family feeling she'd tasted during the storm.

Only it wouldn't be real.

"It would never work," Fern said. Better to pull the Band-Aid off quickly.

He swallowed visibly, opened his mouth as if to argue, and then closed it again. "Then, we should tell her together."

Fern forced herself to shrug and nod. "Sure."

"That way," he said, "she'll be more comfortable. So she can ask questions."

Push him away, push him away. "She'll have a lot of them. Not only about why you weren't there for her first four years, but about why you didn't tell us the truth during the snowstorm."

Carlo closed his eyes for a second and then reached out and took her hand, his expression regretful. "I want to build a relationship with you and I know it got started wrong."

The feel of his hard, large, calloused hand seemed to burn her. Her heart raced and she snatched her hand

back, feeling heat rise in her face. "There's no relationship."

"Why?" He sounded bewildered. "Fern, I know I
was wrong not to tell you my suspicions, but you of all
people ought to know what it's like. We were practically strangers. I didn't know how to bring it up, or if I
should. Things got away from me, but I never intended
to deceive you."

She drew in a breath between clenched teeth. "Stop
it."

"Stop what?"

"Stop acting so nice." Fern's throat closed up, and
tears burned her eyes.

Don't you dare cry. The words of one of her particularly harsh foster mothers echoed in her mind. She'd
learned to hold back her feelings then, and she could
still do it. Again she pinched the back of her hand, hard.

Carlo leaned closer. "Fern. I want to work this out."

"It's not going to work out. How can it? You're her
father, and you have the right to her. She likes you. It'll
be fine for her. I'll just be a memory in her life, someone
who took care of her for a little while until her daddy
could come." Her voice squeaked and she clenched her
mouth shut. Enough talking.

"Fern. I'm drawn to you. Are you sure you won't
consider—"

"No!" He wanted a marriage of convenience, not of
love. He didn't care for her as a woman.

"Why?" He was looking at her steadily. "Maybe
there's a way we can work together. We certainly have
to work together to tell Mercedes."

If she agreed to it, she'd be making a mockery of
something that was supposed to be sacred. And she'd

die a little more every day, living with Carlo and knowing he didn't love her.

She hardened herself to the hurt and concern on his face. "Didn't anyone ever tell you that no means no?"

He gave her a long, pained look and then broke eye contact and slumped back in his chair, seeming to shrink before her eyes.

Lindy approached with their food and Fern used the brief interruption to take deep, calming breaths. She could get through this. For Mercedes's sake, she had to. Had to hand the child off graciously to him, could never let Mercedes suspect that her daddy had broken Mama Fern's heart.

The bells on the front door jingled, and Lindy put their plates in front of them and looked toward the restaurant's entrance. "Hey, it's my mom and brother. If he's feeling okay, can I bring him over for a minute?"

"Of course." Carlo's voice sounded stiff and formal.

"Mom," Lindy called. "Over here."

A tired-looking fiftysomething woman, whom Fern had also seen at the library, was struggling to get a wheelchair through the door. In it was a man who couldn't be more than twenty-one. He wore a hoodie and flannel sweats, and his head rested in a special support.

A couple of men near the front hurried to help with the door, and the older woman looked up, saw Lindy beckoning and headed over, a wide smile creasing her face.

"Mr. Camden, sir, I'd like you to meet my brother. Tom," Lindy said to the man in the wheelchair, "this is the one I told you about, who became a missionary? The Purple Heart, Silver Star guy? Say hi."

The man in the wheelchair didn't seem to be able to move much, but he lifted his eyes to meet Carlo's.

Carlo was out of the booth in a flash, squatting to put himself on the same level as the man in the chair. "My pleasure," he said. Then he lifted his hand in a slow salute. "Thank you for your service."

The man in the chair blinked and swallowed and gave a little nod, and Lindy reached out to put an arm around her mom, whose eyes were shiny.

In the space of a few seconds, the two men seemed to exchange some knowledge that none of the rest of them could share.

"Would you like to join us?" Carlo asked, still kneeling.

The man shook his head, making garbled speaking sounds. He looked up at his mother and tapped his chest.

"He wants me to show you his medals," she interpreted, and reached into a bag attached to the wheelchair. She pulled out a small box and flipped it open. "He got the Purple Heart. We carry 'em all the time."

Fern watched, her food forgotten, as Carlo looked at the medal and then talked with the family about the younger man's combat. He was obviously comfortable with the man's disability and with the family as he walked with them to another table in the diner.

All Fern could think was what a good daddy he would be for Mercedes. And how proud and happy the woman would be who won his love.

He came back in and sat down across from her, looked ruefully at his cold burger and her untouched chicken salad. "I'm sorry about that," he said, still sounding polite and distant.

"It's fine. When...when do you want to meet with Mercedes?" His kindness and heroism just made it harder to think of how he'd probably take Mercedes and go somewhere else. Now she just wanted to get out of the café before she fell more in love with him. More impossibly in love.

"Well," he said, looking down at the table, "given the fact that Gramps already knows, and he didn't hear it from me, I think we should move fast. How about tonight?"

She didn't think she could bear another encounter with Carlo in one day. But she also wanted to protect Mercedes, and after the emotional encounter they'd just had with the wounded veteran, talk about Carlo would be all over town. "Okay," she said, "where?"

"Where does she feel most comfortable? Would that be out at the rescue, since you're staying there, or would it be at your home?"

Fern drew in a deep breath. The last thing she wanted was to have her cozy little retreat invaded by giant, gorgeous Carlo. Once he'd been there, she might never be able to exorcise the memory of him.

But that was the place where Mercedes felt at home, and Mercedes's needs took precedence. In fact, Fern had promised her that they could spend some time at home, among her familiar toys and games, tonight.

"All right," she said with a sense of impending doom. "Why don't you come over after dinner tonight?"

THAT EVENING, CARLO approached Fern's little bungalow as the sun sank below the trees that lined the snowy street. The house was in a neighborhood, but separated from the other houses by a little more land and a row of pines. That was perfect for Fern; she'd want to be able to keep to herself, but she was an integral part of the community, as well. In her quiet way, she helped others, from the kids at the library to the shut-ins at the Senior Towers. She might not know it, but everyone loved her.

He was in a fair way to falling in love with her himself. Which was bad, because she'd given him a definitive no today at lunch. And as she'd pointed out, no meant no. His face heated at the memory.

Seeing lights inside, he tapped lightly on the door, but no one came to open it. He pounded louder and rang the doorbell.

"Sorry," Fern said as she opened the door, her voice breathless.

"We were making a cake!" Mercedes added, popping out from behind Fern. "'Cause Mama says there's a surprise!"

"There *is* a surprise," he agreed, smiling at Mercedes, his heart pounding. How would she react when she learned he was her father?

He'd called Daisy for advice and strategies about how to talk to Mercedes, and she'd offered to call Fern as well, so that they were on the same page. They had to tell her together, reassure her that she was loved, let her know the progression and what would come next.

What *would* come next? Carlo didn't know. He wanted to have Mercedes, to raise her. More and more, he thought he'd like to do it in the little town of Rescue River, where she was already comfortable, where she had friends and a day care and a church home, where she'd have an aunt and a great-grandpa who loved her.

"She'll surely transition to living full-time with you," Daisy had said, "provided all the tests come back positive. But don't promise that. Let her know that the judge will decide what's best for her."

The whole situation had his heart aching and his stomach in a knot. This little girl had already faced so much loss, and he hated the idea of taking her from her very special Mama Fern.

On the other hand, he wanted to know her and love her and raise her. And it didn't look as though Fern would be able to get along with him to do that. He'd screwed up, plain and simple. He should have been easy and honest and up-front, and things might have been different.

But for better or worse—in this case, for worse—he wasn't a trusting guy who could spill his guts at a moment's notice, express a thought as soon as he had it. In that, as in so many things, he and Fern were alike.

"Come on, come see my house!"

He slid out of his snowy boots, catching a whiff of chocolate as he let Mercedes pull him through the little cottage in his sock feet. He got a quick impression of a cozy gas fire, polished wooden floors with colorful throw rugs, and books. Lots and lots of children's books, on shelves and stacked on end tables and in a basket beside Mercedes's booster chair in the dining room. Among the stuffed animals piled in an armchair, he recognized Peter Rabbit and Paddington and the Stinky Cheese Man, who'd made Mercedes laugh hysterically each night during the snowstorm. And there was a Madeline doll; he recognized the character from childhood reading with Angelica.

On a whim, he picked up the doll and made her recite a couple of lines from the Madeline book to Mercedes, and was rewarded when Fern and Mercedes recited the next line back at him.

"Come see the cake!" Mercedes shouted impatiently, tugging at him.

"You keep on surprising me," Fern said, smiling up at him. "Did you read that book to your sister?"

"At least five hundred times." He swallowed, tried to

steel himself to the effect of her innocent smile. "Has Angelica seen this place? She'd love it."

Fern nodded. "She and Xavier have been over here a few times."

Carlo pondered that as Mercedes showed him around the little downstairs. So Angelica and Xavier had been here, not knowing that they were actually related to Mercedes.

The deceit just went on and on. Kath had never wanted to meet his family, and she'd stayed away from Rescue River during their short and stormy marriage, but what had brought her here in the end? He might never know.

"Come see my room and my kitty cat!" Mercedes ordered.

"Okay with you?" he asked Fern.

"Sure."

Mercedes took them both by the hand and pulled them up half a flight of stairs and into a bedroom so sweet and girlie that it took Carlo's breath away.

What he wouldn't have given to be able to provide Angelica with such a room back when they were kids. All pink and ruffly, with books on the shelves and a cozy window seat. More stuffed animals on the bed and a small table with a plastic tea set on it.

He was beyond thrilled that Mercedes had such a wonderful place to live. How could he take it away from her? How could he possibly compete?

Mercedes jumped up and down on her bed. "When you turn the lights off, there's stars!" she said. "Do it, do it, Mama!"

"When you stop jumping on the bed," Fern said, looking stern.

Mercedes clapped her hand to her mouth. "I forgot."
She sat down properly on the bed, hands folded.

"Okay, ready?" Fern asked.

"Ready," Mercedes said.

Carlo found his throat just a little too tight to speak.

Fern turned off the light and the ceiling glowed with
stars. Through the window, the purple and pink and orange shades of sunset showed above the evergreen trees.

"Mama Fern wanted to make my room fancy and
special, like me," Mercedes explained reverently.

Wow.

After a minute, Fern flipped on the lights. "Cake
next, or do you want to show Cheshire?"

"Cheshire!" Mercedes cried.

"He's probably hiding in my room," Fern said. "Why
don't you go pick him up, very carefully, and bring him
in here?"

"Mr. Carlo could come see your room."

Both adults shook their heads immediately. Though
Carlo wouldn't have minded seeing what kind of bedroom Fern had created for herself.

After he'd met the cat, who looked decidedly unhappy to be awoken from his nap and manhandled by
an overenthusiastic four-year-old, they headed down
the stairs, Mercedes running ahead.

He touched Fern's arm, stopping her. "You've made
a wonderful life for her here, Fern, and I appreciate that
more than you'll ever know."

She met his eyes, the muscles in her throat working,
and didn't say anything.

"Look, I decorated it myself!" Mercedes cried from
the kitchen.

Carlo followed Mercedes into the eat-in kitchen complete with old white appliances and blue-and-yellow

curtains at the windows. On the counter was a lumpy-looking chocolate cake, decorated with an overabundance of sprinkles and M&M'S candies.

Fern took a deep breath. "Let's sit around the table and have dessert," she said, her voice just a little shaky, "and then we'll have our talk."

Carlo poured milk while Fern cut cake and Mercedes set out napkins and forks, and just like during the snowstorm, he got a feeling of family. And he liked it. A lot.

If only...

Fern cleared her throat. "So," she said, pushing cake around on her plate, "Mr. Carlo and I have something to tell you."

"When's the surprise?" Mercedes asked, her mouth full. "Is it after the talking? Did you bring it with you?"

"Oh, honey," Fern said with a laugh that sounded forced, "the surprise isn't a present. It's...news."

Mercedes cocked her head to one side and looked from Fern to Carlo. "Okay." Her voice was a little subdued, and Carlo couldn't tell if that was because she wasn't getting a present or because she sensed something momentous.

No point in delay. His heart felt as if it was going to pound right out of his chest. "The news is," he said, "that I'm your daddy."

The child's eyes widened with delight. "I got a daddy? Like Xavier?"

"No," Fern said in a controlled voice, "he's your daddy because once, a long time ago, he was married to your mommy."

Mercedes looked puzzled. "But Mommy went to heaven."

"That's right, and your daddy was far away and didn't know."

She patted his arm, looking concerned. "Were you sad? Because it's okay to be sad."

"Yes," he said truthfully. "I was sad. But when I got here, I found out something very happy. I found out about you!"

Mercedes studied him for a minute as though she was thinking hard. "You could stay with me in my room," she said, "but I think mommies and daddies are s'posed to sleep in one bed."

"Oh, no," Fern corrected, a pretty flush crossing her face. "Mr. Carlo isn't going to be that kind of daddy. He's going to live somewhere else. Like…like Bryson's dad."

"And you can have a room there, too," Carlo hastened to add, wondering if Fern or Angelica would help him decorate it, since his skills were minimal in that department.

Mercedes's lips pursed out in a pout. "I want the kind of daddy who lives in the same house."

Fern reached over to give her a side hug. "Things can't always be just the way we want them to be, Mercy," she said in a low voice.

Mercedes struggled away and stood up, hands on hips, cake smeared across her face. "Wait. Mama Fern's still gonna 'dopt me, right?"

Fern looked at Carlo and he looked back at her. This was the tricky part. What had Daisy advised? He tried to remember the words he'd practiced.

Fern spoke up. "Since you have a daddy now," she said carefully, "you might not need to be adopted."

Mercedes's eyes went huge and she climbed into Fern's lap. "I wanna be 'dopted!"

Fern's arms went around Mercedes and she didn't look at Carlo. "I'll still see you lots and lots, I hope."

"We both love you," Carlo chimed in, his heart aching. "That doesn't ever go away or stop."

"Where am I gonna sleep?" Mercedes asked, her voice rising. "I get scared in the dark. I can't go to sleep without Mama Fern."

"I know." Fern's voice was broken. "It's hard."

Mercedes clung to Fern then, burying her head in Fern's shoulder, crying. Gone was the happy, confident little girl who'd led him all around her house. Carlo sat helpless, staring at the misery he'd caused.

"I don't wanna go with him," Mercedes said through her tears, looking up at Fern.

"Shh," Fern murmured, rocking her a little. "Shh, it's okay. You're staying with me for now. For a little while."

"You said it was a surprise, but this isn't a good surprise."

Fern grabbed a tissue and wiped her eyes and nose, took a gulp of milk. A deep, audible breath. "It *is* a good surprise, even if you feel a little sad now. It's wonderful to have a daddy. Daddies are lots of fun."

"But I want *you*, Mama Fern. I need a mommy!" She paused, rubbing her hand across her nose. "I'm sorry I jumped on the bed. I won't do it anymore."

"Oh, honey." Fern's arms tightened around the little girl. "It's not your fault. You're a wonderful girl."

"Then, why can't I get 'dopted and stay with you?"

"We'll keep talking about it," Fern said. "We'll get to talk to a judge who will help us figure it all out."

"I don't wanna." Mercedes peeked out at Carlo then, her face thunderous. "You go away, mean man."

"Mercedes!" Fern drew in an audible breath. "We use nice words and respect."

Carlo waved his hand. "It's okay. Maybe it's best that I go for now?" He had no idea how to fix this.

He should never have come home. He should have stayed away.

"It might be best," Fern agreed with a slight catch in her voice. "We'll get together with you again…real soon. Maybe meet with Daisy."

"Okay," he agreed, and escaped out the door.

CHAPTER THIRTEEN

"THANKS FOR PICKING me up," Fern said to Susan Hayashi on a cold Saturday morning. The past couple of weeks had been awful, and she'd wanted to beg off from the church ice-skating outing and hole up at home. But the fresh air would be good for Mercedes. And the companionship, because Susan was bringing Roxy, one of the kindergarten-age kids she tutored.

They moved Mercedes's car seat into Susan's little car, and Susan cranked up a CD of kids' music, adjusting the sound to be louder in the back. As they headed down a country road, Fern heard Mercedes laugh in the backseat. She sighed with relief.

"Rough day?" Susan asked.

"Rough two weeks." Since Mercedes learned about Carlo being her father, a reality that the paternity test had confirmed, she'd had tantrums almost every day, along with bed-wetting and nightmares most nights. Mercedes wasn't getting much sleep, which meant that Fern wasn't, either. The strain was showing on both of them.

"Is it about Carlo?" Susan asked quietly. "I don't mean to be nosy, but the news is all over town that he's Mercedes's dad."

"Yep, that's what it is." Fern didn't exactly want to talk about it, but on the other hand, she had to talk to someone. "This is just between us, okay?"

"Sure."

Fern cocked an ear back to make sure the girls were doing okay. When she turned around, she was glad to see them bent together over Roxy's handheld game as the preschool music blared.

"She won't go with him," Fern said quietly to Susan. "He's supposed to have visits every other day, to get her used to the idea of him being her father and to prepare for her possibly living with him. But she hides in her room or has a huge tantrum. If he takes her, I hear her screaming all the way down the street."

It was awful, wrenching. Carlo had rented an apartment just a couple of blocks away from her house, and he'd bought toys and games and tried to make the place comfortable for his child, but she was having none of it.

"Is she afraid of him?" Susan asked. "I mean, he's kind of...large."

"I don't think it's that. He's so gentle with her. I think it's that she sees him as taking her away from me."

"Which he's doing," Susan observed.

"Well, maybe. The hearing might be as soon as next week, and then we'll know for sure how it's all supposed to turn out. But meanwhile, they need to spend time together."

"Is she clinging to you?"

Fern nodded. "Either that, or defying and hitting me. It's crazy."

Susan turned onto a smaller, snow-packed road, handling the car skillfully as it slid a bit. "It's actually pretty normal."

"Really?"

The young teacher nodded. "From all my coursework in special ed, I know that kids lash out at caregivers a lot when they're making a transition. On some level, they feel as though the parent they're attached to is pushing them out."

"That makes sense." She looked out the window at the wintry farmscape, remembering her own multiple transitions between homes. She'd never struck a foster parent, but there had been plenty of times she'd just given up and withdrawn. "I was in foster care myself, so I feel for her," she said to Susan, surprising herself. Mostly, she kept the details of her childhood private, but Susan's accepting friendship made her comfortable, as though she could let down her guard.

"Really?" Susan glanced over at her, eyebrows raised. "That must have been hard. Is Mercedes's situation bringing up all that for you?"

Fern cocked her head as she thought about it. "You're really smart, you know? I've been feeling incredibly blue and awful, and it's mostly about losing her, but it's…it's weird. It feels as if it's me getting abandoned and pushed out, a kind of hole inside I haven't felt in a lot of years."

"Childhood can come back to haunt you like that," Susan said in a tone that suggested she had a few childhood issues of her own to deal with.

As they pulled up to the lake—more of a small pond, really, with lots of children and adults laughing and playing—Fern put a hand on Susan's arm. "Thank you again for getting us out," she said. "I really want Mercedes to have a good time and just be a child. Stuff like this is perfect."

"Stick with me, kid." Susan smiled at her. "Seriously, you should hang out more with Daisy and me. We're the single supernerd girls of Rescue River, and we always have a good time."

"You're friends with Daisy?" Fern's stomach twisted.

"My social worker? Are you going to tell her what we talked about?"

"You didn't say anything bad. But cone of silence anyway." Susan gave her a quick side-arm hug.

The girls started clamoring to join the fun, and Susan and Fern climbed out, too, to help them. "Daisy's great," Susan said. "You'll see, once she's not your caseworker anymore."

Yeah, great. That'll be when I don't have a kid anymore. Fern bit back a sigh. There was no reason she was entitled to have a child, just because she'd befriended Kath. It had been an unexpected gift and an honor that Kath had chosen her to raise Mercedes when she'd realized that she was terminally ill.

Fern had been in almost daily contact with Daisy since the blowup when Mercedes had found out Carlo was her daddy. Daisy had coached her about how to handle Mercedes's emotional storms, and had recommended consistent routines, an extra bedtime story and plenty of attention. According to Daisy, Fern was doing great. And Carlo, while he was visibly upset about Mercedes's rejection, wasn't taking it personally. He understood that a new change so soon after Kath's death was bound to upset Mercedes.

The thing was, though, that Mercedes needed closure. And so did she. Seeing Carlo almost every day wasn't helping her to care less for him. It just made her admire him more. His strength, his gentle patience, his efforts to make Mercedes laugh… It said a lot about the kind of man he was. He was a rock in the midst of a stormy time, and the temptation to cling to him grew bigger every day.

But she couldn't cling to a man who would never really love her.

Keep busy. She'd been following that mantra, working on her writing and illustrating when Mercedes was at Carlo's, putting in extra hours at the library.

Keep busy. Even now she needed to focus on the activity at hand, not go off into her own spinning thoughts.

She laced up her borrowed skates and followed Susan's lead, teaching Mercedes first to take giant steps in the skates on the nonslippery snow, and then heading out onto the pond for some very clumsy skating. Fern was learning right along with Mercedes, and she tried to model good sportsmanship about her own ridiculous lack of skill.

Finally, they got to where they could skate slowly around the pond, holding hands, with only a few falls. Thankfully, Susan had thought of knee pads for the kids. Fern could have used a pair herself.

Treasure each moment. It wouldn't be much longer that she'd have this precious hand in hers.

Afternoon sun peeked through the clouds, casting a golden light on the pond, glinting off the snow. She could smell the bonfire the guys were already building in anticipation of staying through twilight. She didn't know if they would stay; Mercedes's eyelids looked heavy, a reminder that this was her nap time.

They needed to stick with regular routines, as Daisy had been emphasizing. But then again, it was important for them to have some fun time together, to get out with other families and be social.

No matter how short or long was the time she'd parent Mercedes, Fern knew she'd never feel absolutely certain she was doing it right. Parenting was complicated, requiring a million little decisions. She had a renewed respect for all the parents she knew.

And doing it alone was more than challenging.

Fern thought of the time she'd spent with Carlo and Mercedes out at the farm. Thought of the happy moments at her house before the revelation that had shattered Mercedes.

Oh, she wanted that. She'd never known it before Carlo, but she wanted the whole lock, stock and barrel of family. Not just kids and pets, but a man.

Not just a man, but Carlo.

Throughout these past awful weeks, he'd never lost his temper, never yelled, never criticized. Compared to all the foster dads of her youth, he stood out as first-rate. Let alone that he was heroic, and handsome…and that he'd kissed her. For some time, however brief, he'd found her attractive.

It was enough to sweep a shy librarian right off her feet.

Beside her, Mercedes abruptly sat down on the ice—her preferred way of stopping—pulling Fern down, as well. Fern giggled and turned to the little girl. "What happened?"

But the question died on her lips. Mercedes was staring ahead, lower lip trembling, face flushing red. Meltdown warning signs.

Fern followed the little girl's gaze. Carlo.

Her heart thudded and she felt her breathing tighten.

Carlo skated slowly toward them and Mercedes scooted into Fern's lap. "I'm not going with him. Don't make me go, Mama. I'll be good."

Fern's heart constricted at the pain in the little girl's voice. It was pain she understood, but she also knew Mercedes had to get over it. "Tell you what," she suggested. "Let's show Mr. Carlo—I mean, Dad—how well you can skate."

"I don't want to show him. I wanna go home."

Fern struggled to her feet, but Mercedes's desperate clinging pulled her right back down again. "Don't make me go, Mama!"

Fern drew in a deep breath and fought for calm. People were staring, and if this was hard on her, it was twice as hard on Carlo and Mercedes. She closed her eyes and tried to pray, an effort that lasted only a couple of seconds before nerves made her open her eyes again.

"Hey, buttercup," Carlo said, coming closer and tweaking a lock of Mercedes's hair. "What's up?"

"Go 'way."

"She's doing a great job of skating," Fern said, meeting Carlo's eyes over the crying child. He was so handsome, and the pain and worry in his eyes made her ache for him.

"I wish she'd show me how to do it. I'm not very good."

Mercedes peeked out.

"Do you think if I just did it like this, it would work?" He leaned precariously out on one leg and fell.

Fern chuckled, knowing it took more skating skill to do what he'd done than it would to skate more normally. "Should we show him?"

"All right," Mercedes said reluctantly.

She got to her feet with Fern's help and together they took a few shaky, gliding strides across the ice. "See, Carlo," Fern called back, "you have to use two feet."

"Yeah," Mercedes added.

It was the most communication the child had offered Carlo since she'd learned he was her father. "Let's watch and see how he does," Fern suggested.

They turned and watched as Carlo glided on both skates, then lifted one leg out behind him and promptly fell.

"No, Daddy!"

She'd called him Daddy. Fern's world froze.

From the looks of things, Carlo's did, as well.

"Do it like this!" Mercedes demonstrated.

"Do you want to hold his hand and show him?" Fern asked, her heart just about breaking. She pointed Mercedes toward her father, holding her lightly from behind.

"Would you?" Carlo held out a hand from his position, low down on the ice. "I think I need some help."

Fern watched, barely breathing, as the little girl slowly skated away from her to her father.

Letting out a sigh, Fern watched as Carlo carefully got to his feet and took Mercedes's hand.

The pair of them made a couple of rounds on the ice. Fern watched, her mitten pressed to her mouth, the other hand across her belly. What a bittersweet feeling. She didn't want to give up Mercedes, but she knew it was in the child's best interest to have a good relationship with her father. Which probably meant to live with her father. Not with her.

Problem was, she felt as if a hole had been cut in her gut.

She skated off by herself, looking out at the snowy fields. *Father God, I really need You here. I need to cling to You, because I have to learn how to let this little girl go.*

She didn't hear words for an answer, but from somewhere, calm crept over her. God was with her. God would make the outcome right. God would help all of them. Not that it wouldn't hurt, but the Lord would be there for her. She could lean on Him.

When Carlo brought Mercedes back, the little girl was full of pride. "I helped Daddy, Mama Fern! I helped him learn to skate!"

"That's great." Fern smiled and a painful peace, the Lord's peace, settled over her.

"Thanks, kiddo," Carlo said, patting Mercedes's shoulder as Roxy skated up.

"You're welcome, Daddy." She said it loud enough for her new friend to hear. Like Roxy, like most kids in Rescue River, she had a daddy now.

The two girls skated clumsily away, leaving Fern and Carlo alone.

"That went really well," she forced herself to say.

"Yes, I think she's opening up to me. She's precious. Amazing."

"She is." Standing here with Carlo, watching the child they both loved, felt like everything Fern had ever wanted.

"Are you sure we can't—"

He was going to talk about a pretend marriage again. And she couldn't trust herself to keep resisting, not with the way she felt about him. "No. We can't."

A muscle twitched in Carlo's square jaw as he looked away, back toward the crowd at the bonfire site. "Excuse me. I have to talk to someone."

"Okay." She watched him skate away, admiring his grace. Was there anything he didn't do well?

Would she ever stop feeling heartbroken over him?

And then she realized that Carlo was headed toward Daisy. Great. She watched as the two engaged in animated conversation. Carlo seemed to be trying to convince Daisy of something, because she shook her head, and he talked more, and then she cocked her head to one side as if she was considering.

What were they saying? Was he telling her how Mercedes had connected with him, meaning that now he could take Mercedes full-time?

Fern watched, her eyes blurring with tears, until Roxy bumped into her. "Sorry, Miss Fern!"

"It's okay." And then Fern did a double take. "Where's Mercedes?"

The girl shrugged. "She was crying. She didn't want to play."

Fern's Mom Radar turned on. "Where did you see her last, honey?" she asked as she scanned the pond.

"Over there." Roxy waved vaguely toward the wooded side of the pond and skated off.

Fern scanned the crowd at the pond. Pulled out her glasses, which she'd dumped because they kept fogging up, and scanned it again. Squinted to see the area the little girl had pointed out, now darkening in the late-afternoon gloom.

She started skating, searching frantically, a vise tightening around her chest. Where was Mercedes?

CARLO PULLED HIS hood up against the increasing cold and nodded at Daisy. "I'm sure."

"Because if you change your mind," she said, "the judge could get irritable, think you're not stable. Which is the problem you face in your custody case anyway."

"Nope. Fern's her mother in every real sense of the word. I'm making arrangements for a better place to live, out in Troy and Angelica's bunkhouse, but that won't match what Fern has set up for her. I think we can work together and figure out a joint custody arrangement."

Daisy's face broke into a smile. "I love that you're looking at Mercedes's best interests. I'll start the paperwork tomorrow."

A frantic shout from the cluster of skaters in the middle of the pond kicked Carlo's adrenaline on.

"Who's that yelling?" Daisy asked.

"Sounded like Fern." He turned and skated toward the crowd, heart racing. Fern wasn't a yeller, and that hadn't been a fun-loving shout. Something was wrong.

He reached her where she stood in the middle of the pond, face white. "It's Mercedes," she gasped out. "I've hunted everywhere and I can't find her."

Behind him, Daisy skated up while Susan came from the other direction.

"Let me check with Roxy," Susan said, pointing toward the child they'd come with, and skating over toward her.

"I already did," Fern called after her. "She said Mercedes was upset and wouldn't play. Oh, why didn't I keep closer watch on her?"

Carlo's pulse raced as he looked around the pond, trying to spot his daughter. "But she was so happy just a couple of minutes ago, skating with me."

"That's how she's been lately. Her moods have been really up and down." Fern was turning around slowly, shading her eyes, scanning the area. Her breath came in ragged gulps.

"That's normal with all she's been through." Daisy had a hand on his arm and another hand on Fern's. "Maybe she got overwhelmed with feelings. Some kids run off when that happens."

Carlo's heart was racing and his head spun with guilt. Had he caused this, somehow, by pushing Mercedes to skate with him? And it was cold out here, no place for a child to be alone as twilight fell. No telling who was lurking around, possibly meaning harm to a little girl. And the ice had been checked, but there was always the chance a fall or a current had made it thin.

But there was no time for emotions. And as Fern

buried her face in mittened hands, her shoulders shaking, he realized he had to take the lead. Finding Mercedes was up to him.

"Everybody, gather round," he roared out in the same voice he'd used to command a company of soldiers. "Over here. Everybody. Now."

Members of their group skated their way quickly, seeming to recognize the seriousness in his voice.

Quickly he explained the situation to them, described what Mercedes was wearing. "Let's get organized. We need somebody to take care of the kids and keep them happy and together. And ask them what they saw without scaring them."

"I'll do that," Susan offered. "I know the kids."

"Keep them near the bonfire, and keep it stoked up," he said, making the plan as he spoke. "We'll need somewhere warm to bring her if we find her. *When* we find her." Important to keep everyone's confidence up. They *would* find her. They had to.

And they could use all the help they could get. "Someone needs to call the cops. I don't think there's anyone dangerous out here, anyone who could have taken her, but we should cover all our bases."

At that, Fern's sobs increased. He regretted having to say it, but there wasn't time to be sensitive, not now. If someone had taken Mercedes, every second was important.

"I'll call Dion," Daisy said, already on her phone.

People chimed in, offering to help, accepting his leadership without question.

He started assigning territory. "Ralph, right?" he said, pointing to a burly man whom he'd seen skating well. "You get a couple of people and cover this whole pond. Look for breaks in the ice, spots near the edge where a kid could hide or—" his voice cracked a little "—fall in. Here, punch your number into my phone first."

He turned to a woman who wasn't wearing skates, a sporty outdoors type who'd been helping to gather wood for the fire. "You get a group. Even numbers. Go through the woods in pairs. Stay where you can see each other."

She nodded, started pointing at people to help her, assigning them partnerships. Good.

"Parking lot," he said to the two remaining adults. "Look in and under every car. Give your phone numbers to Daisy and Susan."

Which left him and Fern, and she was shivering and sobbing. "Let's think," he said, putting an arm loosely around her. "There's no time for tears."

"But it was my fault!"

"Snap out of it!" He softened the words with a squeeze to her shoulders. "We know her best of all. You do. What kinds of places does she like to hide?"

"She likes to get into little places." She sniffed. "Like that book, *Hide and Seek Sammy*. Oh, Carlo, I'm so sorry."

"It's not your fault. Come on." He guided her over to the gathering area, found her a seat by the bonfire and sat down himself, removing his skates and pulling on his boots. "You stay here with Susan and Daisy and the kids. She'll be drawn to the fire as it gets dark, and I want you here." He gave Daisy a meaningful look. "I mean it, no searching. You stick together and wait for her."

Fern nodded, her shoulders still shaking. This highly competent woman had finally lost it.

"We'll find her," he promised. There was no room

for doubt here, not in this type of situation. You had to keep your confidence up. "Pray. Hard."

He ran off toward the far side of the lake, checking every small spot, praying the whole time. *Lord, help me find her. Don't let me lose her before I've had the chance to be her dad. If You let me find her, I'll give her up, whatever she needs, whatever's right.*

He searched clumps of bushes, checked dry cattails sticking up through the ice. Waved and called encouragement to the other searchers. Went hoarse with calling his child's name.

His fingertips and his toes were going numb, and his face felt raw in the wind, but all he could think was how cold Mercedes must be.

He dipped in and out of the woods, because even though there were searchers there, he knew he was better trained than any of them. His eyes automatically scanned for small footprints and his ears were alert for little-kid cries.

But there was nothing. He'd gone most of the way around the pond with no sign of her. His stomach tightened as he reluctantly concluded that someone might have taken her.

Please, Jesus, keep her safe.

Then he saw the outline of a rowboat, upside down, covered with snow.

In a flash he thought back to one of the stories they'd read together during the blizzard. Something about boats, all the uses of boats.

Upside down, it's a home for a clown. The picture had shown a clown peeking out from the edge of an upside-down rowboat.

Would she really?

He ran to the boat. The wind was fierce now, whistling through the pines, making his eyes tear up. He couldn't tell if the boat had been disturbed. "Mercedes?" he called, quieting his voice.

Was that a sound? Hard to hear over the wind, but maybe.

He heard it again as he lifted up the boat.

And saw a small, pink-and-purple-clad shape there. "Daddy?" the shape said with a little sob.

Thank You, Jesus.

He scooped her up in his arms, checked her limbs for injuries, kissed away her tears as she clung to him. "Are you okay? Do you hurt anywhere?" His heart was racing, now with joy, because she looked okay and she felt wonderful.

"I'm cold," she said, burrowing into his chest, crying. "I called and called but nobody came."

"Come on, let's take you to Mama." He shifted her to hold her even tighter against his chest, trying to warm her.

She nestled in. "I got scared," she said confidingly.

"Me, too, when I couldn't find you." Hugging her, he shot up another prayer of supreme gratitude.

Then, suddenly, she struggled violently to get out of his arms. He let her go, put her down on her skates but kept hold of her shoulders. "What's wrong, honey?" he asked, squatting down in front of her.

"Are you going to take me away now?" Her eyes were round, her voice worried.

After a moment's puzzlement, he suddenly understood her question and shook his head. "I'm not going to take you from Mama Fern," he said. "I'm going to take you back to her."

She hesitated, considering his words. "Really?"

"Really. Mama Fern needs you and you need her."

She held out her arms to him, and as he picked her

up and felt her arms go around his neck, a lump formed in his throat.

Holding her, looking around the darkening pond as it sparkled in the moonlight, he felt God's presence as never before in his life, and with it, a sense of calm came over him. God had it in control. God was making everything right, and He'd continue to do so.

Carlo couldn't even call out, he was so choked up, so he simply held Mercedes tight and set off at a fast walk toward the bonfire.

"Mama!" Mercedes cried when they got there, and Carlo put her into Fern's arms.

"You found her!" came Daisy's voice.

"Praise the Lord," Susan said as the kids cheered.

Fern didn't say one word, but her eyes, lifted to his, were filled with such gratitude and relief that he felt ten feet tall.

"Tell the others?" he asked Susan, whose eyes were wet.

"Of course." She headed off, calling in her strong voice.

"Oh, honey," Fern said, cradling Mercedes close, "are you okay? Let's get you right by the fire. Mama was so scared!"

"I did like the clown in the book," Mercedes said. "But it wasn't fun. And I was cold."

"Of course you were," Fern scolded, holding Mercedes's small hands toward the fire, holding the child herself in her lap. She looked up at Carlo. "Thank you. Oh, Carlo, thank you so much. I'm so, so sorry I let her get lost."

He sat down behind them, wrapped both arms around them. "Thank God. Praise God."

CHAPTER FOURTEEN

A WEEK LATER, as Fern parked in front of the dog rescue where she and Mercy had been stranded with Carlo, her mind played a movie of memories: hot chocolate and burned cookies, Carlo's deep rumbling laughter, his arm warm and protective around her shoulders. His tender kiss.

"My first sleepover!" Mercy bounced in her car seat. "Let's go, let's go!"

Mercy had clung to Fern for a couple of days after the near disaster at the skating pond, but then she'd gotten back into her four-year-old groove: playing hard at day care, eating and sleeping well at home, proving her resilience. And when she'd been invited to sleep over at Xavier's house for his birthday, she was over the moon.

Fern helped Mercy unhook her seat belt and then pulled the overnight case from the trunk.

"I'll carry my new sleeping bag," the child said, holding out her arms for the prized pink item.

Fern thought Mercedes was way too young for a sleepover, but Angelica, calling to invite her, had brushed aside Fern's objections. "She'll be fine here. She'll have Xavier, and her dad will be here, too. Her dad. I still can't believe Carlo has a daughter!"

So maybe it was okay. Fern's own childhood had been a little short on family sleepovers. What did she know about how to raise a child anyway?

Now Angelica opened the door, sank to her knees and pulled Mercy into a hug. "We're so glad you're here, honey! Come on in, it's cold out." She looked up at Fern. "Do you want to drop her off or stop in for a minute?"

Angelica's casual question surprised Fern. Was it normal to just drop off your four-year-old at someone's house?

"We have two other girls and three boys. It's going to get crazy, but I'll have plenty of help. I can handle it." Angelica got to her feet and held the door open, smiling at Fern.

"I'll come in," Fern said, "get her set up and settled and make sure." She met Angelica's eyes. "I'm a little overprotective. I can't help it."

"Of course you are, after the scare you had."

"You heard about that. I feel awful that I let Mercedes get lost. It was all my fault."

"What, that she got lost?" Angelica's voice, which had sounded distracted and light until then, suddenly got focused. "Are you beating yourself up about that?"

"I should have been watching her every minute. I got upset and preoccupied and she was gone." She waited for Angelica's gasp of horror.

It didn't come. Instead, "Did I ever tell you about the time Xavier escaped from the hospital?"

"What? No."

"He got a whole block through downtown Boston. In a hospital gown, no less! And a complete stranger brought him back."

Fern leaned back against the doorjamb. "But that wasn't on your watch."

"Yes, it was. I had him out of his room in the playroom and got talking to one of the other moms. I looked up and he was gone."

"Wow." Fern took a deep breath and let it out in a sigh, some of her tension ebbing out with it. "I feel like such a bad mother."

"I know, right? But we're all bad mothers at times. Now come in and see what we're planning."

The living room where she and Carlo and Mercy had gotten to know each other was transformed with blue and green balloons and crepe-paper streamers. "Of course he wanted a puppy theme," Angelica explained. "Wait till you see the cake."

"It's shaped like a dog bone," Xavier shouted as he ran into the room, another boy racing behind him.

Quickly, Fern turned to check Mercedes's reaction. Would the older boys intimidate her?

But Xavier stopped in front of Mercedes, grabbed her hand and tugged her toward the kitchen. "C'mon, Mercy! We're cousins now, so you can come over all the time. But you're gonna have to learn to play fun games, not dolls."

"I play fun games." Mercy put a hand on her hip as if daring Xavier to disagree.

"Then, c'mon!"

The three kids ran off together without a backward glance.

"I'll, um, just put her stuff down, I guess." Fern set down the birthday present she and Mercedes had wrapped together, checked the overnight case again to make sure her daughter's favorite stuffed frog hadn't been forgotten.

"I'll take good care of her, don't worry. And Carlo will be here all night."

Fern's heart lurched. "Carlo's staying over?"

"Just for tonight, for the party. In fact, he should be here any minute. Troy and I can use the help, and we thought it would make Mercy more comfortable. I'm so excited to have a little girl in the family! I'm going to spoil her like mad."

Troy came up behind Angelica, smiling as he heard what his wife was saying. He put an arm around Angelica and patted her rounded belly. "Good practice for us."

"That's right," Angelica said, her dark eyes sparkling. "Pretty soon, Mercy will have a new baby cousin to play with."

"That's wonderful." Seeing the loving way the two of them looked at each other, Fern felt her heart aching. Maybe she and Carlo could have had something like that, if she hadn't blown it.

"In fact," Angelica said, "did Carlo tell you he's going to be moving into the bunkhouse as soon as the weather breaks? That way, Mercy can have room to run and play and get to know all of us better, and we can help when his new job starts up."

New job? "Great!" Fern tried to inject some excitement into her tone, but her stomach churned.

"You should take a look at the bunkhouse on your way out," Angelica encouraged. "I don't think it's locked. I fixed it up a little when Xavier and I were staying there, and it's really homey. Mercy will be super happy there."

Of course she would. "Okay, I will. Thanks."

Fern found Mercy and hugged her goodbye. "Daddy will be here. You go to him if you need anything."

"I will, Mama. I gotta go play." She struggled away and ran over to where Xavier and the other boy were dumping an army of plastic men on the floor.

Fern watched for another minute, then forced herself to walk out the front door. She waved to Angelica, who was greeting another mother and a pair of twin girls, and trudged toward her car.

"Leave her all day tomorrow if you want," Angelica called after her.

Fern waved back, unable to speak.

Mercy was fine without her. She was being embraced by Carlo's family. And what could Fern, a nerdy librarian, all alone in the world, offer Mercy that would compare with Carlo's wonderful family?

She drove a couple of hundred yards, but tears blurred her vision and she stopped to find a tissue. There was the bunkhouse. She blew her nose. Well, sure, she'd stop and take a look. It wasn't as if she had anything else to do.

She walked inside and looked around, immediately aware of how the pine-paneled walls, bright area rugs and colorful curtains said *home*. There were two small bedrooms and a kitchen along one side of the living area.

It was perfect for Carlo and Mercy.

A spasm of pain creased her stomach and she sank down into a rocking chair, wrapping her arms around herself for warmth, still in her winter coat.

She was going to lose Mercy.

Just as she'd already lost Carlo.

By ignoring his offer of a marriage of convenience, she'd given up all she'd ever wanted in life. Now that he saw what a bad mother she was, he'd never take her back. He'd never let her keep Mercy. What claim did she have on the child anyway?

And what claim did she have on Carlo?

She'd judged him and pushed him away. She'd been so harsh, refusing to accept his apologies even when he was so kind to her and Mercy. And then that horrible experience at the pond. Even now she remembered the terror she'd felt, thinking Mercy might have been drowned or kidnapped. And she remembered the sternness in Carlo's voice as he'd called everyone into action, worked to solve the problem, while Fern had fallen apart.

Now he was settling into the bosom of his family, and rightly so. He'd find another woman, someone who was outgoing and more motherly, someone who wouldn't let a child get lost, wouldn't pass judgment, wouldn't act shy.

And Fern would go on alone.

She'd lost it all.

She let her face sink into her hands, and in the despair of an aloneness she'd created for herself, she cried out to God.

"Isn't that Fern's car?" Troy said to Carlo an hour later. They were walking out to the kennels to get puppies for the kids to play with, having decided that Brownie and her pup needed to stay sequestered from the over-enthusiastic kids.

Carlo glanced over, and just seeing her little subcompact stabbed him in the gut. "What's she doing at the bunkhouse?"

Troy shrugged. "You should go see."

Longing tugged at Carlo's heart, but he tamped it down and shook his head. "She doesn't want me anywhere around." He was trying to accept that no meant no, but it wasn't easy.

They walked to the kennel, where the silence between them was broken with loud barking. Troy grabbed a couple of leads and opened a kennel. "Leash up those two," he said, "and I'll get a couple more. We need sturdy pups for this crew."

As they brought the excited dogs to the house, Troy spoke up. "Seemed as if you and Fern had some feelings for each other. Might be worth a second try." He cleared his throat. "I'm not much on talking about my faith, but the second chance God gave me and Angelica has meant the world to me."

Carlo thought about that as he opened the front door and held it for Troy, laden down with a crate of three yipping pups. Could he open himself up to more rejection from Fern? And where was the line between hope and harassment, when she'd already given him a clear no?

"Daddy!" Mercy ran to him, hugged his leg and then squatted down to pet the dogs he'd brought in.

Troy met his eyes over the crate. "Might mean the world to her, too," he said quietly, nodding down at Mercy. "This back and forth from one house to the other can't be easy on her."

That was for sure. It wasn't easy on any of them. "I'll give that some thought," Carlo promised.

FERN DIDN'T KNOW how long she wrestled with herself, tears running down her face, praying for forgiveness.

Finally, the setting sun cast its rays through the bunkhouse windows, and she lifted her eyes to see God's glory painted across the sky in pink and purple and orange. At the same moment, she felt warmth and love embracing her.

Her heavenly father seemed to speak through the sunset, expressing His extravagant love for her. Forgiving her the faults that a childhood tainted by human sin had wrought in her. Offering the hope that she could learn, could grow, could love.

She wiped her eyes and let the forgiveness wash over her, soothing some of the heartache and loss.

A knock on the bunkhouse door had her blowing her nose and wiping her eyes again, running her hands over her hair.

"Fern! Are you in there? It's Daisy and Susan. We stopped in to wish Xavier a happy birthday and saw your car."

She drew a deep breath, waited for her usual anti-social desire to shoo away human contact. But it didn't come. She actually wanted to see them. She hurried to the door and opened it.

"You've been crying!"

"What's wrong, honey?"

They wrapped her in hugs and worried questions, and soon all three of them were sitting at the bunk-house's small dining table, drinking from juice boxes that were the only thing they'd found in the refrigerator.

"Did anyone check the expiration on these?" Susan asked, studying her box.

"They're full of preservatives. It's fine." Daisy waved a hand. "Fern. Are you going to tell us what's going on?"

"I'm just emotional about leaving Mercy overnight, that's all." Fern looked at her friends' skeptical faces and added, "Mostly."

Susan smiled sympathetically. "Get used to it. As a single mom, you've got to embrace time to yourself when you can find it. In fact, once you start dating, I'll gladly take a turn at babysitting."

"Me, too," Daisy said. "We're like the best babysitters in town."

"Because we love kids and I, for one, am never gonna have kids of my own."

"Me, either," Daisy said.

Susan nudged her. "Don't be too sure. With the vibes I'm feeling between you and Dion, I'm thinking you might have yourself a white picket fence and a couple sweet little babies before you turn thirty."

"Susan!" Daisy's fair skin went pink. "That is *so* not happening."

Fern's memory conjured up the speedy way Daisy had contacted the handsome African-American police chief and how they'd shared a spontaneous hug when Carlo had come rushing across the frozen pond carrying Mercedes.

Daisy cleared her throat. "Change of subject. You heard that Carlo needs to adjust the schedule for Mercy's care, huh?" Her voice was businesslike as she switched into full social worker mode.

Fern could understand wanting to keep your personal life to yourself. "Yeah, only I don't quite understand what happened. When's the custody hearing?"

"Um, unless there's a problem, there's not going to be one."

Fern frowned at Daisy. "Why not?"

"Didn't he tell you he's not fighting for sole custody anymore? That he wants to do joint custody?"

"Nooo," Fern said as her world spun.

"You're kidding." Daisy stared at her, then slapped her own forehead. "I'm so sorry, Fern. I should have told you, but I assumed that the two of you had talked it through. All we need to do is finalize the arrangements, figure out what days she's with you and what days she's with Carlo. In fact, I have papers for you to sign back at the office, if you're game."

Fern stared at the other woman, stunned. "You mean," she said faintly, "I can still be Mercedes's mom?"

"Yes! Yes! Oh, honey, I'm so sorry."

Fern buried her face in her hands, overwhelmed. Just like that, she was back to being Mercedes's mom. She had everything she'd hoped for. Only...

She felt a hand gently rubbing her shoulders from one side, and heard Daisy slide her chair over from the other. She looked up to see both women leaning toward her, concerned expressions on their faces.

"Are you okay?" Susan asked. "Isn't that what you wanted?"

She nodded quickly, blinking back tears. "I can't believe it. I can't believe I get to mother that wonderful child. Even after I screwed up so bad at skating."

Daisy patted her arm. "That could've happened to anyone. You're a wonderful mom, Fern. You and Mercedes will be great for each other long-term. I'm so happy it turned out this way."

"Is it going to be weird," Susan asked, "working out joint custody with Carlo when you weren't even married to him?"

Fern nodded. "Yeah, especially when we're...basically not speaking to each other."

Susan gave her a hard look. "Does that bother you?"

"Well, of course it does." She opened her mouth to say something about communication being important for Mercedes's sake, but what came out was different. "I like him. A lot."

Susan lifted an eyebrow. "As in *like* like?"

"I'm not totally surprised," Daisy said. "You should let him know how you feel."

Fern heaved a sigh. "Easier said than done. He's just

so *nice*. He'd do anything for Mercedes, but… I wish he liked me for me, you know?"

Daisy and Susan exchanged glances.

"It'll never happen," Fern said to forestall a pep talk. "I'm just not the type of woman men go for. And someone like Carlo, all handsome and hunky and kind? There's no way." As she said it, a heavy weight seemed to settle atop her heart.

Susan looked at Daisy. "Chatterbox?"

"It's two-for-one appetizers tonight," Daisy said.

"Come on, Fern," Susan said, reaching for Fern's hands and pulling her up out of her chair. "This calls for a lot more girl talk."

"Yeah," Daisy added, patting Fern's shoulder and then slipping into her coat. "Let's go get some dinner. It's five thirty and still a little bit light out. Spring's only a heartbeat away."

"The Chatterbox's fried zucchini will make everything better," Susan said.

But as she walked out of the bunkhouse with Susan on one side and Daisy on the other, Fern's heart ached.

She had Mercedes. She had friends. Life should be good.

But she didn't have Carlo. And wouldn't. Not ever. "I'm going to have to take a rain check, guys," she said.

Daisy eyed her sharply. "You going to be okay?"

Fern nodded. "I think… I just need a little time alone." And not just alone; she needed time with the Lord.

CARLO AND ANGELICA were sitting at the kitchen table the next morning when a car door slammed outside.

Troy, spatula in hand, stepped from the stove to look out the window. "It's Fern," he said.

In the cool of the slightly drafty kitchen, Carlo started to sweat. He was about to do one of the hardest things he'd ever done in his life.

Fern knocked on the kitchen door and then opened it, sticking her head in. "Hey," she said with just a trace of librarian shyness.

Carlo's heart constricted at the sight of her. She looked stressed, as though she'd been crying. The fact that he'd caused more than some of that stress bit at him.

At least now he knew he was going to alleviate it.

Inside, she accepted hugs from Troy and Angelica and peppered them with questions about how Mercy had done and how they'd survived the party. She was coming out of her shell, and he knew without a doubt that every unattached guy in Rescue River would want her. What would it be like if she started seeing other guys? If she found someone special to be with, to help her raise Mercy?

The very thought made him nauseated.

"Sit down, I'll fix you some pancakes," Troy said. "You'll need your strength for the rest of the day. The kids didn't get much sleep last night."

"Aw, thanks, but I'm not hungry. Where are the kids anyway?"

"They're watching the end of a movie." Angelica lifted her hands in apology. "Sorry, I know you don't let Mercy watch much TV—"

"No problem! I totally understand." She turned to Carlo. "We need to talk," she said.

Dimly he wondered what she had to say to him, but whatever it was, it couldn't be as world changing as what he had to say to her. If she was going to tell him he was around too much, that he needed to back off, or that she'd decided to sue for full custody... Well, he could trump that.

Oblivious of the undercurrents, Troy flipped pancakes like a short-order cook. "So, Fern, what have you been up to?"

She shrugged, smiled at the man. "Actually, I've been writing and painting like crazy."

"That's so cool," Angelica said. "Our local librarian is going to be famous!"

She blushed and shook her head. "I doubt that, but it helps me to think."

"Did you hear about Carlo's new job?" Angelica asked. "Tell her, bro!"

Fern looked surprised and interested. "Where? Doing what?"

"A nonprofit that helps some of the migrant families," he said quickly, wanting to get the unimportant stuff over with. "They needed a Spanish speaker, someone with field experience in the country. I start next week." He looked over at his sister, his stomach churning. "Would you mind if we went for a little walk?"

"Go for it. Troy and I will finish cooking, and the kids are content here with the dogs." She gave him a tiny grin and a subtle thumbs-up.

Whatever that meant.

So they headed out the door and into the snowy countryside. The sky was a brilliant blue, and long icicles dripped from the eaves of the barn. In the distance, a farm truck chugged down the highway.

It was as good a time as any. "I've been thinking about something—"

"I've made a decision—" she said at the same time. They both laughed, awkwardly. "You first," she said.

He swallowed. "Okay. Fern, I've gone over and over

this situation with Mercy. I've thought about it and prayed about it and I can only think of one thing that's really best, best for both of you." He paused, his heart hurting, and then forced the words out. "You should take her full-time."

She'd opened her mouth to speak, but with her words, her jaw dropped open and stayed that way a good few seconds.

He rushed on, wanting to get this over with. "It's not right to have a child go back and forth between two houses. She's happiest at your place, with her books and her cat and her stars on the ceiling. And with...with you, Fern. You're the best mother a little girl could ever hope for, and I trust you completely with her."

She was still staring at him.

Why wasn't she saying anything? "Of course, I'd hope you would let me have visitation rights. I want to be in her life," he said. "I mean, who am I kidding? I *want* to raise her. But for her sake—and for yours—I'll gladly give that up."

Silence. He couldn't interpret the look in her eyes. "What do you think?" he asked.

"Carlo." She took his hand in her smaller ones, staring up at him.

Being this close to the woman he loved made him a little dizzy. "Yeah?"

"You'll never believe this, but... I was going to offer the same thing. I've been up all night, reading my Bible and thinking about it, and I realized that Mercy would do fine being with you full-time."

"But—"

She stopped his protest with a finger to his lips. The touch was quick and soft, like the feather of a bird, but it took his breath away.

She went on, her voice resolute. "You have a great family. I mean, look at all this." She waved a hand, encompassing Troy and Angelica's house and the rescue barn and the snowy fields around them. "But more than that, you're a great dad. And, well, it's time to think about what's best for her, not for me."

He couldn't believe what he was hearing. He cocked his head to one side. "You'd sacrifice what you want for me and Mercy?" he asked.

She nodded. "Once I got my head on straight, yeah. I would. It's the only thing to do. When you care about someone, you want the best for them."

"That's what I thought, too."

They were quiet for a minute, staring at each other. Around them, sunlight sparkled on snow.

A chilly wind loosened a lock of hair from Fern's red cap. He brushed it back with a finger, thinking he'd never seen anything so beautiful as her face. "What part of the Bible were you reading?"

She cocked her head to one side. "King Solomon?"

Of course. He nodded slowly. "It just doesn't seem right to divide the living child in two, not when she has a perfectly wonderful mother and home."

"What happens," she asked in a voice that was barely louder than a whisper, "if *both* parties want to keep the child whole?"

The question hung in the frosty air between them.

Her bare hands looked cold, so he encased them in his larger ones. "I asked you before if you would marry me," he said, "but you turned me down. Would you… Could you reconsider?"

When she shook her head decisively, his heart sank.

"No, Carlo," she said, squeezing his hand, her eyes

going shiny. "No! I just can't. I can't pretend about something as important as marriage."

"I wouldn't be pretending," he blurted out.

Her eyebrows shot up into her hairline. "You wouldn't?"

He shook his head. "I think I fell for you the first night I saw you, taking such good care of a little girl I had no idea was mine, bringing me soup in a storm." He smiled a little, remembering. "That feeling's only grown over time, as I've gotten to know you. You had a bad start, Fern, just like I did, but you didn't let it stop you from loving and helping and being part of the community." He paused, unaccustomed to making such a long speech, but he felt as if his life and his future depended on it.

The occasion demanded something else, too. He sank to his knees in the snow. "The fact that you'd be willing to give Mercy up, for her own good… That just seals it, Fern. You're the woman I want to spend the rest of my life with. I know you said no before, but do you care at all about me? Maybe even enough to marry me?"

"For Mercy or for real?" she asked, her eyes wide and insecure.

"For real." He kissed her cold hands, each one, and then wrapped them together in his own larger ones. "Totally for real." He held his breath.

"Then…yes!" She sank down to her knees, facing him, as his heart soared. "Oh, Carlo!"

He clasped her to him and felt that everything he'd ever dreamed of was right there in his arms.

Moments later, she lifted her head. "Do you want to go tell Mercy?" she asked. "As her daddy, I think you should do the honors."

Carlo stood and pulled her to her feet. He tucked her under his arm and pressed her close to his side. "I think," he said, "we should do it together."

EPILOGUE

"I AM SO not a party person." Fern taped the end of the last crepe-paper decoration into place and surveyed it, frowning. It looked crooked.

"It's for a good cause," Carlo said as he dumped a load of firewood into the holder beside the fire.

She smiled at her husband, taking her time to enjoy the view of his muscular arms emerging from rolled-up flannel shirtsleeves. "Two good causes. And it's my favorite kind of party—small."

She looked around the room with satisfaction. They'd bought this little farmhouse only two months ago to accommodate their growing family, and it was absolutely gorgeous. Fern had brought all her favorite things from her little cottage, and they'd hustled to get the decorating done in time for the holidays.

Right at the edge of town, the place perfectly accommodated her need for both social and quiet time.

Mercedes called from the living room, "Sissy and me are gonna go build a snowman to meet everybody, 'kay?"

Fern met Carlo's eyes. "Could you help them?"

"I'd love to."

And it was true, Fern thought as she watched him usher the two little girls outside. Carlo was a natural father. To Mercedes, of course, but he was the one who'd heard about Paula in his new job reaching out to migrant groups.

Adoption. It came naturally to Fern anyway, with her background and with the way she'd come to love Mercedes. There were so many children who needed homes. And Paula was exactly Mercedes's age. They'd had her for six months, and of course there were issues, but the two girls were already inseparable.

Carlo helped Paula form a snowball and then roll it into a snowman. The little girl's dark eyes shone as she emulated Mercedes and stared up adoringly at Carlo.

Smiling, Fern hurried back into the kitchen to stir the tortilla soup she'd prepared for this double celebration—housewarming and adoption. It was comfort food for Paula. And then she returned to watch her family out the window, sketch pad in hand.

She'd gotten the go-ahead on a new picture book, and she'd deliberately chosen to work with snowy landscapes and with a family much like her own. Far from halting her creativity, being a wife and mother only added to it.

Time was an issue, but with Carlo's encouragement, she'd gone down to half-time at the library. That way, she had some time to paint while the girls were in school, and time to nurture them when school was over.

Pretty near perfect.

The gates to their front yard opened and Susan and Daisy came in. Angelica and Troy were right behind them, carrying presents, with Xavier running ahead to meet the girls. They'd also invited Lou Ann Miller, Gramps and Miss Minnie Falcon, but the older generation had a birthday party to attend at the Senior Towers and they were coming later.

Fern put down her sketch pad and went out onto the

porch. Carlo came to stand beside her as the girls ran ahead to greet the new arrivals.

Fern looked up at her husband and shut her eyes for a two-second prayer of thanks. Carlo squeezed her shoulders and kissed the top of her head. "See, a party isn't so bad," he teased.

"Not when it's all the people you love." Fern slid an arm around his waist, and together, they went to bring their friends and family into their new home.

* * * * *

We hope you enjoyed reading
Mercenary's Woman
by *New York Times* bestselling author
DIANA PALMER
and
His Secret Child
by LEE TOBIN McCLAIN

Both were originally Harlequin® series stories!

From passionate, suspenseful and dramatic
love stories to inspirational or historical,
Harlequin offers different lines to
satisfy every romance reader.

New books in each line
are available every month.

*Clancey Lang's irascible boss, Texas Ranger
Colter Banks, gets under her skin like no other man
can. She resolves to keep her focus on her little brother
and outrunning her past—not on her all-too-alluring
employer. But there's something about the Long, Tall
Texan that might just change her mind...*

Read on for a sneak preview of
Unleashed, *available in July 2019 from*
New York Times *bestselling author Diana Palmer.*

"Where did you learn to shoot a gun?" he asked curiously.

"My grandfather taught me about big guys, but Cal taught me how to shoot a pistol," she said. "He took me out to the firing range and let me practice." She winced. "It made my hands so sore. He said I had to learn to fire with either hand, like the FBI teaches you."

He scowled. "Why did he teach you?"

"It was just for fun," she stammered, and then flushed. That wasn't true. Cal had started teaching her right after Morris beat up her and Tad, while Morris was still living at home. Cal had even given her a little .32 caliber pistol. She'd assured him that she could never shoot anybody. He'd assured her that there were times when a gun might be the only way to save lives. And he added a rider about how Morris was drugged up half the time, and dangerous to both her and Tad. That was while Morris was waiting for his court case to be called. It didn't go to trial for several months after the assault that had cowed Clancey.

"Does he still take you out to the range?" he wondered aloud, and could have kicked himself for asking the question.

"Not anymore," she said. There was no need, since Morris had been locked up. She handed him the bag. "The cartridges," she added.

He took the bag from her cold fingers. He noticed that she had pretty fingers, but that she wore no polish on them. He looked at her hair, as well, with a frown.

"What's wrong?" she asked.

"You don't wear fancy nail polish or put green in your hair," he noticed. His black eyes began to twinkle. "No tattoos, either?"

"I don't like needles," she replied. One side of her pretty bow mouth pulled down. "And I can just see me trying to wear green hair and a tattoo in this office! The first time the lieutenant saw me, I'd be standing in the unemployment line!"

He pursed his lips. "The lieutenant has a tattoo. But if you ask him where it is, he turns red and finds an excuse to leave the room."

"What?" Her eyes danced and she laughed.

Her whole face lit up when she laughed, and her pale silver eyes glimmered like sun on steel. He smiled unconsciously at the picture she made, like that.

Don't miss
Unleashed *by Diana Palmer,*
available in July 2019 wherever
Harlequin® books and ebooks are sold.

www.Harlequin.com

Love Inspired

Save **$1.00**

on the purchase of ANY

Harlequin® Love Inspired®

book.

Available wherever books are sold, including most bookstores, supermarkets, drugstores and discount stores.

- ✂

Save **$1.00**

on the purchase of any Harlequin® Love Inspired® book.

Coupon valid until August 31, 2019.
Redeemable at participating outlets in the U.S. and Canada only.
Not redeemable at Barnes & Noble stores. Limit one coupon per customer.

52616394

Canadian Retailers: Harlequin Enterprises Limited will pay the face value of this coupon plus 10.25¢ if submitted by customer for this product only. Any other use constitutes fraud. Coupon is nonassignable. Void if taxed, prohibited or restricted by law. Consumer must pay any government taxes. Void if copied. Inmar Promotional Services ("IPS") customers submit coupons and proof of sales to Harlequin Enterprises Limited, P.O. Box 31000, Scarborough, ON M1R 0E7, Canada. Non-IPS retailer—for reimbursement submit coupons and proof of sales directly to Harlequin Enterprises Limited, Retail Marketing Department, Bay Adelaide Centre, East Tower, 22 Adelaide Street West, 40th Floor, Toronto, Ontario M5H 4E3, Canada.

U.S. Retailers: Harlequin Enterprises Limited will pay the face value of this coupon plus 8¢ if submitted by customer for this product only. Any other use constitutes fraud. Coupon is nonassignable. Void if taxed, prohibited or restricted by law. Consumer must pay any government taxes. Void if copied. For reimbursement submit coupons and proof of sales directly to Harlequin Enterprises, Ltd 482, NCH Marketing Services, P.O. Box 880001, El Paso, TX 88588-0001, U.S.A. Cash value 1/100 cents.

5 65373 00076 2 (8100)0 12423

® and ™ are trademarks owned and used by the trademark owner and/or its licensee.

© 2019 Harlequin Enterprises Limited

BACCOUP01516

SPECIAL EXCERPT FROM

*Read on for a sneak peek at
the second heartwarming book in
Lee Tobin McClain's Safe Haven series,*
Low Country Dreams!

Yasmin shifted on the glider, set it rocking with one foot and tucked the other foot up under her. The air was cooling now, a slight breeze bringing the fragrance of oleander flowers. It seemed only natural for Liam to shuffle closer on the glider. To let his arm curve around her shoulders.

Yasmin's breath whooshed out of her. Talking with Liam about her brother had made her feel vulnerable, but also relieved. Less alone. She remembered when she could share anything with Liam and he would always have her back. Such a wonderful feeling, especially after her brother had stopped being able to be that rock and that support to her.

Now Liam turned to meet her gaze head-on. His hand rose to brush back a curl that had escaped her ponytail. "I like your hairstyle," he said unexpectedly, his voice a tone deeper than usual. "Reminds me of the old days, when we were in school."

"In other words, I look like a kid?" Her words came out breathy, and she couldn't take her eyes off him.

Slowly, Liam shook his head. "Oh, no, Yasmin. You don't look like a kid at all." His eyes flickered down to her mouth, then back to her eyes.

Yasmin's heart fluttered like a terrified bird. Her stomach, her chest, all that was inside her felt squeezed by warm hands, melting.

How she wanted this. This opportunity to talk to Liam in a low, intimate voice. To feel that sense of promise, that there was something happy and bright in their future together.

She tried to grasp on to the reasons why this couldn't happen. How she didn't dare to have children, because the risk of them developing a mental illness was so high. Not only because of Josiah, although that was the main thing, of course. But also because of her mother's issues.

As if all of that wasn't enough, Yasmin knew she wasn't past the safe age herself. What if she got into a relationship and then started having delusions and hearing voices?

It was hard enough taking care of her brother, her blood relative. She owed him and bore the burden gladly. But she couldn't expect a romantic partner to do the same for her, wouldn't want someone to.

Wouldn't want Liam to.

If she let things go where they were headed right now, if she let him kiss her, she wasn't sure she would have the strength to push him away again. Doing it once had nearly killed her. Maybe she could be strong enough, but only if she put an end to this before getting closer. "I think we should go."

His head tilted to one side, his eyes steady on her. "Do you really think so?"

She hesitated, clung for just a moment to the possibility of not being the responsible one, the caretaker, the one who took charge of things and tried to make everything work out. She could let herself do what she wanted to do every now and then, couldn't she? She could be spontaneous, go with her emotions, her heart.

But no. Her duty was clear. Her life was about taking care of her family, not about indulging in something pleasurable for now, but ultimately dangerous to someone she cared about. Liam was too good of a man, had suffered too many of life's blows already, to be shackled with Yasmin's issues. "Yes," she said firmly. "I really think so."

Don't miss Lee Tobin McClain's
Low Country Dreams, *available June 2019*
wherever Harlequin® books and ebooks are sold.

www.Harlequin.com

PHLTMEXP0619

Reward the book lover in you!

Earn points on your purchase of new Harlequin books from participating retailers.

Turn your points into **FREE BOOKS** of your choice!

Join for FREE today at
www.HarlequinMyRewards.com.

Harlequin My Rewards is a free program (no fees) without any commitments or obligations.

MYR18